TRUST IN YOU

For Jennifer

Happy reading

Julia Firlotte

www. juliafirlotteauthor. com

Trust in you

PART ONE IN SERIES:
FALLING FOR YOU

JULIA FIRLOTTE

enquiries@juliafirlotteauthor.com

ISBN 978-1-9161670-1-8

Also available as an ebook
ISBN 978-1-9161670-0-1

Cover design and typeset by Hybert Design

For Justin, Lee and Emma.
I love you always and forever.

Chapter One

Some mornings you wake up and just know that something has got to change. Not that things haven't changed for me recently. I've lost my dad, finished college, moved to a new country, started a business; there's not much more that possibly *could* change in my life right now, but that's beside the point. I'm talking about things that you've got to change about yourself.

I was bullied as a kid by the boys that lived on our estate, so I hung out with my older sisters and Hannah from next door rather than make friends of my own. It didn't mean I was happy, though; I didn't want to always be treated as the baby of the family that everyone had to look after. I wanted to be that confident girl who could saunter up to those boys hanging out at the end of my street and cut them dead with just the arch of a carefully plucked eyebrow, but I wasn't that girl back in school, and at almost nineteen I'm still not that girl.

Just now was no different.

We pulled up at a petrol station on the way to the market and while Rose was re-fuelling the van, she sent me inside to pay the cashier. And he was gorgeous. Stunning eyes and a warm smile for me as I passed him the money, he could have come straight out of the pages of a Harlequin romance novel. He started the conversation with, 'I haven't seen you in here before, I'd have remembered you,' and my pulse did that weird racing thing as I realised he might have been flirting.

All great, huh? Not so much.

Did I smile and reply with something cute and witty? Of course not. I blinked at him, mumbled 'no' and scurried out of the shop before realising I'd left my change on the counter and had to go back in again. By then I was blushing a shade of red that a London bus would be proud of.

It's the story of my life.

When I returned to the van, I plummeted into the seat next to Hannah with a thump that gained me a concerned look, but I just stared out of the side window, desperately trying to catch the breeze on my face from the open window as we started to drive again, still lost in my thoughts.

I want what most girls want, a boyfriend who I can love and trust. Oh yeah, and a fabulous career in song writing wouldn't go amiss, would it? But not me, I can't even talk to a cute guy in a petrol station. What am I, still at school?

But one day, I'm going to be that confident independent girl who can stand up for herself and flirt with a cute guy.

One day.

The van bumps over a rut in the road as Rose pulls into the car park for the warehouse where the market is held; it literally jars me out of my thoughts. Well, today is the start of a more independent me. I've invested everything I had left in my savings to set up this new business and I'm determined to make it work. It's *got* to.

Rose parks in a vacant unloading bay just as a commercial van reverses out, and she cuts the roar of the engine. Traders are carrying boxes of merchandise, and some are using trolleys; it looks like the market sells everything from gardening tools to toys. It's still early and I can already feel my ponytail sticking between my shoulder blades. Urgh.

'So, if you two unload the van, I'll go and find the manager about our pitch,' Rose says, opening the van door and jumping down before either Hannah or I can object. We just look at each other. Typical Rose, making us do all the work while she pretends to be busy.

Hannah swings the passenger door open and jumps out. Four men are standing a short distance away carrying crates of groceries, and a dark-haired Latino man with a small beard wolf-whistles at her. I see her smile at him and flick her long dark hair over her shoulder. I immediately admire her confidence. Due to the excessive heat she's wearing almost the same as I am, snug denim shorts and a strappy cream camisole, and she looks gorgeous as she always does. As I get out of the van after her, the guys whistle at me and it makes me blush, as I knew it would. Why can't I play it cool like Hannah?

I quickly tilt my head to let my fringe hang over my burning cheeks and concentrate on helping Hannah unload the large wicker basket we've carefully packed with eggs. As we carry it to the front of the van, I can feel the men's gazes focused on us from a few feet away. I risk a glance in their direction and then wish I hadn't. They're an attractive group and all clearly older than me, dressed casually in khaki shorts and sleeveless vests, one has *Wildcats* printed across a T-shirt. Most look like they haven't bothered shaving this morning and some have tattoos; to say they are a little intimidating is an understatement. I unintentionally make eye contact with one of them and swiftly turn away; it makes me cringe as I hear him laugh. After that I successfully keep my eyes diverted from them as I unload the egg boxes. I must be doing a reasonable job as I don't get any more whistles; my dad would have approved.

Rose comes back out and sidesteps around the men.

'Son of a bitch, they're multiplying!' one of them jokes loudly and the others chuckle. Rose pauses to raise her eyebrows at them before turning back to Hannah and me, fluffing out her brown bobbed hair as it's gone a little frizzy with the heat.

'I found him, he says there's a table near the roller door, just inside this entrance,' she says and the guys' interests are spiked as they hear her accent.

'Are you from England?' A man with dark blond hair hanging in his eyes calls over to her as his friends watch on amused.

'Obviously,' Rose answers before gesturing to me where I should take the boxes like she's in charge. Hannah catches my eye and looks at me understandingly; Rose can be more than a little bossy at times. I roll my eyes at Hannah and pick up the nearest box. Sometimes it's easier to go along with it than argue.

'So are you new to the area?' I hear another man ask either Rose or Hannah behind me, initiating a conversation. I don't wait to hear the reply and hurry inside before I have to join in.

The warehouse is a large brick building with a concrete floor. Thankfully, our allocated table next to the unloading bay entrance allows for a slight breeze in the stuffy interior. As I'm unpacking the egg boxes onto our stall, I pretend not to notice the men walk past, each carrying three large crates of groceries. It's quite impressive to be frank. The guy with the dark blond hair deliberately catches my attention and smiles at me as he passes. A tingle of excitement ignites inside me. He's quite good looking, but I think it's the tattoos of naked women up his arms which put me off and makes me decide not to smile back.

As Hannah and I finish setting up the stall, Rose is standing around doing nothing and it's beginning to get on my nerves. Hannah grins at me.

'Rose, it would be great if you could get Ella's bike for her,' she says overly sweetly. Rose looks surprised but turns to do as she's asked, leaving Hannah and I smiling at each other behind her back. We both know that if I'd asked, Rose would have refused. 'It won't kill her to do something to help,' Hannah whispers to me in a spirit of camaraderie just as a man walks into the warehouse past our stall.

'Thanks!' I say giggling as I bump my hip into hers deliberately. The guy passing us pauses to glance sharply in my direction. I look up at him out of curiosity as I feel his eyes on me.

Oh wow!

It's like someone's suddenly turned off my oxygen supply and my breath catches in my throat. A warm sensation shoots up my spine and my tummy free falls through the floor. I swallow before dragging some air into my lungs as his gaze locks on mine. He has the most attractive warm hazel eyes, set handsomely under eyebrows that draw attention to them. He has a strong jaw and lips that make you want to press your mouth against them. His beard is trimmed and he has short dark hair, which shows off his powerful frame, but he wears it longer and gelled on the top and it suits him. He's at least six foot three and broad shouldered like he works out a lot.

I realise I must be staring at him as he's looking at me intently. It's only been seconds, although it feels like minutes, but I can't seem to look away, my eyes inexplicably glued to him.

He's wearing cream knee-length shorts that hug his thighs, a brown leather belt and a navy blue T-shirt that stretches tightly across his shoulders. It's a casual outfit but he pulls it off like he's advertising clothes, although he's not polished like a model, with black tattoos poking out from under his sleeves and another on his neck. As I look at him I notice the slight green of what could be a fading bruise over his left eyebrow.

He casts his disturbingly attractive eyes over my face and then blatantly flicks them to my cleavage, sending shivers of excitement racing from my fingers to my toes. His lip curves up a little in a mildly bemused smile and he winks at me. It's the sexiest thing ever. My body's reacting to him before my brain has a chance to catch up.

I feel my cheeks start the familiar burn of embarrassment and hurriedly look back to Hannah. From the corner of my eye I see him walk away, and I try to act like my heart isn't slamming painfully hard against my ribs. Hannah doesn't seem to notice my reaction and continues talking to me; I pretend to give her my attention, but my thoughts are on *him*. I've never felt *that* before. I risk a glance across the warehouse, trying to see where he went but I don't spot him.

It takes several minutes before my pulse returns to normal and my hands stop trembling.

Rose brings my uncle's old bike up to the door of the warehouse and I take the chain she offers me and lock it up outside. When I return she passes me a bum bag with float money, my rucksack and a shoulder strap we made so I can carry the basket home. In the far corner I see a door with both a male and female sign so I use the toilet before the girls leave. The door lock catches a little as I bolt it. The room is L-shaped with a toilet and a sink on the right and a shower cubicle around the corner. I splash blissfully cool water on my cheeks after I've washed my hands and look back at myself in the mirror, pleased that I wore waterproof mascara due to the heat. I smooth my ponytail down before hurrying back to my stall.

As I walk, I hope to catch a glimpse of *him* among the bustling traders rushing to finish setting up. It's a rectangular warehouse and our small stall is in the centre of the longest side, with the largest pitch at the far end selling groceries. I guess the size of the stall would explain why it takes so many guys to run it as there are six men efficiently unloading the produce. My heart jolts into life as I lay eyes on *him*, working alongside the others. He's gorgeous! I could stand here gawking at him all day. I make myself turn away quickly, though, in case he catches me staring again. That would be embarrassing.

When I reach our stall, I hug the girls and wish them luck. They're driving to the next town where it's also market day and they have their own stall to run. It's only a morning market there, so we've decided I'll cycle home providing I can sell most of the stock. It'll be cheaper on fuel.

'Are you going to be ok?' Hannah asks, so I nod.

'Sure, go and sell lots!' I reply brightly. She smiles at me while Rose nods briskly.

'Well Rose will, I'm just keeping her company, remember?' She winks at me. Oh yeah. Hannah's here on a tourist's visa so mustn't work.

'Come on, Hannah, I've got to move the van,' Rose says, steering Hannah towards the exit. I watch them leave, a bubble of hope tinged with desperation lodging in my throat. This new venture really needs to earn some money, and soon. Since we arrived from England six weeks ago, we've been living off our savings and they are running out fast. So far, despite substantial efforts, only my sister Sarah has managed to find a job. It's part-time in a supermarket so doesn't pay that well, but the staff discounts are appreciated. We had to borrow money last week to pay for the market licence and let's just say it wasn't from a bank, so now there are some scary men we don't want to not pay back on time.

I sit on the stool the girls found for me, waiting for the market to open when an old lady speaks to me.

'I haven't seen you here before,' she says cheerfully as she's setting up the stall next to me, she's selling hand-made baby clothes. I smile at her.

'No, I'm new to the area.'

'Grace,' she says holding out her hand so I shake it.

'Ella,' I answer and then shake her husband's hand who's introduced as Nicholas. I notice the worn cowboy boots he's wearing and hide my smile. He looks like he'd be more at home on a cattle ranch than selling baby clothes.

'Are you from England?' Grace asks me cheerily. 'What brings you to Kansas?'

'Yeah, I moved over with my sisters to our family home last month.'

'Oh, who's your family?' she asks curiously. I get the impression she probably knows every family in twenty miles.

'Robin Peterson, of Home Stead Farm.' Her expression changes a little; she must have heard about the accident. 'He… was my uncle.

7

My dad grew up here before he moved to the UK,' I mumble, my voice catching on the use of the past tense.

'Oh, I knew Robin. I'm real sorry for your loss, although I don't know the specifics,' she says and puts her hand on my arm. 'That must be real hard on y'all.'

I clear my throat and nod. She seems genuinely sad for us, so I volunteer a little more information; I figure I have to start getting used to talking about it at some point.

'Uncle Robin came to visit us in England for a holiday,' I say trying not to choke up with happy memories. 'He and my dad decided to go on a fishing trip… The coast guard searched for three days, but they were found a few weeks later by dog walkers, washed up on a beach fifty miles away.' I take a deep breath, desperately trying not to get emotional.

'Oh, how terrible!' Grace exclaims, shocked and sincere.

I shrug, trying to give Grace the impression that I'm in control of myself, although I'm not.

'There was nothing that could be done.' And that was that. My wonderful dad and dear Uncle Robin were gone, and my world changed forever.

'So, you decided to move to the States with your sisters?' Grace asks me, trying to move the conversation on and I'm grateful to her.

'Well, Dad was self-employed, so when we lost him, we couldn't afford the rent and had to move anyway, so we decided a fresh start was what the family needed.'

She nods. At least here with the ranch bought and paid for, we have a guaranteed roof over our heads. At eighteen and fresh out of music college, like my older sisters, I wasn't earning much from my Saturday job and my dreams of becoming a lyricist are still a long way off.

I glance up and find myself looking straight into the eyes of the handsome stranger who's watching me talk to Grace. Oh God, my insides light up like petrol on a bonfire and I turn away so quickly it's ridiculous. Grace glances up and registers who I was looking at and smiles a little. How embarrassing.

'Well I hope it's the fresh start you need, honey,' Grace says before asking her husband to do some final tasks as the market will open soon.

I sit on my stool and try hard not to look over at *him* again in case he sees me. I try to think of something else and my thoughts land on my dad as they usually do. I miss him like crazy. I think as I'm the youngest and so shy, he would have been protective over me anyway when Mum died, but it didn't help that Tom and his crew picked on me growing up.

The doors open in the far corner of the warehouse and provide a welcome sight as potential customers start coming in. I realise immediately that the large grocery stall is in the prime position right next to the entrance and people flock to it, not through the car park entrance I'm next to, which isn't used at all. Oh well, as a complete newcomer, I could hardly hope to get the best spot.

Trade is slow, although the coffee and hotdog stand opposite me has a constant queue. Throughout the morning I can't help but notice that the team on the grocery stall are frequently looking over at me, the attention is making me self-conscious. It's mid-morning when two of them buy coffee from the stand opposite mine; they pretend it's casual but come over to my stall afterwards. One is balancing several cups and the other only has one, it's the blond guy who smiled at me earlier. I stand up as they approach and hope they'll speak first.

'Hey darlin',' the dark blond man says, flicking his head so his hair is no longer in his eyes. He has a remarkably strong southern accent. I decide he has nice eyes but the way he's looking at me is making me nervous.

'Hi, can I help you?' I ask.

I'm hoping they'll buy lots of boxes of eggs and then leave me alone. He smiles at me like he likes my accent. I notice that his unshaven friend with dark hair hanging almost to his shoulders is looking over the top of the table blatantly checking out my legs. I move closer to the table and pretend it's a natural inclination; although my shorts finish several inches above it, it's better than nothing.

'How much are you charging for your eggs?' he asks, his accent sounds so strange to me even though I'm getting used to it.

'One dollar for six.' I can see from the glint in his eyes that he's amused by my voice rather than actually interested in shopping. It's unnerving. His friend grins like he's been drinking although I don't think he has. He's clearly just enjoying my accent too, and also, if I'm not mistaken, my cleavage.

'I'll take a box,' the blond one says and casually flips me a few coins from his pocket. I bend down and fill an egg box from the basket under the table and when I stand up, I catch them staring down my top. I pass the box to him and pretend I didn't notice. He grins at me and shows little intention of leaving. 'I'm Dan,' he says, holding out his hand to me. It puts me on the spot and it would be rude to ignore it, so I shake his hand, deliberately trying to avoid giving him my own name. His hand is strong and warm, slightly callused too like he works hard, and it engulfs mine. He keeps hold of my hand longer than necessary. 'And you are?'

'Ella,' I answer reluctantly, and his eyes light up like he's won a little battle. I pull my hand away and notice his friends are mostly looking over at us, including *him*. Don't they have customers to serve?

'Carson, you need some eggs, bro?' Dan's gaze remains focused on me.

'Nah, I'm good,' Carson says in an equally deep accent and indicating the several plastic cups he has in his hands.

'See you in a bit then,' Dan says smoothly. I blink in surprise. Why, will he need another box of eggs in an hour?

I don't look at them, and as they walk back to their end of the market I breathe a sigh of relief, glad to turn my attention to my next customer. I hear the deep rumble of laughing over the din of the market when they reach their stall and I suspect it will not be the only visit I receive. I wonder what they're laughing about but have a sinking feeling that I'll find out at some point later. The old lady I'm serving looks up scornfully in their direction and then pats my hand.

'You just ignore them,' she says kindly. 'They sure do like to tease pretty young women.'

I smile serenely at her, pretending I didn't notice. I don't sell as many eggs as I'd hoped as the day moves on, but at least I've broken even. After lunch the market manager, Mr Jackson, stops by to check how I'm doing. He's a nice man with a stomach that overhangs his trousers and I talk to him for a few minutes before he continues his rounds. When he stops by the grocery stall, he pauses to chat for quite some time and I get the impression they are questioning him about me. Of course, he knows quite a bit about us as Charlotte and Rose have been in contact several times to fill out the paperwork. When I look up, four of them are looking over as they talk and it's clear that I'm not being paranoid.

Oh, to hell with this! Feeling flustered, I turn to Nicholas and ask him if he would keep an eye on my stall while I buy a drink. Of course he agrees, he's a sweet old guy. I join the queue at the coffee stand opposite and consider whether I'm rapidly becoming over sensitive. It's so hot I scoop my hair up into a messy bun, and am fanning my face with a piece of paper when a deep voice with a Spanish twang speaks from behind me.

'It's hot as hades around here,' he says, and I know he's talking to me. I turn around and look up at the two guys who literally tower over me. It's the Latino man with the beard who spoke, and my tummy lurches, again, as my eyes land on who's standing next to him. *He* is looking directly down at me. I blink at him and shove my hands self-consciously into my shorts pockets. Say something. Think. Don't just stand here. As usual, though, I come up with nothing inspiring, so look back at the guy who spoke to me. 'Your friend didn't stay?' he asks, presumably talking about Hannah.

I swallow, it's like I've got stage fright. I shake my head rather than speak, not daring to glance at his stunning companion who is watching me curiously. I quickly turn to face the direction of the queue, making an effort to appear more at ease than I am and kicking myself that I didn't even say hello. What's wrong with me? I can't even say hello!

The people in front of me move away from the counter and I then struggle through an embarrassing conversation with the woman serving before we establish that they don't sell hot tea, so I order a can of Coke instead. I put my purse down after tipping the coins out so I can check I give her the right money and I hear chuckling behind me. I pick up the can and hurry away. Back at my stall, I put my can down and a minute later the same guy speaks to me again, making me nearly jump out of my skin. God, have they've followed me back here? I spin around and find myself facing them both.

'Pardon?' I ask, flustered and showing it.

'I said have you forgotten something?' the guy repeats, humour in his voice.

What? I'm about to say no when I notice *he* is holding out my purse to me which I'd clearly left at the drinks stall. He flicks his eyes over me and my tummy feels instantly like I'm on a roller coaster.

'Oh, thanks,' I say snatching my purse self-consciously. A spark of electricity shoots up my arm as our fingers briefly touch.

They amble back to their group and I try not to stare at *him*, but it's hard. Grace turns to me and her eyes are twinkling at me kindly.

'You want to go and chat with them while I watch your pitch for a bit?'

It's that obvious? I shake my head hastily and scramble behind my table, taking my sandwich out of my rucksack as a distraction, although it's some time before my nerves calm down enough for me to eat it.

As the customers dwindle away with the rising heat of the late afternoon, the team from the grocery stall start to trickle over to buy eggs from me. They must be as bored as I am and every time they ask me what the price is. I know they're all laughing at me. There's no way any of them actually want that many eggs. Aside from the blatancy of what they are doing, though, I can't see the joke.

All of them pay me a visit, all except *him*. He just lounges behind his stall and watches. At least it reduces the stock sufficiently for me to carry home what's left. It's getting towards packing up time when Grace goes over to the grocery stall to buy some things and finally puts me in the picture.

'Ella, I just wanted to let you know, the grocery stall is also selling eggs. I'm not sure you knew? They have a sign up saying one dollar twenty and it's been crossed out. They're selling them at eighty cents a box. I guess they've been at it all day and taking the customers as they walk in the main entrance.'

I can't believe they're willing to make a loss just to spite me. My mouth drops open and my cheeks burn with humiliation. Finally, I know what the source of entertainment was.

My naivety apparently.

It upsets me more than it should; I guess it hits a nerve from being picked on so much growing up. I already knew they were laughing at me, but it's embarrassing all the same.

'Thank you,' I say hoarsely and squeeze her hand. She pats me on the arm and continues to pack away the baby clothes they've been selling.

I sit down dejectedly and sip the can of drink I bought earlier. It's a treat to have something fizzy after weeks of reducing the shopping bill to essentials only, so I'm determined to enjoy it.

Quite a few traders have already left so before Grace and Nicholas leave, I cross to the toilets to freshen up. I pause at the mirror; my eyes look dull and tired. Tendrils of hair are escaping from my bun down my back and my fringe is hanging in my eyes. I feel as drained as I look and wipe the perspiration from my cleavage with a sigh.

Grace and Nicholas say goodbye when I return and I watch the market manager close the doors to the public. The remaining traders start packing up more quickly, all having other places they want to be on a beautiful Saturday evening, unlike me.

I notice that the grocery stall has very little produce left and remember the dozens of crates they unloaded this morning. They must have made a fortune here today and I'm more than a little bitter they were undercutting my price all day and laughing every time one of them came over.

I'm not looking forward to the long ride home as I gather my things. We're supposed to fold the tables and stack them against the far wall, so I crawl underneath trying not to look like an idiot as I sit on the floor to figure out how the mechanisms work. Several minutes pass but I'm no wiser and getting irritated. I decide to lay it on its side, but it slips from my grasp and slams down with a resonating bang. It's so loud it makes my cheeks flame as people look over at me. Great. Tears of frustration start to prick my eyes as I kneel down and stare fixedly at the table, pretending nothing happened. You'd have to be superman to pull these metal clips apart! I wipe some tears off my cheek crossly with the back of my hand.

I've been so busy looking at the table leg fastenings that I haven't realised someone is standing on the other side, in fact I think he's been there for some time. I know it's *him* before I even look up, the tell-tale race of my pulse is my body's own little alarm system. When I do peek up, it's straight into those disturbing hazel eyes. He's got a towel in his hand and is clearly returning from freshening up like I did not long ago, his dark hair is slightly wet on top and it makes him look drop dead gorgeous.

'Need some help with that?' he asks and his voice does strange things to my insides, I notice his accent is not as southern as the others, though. It's the first time he's actually spoken to me directly and here I am, kneeling in the dirt with tears on my face.

Fabulous!

14

Well they've already had their laughs out of me today; I'm not going to give them any more and can damn well dismantle a table on my own. I shake my head and look back at the table to avoid his eyes. My heart is pounding erratically, I can't believe the effect he has on me and I don't even know what his name is. Perhaps if I ignore him, he'll just go away.

He doesn't.

After a minute of him watching me struggle and me pretending he's not there, he leans forward over the table. Embarrassingly it makes me freeze; he's so close I can smell his deodorant. Oh my God, he smells amazing. He reaches one hand towards mine and slowly presses one finger on the edge of the metal bar. A button releases and the table leg loses its tension. Heat burns my cheeks and I stare at it. Then another tear rolls down my face as my emotions get the better of me. How embarrassing. I want to just roll over and die. I hope he hasn't noticed, but he'd have to be blind not to, as he's still bending over the table and watching me.

'Tables must be different in England, huh?' He smiles at me. I think he's teasing me and the butterfly farm in my tummy goes crazy. There's such an air of confidence about him that is deeply appealing. I only manage to nod in reply. Then he reaches forward and gently wipes the tear away with the side of his thumb. My cheeks flush scarlet. I wish the ground would swallow me whole. 'You're welcome, Ella,' he says quietly, remarking that I haven't thanked him. He knows my name!

He drifts off towards his friends where their own stall has now been fully dismantled, leaving me to unclip the other table leg swiftly and pretend my hands aren't trembling. I balance the table against my leg with my back firmly to the group and wonder how on earth I'm going to lift it. It's far too heavy for me, but I'll be damned before I ask them for help. I start dragging it and a high-pitched screech emanates from where the metal scrapes the floor like nails down a blackboard. The remaining traders wince as eyes are drawn sharply in my direction from all over the warehouse. I think I'm about to have a meltdown in the middle of the market place, I hate being the centre of attention. I stagger a few paces dragging the table along the floor, no longer caring about the noise, then suddenly it's out of my hands and I look up amazed. *He's* back. He's taken one end of the table out of my hands; Dan is carrying the rear. They don't even look at me as they walk away with it, continuing their conversation like I'm not even here. I can't thank them without calling after them, which I think would make me look pathetic, so I spin around, pick up my things and stride out into the car park without a word. Could this day get any worse?

My bike is chained to the fence right next to a jeep and two flatbed trucks which the men from the grocery stall are climbing into. Oh great. They are unusually quiet and watching me as I approach. Then I realise why. The rear tyre on my uncle's old bike is flat and I can't help wondering if perhaps one of them thought it would be funny to let it down.

Yes, apparently the day could get worse.

I'm an emotional mess, tired and want to go home, but I'll be damned if I'm going to sit on the pavement and cry in front of them. I walk past the men in the vehicles and keep my eyes fixed on my bike. As I put my things down I hear the men calling out to the last two joining their group with exclamations of 'finally!' and 'we're going to quit waiting on you two!'

I kneel down on the pavement to inspect my rear tyre without looking around. I hope there's no damage, I really can't afford to replace it. I take out the bike pump I packed and my heart sinks as I notice the connecting hose is missing from the end. It's useless without it so I start rummaging around in my bag to see if I can find it.

Someone crouches down right beside me, and my heart stalls. It's *him*. His friend Dan is next to us. I glance at them, but although Dan is looking at me like he wants to eat me, his gorgeous friend is looking at my tyre. He speaks first.

'I have an adapter that'll fit the valve, want me to air it up for you?' he asks turning to look at me. His eyes almost knock the breath out of me and I stare at him for a moment before coming to my senses. I take a steadying gulp of air.

'If I could borrow it, that would be great, thank you,' I reply hoarsely, my pride getting the better of me.

My pulse is out of control with him so close. I hastily concentrate on my tyre, trying to keep my eyes wide enough so that the tears don't spill over again. He looks at me for an excruciating moment; it couldn't be more obvious that I'm upset and trying to hide it.

'No problem,' he says brusquely, walking back to the newest flatbed truck parked alongside us amid jeers coming from the other vehicles.

I can't quite believe he's being so nice. Perhaps he's feeling guilty that they've been acting like pricks. Why couldn't they have ignored me and left the price of their eggs as it was? That would have been a thousand times better.

'Go on, we'll meet y'all there,' Dan calls out to the others and immediately the jeep is slammed into reverse, then turned to accelerate out of the car park with the wheels kicking up a cloud of dust. The other truck follows it the same way and I can't help wondering what's with the testosterone-fuelled driving.

The Latino guy with the beard seems to decide it's too hot to wait inside the remaining shiny blue truck and gets out, leaning on the cab door and looking over to his friend who's pulling out a tool box.

'Adam, are you going to need the tyre levers? They're in the other one,' he calls out, pointing to a different box.

Well at least I know what *he* is called now.

Adam.

It suits him.

'Nah, the bastards probably just let it down as a prank,' he calls back well within my earshot. I can feel my cheeks flame to hear my suspicions corroborated and pretend I didn't hear. Dan's eyes are focusing on me and I'm pretty sure he's looking down my top, so I move my shoulder a little hoping it blocks his view and concentrate on unlocking the padlock on my bike chain.

Adam comes back with a battery-powered pump with a special adapter fixed to it and kneels on one knee next me to unscrew the dust cap.

'It's ok, I'll do it,' I say quietly and take the pump from him. Goosebumps tingle up my arms at his proximity and I try not to make it obvious as I cast my eyes sideways over his muscular forearms.

I try to attach the adapter to the valve but fumble with it, nerves at being so close getting the better of me.

'Let me,' he says softly and puts his hands over mine to take over. His hands are callused and warm and I belatedly jerk mine out of the way.

'No, it's fine, don't worry,' I respond quickly, determined to do this myself. I refuse to play the damsel in distress and thankfully manage to attach it to the valve.

The tyre blows up quickly and I take a second to look at his face and decide the fading green over his eyebrow was definitely a bruise. He has a strong neck and his Adam's apple protrudes a little; I have to fight the overwhelming urge to press my cheek against his skin. He's definitely older than me, at least upper twenties I'd guess. My thoughts are interrupted when the pump beeps after barely seconds, it's clearly intended for car tyres, and I detach it and reapply the cap.

'*Thank you*,' I make a point of saying before passing back the pump. At least this time he can't imply I'm impolite. He looks sideways at me and smiles, catching on immediately that I'm being more flippant than grateful.

'You're welcome.' He grins, his eyes sparking at me. I'm surprised he gets my sarcasm, most Americans I've met so far don't really relate. I look away quickly and I'm sure I hear him chuckle as he walks back to his truck to put the pump away. I get to my feet and find that my rucksack is now far too heavy with the chain inside, so I let it plummet back to the pavement again.

Dan is still watching me. I have no idea what to say to him and wish he'd stop, so I busy myself with taking my bike chain back out of my bag again, feeling flustered.

'You coming, Dan?' the other guy calls over.

Dan hesitates. 'See ya,' he says before walking over to the truck. Adam is already in the driver's seat and starting the engine up. I can feel his eyes on me as he waits for Dan to get in and as I glance up, he holds my gaze. I'm frozen to the spot, unable to pull my eyes away; the moment lasts longer than it should, until Dan closes the truck door and he turns away.

I hastily focus on wrapping the chain around my bike frame while the truck's tyres crunch the ground as it reverses slowly and drives off. Once I'm sure it's gone, I slump onto the pavement, the tarmac still hot and warming my bottom through my shorts. I pull my hair loose and as it tumbles down my back I move it about in the breeze. I can't wait to have a bath when I get home. The market manager has just locked up the warehouse doors when he sees me.

'You're pretty darn popular, ma'am.' He greets me cheerily. 'The Brook guys couldn't hear enough about you,' he says before continuing towards his vehicle.

Hmm, why does the name Brook sound familiar? Perhaps I should be flattered I seem to be that interesting, but after the way they've laughed at me all day, *flattered* is not the sentiment I would choose. It's on the tip of my tongue to ask him what was said, but I decide against it. I'm hungry and want to get home.

As I swing my leg over the high cross bar of Uncle Robin's old town bike and balance the large basket off my hip with the shoulder strap, I can't help feeling at least a little bit proud of myself. I've completed my first day of trading in my new business! Admittedly, I didn't make as much as I could have, but it's a start, certainly something to be positive about.

I've memorised the way home and head for the footpath which will take me all the way to the big commercial farm backing onto our land. It's really the only obvious route unless I want to risk life and limb on the highway.

The fresh country air as I cycle home is refreshing, despite the heat of the sun warming my face. With this prolonged heatwave a lot of the farmland is looking noticeably wilted, but it's still beautiful. Vast fields of amber grain are intermixed with the different shades of grasses and the occasional cattle farm. Against the clear blue sky, the flat landscape has few borders, interspersed only with electricity cable pylons and occasional trees. I'm not used to so much space without hedges or fences to break it up into sections and I miss the patchwork landscapes of England, but I have to admit the land here has a certain charm to it. We have acres of land ourselves, surrounding the family ranch, but frustratingly it's been decades since it was harvested for crops and is in a dire condition. The cost to hire machinery and irrigate it prevents us from putting it to good use. Its contrast to the huge commercial enterprise of DB Produce Corp, which neighbours our land, is stark. Their fields of wheat stretch as far as the eye can see outside their perimeter fencing and inside it; they must have spent a fortune on crop dusting systems, greenhousing, labour and machinery.

A few miles from home, I see a large gathering up ahead where a sports game is being played in a particularly flat open space next to two large natural rocks. There must be around forty people there and many vehicles are parked up along the edge of the highway. As I get closer I can see that the people gathered are mainly in their twenties or thirties, there are no kids or old people, it seems to be the place to hang out on a Saturday evening for those without families. My spirits sink knowing that I'll have to cycle past them with my huge basket and old man's bike.

The game looks similar to rugby and although I can see various women sitting on the hoods of the vehicles parked up, predominantly it's men in the group. I have a sinking feeling that I'm likely to run into the grocery stall crowd and pause to take out my map to see if there's another way around, but there isn't. I take a breath for courage, knowing this is going to be humiliating, and decide to race through and draw the least attention possible.

The path runs along the south of the ball game and between the two large rocks which people have climbed on to watch. As I reach the group, many people are drinking beer and I recognise the Latino guy with the beard from the market. He calls out to me, but I don't hear what he says and am too self-conscious to stop, so I continue until the path narrows between the rocks. Here a lot more people are gathered and I have to slow my bike down to navigate through the crowd with my basket. Frustratingly I'm almost clear when someone inadvertently steps in front of my bike, causing me to stop.

'Hey, watch it,' he says sharply like it's my fault, but it draws the attention of the surrounding people who would have otherwise not noticed me. Great.

'Sorry,' I mumble, hopping awkwardly to balance. I turn my front wheel and thankfully he moves back so I can pass. I glance ahead to see where the path is and find myself looking directly into Adam's eyes. My tummy somersaults. It's like my body knew he was there before my mind did. He and Dan are leaning against the side of the rock in front of me, drinking from cans and talking to two pretty women in short skirts. The group stop talking as they see me and I'm intending to look away quickly when Adam smiles warmly at me. In that split second our eyes hold and he winks at me, it's a slow and intensely sexy gesture and sends hot waves of desire crashing through me. I flush, feeling star struck and cumbersome. Oh my, he's good looking! I push my foot down hard on the pedal to start the bike moving again. Then just as my embarrassment is overwhelming, the guy called Carson from the market appears beside me.

'Eggs for sale! A dollar a box!' Carson calls out.

Laughter fills the air and I stand up on my pedals and cycle away faster, a few tears springing to my eyes. It's like I'm thirteen again, but it's no longer Tom and the lads from my neighbourhood making the jokes.

Finally, I reach the end of the path and come out opposite the main entrance to the commercial farm that neighbours our land. The security guard on duty at the main gate nods at me, looking bored. There are a number of commercial buildings up ahead, it's a big operation and I can't help thinking they must supply the entire state with that much produce. It's more than a bit frustrating to know they probably have hundreds of employees and they can't even reply to our emails enquiring about work. I nod at the man in the cabin and turn my bike right, finally nearing home.

I cycle up our rutted driveway, avoiding the deepest holes, and pass the family van. It's a typical looking ranch for the area, not very big, with a fenced in veranda running along the front and around the sides with shutters at the windows. The paintwork desperately needs to be redone, but its structure is solid. There are no bushes or fences or even pot plants out the front, though, Uncle Robin really wasn't into gardening or making things look attractive that's for sure. The land around the property stretches out for acres in a vast expanse of dried mud and wilting weeds.

At the back of the ranch, there's a neglected vegetable patch and an old garden tool shed that's half falling down and further back is our makeshift chicken coop. It has wooden fencing at the bottom and wire netting on top, which stands a few feet off the ground, and has a few wooden hen houses inside and a gate at one end. We've got about seventy chickens and I spent all my savings to buy them and put the coop together. I know today's grand launch wasn't the roaring success I had hoped it would be, but I'm still rather proud of myself. Not many girls my age would be able to set up their own business and fund it themselves. I'm planning on asking some of the shops in town if we could sell to them too.

I leave the old bike propped up against the veranda rail outside and open the front door.

'Hello!' I call out as I enter. David jumps up from the sofa excited that Aunty Ella is home. I swing him up into my arms and give him a kiss before setting him back down, at four years old he's a bit big to keep picking up, but I can't resist cuddles with my nephew. The smell of pasta sauce is the next thing I register as I walk in, my tummy rumbling impatiently. It's the same plain and inexpensive food we always have these days, but at least it's hot and filling and not omelettes. I'm sick to death of omelettes.

The house is open plan with the kitchen area on the left. My sister Charlotte is standing at the sink looking out of the window and turns and smiles at me as I enter. The glass-panelled back door next to the old-fashioned wooden kitchen cupboards is open wide to let some air in on this hot summer's night.

A central island with several tall stalls alongside serves as a natural break in the open space; it sounds modern and fashionable, but it's not. It's battered laminate and probably original to when the old house was built. I leave the basket inside the door with my rucksack and slump down on the nearest stool.

'You're back late,' Charlotte says.

'Yeah,' I sigh. We lost my mum to cancer when I was a toddler and at seven years older than me, Charlotte's the closest thing I've had to a mother.

'You didn't have a good day?' she asks.

'Let's just say that I didn't sell as many eggs as I should have because a large group of idiots decided they would undercut my price and laugh about it at my expense all day. And they let the tyre down on my bike, so I almost had to call you to come and get me. Then I had to cycle past them on the way home and I felt like an utter idiot with the basket!' Ooh that feels better, ranting to Charlotte always helps. 'Anyway, sorry, it's not your fault.'

'Oh El, I'm sorry,' she says, turning off the cooker and coming to sit on the stall next to me. David comes over to hug his mum's leg and she ruffles his hair. 'How'd you get home then?'

'One of them, called Adam, took pity on me and lent me his pump.' I sigh and close my eyes. 'And he was completely gorgeous, Charlotte. And I was a mess. Could hardly string a sentence together.' My words come rushing out.

'Gorgeous huh?' she repeats, her eyes twinkling mischievously at me.

'Don't you start.' I retort, but fail to stop the shy smile from lighting up my face at the thought of Adam. 'I've already had half the old people in the market notice. I nearly died of embarrassment. And to say I'm hot, sticky and in need of a long bath is an understatement.'

'Oh,' she says with a little pause, implying I'm not going to get my wish.

I look up at her sharply.

'What?' I ask, praying that I've misunderstood. She holds her hands up palms facing me in a gesture of surrender.

'It's not that bad, but we finally managed to get through to the water company. They told me the price to refill the water tank… it's a lot.' Her tone is loaded.

'Meaning?'

'That we're saving water where we can, so it'll have to be a quick shower instead of a bath.' Her eyes are apologetic and I nod, accepting yet another thing to cut back on.

'Shall we count up the eggs money then?' I suggest, my tone blossoming in hope, and I fetch the bum bag and pour its contents onto the worktop. It takes us a few minutes to count and we've made a profit, but it's lower than we'd hoped. I'm determined not to be disheartened, though, it's only the first day after all. Next week, perhaps I'll ask Mr Jackson if I can change my pitch location to increase traffic flow past my stall. 'How did Rose and Hannah do at the other market?' I ask.

'You mean how did Rose get on?' Charlotte corrects me and then shakes her head in answer to my question. The other market clearly wasn't a success. Damn. I refuse to let my spirits drop. Nope, not even a little bit. Not going there.

Hannah lived next door to us and had a turbulent upbringing, so practically grew up at our house and is more of a sister than a friend. When we told her we were leaving, she decided to come. She doesn't have dual citizenship like we do so can't work due to her tourist's visa, but she pulls her weight. And she contributed to our moving costs. As a trained baker, Charlotte is the most qualified among us, so it makes sense for her to find work and bring in a higher wage. The intention is that Hannah looks after Charlotte's children as her way of contributing until she's got a work permit. Sarah, Rose and I having already found full time jobs of course. Hmm, like *that* is looking likely in the near future.

'On a positive note,' I say trying to cheer up, 'I'm planning on sowing more seeds in the vegetable patch out the back to help with the food bills.'

Charlotte squeezes my hand encouragingly, she's being supportive, but her eyes are concerned.

'Then you'll have to start reading some of Robin's books about farming,' she says brightly.

I nod and Charlotte rises to dish up some pasta they've saved for me.

Chapter Two

The week passes slowly and Adam plays heavily on my mind. I wonder where he lives and if he's single. Is the market his main job? What do his tattoos look like without a T-shirt over them? I remember how my insides caught fire when he winked at me. To be frank, I can't seem to get him out of my head. He had such a confidence about him and it was magnetising. I know he's probably too old for me, my dad would have said so, but I tell myself a girl can look. I mean, where's the harm in that? Ironically, I spent most of Saturday avoiding looking at him. Once more, I'm frustrated with myself. So much for becoming more confident. If I see him again, I'll try harder to talk to him and not clam up like a school girl. Let's be honest, though, considering I was an emotional mess and hardly spoke to him, the likelihood of a guy like him wasting his time speaking to me is unlikely.

Early on Thursday morning the household is woken up by the hens making a racket. Charlotte, Sarah and I rush outside in our pyjamas just as the sun is coming up and find a large hole under the fence of the chicken coop. There are feathers all over the place and several dead birds on the ground. *That's all we need.* We clear up the mess then I send my sisters back to bed. I get dressed and sit by the coop for the rest of the morning in case the animal comes back before we can fix the hole. I'm sad for the birds but more concerned about our livelihood being taken away from us, I can't afford to replace them.

Later that day the girls assure me that they will watch the coop, so Charlotte drives me over to a small dead tree on our land by the highway. We can't spare the money right now to buy planks from a store to mend the fence, so with a bit of effort, the wood from the tree will have to do. It needs to be cut down anyway, so Charlotte drops me off with some tools and a wheelbarrow and says she'll give me a hand when she picks me up later.

By the time the small tree is down, the sun is hot on my back. I'm stripped down to a pair of denim shorts and a white crop top that exposes more of the curve of my hips than I'd like, yet I'm still sweltering in the heat. I can't take off anything else, passing vehicles have already started tooting at me, so I scoop my hair up under a baseball cap and put on sunglasses, hoping I won't be recognised.

The quiet time to think is welcome, even if the exercise is tough. Since studying music at college, my dream is to be a professional lyricist and I'm finally getting a chance to finish some songs I've been humming in my head. I'm resting a hiking-boot against the main trunk of the tree, taking a break for my aching arms to recover from sawing off a large branch, when I hear a vehicle crunch the gravel behind me as it pulls up to the kerb. I half expect to see our van, but instead find myself facing a shiny light blue truck like the one Adam had at the market. The sun is shining from that direction, and despite my sunglasses I have to squint to see who's getting out as both the doors swing open.

It's Dan and… *him*. Adam.

Oh jeeze! I must look a sweaty mess.

I put the saw down and take my foot off the tree so I can face them. What are they doing here? My heart is pounding and I decide to let them speak first, hoping like hell they haven't stopped to make fun of me.

'Hey there,' Dan calls as his eyes drift slowly down over my figure. Does he have to be so blatant? Goosebumps prickle my skin and I glance at Adam. He's doing the same, just trying to be more discreet about it and this time it makes my pulse race. I fold my arms over my chest nervously.

They're both dressed in short-sleeved shirts, light trousers and shoes. It's quite a transformation from their casual clothes on Saturday. I can't help but notice Adam's upper arms stretch his sleeves tight and he has the most fantastic shoulders. My memory didn't do him justice.

'Hello Ella,' Adam says smoothly; it sends a small thrill through me to hear him use my name. Is that a little pathetic? Probably.

'Hi.' I fight my natural inclination to try and get them to leave as I remember my resolve to make an effort to speak to him.

'We saw a cute backside sticking up in the air and thought it must be you,' Dan says.

What?

My intention to make conversation rapidly flies out of the proverbial window. I'm hot, I'm due on my period and I'm more than a little tetchy.

'Is that supposed to be funny?' I ask. 'Because it isn't.'

Dan grins at my reaction. 'Not particularly, just stating how it is, honey,' he drawls.

'Well I'm not in the mood to be the butt of your jokes again right now.' I pick up my saw, intending to resume cutting up the wood. I think Dan is about to respond, but Adam knocks him on the arm.

'Cut it out, will you?' he says before turning to me. 'Actually, Ella, we were going to ask if you needed a hand with that.' He nods towards the pile of wood. I blink at him. He's offering to help?

'Umm, that's nice of you but I can manage thanks,' I mumble, far too self-conscious to accept the offer.

'Ok,' he says still watching me, the eye contact he's maintaining is making my pulse race faster.

'My sister's bringing the van up soon,' I add for something to say and then almost kick myself realising I've practically just sent him packing when I could have spent some time with him. God, do I suck at this!

Luckily, he smiles at me instead, a definite glint of appreciation is on his face which I don't know how to react to. I'm glad my sunglasses are helping to hide my expression.

'So what part of England are you from?' he asks, hooking his thumbs into his trouser belt loops. His interest catches me off guard.

'The south coast, near Portsmouth.' I knock my fringe out my eyes nervously with my free hand.

'Near London?' Dan asks. I get the impression that he doesn't like Adam getting more of my attention. Huh? If he wants my attention, why was he so obnoxious? *Cute backside* indeed! Guys are so strange. It's like a flashback of Tom all over again.

I break my gaze away from Adam and look at Dan. It strikes me again that he's not bad looking, in fact his eyes are rather attractive, but next to Adam I think even Adonis would pale in significance.

'Not that close.' I feel a little awkward and wonder if the real reason they stopped was to talk to me.

Adam gives me a sexy as hell smile. Christ. I practically drool.

'Portsmouth is, like, just a few hours from London. You guys call that *not close*?' he exclaims, looking at me amused.

'Well, it's not that close in our eyes,' I say quietly, a little fazed by the way he's focusing on me. 'England's smaller than the States.'

I'm starting to recognise that look the guys around here get when they like my accent. Right now, Adam's got it in spades. My eyes seem to have become locked to his, so I switch my attention to Dan to give myself a breather.

'So, who's in charge of your stall?' I ask. If they can be friendly for five minutes then I want to know who makes their pricing decisions.

Adam is entertained at that question and Dan raises his eyebrows a little.

'Dan runs the grocery stall,' Adam says and he smacks Dan on the arm. Dan scowls at him in a manner that clearly means something between them, and I wonder if Adam is lying.

'Do you?' I ask Dan.

'Yeah,' he replies. Hmm, perhaps he is the manager then. I can't tell.

'Well, why did you drop the price of your eggs?' I ask him. Dan smiles at me.

'Why did you price yours below ours to start with?' he responds tilting his head to one side with a cocky expression on his face. It gets my back up.

'I didn't. I didn't even know you were selling eggs until late in the day.' Oh shit, I mentally kick myself; I might as well have said *you got one over on me, well done you*.

Adam is looking at Dan and appears to be enjoying this. The way his trousers fasten up against his flat stomach makes me want to undo the buttons to see if he's as toned as he appears. God, he's hot! I blink, startling myself with my own thoughts. What's wrong with me? I'm practically undressing him with my eyes.

'Dan, the lady asked you why you dropped the price of the eggs,' Adam says.

The lady? I'm a *lady* now? I thought I was the simple girl who couldn't dismantle tables…

Dan shoots a glare at Adam who doesn't look remotely bothered by it and instead folds his arms over his broad chest, smiling serenely. His tattoos inked over his impressive biceps catch my eye as they sneak out in black lines from under his short sleeves.

'It's just good commerce,' Dan shrugs.

I bite my lip as I ponder this. 'So, if I charge eighty cents on Saturday, you'll drop yours to sixty?'

'Perhaps.' He smirks, but his eyes are watching me like a hawk and I realise it's got nothing to do with trading, but everything to do with me.

Right now, though, I'm so not in the mood to play games. Financially, we're already in deep water. The money Rose made at the other market on Saturday barely covered the pitch fees and I'm scared to death of the man with the shaved head and spider's web tattoo who we borrowed the licence money from. We have to pay an inflated sum back soon and I doubt we'll manage it, but with no credit history here and only Sarah with a job, we didn't have any choice.

I sigh. I need Dan to listen to me.

'Look, I know this is a game to you, but it's not to me. Can we come to an arrangement?'

'Sure,' he says smoothly, but his eyes are lingering on me so much it sends my nerves tingling and I can't work out if it's in a good way or not. 'I'll tell you what, let me take you out for a drink on Friday night and we can talk about it.'

Huh? He just asked me out? A part of me is flattered even if my answer is no.

'Pardon?' I ask him, a little stunned.

'You heard. You can help persuade me to *come to an arrangement.*' It couldn't be clearer what he's implying as he arches an eyebrow at me. My cheeks burn with humiliation; for a second I thought he was being serious. I lower my gaze immediately so he doesn't see he's struck a nerve. 'Or you can say no,' Dan continues confidently, 'and I can check with the business owner if I can raise our price while you undercut us, I'm sure he'll agree.'

Now he's being a jerk.

My mouth opens to reply but I find there are no words, so I close it again and just stand there feeling like a dork. I daren't even look in Adam's direction. Eventually I find my voice.

'You're giving me an ultimatum?' I'm shocked and I know I sound it.

'No, he's not,' Adam says firmly, so I finally glance at him and the tension in his brow tells me he's far from pleased with his friend at this moment. Dan ignores him.

'You haven't answered,' Dan says to me.

'What exactly are you expecting me to say to such a *lovely* offer?' I'm trying, and probably failing, to hide the hurt inside me. It's the first time I've been asked out in over a year… and it's a joke. Although he's good looking, I wouldn't have said yes even if he was serious, but it still upsets me that he recognises I'm such an easy target. I long to have the impetus to rant that I'd not even consider going out with him after he almost ruined my first day of business and embarrassed me, but I don't. It's like my tongue is made of lead, so instead I look at him uncertainly, feeling out of my depth. When he doesn't answer, I spin around and start sawing at my tree again, ignoring that my hands are trembling with frustration. At myself.

'You don't have to answer that, Ella,' Adam says now in a tone that's authoritative and clearly implying to Dan 'that's enough'.

I hear the loud rumble of a familiar engine and see our van pull off the highway and lumber to a grumbling halt with Charlotte driving. Oh, thank goodness. I'm feeling well outside my comfort zone with these two. She parks behind Adam's truck and as she approaches us, there's curiosity on her face.

'Hello,' she says brightly to them. 'Who are your friends, El?' she calls over just before she reaches us.

I want to say they're not my friends but it would be childish.

'Hey,' Adam says taking the initiative. 'I'm Adam.' He holds out his hand in introduction.

Hmm, it's petty of me I know, but I'm peeved that I didn't get an introduction. The first thing he said to me was something about my ineptitude at dismantling tables.

Charlotte shakes his hand and looks at me. 'Adam? The same Adam who fixed your bike?' Her eyes twinkle with mischief as she clearly remembers my gushing description of him. I nod and silently beg her not to repeat my words. It's bad enough he knows I was talking about him. I deliberately don't look up at Adam, my pulse pounding in my head. 'I see what you mean.' She smiles, winking at me playfully. My knees almost give way. Did she seriously just do that? *Right in front of him?* I feel Adam's eyes focus on me and I clear my throat meaningfully at Charlotte. She takes the hint quickly and shakes Adam's hand. 'I'm Charlotte, El's sister,' she says in a friendly way and then holds out her hand to Dan.

'Dan,' he replies and Charlotte nods.

'Dan was just asking Ella out to a bar,' Adam says, and I look at him sharply. He meets my gaze unwaveringly and my palms break out in a sweat. Oh wow. I turn to Charlotte who raises her eyebrows at me as her eyes ask me silently 'do you want to'?

I shake my head a tiny bit at her, thankful that Dan is looking the other way even if Adam isn't.

'Well, please don't take offence, but I think you're a bit old for her,' Charlotte says to Dan. Her voice clearly depicting that of a protective big sister.

Some people might find that embarrassing, but not me. She can tell I'm nervous and is trying to help me out. I throw her a grateful look. I'm conscious that statement could also apply to Adam as he looks a similar age to Dan, but honestly, the way I react when he looks at me is scaring the life out of me. If my age puts a natural barrier between us, then I'd be relieved.

'She sure doesn't look too young.' Dan huffs, a little put out. I almost gasp as the realisation hits me. From his tone it's clear that he might have been serious about taking me out after all.

Adam hasn't taken his eyes off me for some time, and jumps in before Charlotte can answer Dan.

'How old are you, Ella?' he asks.

'I'm almost nineteen,' I reply looking Adam in the eyes for once and ignoring the way my tummy is bungee jumping. He considers my age for a moment, then deliberately lets his gaze run slowly down my figure, blatantly checking me out when he knows I can see what he's doing.

Whoa!

He's doing that in front of Charlotte? My heart rate takes off like a drummer in a beats per minute competition and I stare back at him. Adam is the one to break the agonising pause in conversation.

'No, she doesn't look too young,' he says confidently, agreeing with Dan's earlier comment, 'but she is, so you better back off, Dan.'

The obvious undertone to his voice makes the hairs on my arms stand up. Is he really saying that I'm too young for Dan and therefore, presumably, also for himself? Or is he just telling Dan to back off? Does that mean *he* likes me? God, I wish I was more used to dealing with guys.

I can't take this anymore and turn away, abruptly flicking my ponytail and putting my saw down. I start putting the small logs I've already cut into a pile. Charlotte clears her throat a little awkwardly.

'Well we must crack on,' she says brightly. 'It was nice to meet you Dan,' she says to him as she passes, and she pauses and looks at Adam for a second longer than strictly necessary. 'Adam,' she acknowledges him, before coming over and helping me stack the wood. A moment of silence passes.

'Yeah,' Dan says turning to leave and then hovering as Adam doesn't move to follow him.

'Ella?' Adam says to get my attention. I have little choice but to look up at him from where I'm bending down. When our eyes meet electricity races through me. Can he feel this too? Is it just me?

'See you Saturday,' he says in goodbye.

'Yeah, see you later,' I say self-consciously and return to my wood gathering, hoping like hell that my trembling hands are only noticeable to me.

'And Ella?' Adam says, deliberately making me look up again.

'Yes?' I snap, becoming flustered.

'I like your hot pants, you should wear them Saturday,' he says smiling at me with a teasing glint to his eyes.

Wow!

I gawp at him and blush quite considerably and it makes his smile widen. Christ. I have to gulp in some air. Did he really just say that? I guess the girl at the sports ground on Saturday wasn't his girlfriend then.

I look at Charlotte; she's raising her eyebrows at the wood pile, clearly having heard what he said but not looking up.

In stark contrast to me, Adam laughs a little and then ambles off towards his fancy truck before climbing in. Dan gets in beside him.

Charlotte and I stand to watch the truck start to pull away. It draws level with us and Adam smiles at me; I can't help but stare at him as he checks his wing mirror and drives out onto the clear highway. Charlotte and I both wait until the truck is well out of earshot and then turn to look at each other. Immediately we burst into a fit of giggles which take some time to subside.

'Oh my *God*, Ella, what did you *do* at that market?' She squeals at me in such a carefree way that I haven't heard her talk like that in years. She's always the responsible mother of two, guiding the rest of us, so for her to giggle like a girl is pretty rare.

'You know what, Char, I have no idea,' I say. 'No idea whatsoever.'

It's market day again and after helping set up, Hannah and Rose have just left in the van. There seemed little point in making them hang around when they could be at home securing the chicken coop a little better. We worked on it yesterday with the wood I'd cut, but it's not that secure. The Latino guy who was here last week (who I've found out is called Miguel), Dan and Carson hung around earlier drinking coffee while Hannah and Rose were still here. We aren't stupid, it was clear they were just ogling us, but where I felt conspicuous and shy, the girls didn't seem to mind and even smiled at them.

Adam isn't with the group this morning and I won't lie, I'm disappointed. After his hot pants comment, I'd got my hopes up that

I might see him. Stupid really, I probably would have spent most of my time avoiding him anyway.

I've priced my eggs at one dollar per box, as Dan confirmed this morning that he would do the same. I look over at their packed stall; they must be making a fortune. Clearly, they can afford to make a loss on a few boxes of eggs if he decides to undercut me again. I'm not willing to take that risk, so as Nicholas and Grace are set up next to me again, I ask Grace to do me a favour and go on a spying mission to check their prices. I rang Mr Jackson during the week and he couldn't change my location, so I have a back-up plan for that in my bag also.

When Grace returns, she has a mischievous grin on her face.

'He's undercutting you, honey, they've priced their eggs at eighty cents again,' she whispers to me in a spirit of camaraderie. I get the distinct impression she's thoroughly enjoying herself.

I smile at her smugly and deliberately pull out a different sign from my rucksack and put it on the table. It states, buy two and get one free.

'Better to come prepared,' I whisper and wink at her. She grins at me and then when I pull out a large cardboard sign, which is folded in half, and a roll of Sellotape, she starts laughing. 'Would you be a tremendous friend and go and attach that to the entrance wall outside, but not let them see you?' I whisper.

She nods, still laughing and goes off to do as I ask. The sign will advertise the offer and state my location at the back of the market. It's not long before Grace returns; mission successfully accomplished.

It's late morning when I look up from the book I'm reading about farming, sensing a customer at my table and find Adam standing there instead.

'Hello,' I exclaim and stand up. He smiles at me and I'm sure my tummy relocates itself in response. God, he looks hot this morning in a white distressed T-shirt stretched across his shoulders.

'Good morning,' he says smoothly and passes me a lidded plastic cup from the coffee stand and a stirrer. 'I got you a chocolate, they didn't have *tea* and you didn't seem keen on coffee,' he says, pronouncing 'tea' in an English accent and smiling at me. I don't mind in the least that he's teasing me. It's sexy as hell. My megawatt smile could light up the warehouse, so I bite my lip as I take the cup. I hadn't realised he'd paid so much attention last week. He stares at me for a moment before glancing at the book I've left face down on my stool. 'You're starting farming?' he asks, raising an eyebrow. I shake my head.

'More like considering a vegetable patch.' I smile, still glowing that he bought me a drink. An expression flits across his eyes that I can't interpret as he watches me. Hmm, what's up with him today? 'You're here late,' I say to fill the silence. 'Won't Dan tell you off?'

'I'd like to see him try.' He chuckles, sounding supremely assured of himself. I wonder what I said that might have been funny. I see him glance at the sign on my table, stating buy two and get one free and I almost kick myself. I should have paid more attention, seen him coming and hidden it. Damn! He's bound to tell Dan and I can't afford to drop my prices further. Adam doesn't mention it, though, and turns to head towards his own stall; I admire the way his bum fills out his jeans from the back with perfect curves.

'Thanks for the drink,' I say to him.

'No problem. Oh, and I like the shorts, Ella,' he adds as an afterthought to me over his shoulder as he starts walking off. I'm glad he has his back to me as the smile spreads across my face that he noticed, because it wasn't deliberate that I wore the same shorts. No sirree.

At lunch time trading is quiet. I imagine the even hotter weather has put people off going shopping. I notice Dan looking in my direction and when he starts walking towards me, I quickly swipe my Buy Two Get One Free sign off the table, leaving the One Dollar price sign there. The offer has been doing well all morning.

'Hey, Ella?' he says as he reaches my stall. 'A few of us are going to the diner; you wanna join us if Nick can watch your pitch?' Is he asking me out or making a joke?

'Oh! I can't today but thanks for asking.' I'm unwilling to leave myself exposed to teasing by accepting the offer.

'You not eating?' he asks, clearly trying to find out if I'm saying no to him specifically.

'No, it's too hot for me to eat,' I answer, adding a smile to appear friendlier. I don't mention that I can't afford to buy lunch out and have another unappealing cheese sandwich in my bag. 'I'll just buy some fruit later.'

His face lights up.

'Well *that* I can help you with,' he says. What a surprise. 'Come on.' He holds out a hand to me, implying I should go with him. I look at Grace in enquiry about my stall and she nods at me with a smirk on her face, so I cross the market with him, but I don't take his offered hand.

When we reach the stall, Adam is sitting towards the back talking to Miguel and looks up as I approach with Dan. He's not exactly working, just sitting at the back chatting. Hmm, nice life if you can get it.

'What'll it be?' Dan asks me.

'Just a small bunch of bananas and some carrots.'

I glance over the stall and deliberately don't look up as I can feel Adam watching me.

Dan gestures to some quantities that he's picked up, so I nod before he bags it up and tells me the price. I put my hand in my bum bag to pay him.

'No charge,' Adam says to Dan. I glance at him; it feels like a trap door opened under me the way my tummy drops. Dan doesn't react but also doesn't accept my money when I offer it to him. Hmm, I thought Dan was the manager…

'Thanks,' I answer, surprised, but Adam has already turned his attention back to Miguel.

I look around and automatically my eyes fall on their eggs. They are priced at eighty cents per box just as Grace told me they were. I know Dan has seen me clock the price, so I arch an eyebrow at him in silent accusation.

'We said eighty cents per box, didn't we?' Dan asks in mock innocence. I hear a few light chuckles from the other guys behind the stall, but they die away quickly as I look at Dan and remain deliberately quiet.

It works a treat and he soon starts looking more uncomfortable. Good.

Fucking A!

It also means that Adam hasn't told him about the offer I've been advertising. I glance at him and he holds my gaze. I expect him to say something, but he doesn't.

'What? You're not going to pout and throw a hissy?' Dan drawls. 'I like your accent when you're mad.' He says this loud enough for everyone to hear and I lose the composure I was becoming so proud of maintaining and flush pink in embarrassment. Damn.

'Really,' I exclaim dryly, wondering if the sarcasm will be lost on him. It is.

'Yeah,' Dan replies openly.

'What did you agree? It clearly wasn't eighty per box,' Adam asks Dan from where he's still sitting at the back of the stall.

'We agreed to charge one dollar,' I reply, catching Adam's eye to see if he's going to give up my secret. A smirk lifts up at the corner of his mouth.

'Well Ella's charging one dollar, I saw her price earlier,' Adam says, an underlying challenge to his voice. I almost gulp in shock. He's covering for me?

Dan clears his throat, picks up the price ticket and replaces it with one Miguel passes him stating One Dollar. 'Sorry, Ella.' His voice *sounds* sincere, but he's smirking.

Did Adam just tell him to higher the price? Is Dan the manager or not? Carson is blatantly not listening as he's checking out my legs over the top of the stall and looks up guiltily when he realises I'm staring at him.

'Who's in charge of this stall?' I ask.

He nods towards Dan immediately. I frown at him, something here doesn't add up. Then I'm distracted as Grace calls out from behind me.

'Ella honey, there are some men at your pitch who want to talk to you.'

I look towards my stall; there's a white man in his late thirties with a shaved head and a spider's web tattooed up his neck looking at me. A taller broad-shouldered black man with a beard is next to him. They're both wearing dark jeans and long-sleeved shirts despite the heat and look as they are supposed to. Intimidating. Oh fuck. I take a gulp of air.

'I better go,' I mutter to Dan without looking at him (or anyone else) and start to follow Grace. I know who they are and what they want but I haven't got enough money to pay them.

I stop a couple of feet from them, because, frankly, they scare the living daylights out of me.

'You owe fifteen hundred dollars. Do you have it?' Reece's curtness has me drawing breath. I shake my head.

'I can give you what I've got,' I say, putting my things down and handing over my bum bag containing our money. 'But can we go somewhere else, *please*?' I almost plead, acutely aware of the weight of several pairs of eyes boring into the back of my head from a particular stall behind me.

He flicks his eyes over my shoulder and his gaze lingers there as he smiles insolently at someone, then he turns me towards the car park entrance and escorts me outside like a detainee under police arrest. When we get outside Reece rummages around in the bag and pulls out the few notes.

'You've got three hundred dollars in notes, and another thirty in coins,' he says, putting the money in his pockets. 'And the rest?' He's unimpressed and returns an almost empty bag.

'We don't have it yet. I'm really sorry, we're working on it and trying to get it for you, it's just the market isn't—'

He holds his hand up abruptly and stalls me mid-sentence.

'When?' He's clearly a man of few words. I shake my head.

'We just need a bit longer. Maybe a month?' I propose hopefully, biting my bottom lip so he can't see it tremble.

'One week. And then it will be two thousand dollars.'

I desperately want to argue but one look at their faces tells me not to.

'Will you come to the market?' I ask, concentrating my eyes on Reece's web tattoo rather than his eyes.

'No, we'll come by your house on Sunday afternoon.' They know where we live?

Shit.

'And my advice, sweetheart, is that you pay up. You don't wanna find out what happens to pretty young women who don't.' He practically breathes in my ear as he leans forward. Every hair on my arms stands up on end. I don't dare say anything. Then his companion elaborates further, even though I could have happily lived without the added detail.

'We make them work for it.' The big man almost growls, his voice is deep with a Spanish accent. My heart pounds and I stare at the ground.

'Ella, you alright?' Adam calls loudly from somewhere behind me and I almost jump a foot in the air, but thankfully Reece and his friend back off a little. I turn and see Adam standing in the warehouse entrance watching us with his arms folded, Dan and Carson are with him.

'Yeah, just coming,' I call back to them brightly, knowing I'm failing miserably to fool anyone.

'See you Sunday then,' Reece croons, so I nod stiffly and stride back to the warehouse, noticing as I walk that Adam, Dan and Carson are not watching me, but keeping steady eye contact with the two men behind me. Do they know each other?

Once I reach them, I turn also to watch Reece and his hulking companion walk away. The back waistbands of their trousers are bulging and an icy chill runs through me. Do they have guns under their shirts? Fuck. It's a wakeup call. My heart is beating erratically and I try to discreetly drag more air into my lungs. I suddenly pine for my dad and I'm bitter that he isn't here to tell us what to do.

'Are you ok, honey?' Dan asks me. For once his voice shows no undertones of the usual banter.

'Yes, I'm fine, thank you.' I try for nonchalance but know I must fail as Adam puts his hand on my shoulder supportively. The contact sends my emotions into turmoil and I know I need to get out of here before I make a fool of myself. So I smile brightly at the guys and walk away as calmly as I can, knowing half the market must have witnessed that, and avoiding eye contact with everyone.

In the late afternoon, a smartly dressed man comes to my stall and shows me ID stating he works for the state authorities. He requests our trading licence, looks at it briefly and then puts it on the table, saying it's not the right one. It's the only licence that we were advised we'd need, so I look at him blankly.

'Oh! I'll need to check with my sister then. It must be at home. Err, what are the implications if we don't have the right one?' I'm trying to hide the anxiety in my voice. I get the impression he doesn't like his job and goes into a dull recitation of stall holder responsibilities and infringement of state trading laws and fines applicable. Blah blah blah. I tune out feeling numb. It makes little difference what the fine is, we can't pay it. We also can't trade without a new licence, which we can't afford. Then another thought occurs to me.

Oh. Dear. God.

The licence is in Charlotte's name, what if she's sent to prison for not paying the fine? Panic rushes through me and I shove my shaking hands into my pockets and try to focus on what's being explained to me. Then out of nowhere, Adam appears at the man's side, clapping him on the back like they're old friends and I want to slump through the floor again. The man's timing is something to behold!

'Geoff.' Adam greets him and the two shake hands.

'Hello sir,' the man says in a significantly more personable tone of voice.

'Is there a problem?' Adam asks pleasantly. The man pauses and looks at me. 'It's ok Ella won't mind you telling me.'

Pardon? I raise my eyebrows; that's quite an assumption. Geoff, however, takes my silence as confirmation.

'It seems Miss Peterson has the wrong licence.'

Adam spins the form around so he can read it and then raises his eyebrows at me. His eyes send sparks shooting through me and I momentarily have trouble focusing. I shake my head in answer to his silent query, hoping he doesn't notice I'm upset. Fat chance of that, he's so sharp, I get the impression he never misses anything.

Now the groceries team can celebrate I'm out of business. Dan will likely be elated. My heart plummets at the thought that I've wasted all my savings and was trading for just two weeks. So much for the new independent Ella. I feel like a complete joke and want to crawl under the table.

'Well, Geoff, my licence will cover her stall until she gets the paperwork sorted. Write it down to me and I'll get Sally to give you a call during the week, no need for the fines,' Adam states firmly.

What?

That was unexpected.

Geoff blinks at Adam in surprise and so do I, particularly when Geoff agrees. He turns his attention back to me, though.

'Pardon me ma'am, but I also need to see your ID and Employment Authorisation Document.' I start to pull my American passport out of my bag when Adam answers for me.

'She's old Robin's niece; Jackson's got copies of the ID in the market office if you need them.'

My eyes widen in surprise, but Adam is looking at Geoff so doesn't see my expression. Has the market manager shown him our papers? Surely that's confidential.

I offer Geoff my passport, but he sees its American and waves it away instead. Adam's word is apparently good enough.

'I was real sorry to hear about your relatives, ma'am,' Geoff says.

'Thank you,' I reply a little hoarsely, sliding my passport into my shorts.

'You have a good day now.' He nods at Adam in farewell, and I get the impression that he's relieved he doesn't have a pile of paperwork to fill out.

I look at Adam, but he's already turned away so I watch him leave with more than a few questions left unanswered.

At almost closing time, Grace asks me if I wouldn't mind taking out a sack of rubbish for her, so I nod and head across the car park to where the skips are.

As I'm returning, I sigh to see Dan. Great. He looks at me sharply and I think I caught him checking out my bum as I stretched up to throw the bag in the skip. He's carrying a few trays of produce and heads to a truck that I recognise as belonging to one of the team. I cast my eyes over the trays; they would feed my family for over a week.

'Are you giving those away?' I ask after we pass one another, and he nods as he puts them in the back of the truck. 'Would you trade them for eggs?' I ask hopefully, walking over to him.

'We sell eggs too, sweetheart.' He arches an eyebrow at me like I'm a bit simple. Hmm fair point.

'Can I buy them then?' I quickly pull a ten-dollar bill out of my bum bag.

'Nah, trading's finished.' He casually flicks his eyes down over my chest. 'Unless you come out for a drink with me, then I might change my mind.' Oh, so it looks like we're back to this again.

I hold the money out to him. 'I'll give you ten dollars. It's better than giving it away.' I try to persuade him.

'And the drink?' he asks leaning his hip casually against the side of the truck and glancing over my shoulder towards the warehouse.

'I don't get the impression it's just a drink you want,' I retort, but instead of being offended, he laughs at me.

'That's true,' he agrees, and my cheeks flush at his blatancy.

'Please?' I leave my arm outstretched. 'Or are you going to make me beg?' Oops, did I really say that out loud?

'Oh, I'd love to make you beg, Ella.' He flirts with a lazy half-smile on his face and I know he's making fun of me.

'I haven't got any more money, or I would have offered it to you.' I sound a little desperate even to my own ears. It's really a lot of food and I can't believe he'd rather give it away than sell it to me.

'I don't want your money, Ella,' he says smoothly and reaches out to caress my bare shoulder with his fingertip. Nerves shoot through me and it annoys the hell out of me, so I pull my shoulder back out of his reach.

'I'm not going to sleep with you for some vegetables,' I snap and shove my money back in my bum bag.

He smirks at that and takes great pleasure in methodically securing a plastic sheet over the trays in the truck, making it clear he definitely won't change his mind now.

My shoulders slump as my anger leaves me. Crap.

A stillness settles between us as I look at him. The sensible thing would be for me to go back inside, but the strain of our money worries and that he's been winding me up for two weeks takes its toll.

'I don't understand what I did, Dan. Why do you dislike me so much?' I blurt out without thinking.

'I don't dislike you,' he exclaims.

'So being mean to me is just entertainment for you?' My voice raises an octave as my pulse pounds in my ears. I rake both my hands through my fringe and gasp as my emotions start to take over.

'*Mean* to you?' he repeats raising his eyebrows.

'Christ. I thought I'd moved away from guys like you. Why are men such fucking arseholes sometimes?' I snap and take a step back. It's the first time I've actually had a go at him and his expression is nothing but stunned.

'Ella.' He starts to say something in a more serious tone, but I don't want to hear it. I've put up with Tom and his friends picking on me my entire childhood and I've no intention of going through it all again with Dan. I spin around, intending to march back to the warehouse and instead slam straight into Adam who's standing right behind me. It sends me reeling backward and he catches me with large strong hands by my forearms before I land on the concrete.

'Whoa, easy!' he says.

'Oh sorry,' I mutter, stunned, and looking up at him. He removes his hands and his expression is… thoughtful. I drop my eyes and scoot around him, intending to pack up, freshen up and then get the hell out of here.

Grace and Nicholas help me put my table away before they leave, so I pile several boxes of eggs into their hands and they joke about how many flans they'll have to eat, which lightens my mood a little. I know the feeling.

Most traders have left by the time I've packed up and head to the toilets to freshen up. It's been one hell of a day and I'm emotionally shattered. The visit from Reece, the licence issues and then Dan refusing to sell to me really have got me down. I bang on the bathroom door, which is ajar.

'Hello? Anyone in here?' I call out and there's no reply, so I enter. The commercial light is on and the rear of the bathroom is steamed up but it's dissipating. I fumble with the door lock, which doesn't close properly, and decide to prop the bathroom's plastic chair in front of the door instead. I leave my fresh top, tampon, hair brush and towel on it and finally let myself exhale a sigh of relief. God, it feels good to be alone. Maintaining a pretence of being ok when I'm not is so draining.

What are we going to do if we can't pay Reece back? Where are we going to find two *thousand* dollars from in *one week*? The licence issue is serious too, it's all money we simply don't have. I decide to vent my frustrations at Dan. If he wasn't playing pricing games, we'd be further ahead than we are.

I pull my camisole off, drop the sweaty material in the basin and turn on the tap, then shake my hair free from its band so it falls loose to my lower back. Tears slip down my cheeks as I lean on the sink, but it's such a relief to finally let my bottled-up emotions out. I turn the tap off and look down at my changing body shape; with all the cycling and cutting back on non-essentials I've dropped a dress size recently and my waist noticeably curves in above my hips now. Most girls would be thrilled, but I'd rather have the occasional chocolate bar. I wring out my wet top and use it as a flannel before pulling the brush through my hair and scooping it into a high ponytail.

I can't switch my mind off from our problems, and the tears continue to flow freely as I dry myself with my hand towel. Having my period doesn't help either; I'm always emotional when it's my time.

I pick up my top and sink dejectedly onto the chair, resting my head in my hands and all of the pent-up worry inside me escapes in a flood of tears. Sobs wrack through me for a minute and when I finish crying, I feel slightly better. Breathing deeply to calm down, I wipe my towel around my face to dry my tears and sit up.

It's time to be strong and think positively. Perhaps I could go to see the manager of the large farm neighbouring our land instead of just calling. I look up as if inspiration is going to fall out of the commercial ceiling tiles. Perhaps some of the local farms will want to buy eggs. I fan my fingers in front of my face attempting to make it less obvious I've been crying.

I'm starting to feel better when something moves at the back of the room. My heartrate surges and I jump off the chair like I've been electrocuted.

Jesus Christ!

I squeal with fright and clamp a trembling hand over my mouth.

Adam is leaning against the far wall, watching me. I'm not sure whether to scream, run or apologise.

'Oh my God, Adam!' I finally exclaim, panting in response to my thundering pulse. 'You nearly gave me a heart attack.'

He's got one leg bent to rest the sole of his shoe against the white tiled wall, and his hands behind his back. He's clearly been there since before I entered the bathroom. Oh good Lord, he's just witnessed all that crying! I'm mortified.

His towel and fresh T-shirt are on top of a bag by his feet and he's wearing jeans, but his chest is bare. And I'm suddenly mesmerised. He's got the figure of a Calvin Klein underwear model, but with black tribal tattoos on his arms, neck and chest.

Mmmm.

Yummy.

I'm lost for words and my heart is thundering. I drag my gaze from his body and finally meet his eyes. He looks concerned.

'Sorry, I didn't mean to make you jump,' he says in a gentle voice and starts to cross the room towards me. I stare at him for a moment then belatedly realise I'm only wearing my bra so clutch my top hastily to my cleavage like it's a lifeline. When he stops walking, he's practically in my personal space, so I side step the chair and back up against the wall to create some distance, but he takes a step forward and follows me.

He follows me!

My adrenaline kicks in, spilling a tear down my cheek. He goes to wipe it off but then checks himself and drops his hand back to his side.

'Did I scare you?' he asks. My eyes are naturally on a level with his shoulder. What a shoulder!

'Yes,' I squeak at him. 'Y… you… could have said… you were there,' I stutter and then mentally kick myself. There's nothing like playing it cool when the man of your dreams corners you in your underwear. I can't take my eyes off him.

'Sorry.' His expression is kind and my heart thuds so loud I wonder if he can hear it. 'At first I was admiring the view,' he says.

Pardon?

Now he does touch me. He runs a single finger tip from my shoulder slowly down my arm to where I'm clutching my top to my chest and his finger pauses there, making it clear what he was looking at. My skin burns fiercely at his touch, but I hold his gaze. Adrenaline is still pumping fight or flight instincts through me. Then he retraces the line back up my arm, over my collarbone to my face.

'But I can't say I was enjoying seeing these,' he says, wiping away a tear off my cheek and being careful not to touch me with anything but his finger. His accent sounds stronger now and I'm transfixed by it. He leans closer so his face is inches from mine. The tickle of his breath on my cheeks makes me light-headed. I'm glued to the spot; I don't know whether to smack him, burst into tears or throw my arms around him at the shock he's just given me.

Hmm… maybe *not* the last one.

'Will you tell me what's wrong?' he asks softly. I shake my head and can't seem to stop shaking. I take a deep breath and try to calm down, perhaps then I can get my legs to start working again and I can leave. 'Perhaps I can help?' I know he means it as his hazel eyes are intent on my reply. I'm about to say that he's already helped me with the licence fines, but the words fly out of my head as he puts one hand against the tiles above my shoulder and leans against it.

He's so close he's almost pinning me against the wall!

My pulse explodes into life. Even though he's not touching me, I'm turned on and excited, but, if I'm honest, also scared. I've never even had a relationship and now this gorgeous, strong older man has me half-naked against a bathroom wall in a warehouse. Panic is starting to set in and my eyes flit nervously to the door and then back to him.

'It's ok, Ella, I just want to know if I can help.' He registers my glance towards the door but he doesn't move away.

I shake my head, words beyond my capability with him so close to me like this. On the one hand, my skin is burning in anticipation of his touch, but on the other I'm terrified he might actually do it… and even more so, how I might react. So I stay frozen, staring up at him and trying not to broadcast the turmoil raging inside me. So much for becoming more confident around guys. I shiver as he tenderly strokes his finger tip down my neck and I see in his eyes he knows exactly how he's affecting me. Oh damn! I turn my face to the side and concentrate on the wall to my left. Should I push him away? He's hardly even touching me. Would that be overreacting? Christ! What if he pushed me back? He's so much stronger than me. A lump forms in my throat.

'Tell me, are you trembling because I gave you a shock, Ella? Or because you're nervous to be alone with me?' he asks me quietly. His breath smells amazing and I have an overwhelming urge to kiss him, so I bite my lip, but I'm practically panting. Why does he have to be so astute?

'Go and give someone else… a hard time.' I struggle to get my words out. Instead of moving away, he smiles and leans even closer, so his lips are almost touching my ear.

'I'm not giving *you* a hard time,' he whispers making my heart pound erratically. 'Personally, I think you're trembling because I make you nervous, but there's no need to be nervous, Ella, not with me.'

I look sideways and I'm startled to see his eyes are soft and kind. It overwhelms me more than if he'd been threatening and I shuffle left along the wall, but he puts his other arm out to cage me in. Panic is bubbling away inside me.

'That's enough, Adam.' I turn my face back to his but he's much too close and our lips touch. I jerk my head back, flattening myself against the cold tiles and giving us barely an extra inch of space. I'm beginning to get upset and I think he can see it.

'Ok,' he says, withdrawing slightly but leaving his arms exactly where they were.

'Move your arm!' I choke out. Oh my goodness, he smells so wonderful my head is buzzing, but he doesn't move. I ask myself if I'm secretly pleased about that or freaked out.

'No. Tell me why you were crying, Ella,' he asserts.

'*Why?* Don't pretend to care. And Dan will only use it to pick on me; it's what guys like him do.' I turn my shoulder to him, still clutching my top to my chest. The butterflies in my tummy go positively berserk.

'Hell, that's not true.' His voice is soft but firm. I try to duck under his arm, but he scoops a strong hand around my waist and actually lifts me to back to where I was. My insides spasm at the contact and I gaze up at him; did he seriously just lift me up like a bag of sugar?

Big hands envelope my wrists and my arms are suddenly pinned gently against the wall level with my head. I drop my top as my hands start to tremble, but I see no point protesting, he's far too strong, so I just stand there flushed with embarrassment that I'm wearing only my bra.

'Ella, I care. Trust me, I care.' Oh jeeze, is this really happening? 'Now tell me what's upset you and I'll let you go.' He's leaning more weight against my wrists. As if I could have pulled my arms free anyway. Should I be scared? I look at his eyes and don't feel threatened; he looks concerned about me, protective even, not like he's going to hurt me. He's also keeping his eyes on my face, not my chest, which is a relief. 'I want to help you, woman!' He sighs and rolls his eyes in exasperation.

I cave and figure what harm can it do to offload to him? I look up at the ceiling as if not meeting his eyes will make it less humiliating.

'You heard what the authorities' man said. We need a new licence and we can't afford one. We're really struggling, Adam. And Dan thinks it's *amusing* to drop his prices so much we're hardly even covering our costs. So, in a nutshell, we've just lost our income and I've wasted a year's savings. That's why I'm upset. Now let go of my wrists.' My words tumble over each other and I gasp for breath. Why mention the loan sharks he saw me talking to earlier? He can fill in the blanks on his own.

He lets go of my wrists but puts his hands on my hips instead and my skin tingles above my shorts where his hands make contact. My heart hammers erratically and I rub my wrists even though he wasn't hurting me. The tattoo on the upper right of his toned chest is directly in front of me, it's of a lady's hand making some sort of signal. He must work out all the time to keep that in shape I muse, then realise my mind is taking off on a course of its own, so I look up at his face and try not to be distracted.

'You could go for a drink with Dan,' Adam proposes quietly. I get the impression he's floating the idea to see my reaction.

'As if I'd do that.' He nods, like he knew I'd say that.

'If you like, I could sort your licence out,' he offers. I blink at him, my mind reeling.

'Why would you do that?' I accuse him defensively. He raises his eyebrows at me.

'Because I like you, obviously.'

Whoa.

My mouth drops open and heat creeps up my cheeks. Do dreams really come true?

'Don't look at me like that, Ella,' he says plainly. 'I know you like me too; I've got eyes in my head.'

His confidence floors me. It might be verging on arrogance even... if it wasn't true. I'm rendered speechless. My eyes dart away from his, trying to find a safe spot to concentrate on which isn't him, but his presence fills the whole room. My heart rate soars through the roof.

'You don't know anything about me!' I protest.

'Yeah I do,' he rebuffs me gently. 'The question is why are you pretending real hard that you're not interested in me? Are you just shy or do you have a guy already?'

If I wasn't such an open book, I might consider lying, but instead I shake my head.

'No, I don't have a guy already,' I mumble, my cheeks burning. I push at one of his hands on my hip, but he doesn't release me.

'Or perhaps that's the issue,' he says, his eyes glinting as a thought occurs to him. His expression takes my breath away. 'Yeah, I reckon it is, isn't it?'

'What?' I snap, not understanding what he means. God I wish I could play this cool, but instead I'm a nervous wreck.

He leans his face down to my level and his lips skim mine. I jump in response. Oh Jesus! Is he really doing this? Is he kissing me?

'That's it, isn't it? That's the reason why you're pretending you're not interested,' he murmurs against my lips. 'You're... inexperienced with men, aren't you, Ella? You're feeling out of your depth,' he says astutely.

My intense blush is answer enough for him and maintaining eye contact, he presses his mouth softly against mine. The room sways. My knees buckle. I should probably back away, but with the wall right behind me there's no room. His body pins mine dominantly and when I gasp, he pushes his tongue inside my mouth.

I let him.

Oh boy, it feels out of this world. Desire courses hot and wanton between my legs and a little moan escapes as my body melts against his of its own accord. I've never felt anything so amazing, my breathing stalls and he kisses me harder, like he's starving and I'm dessert. It's as though nothing else exists for that moment, just him and me. He slips one arm around my lower back and tugs my waist up against his hips; thrills race through me like never before. Our tongues clash against each other and I wrap my arms around his neck and pull him closer, making him groan in response. His hand slides from my waist up my side leaving a burning trail in its wake before covering my breast.

Oh God!

My nipples harden like bullets under my bra and my blood rushes south leaving me light-headed.

A loud rap on the bathroom door catapults me back to my senses and I pull my mouth away from Adam's, feeling flushed and panting. Christ, the man can kiss!

'Anyone in there? Locking up now!' It's Mr Jackson calling. I'm dazed and literally can't speak. Luckily Adam answers for us so we don't end up locked in… together… all night. Hmm.

'Yeah, be out in just a minute!' Adam calls confidently, his voice under complete control, but when he looks down at me his eyes are searing with lust and he has the most wicked smile on his face. He's a man who's just got exactly what he wanted, and he knows it. My tummy turns over as unsettled as it always is when he looks at me. I wonder what I've started by returning his kiss.

His hand moves from my chest back to my waist and he spreads his fingers out possessively holding me against him. I know he can feel me trembling, but as embarrassing as it is, I can't control it. I try to blink so I'm not staring at him quite so openly and drop my arms to my sides. I think I should move away, but my feet won't cooperate.

'You kiss like an angel,' he murmurs huskily, smiling at down me. It's like my blood catches fire at that.

He releases me and then bends down slowly, deliberately pausing with his face near my cleavage as he takes hold of my top from the floor and then straightens up again. He knows exactly what he's doing and it sends my hormones into chaos. Very slowly he gathers the material in his hands and pulls it over my head, so I hastily push my arms through the holes before he pulls the material down over my tummy. He then passes me the rest of my things, including the tampon. I wish the ground could swallow me whole, and I take my things silently with shaking hands. He kisses me once on the lips, clearly amused by the wide-eyed and flushed look on my face.

'I'll see you real soon,' he whispers with a glint in his eyes, which tells me he hasn't finished with me yet, not by any means. I blink at him as words fail me and then dart from the room like it's on fire once he moves the chair aside.

Smooth, Ella, really smooth.

I'm supremely conscious of the two people left in the otherwise deserted warehouse. Mr Jackson is by the bathroom and Dan is standing with his arms crossed leaning on the wall by my things. I know I look flushed and tear stained and I avoid looking at either of them. If it was possible to grow wings and fly out of there right now, I would.

I reach my bag and stuff my things inside, conscious that Dan is studying my face intently. When I pick my basket up, though, he wraps his hand around my forearm to make me wait. I flinch at his unexpected touch and don't look up at his face.

'Ella, have you been crying? Did he hurt you?' he asks, a definite edge slipping into his voice.

Oh damn!

I shake my head firmly, pull my arm free and speed walk out of the warehouse. As I head across the car park, I've never been more relieved to see my bike has two fully inflated tyres. I unlock it, throw the heavy chain recklessly on top of the eggs in my basket and get on. I hear the men talking behind me as the warehouse shutter door closes and I know I'm being watched and don't look back, just cycle away.

Am I dreaming? I must be. I seriously can't believe the most gorgeous guy just told me he liked me, as if it was the most obvious thing in the world, and then pinned me against a wall and kissed me. He rocked my whole world off its axis and my hands are still trembling as I grip my handlebars. Perhaps my dad was right, older guys are more than a little overwhelming and maybe best avoided.

Like *that's* going to happen.

Chapter Three

I'm halfway home when my front tyre hits a rock on the path so my bike lurches sideways. I just manage to put my foot down as the heavy basket and bag unbalance me. I dismount to inspect the damage, admittedly a little grateful for the rest in the heat of the early evening. The front tyre is flat and the wheel looks buckled. Great. I daren't ride it in that condition, but it's fine to push. I look at the countryside around me and can't see any buildings, just the tallgrass of the prairies, which are wilted due to the heatwave. I don't want to be out here in the dark on my own, but there must be an hour of sunlight left for me to walk home. I sigh, attach the basket to the handlebars and resign myself to pushing it the remaining few miles.

Before long I reach the sports field, the locals are there again tonight, but this week there are more of them. They're milling about and haven't started playing yet, their vehicles parked up by the road. I can hear music from a car stereo even from this distance.

I consider walking along the edge of the highway, but then two lorries go roaring past and I decide I'd rather be embarrassed than dead, so resume my trudge towards the crowd. My heart speeds up a little at the thought of maybe seeing Adam here, but although my cheeks are glowing with embarrassment that I ran away like a school girl because he kissed me, it doesn't stop the grin that is spreading across my face.

By the time I reach the group, people are turning their attention to me and remarking on my appearance. I know I look out of place;

they don't need to rub it in. It's mainly men again. Are there no women around here? It's something I've noticed at the market too, a significant lack of younger females. I had hoped I might have made some friends by now. Then my heart stalls and resumes at twice its normal speed as I spot Adam walking towards me with several other people.

Adam flicks his eyes over my buckled front wheel.

'Hello, Ella, are you ok?' he asks. I raise my eyebrows in surprise at seeing him so soon but nod in answer. 'Awesome.' He smiles at me so warmly a hot flush shoots through me and I tell myself to calm down. 'Yeah, it sure is a coincidence meeting you here,' he says, amused. He makes it sound like he was expecting me to come through and has been waiting for me, or perhaps I'm reading too much into this.

Carson walks over, takes my bike with the basket from me and starts pushing it along. His brown hair hangs below his T-shirt collar and he's unshaven like last week.

'Looks like you've tore slapped up your bike, Ella,' he says gesturing to the wheel. I look sideways at him and nod, not really understanding him.

'Shall I take that?' I offer, holding out my hand and managing to find my voice.

'Nah, he's got it,' Adam answers smoothly on Carson's behalf. I wonder where I'm going and am about to ask when a pretty blonde girl who's now walking next to Adam speaks. I recognise her as the same one Adam was talking to last week.

'So, this must be Ella?' she asks.

What? Have I been a topic of conversation?

'Yeah. Jenny, meet Ella. Jenny's my cousin.' Adam introduces us. Cousin? Oh that makes me feel better. Jenny walks ahead so she can see me and gives me a radiating smile. I smile back shyly before being distracted by seeing Adam's truck ahead of us.

'Err, Adam? Not that I'm not pleased to see you, but... I'm on my way home,' I mumble lamely. He slips a heavy arm around me and it feels wonderful, but I need to get back before the light fades.

'Don't worry, I'll drive you back later,' he says as we reach his truck parked alongside several others I now recognise. The tailboards are lowered and many faces from the market are sitting on the backs, drinking from cans, smoking and lounging about as they wait for the game. I receive a few grins and a hello from someone I don't know.

'You don't have to drive me back.' I'm hypersensitive that people are watching.

'I know, but I'm going to.' Adam leaves his arm around me. My heart is banging insanely against my rib cage at the contact. With so many ears listening, I refrain from arguing, although I catch a glimpse of Jenny's expression and she's smiling like her cousin is amusing her. There are two other women sitting with some of the guys on the bonnet of an old jeep a few vehicles down, but otherwise Jenny's the only girl with the group.

I notice Dan with Miguel on the back of the farthest truck and I get the feeling he's deliberately not looking our way. Various crates left over from today's market are strapped together in some of the trucks and Carson lifts my bike and basket into the back of Adam's before wandering off.

'Adam, I'd better get going,' I protest quietly, my voice a little strained with the embarrassment of the afternoon and knowledge that I practically ran away. 'You really don't have to drive me.'

To be honest I don't feel like I fit in here, it's not just that I'm English or not used to hanging out with guys, I'm the youngest one here by far. Adam lowers the tailboard at the back of the truck and climbs up effortlessly like he didn't hear me. Jenny climbs up on the back too and offers me a hand to pull me up. I don't feel like I have much choice, so I accept and climb up, making Adam grin.

'I see what you mean about her accent, it's hella cute,' Jenny says to Adam.

I turn around in the truck feeling self-conscious and drop my bag next to my bike.

'Yeah it is,' Adam agrees, looking at me. My tummy does a back flip and I rapidly turn my attention away. Another guy I recognise from the market stall gets up onto the back of the truck carrying a plastic bag of drinks.

'Hey Ella, I'm Owen,' he says smiling at me, 'don't think we've been introduced yet.' His smile is friendly; he's African American, tall and wears his hair cropped short.

'Hi,' I mumble feeling awkward. Jenny sits down closely next to Owen and helps herself to a can, clearly they're a couple. Adam winks at me and pats the truck bed next to him.

'Come and sit yourself down,' he says. I gulp. Oh that does sound tempting.

'I was on my way home,' I protest, but it's half-hearted.

'Well you still are, just taking a re-route. Why, you wanna make a call or something?' he asks, his eyes glinting at me warmly. I nod, and he looks at me, waiting expectantly.

'I don't have a mobile,' I say apologetically after a short pause. 'Can I borrow yours?'

Owen repeats 'mo-bi-le!' clearly entertained and Jenny grins.

Adam's eyes are telling me he's amused too and also surprised I don't have a phone, but says 'sure' and leans back to pull his phone out of his jeans pocket.

'Heavens to Betsy! *How* can you not have a cell?' Jenny exclaims raising her eyebrows at me; I shrug. Besides the obvious lack of funds, the only people I know here are my family and we're always together, so there hasn't been any need for me to have one. We bought a 'family mobile' when we arrived for any calls we need to make as the landline got disconnected.

Adam unlocks his phone and passes it to me and I decide to text, feeling self-conscious about my accent. I've not used this type of phone before and immediately open several apps I didn't mean to, so I crouch down and ask Adam to show me how to use it.

'What, the cells are different in the UK?' he teases and I nod, cheeks flushing. 'Like the tables?' he adds. I can't help it, a shy smile creeps onto my face and I concentrate on his phone, hyper-aware of his proximity.

'Yeah, like the tables,' I say, being a good sport.

He takes hold of my wrist and gives me a little pull so that I find myself sitting haphazardly against him. My heart goes into meltdown and I'm barely breathing, trying to hide how I respond to him. I think it's obvious, but he's a gentleman and doesn't mention it, just takes his phone back and opens a text.

'What do you want to say?' he asks.

'Just, something like *It's Ella, my bike's broken so Adam from the veg stall is giving me a lift home later* or something like that so they don't worry.' I say concentrating on his phone and not daring to look up at his face as I'm practically sitting on his lap.

'Adam *from the veg stall?*' he repeats back to me, unable to contain a grin. Jenny and Owen start laughing. I glance at his face and immediately change my position so I can lean back a little. He raises his eyebrows and his eyes are dancing at me. Am I really that amusing? I look at him blankly.

Jenny kneels up next to me and gives me an affectionate hug, making me jump. I don't even know her!

'She's just adorable,' she says looking at Adam. I look at her a bit defensively. Is she being patronising? She seems genuine, though. This is weird.

I bite my lip, confused, and Jenny returns to Owen. Adam's still smiling at me, like he's got a secret or something.

'What?' I ask, more than a little self-conscious.

'Nothing, baby,' he murmurs, then averts his gaze and taps out my message on his phone.

Baby? Coming from *him*? I could get used to that really quickly. He hands me his phone, he's tapped out my message exactly.

I enter the number for the family mobile and press the send icon, passing it back without making eye contact. There's a pause in conversation so I watch various guys wearing catching gloves start scattering around the field as another team throw down bases in a diamond shape.

Adam leans across my lap and reaches the plastic bag with drinks in it, his shoulder deliberately bumping into me and far too close to be a casual oversight. I lean back, still disconcerted they were laughing at me.

'Would you like me to pass you the bag?' I ask him pointedly.

'Nah, I got it,' he says as he snags it and takes out a can of Coke. I'm relieved as he said he'd drive later. He opens the bag to me, there's a mix of soft drinks and beers. 'You want one?' he offers. I nod and take a diet Coke. His phone beeps as a text arrives and he reads it.

'It's for you.' He holds the phone out for me, but doesn't let go when I try to take it, making me look up at him deliberately. His eyes are alight with humour. Oh God, he's so damned attractive. I lean in to read the message as he intended.

Char wants to know if it's the same Adam she met at the tree? Huh? Oh, and do u want us 2 pick u up? H x. I grin.

'Want me to reply?' he asks.

'Just type *yes and no it's fine* please.'

He does and presses send. I turn my attention to the pitch, conscious from the side of my vision that Adam isn't watching them; he's still looking at me. He shuffles back to lean against the side of the truck and slots a leg behind me to sandwich me between his knees. I raise an eyebrow at him and he laughs as he wraps his arms around my waist and pulls my back up against his chest. I gasp in surprise but he stops me from moving away by hugging me tightly and then resting his chin on my shoulder, his beard tickling my skin a little. I don't know how to react naturally and my shoulders are tense. Perhaps he can tell as he whispers in my ear.

'I told you earlier, Ella, there's no need to be nervous with me.' I swallow and stare forward. 'This way we can talk easier. You're a real great kisser by the way,' his voice is deep and sexy and I blush immediately, making him chuckle.

My heart is pumping wildly. He smells of some amazing deodorant and I breathe in deeply, unable to stop myself.

'Do you always pin girls up against bathroom walls?' I ask a little defensively, trying desperately to get my breathing under control. I glance over at Jenny and Owen and they're completely unperturbed by Adam manhandling me at their side.

'Only when they ask me to,' he replies casually. I shift my position so I can see his expression. He's smiling at me, but I can't tell if he's teasing me. I feel like he's constantly talking in riddles. 'Well you aren't pushing me away now,' he observes quietly and pulls me back to where I was, placing his chin back on my shoulder. His breath sends delicious tingles down my neck. 'So, by that I figure you were telling the truth earlier and you haven't got a guy already?'

I'm so nervous words fail me so I just shake my head.

'Good,' he answers. 'And if anyone asks, you can say now you have, right?'

My breath catches in my throat; the thought of being alone with him excites me beyond belief but also pushes me well outside my comfort zone. He tightens his arms around my middle, somehow managing to push them up under my cleavage and I think he must have one hell of a view down my top. Jesus Christ, my heart feels like it's thundering so hard I could go into cardiac arrest soon and despite my efforts, I'm definitely trembling.

'Right?' he prompts me, nuzzling his lips into the side of my neck so I melt back against him without thinking. Oh that feels amazing.

'Adam, I don't usually date,' I whisper, overwhelmed.

'So? Start.'

'I know almost nothing about you,' I croak.

'Do you want to get to know me?' His lips are still moving against my over-sensitised skin and sending delicious trembles through me. I nod. 'Good, then say yeah, that you'll be my girl.'

I gulp. Jeeze! Talk about full on. I can barely breathe. My dad's voice is going around my head *he's too old for you, Ella*. But, oh my goodness, one thing I do know is how I react to Adam. I nod; words have deserted me.

'Was that a yes?' he murmurs against my neck. I nod again wondering if I know what I'm doing and take a deep breath feeling decidedly light-headed. 'Awesome,' he exhales, pleased.

Oh my!

I turn in his arms and manage to create enough space to look at his face. He gently puts his palm on my cheek before sliding it round the back of my head, effectively holding me still and I know he's going to kiss me.

His lips fuse to mine, gentle and probing and my world tilts around me. I kiss him back and heavenly tingles ripple along my scalp from his hand in my hair. Oh my goodness, is anyone watching? From the general chatter, I don't think so, but when we break I try to turn around to look, feeling exposed.

'Relax, baby,' he murmurs softly to me and my cheeks flush as I return my eyes to his. 'Was I right earlier? Are you inexperienced?' he asks, inclining his head to indicate my expression. Christ, is it that obvious I'm not used to this? A rush of sensation pools in my stomach and I try to edge back a little, but his hand still holds me gently where I am. 'It's ok, it's nothing to be embarrassed about, you're sure younger than me.' He shrugs casually, but his eyes are watching my every reaction intently. I swallow and stare back into his eyes. 'Tell me, how many guys have you been with?' he asks directly.

Oh fuck! My cheeks flame.

'Are you always so direct?' I ask defensively.

'Generally, yeah,' he answers, not breaking eye contact. 'Answer me.'

'I haven't,' I mumble so softly it's barely audible. His eyes glint like he likes my answer. No, scratch that. Like he *fucking loves* my answer. Oh dear God. I feel like my nerves are going to send me into palpitations soon. Am I seriously having this conversation... with *him*? He leans forward and plants a kiss on my forehead then wraps his arm securely back around me, pulling me sideways against his chest. I bring my knees up in front of me and snuggle against his warmth, I just can't resist the soft cotton of his T-shirt or the subtle scent of leather, it's distinctly masculine and *so* good.

'It's good you told me,' he murmurs so only I can hear.

'Why?' I whisper.

'It's just good I know, so I can try not to fuck up,' he says with feeling. I gulp and wonder what he means.

'How old are you?' I ask finally having the courage to voice my curiosity and he chuckles a bit.

'Twenty-eight,' he says. Oh, I'm so far out of my comfort zone, I can't even see it in the distance, he's so going to want more than I can give him right now. 'That's a problem?' he asks me softly, cradling me against his chest and pressing his lips into the top of my head. I want to act cool and shrug it off, but my God, I need to be honest about this.

'Probably, yes,' I whisper back, glad my head is under his chin where he can't see my face.

'Why?' he asks quietly.

'I think you can guess why,' I mumble, squeezing my hands nervously between my legs. He shifts back to look at me and if I were to describe his expression, I'd say he was giving me sex-eyes. A look so heated and filled with desire that I'm sure I've never been on the receiving end of before. Tremors of both excitement and unease paradoxically race through me, it's like he wants to take me to bed... right now. I'm so out of my league. And deeply aroused.

'It's only sex, Ella,' he reassures me, hugging me close. I feel dazzled by him. Overwhelmed. 'So, are you going to tell me what else upset you? I'm guessing it wasn't just about the licence,' he asks, perhaps sensing my growing panic and changing the subject. I shake my head. 'You don't owe Reece and his douchebags money then?' he murmurs against the top of my head. I freeze and don't answer. I think it's confirmation enough for him. 'How much?'

'Don't get involved, Adam,' I say back softly.

'Too late, we're together now, right? So how much do you owe?' he asks again, so self-assured it makes me blink. I'm too uncomfortable with the subject to provide the details, though. 'Is it just in your name or your whole family?' Oh sweet Jesus, he's full on! Is that an American thing, or just Adam?

'The whole family,' I mumble reluctantly.

'Shall I pay it off for you?' I blink in shock and shake my head firmly. He doesn't even know how much it is.

'No, thank you,' I say emphatically and clearly embarrassed, so he lets the topic drop.

Our eyes drift to the baseball; after a while the tension eases again and we talk about the game. He explains the rules for me, smiling like I'm amusing him. He's great company and I'm drawn to him. As we watch the match I notice that in comparison to back home, Americans are all so much more expressive, it lends a certain air of confidence to Adam in particular that's appealing and masculine.

When the light fades the game finishes and people talk about meeting at Dan's place, it sounds like it's a regular thing. Even though the others around us are getting up and putting their empty cans away, Adam seems perfectly happy to stay where he is, with me wrapped in his arms. I go to sit up but he holds me still.

'Do you want to come to Dan's?' he asks.

I'm surprised and flattered that this gorgeous man is asking *me*, but I really should be getting back.

'Maybe another time,' I say quietly. 'I should get home; my sisters will be worried.'

'Are you always such a good girl?' he teases me. 'You don't date, you don't stay out late, you don't pick a beer.' I nod, ignoring the glint in his eyes. He leans slowly forward and smiles at me. 'I'm sure looking for a good girl,' he whispers and kisses me on my lips.

'What?' I ask hoarsely.

'You heard me,' he says confident and serious. I blink at him, finding no words. 'I want a good girl, Ella. And just so you know, even if you did have a guy, I'd have made sure you changed your mind until you said yes to me.'

Whoa!

I turn away feeling like my heart is in my throat. He's a lot to take in. When he loosens his arms, I shuffle forward and get off the back of the truck. Adam follows and jumps down agilely, before reattaching the tailboard. I look at his hands and notice there are various scars across his knuckles and I wonder how he got them.

I'm beginning to worry if he's going to drive me home on his own and I'm wary. It's not that I don't feel safe with him, I do, but I have to be honest, I hardly know him. When he puts his arm around my shoulders and starts steering me towards the cabin, I glance up at him apprehensively.

'Is Jenny coming too?'

He blinks at me in instant comprehension of what I'm saying and smiles like I'm being cute. Then he calls out confidently to his cousin who's about to climb into the truck parked next to us.

'Yo, Jen, get your butt over here, you're riding with us.'

She looks up surprised as Owen is already in the other truck but nods and walks over to us and I breathe a sigh of relief.

She gestures for me to climb into the middle seat ahead of her and then she gets in after me. The truck lurches over the rough field until we get to the highway.

Jenny grows on me on the way home as she peppers me with questions about how I'm finding life in America. I'm thankful it's only a short drive and Adam negotiates the truck expertly down our driveway, managing to avoid the bigger holes.

We pull up outside and Adam retrieves my things. Jenny gets out so I don't have to crawl across her lap, then hugs me goodbye like we've been friends for years. I'm not oblivious to the twitching of the living room curtain as Adam leaves my bike and basket resting against the veranda. Then he puts his hands on my shoulders and kisses me full on the mouth before I realise he was even thinking of doing it. My heart hammers in my chest as I know at least one of my sisters saw that out of the window. He keeps the kiss short, but it leaves me flustered.

'Good night,' he says then he strokes my face before striding back to his truck and getting in. I watch as he restarts the engine, turns the lights on and negotiates our bumpy driveway back to the main road. My mind is in a whirl and my heart's pumping hard so I take a steadying breath before I see my sisters. I try to stop the ecstatic grin spreading across my face as I stand on the driveway watching his taillights, but I can't.

It's Sunday afternoon and another scorching day so for once we decide to take some time out as a family in the sunshine. Sarah and I are stretched out on a blanket in our bikinis in the back garden. She's been asking me questions about Adam and how come he drove me back last night, so I'm pretty sure she was the one looking out of the window and would have seen him kiss me. I don't mention that Adam and I might be more than friends; I'm still psyching myself up to that bombardment of questions, and I've never been known for sharing… except maybe to Charlotte.

Long ago I turned onto my front and took my bikini top off to avoid tan lines. I guess that's one advantage of living in the middle of nowhere, just us girls.

Charlotte, Hannah and Rose are also wearing bikini tops and shorts while entertaining the children in a paddling pool with several inches of water as a treat. We justify the water usage as the truth is that the children really deserve a treat. Things are getting desperate and the news that we now owe two thousand dollars, payable next Sunday, is frightening all of us, so we're doing what we do best and avoiding the subject.

The licence issue is also a massive blow and I can't let Adam pay for a new one even though he offered, so Charlotte's come up with a new idea for the market. We also desperately need to go food shopping but are trying to delay.

It's disheartening we've had no luck finding work after trying so hard. Hannah is the only one not looking due to her visa, but she more than pulls her weight, in fact if it wasn't for her aunt's cheque that arrived from England three weeks ago, we would have been in trouble earlier. Tomorrow I'm definitely going to head over to the large farm to try and see the manager, clearly voice messages to Mr Sims are not working.

Sarah asks if I want a drink before going inside.

'No thanks,' I say, relaxing in the warm sun and listening to the children. A while later I think I hear the sound of an engine, but over the squeals the children are making, it's hard to tell. Then Sarah comes back out of the house calling out to me.

'Ella? There's someone here to see you. Put your top on.'

I hear the deeper tones of a man, so jerk upright and hastily put my bikini top back on as my hair tumbles haphazardly down my back.

'She decent?' I hear a familiar deep voice. Oh shit, is Adam here? Then the backdoor shuts. He must be outside already. I look around frantically hoping to see some of Sarah's clothes lying about that I can cover up with, but there's nothing. I scoop my hair hastily over one shoulder, jump up quickly and turn around, thankfully my sunglasses hide a little of my embarrassment. Adam and Sarah are already halfway across the yard and Charlotte, Rose and Hannah stop playing with the children and watch curiously as he approaches. I cross my arms self-consciously; I might as well just be wearing underwear. I notice that Sarah has pulled on a long T-shirt which covers her bum.

'Hello, Ella,' Adam says, stopping a few paces away, smiling as he blatantly looks me up and down, it sends my pulse racing. He's wearing khaki shorts, casual shoes and a tight-fitting blue T-shirt, which enhances his biceps. He has styled his hair, with sunglasses pushed up onto his head and looks sexy as hell.

I get the impression Sarah might think so too the way she's gawking at me from behind his back. I flick my fringe out of my eyes while shuffling into my flip flops.

'This is a surprise.' I smile. An embarrassing one!

'Uh huh.' He grins; his expression says it all. 'I'll have to turn up unannounced more often if I get greeted with this view,' he says quiet enough for only me to hear as he closes the gap between us and kisses me lingeringly on the lips in front of my sisters.

Gulp.

I look instinctively at the girls. Charlotte and Sarah blink and look away, Rose gapes and Hannah grins. I clear my throat awkwardly.

'Err, you've met Charlotte already,' I say flustered and indicate with my hand that we should go and speak to my sisters. He nods at Charlotte.

'Afternoon,' he says in the sexiest of American accents. Charlotte smiles. Of course she does. Who wouldn't? It's almost panty peeling.

'And of course, Sarah just let you in, so you've met her too,' I mumble and they both nod. 'And this is Rose my other sister, and our friend Hannah.' I introduce them and they all shake hands. I can't help but notice the girls stare a little and a small part of me is thrilled that it's *me* he's here to see. 'And these two are Charlotte's children, David is four,' I say and then ruffle my niece's hair, 'and this is Amy who's two.'

The children are thankfully wearing bottoms along with their sunhats so we don't look like complete naturists. They sit in the water where they've been playing with bath toys and bottles and blink up at him.

'I hadn't realised you had such a big family here,' he says looking at me curiously. 'When did you arrive?'

'Last month,' I answer as the children resume playing and the girls pretend to give them their attention. 'Err, would you mind if I just pop inside and grab some clothes?' I say, folding my arms over my chest.

'Sure thing.' He replies smoothly, but his eyebrows flash upwards implying to me that he's thinking something entirely different.

I dart off into the house, my flip flops flapping on my feet and I don't need to look behind me to know he's staring at my bum. I hear the girls start up a conversation with him as the door closes behind me.

I rapidly towel down and pull a brush through my messy hair, change into some proper underwear and a short strappy but casual summer dress in yellow. I also apply some mascara and feel a lot more decent when I return to find my unexpected visitor. The way the girls reacted to him makes me half expect to find him lounging in a chair with my sisters fanning palm leaves at him, but thankfully when I return they're all just as I left them.

He holds his hand out as I approach so he can put his arm around me and it gives me a buzz of excitement. He's wearing aftershave and I resist the urge to bury my nose into his collarbone and inhale.

'Adam's just been telling us he lives at the large farm,' Sarah says to me. I look up at him in surprise, realising again that I barely know anything about him.

'And he told us that you're seeing him,' Rose says in a tone deliberately too light and airy so as not to fool anyone that she's teasing me.

'Uh huh,' I say focusing on wiggling my toes into my flip flops. 'It sounds like you've had quite a chat!' I say innocently enough, and I can tell Adam is amused by that even though I don't look up at him.

'Yes, it was quite a chat, especially when I mentioned already on Wednesday that *Dan* might be a bit old for you,' Charlotte says.

Hmm, warning. Protective big sister nearby.

I glance at her and see she's trying hard not to smile, though, so I relax again; she's also teasing me.

'I thought I'd come by and see if you needed help fixing your bike or with your new licence application,' Adam says, I think deliberately giving me a way out of my sisters ribbing me for having a guy come around for the first time... Well the second time maybe, if you count when Tom took me to my college graduation party just before we left the UK.

'Oh, could you fix my bike? That would be amazing!' I gush then add hesitantly, 'I think the wheel is beyond repair, though.'

'And the licence?' he asks.

I don't need to glance at my sisters to know already that we don't have the money for the new licence.

'Not right now, but it's really nice of you to offer.' I decline, knowing he's already offered to pay for it.

'Ok. I'll get some tools out of my truck then,' he says and I lead the way around the side of the house to where his truck is parked. We walk close to each other but not touching and it's like there's an electrical current running between us. I'm conscious again how tall he is as we walk along. I barely come up to his shoulder, but then again, I'm quite petite.

'I brought you some groceries by the way, I kinda overheard your conversation with Dan,' he says as we near his truck and glances at me sideways with a half-smile on his face. Yes, I bet he did 'overhear' as he was right behind me.

'You didn't have to do that,' I say, surprised. 'Would you like any money for them?' He frowns at me, momentarily taken aback.

'No, Ella, it's not your money I want,' he states firmly. My heart skips a beat. *What*? Was there a double meaning to that? He looks me straight in the eyes and doesn't look away. I have no idea what to say, perhaps if I was older or more confident I could come back with some witty response, but I'm not.

'Well thank you, but tell me if you change your mind,' I improvise. He smiles at me in a way that I don't fully understand and retrieves a huge crate from under a plastic sheet.

'If I'd known you had such a big family with kids here, I'd have brought some more,' he says turning to face me and lifting it with ease. My eyes scan the crate; it's stacked with not only fruit and vegetables, but also packs of sausages, ham, cereals, milk and bread. My mouth drops open.

'Oh wow! You didn't have to do that,' I gush.

'Yeah I did,' he clears his throat a little. 'We weren't exactly fair with our pricing if I recall. So, I'll put it in your pantry?'

We weren't fair with *our* pricing?

I nod, quickly closing my mouth. He looks at my face for a moment and winks at me before walking towards the house. I jump to my senses and run past him to open the door. Charlotte and Rose are in the kitchen and stop talking suspiciously quickly when they see us enter, their eyes widening at the food Adam is carrying.

'Adam's brought us some things,' I announce. 'Isn't that nice of him?' I say brightly.

They both nod and say thank you like robots as Adam deposits the crate on the floor in front of the pantry door.

'No problem,' he says looking around. I glance about also, feeling self-conscious that our home isn't more stylish.

In comparison to English houses the room could be considered large, however, with seven of us living here and this being the only communal space, it could also be called crowded. It's impossible to find space alone. Impossible.

With only three bedrooms, Sarah and I share the smallest one. Rose and Hannah beat us to the slightly larger room when we arrived. Of course, Charlotte shares with Amy and David and as they have all the children's toys understandably they got the biggest room.

'Would you like a drink?' I ask Adam trying to distract him.

'No, I'm good thanks,' he replies, turning to me and smiling. His eyes are so sharp, I get the impression that they've taken in every detail of our surroundings.

The house is clean and tidy as always, but it's crammed full of things we brought from England which wouldn't fit in our bedrooms. The laminated breakfast bar is cluttered with toys and paperwork and I cringe to see our bills spread out with several stamped OVERDUE and FINAL NOTICE in bold print. Oh Christ. I move quickly to stand in front of them in case by some stroke of luck he hasn't already noticed them.

'Shall we go outside then?' I ask him cheerfully.

'Sure,' he answers and glances quickly towards our living area as we head for the door. He turns his eyes too quickly in my paranoid opinion, confirming that he spotted the paperwork.

I follow his gaze towards the living area and cringe a bit as I try to see the room through his eyes. The worn-out sofas and rug are long overdue to be replaced and the sturdy dark wood furniture is marked after decades of use. Uncle Robin wasn't one for living in a show home that's for sure. I wonder what Adam's house is like and what he's thinking about ours. I realise how much his opinion really matters to me, perhaps I like him even more than I thought.

Over the next hour, I sit on the veranda and watch while Adam straightens the front wheel of my bike and re-tensions the spokes. He's not that thrilled with the results as the wheel isn't perfect, but I'm delighted. It means I don't have to walk everywhere. It's frustrating considering I have my driver's licence, but we simply can't afford the extra insurance on the van.

'You'd be better off buying a new wheel,' he says as he packs his tools away.

'Uh huh,' I say.

He looks at me astutely and asks simply, 'Want me to get you one?' I shake my head quickly. 'Are your sisters working?'

'Sarah works part-time at a supermarket, but they can't give her any more hours,' I answer quietly.

'And?'

'And the egg business isn't exactly thriving; I think a fox has killed over half my chickens anyway.'

He raises his eyebrows. 'It'll more likely be a racoon or a coyote around here, baby,' he says amused.

There's that word again, *baby*. A little flame lights up inside me.

'And?'

'Well the truth is we've all been looking, except Hannah who's on a tourist's visa, there just seems to be no jobs near here. Charlotte's got an idea for the market this Saturday that fits with the licence we do have, so hopefully that will bring in some money and we can hire the pitch for the following weeks.'

'Is there a "but" coming?'

'It's the same "but" as there always is.' I sigh.

'What do you need?' he asks me.

'I'm not asking to borrow money, Adam,' I exclaim.

'I know,' he says, 'that's why I'm offering.'

'No it's ok.' I shake my head firmly. 'You shouldn't feel obliged to keep offering to pay. It's sweet of you, but we'll sort something out.'

'Sort something out like borrowing more from Reece?' he asks, his eyes meeting mine. There's a strength of will in his expression that makes me blink. 'Ella, they're bad news, don't get tangled up with them, I know what I'm talking about, you'll get hurt.' Oh God, he's warning me. Panic surges through me again that we owe so much money and need to find it by Sunday.

'So how much do you need?' He pulls out his wallet from his back pocket. 'It's better from me than from Reece, trust me, Ella.'

'I don't want to take money off you. Really, Adam, it might leave you short,' I say quickly.

He laughs a bit. 'You worry too much,' he answers like it's of no consequence.

'What if I can't pay you back?' I fret.

'Well if you can't pay me back in money, you can pay me back in sex,' he says calmly and looking at me. I gape at him. Is he flirting or does he think I'm a slut?

'Are you joking?' My heart is beating a million times a minute.

'Only if you want me to be.' He smiles at me; his eyes alight. Is that a yes or a no? Then he bursts out laughing and I realise he was joking after all. Oh this man is going to kill me! I punch him lightly on his arm in response.

Still grinning, he opens his wallet. There's a stack of notes inside. Jesus! Does he always carry that much on him? I'm astounded as he pulls out the money, counts out five hundred dollars and wraps my fingers around it.

'Take it,' he says. 'Pay me back if it makes you feel better, but just ask if you need any more, it's no problem.'

Is he for real?

'Put it in your pocket then,' he says.

'I can't take that, Adam.' I hand it back to him.

He takes the money back, folds it in half and slips it into the upper cup of my bra. I jump and then flush pink in embarrassment. Talk about forward. I'm about to argue but he rests his finger on my lips to silence me.

'Have you tried DB Produce for work?' he asks changing the subject. If he lives there, perhaps he knows Mr Sims.

'Yes, I've left the manager, Mr Sims, four messages.' I'm trying not to think about the fact that he's just put money in my bra. 'I was actually thinking of going tomorrow to ask in person.'

'Come by in the morning around nine, say your name at the gate or ask for me and I'll find you some work.'

'Really?' I say, astonished. 'What do you do there?'

'Sure,' he says but doesn't elaborate as his gaze focuses on a jeep bumping up our driveway. As it gets closer, I see Miguel is driving with Dan in the passenger seat. 'Are you expecting visitors, Ella?' Adam raises his eyebrows at me. I look at him blankly.

'No offence, Adam, but if I'd been expecting visitors, you wouldn't have found me wearing a bikini,' I reply dryly.

'Well that's just affirmed my desire not to call ahead next time.' He grins at me. I widen my eyes at him, but he holds my gaze, so I spin around to face the jeep which has now parked. God, he can be unsettling sometimes.

Dan and Miguel are looking at Adam through the windshield and their expressions tell me they were not expecting to see him here. I walk over as Dan opens the door. He looks me up and down and I'm relieved I got dressed earlier.

'Hey, Ella,' he says so I smile, a little perplexed at what he's doing here.

Miguel gets out and joins us then Adam slips his arms around my waist from behind me. It's a clear statement. My heart hammers in my chest that he's being so blatant. He might as well hold a sign up against my chest stating *mine*. Dan averts his gaze immediately towards the house and I feel suddenly thrilled and awkward at the same time.

Miguel nods at Adam then turns to me. 'Ella, is Hannah home?'

Adam is pulling me up hard against his hips and it makes me flush. I'm slightly relieved to pull away. It's overwhelming… and an immense turn on.

'Yeah sure, I'll go tell her you're here.' I head back into the house. I hadn't realised Hannah and Miguel had talked that much when the girls had been at the market.

A minute later, I follow Hannah, Rose and Sarah outside. They're still wearing bikini tops and shorts with Sarah still in the long T-shirt. Charlotte stayed in the garden with the children.

To say Miguel and Dan's eyes bulge when the girls walk out dressed like that is an understatement. It's almost comical and I stifle a smile. It's not lost on me that Dan throws an incredulous look in Adam's direction, which I interpret to imply 'trust *you* to be here already when there's a group of half-naked girls around'.

Miguel smiles and exclaims, 'Hannah!' in a warm greeting. He walks over and kisses her on each cheek in a very South American manner. Hannah blinks at him, surprised, but looks pleased.

'Hi,' she answers and glances at me a little bemused. 'Miguel, is it?' she queries, checking she knows his name.

'Yeah. I wondered if you wanted to come to a street party at Dan's on Saturday?' he asks smoothly, his Spanish accent blending with American.

'Err, maybe.' Hannah flushes, but it's obvious she's thrilled with the idea. 'Where is that?'

Wow, that was smooth… and quick! First sentence, what's your name, second sentence, he's got a date. I continue to watch, quite impressed to be frank.

'Over at DB Produce, y'all are real welcome,' he answers glancing at Rose and Sarah. I notice Dan is looking at Sarah appreciatively.

They make more introductions, but I don't pay attention. Adam has slipped his arm around me again and my head is filled with only him as his hand slides down over my hip and under the back of my short dress to squeeze my bottom. I jump and look up at him and his eyes hold mine unwaveringly. I squirm and look back at the others, having no idea how to flirt without making a fool of myself. Should I squeeze his bum too?

He leans down and whispers in my ear, 'You're real pretty when you blush.'

Of course that only makes my cheeks burn brighter and he chuckles, shifting me against his side now.

Oh wow, I could get used to being this close to him. I slip my arm around his waist and hug him back, trying to act cool. I get a kiss on my forehead in response, which makes me light up inside. Am I seriously standing here with Adam's arm around me? Things this good don't usually happen to me.

'Will you come to Dan's?' Adam bends down to me, his breath tickling my ear.

'Maybe another time,' I answer. Or maybe not... I'm not comfortable with going to Dan's house considering I pretty much called him an arsehole yesterday and have turned him down twice for a date this week. 'Dan and I aren't the best of friends,' I add, a little too self-conscious to look up at him.

The girls invite Miguel and Dan inside and their faces light up. I go to follow them, but Adam keeps his arm clamped around my waist, preventing me. Once the door swings shut behind them he turns me to face him.

'You didn't want to go inside?' I ask.

'No, I want you all to myself, I'm greedy like that,' he answers me and I register the intensity in his eyes.

'Oh,' I mumble a little dazed as he presses his body against me and slowly lowers his mouth to mine. His lips are warm and soft, like they were made with the sole purpose to massage mine. He coaxes me to respond, and then his tongue slides slow and deep into my mouth, claiming me as his arms clamp around me possessively. I cling to him as he kisses me and when he pulls away I'm breathing hard and stunned. Desire throbs through me, raw and unsated.

He holds my face in his hands and smiles a little smugly as he can see how flustered he's made me.

'Come on, let's test your bike before I leave.' He takes my hand and leads me back to the bike. I follow him on legs which are significantly shakier than before. He holds the handle bar out towards me. 'Get on then,' he says, and I take the bike and swing my leg over the high cross bar. 'Looks good!' He smirks as he watches.

'Do you mean the wheel?' I ask innocently.

'No!' He grins.

Why is he always talking in riddles? Then I realise I'm wearing a very short skirt and he's been enjoying the view. I blush belatedly and roll my eyes in exasperation and he laughs that it took me a moment to catch on. Then he steps in front of the bike, clamping the front wheel between his knees and leans over the handlebars to put his hands on the tops of my exposed thighs.

'Steady!' He grins as I was hopping a little. He's pretending to help me stabilise the bike which is clearly too large for me, but it's a blatant excuse to smooth his thumbs increasingly higher up my thighs. His eyes are glinting mischievously at me, testing me to see if I push him away. In truth I'm not sure if I want to.

'I know what you're doing!' I accuse him. Instead of backing off, though, he laughs again.

'Oh, I sure hope so, Ella,' he says amused. I can't help but smile too as I look away, his teasing is infectious.

'Step back then or I'll run you over,' I threaten playfully and he grins before moving aside. I push down hard on the pedal in my flip flops and lap the house once. The bike rides well.

It's not long later that Hannah and Sarah follow Miguel and Dan out of the house to wave them off. Adam turns to me.

'Actually, baby, I've got to shoot too, I've got work to do,' he says. On a Sunday? I wonder what he does.

I nod and try not to show that I'm disappointed he's leaving. He leans down while the others are getting into the jeep and kisses me on the mouth again. When he breaks away, he suggestively trails a fingertip down my neck and over my collarbone, making me flush when he slots two fingers into the top of my bra cup and pulls out the money he put there. I take a shaky breath but don't break eye contact with him.

'Don't lose this,' he says handing it to me, his eyes playing their usual games. 'And you just ask me if you need more, don't go to Reece again, right?' He's serious. I nod and he places the palm of his hand on my cheek affectionately.

'See you tomorrow then,' he says. I'm a little awestruck and it takes me a moment to remember I need to ask for him when I arrive at DB Produce in the morning. He waves a casual goodbye to the girls and gets in his truck and both vehicles leave at the same time. Sarah, Hannah and I all exchange a look before walking back into the house arm in arm; we're all smiling.

Chapter Four

It's eight-thirty when Rose and I set off for DB Produce. We're wearing smart trousers and short-sleeved blouses but by the time we arrive, dust from the fields is clinging to our damp skin as much as our shoes.

'Do you think we've got a real chance of finding something?' Rose asks me, trying to dust down her trousers as we walk along the industrial perimeter fence to the front security gate.

'I really hope so.' The truth is I have no idea what Adam does here or if he's able to find us some work.

'I do too,' Rose whispers anxiously and surprises me by giving my hand a squeeze. I put her uncharacteristic sign of affection towards me down to nerves.

Inside the security cabin a man wearing a grey guard's uniform gestures for us to come inside as he finishes a phone call.

'How can I help you?' he asks.

'We're Ella and Rose Peterson, we've come to ask about some vacancies, Adam said to ask for him,' I answer, realising I don't even know what his surname is.

The guard nods, checks his computer and hands us each an ID badge stamped *Visitor* then pushes a clipboard towards us so we can sign in.

'Stick to the footpath as the road is busy,' he says pointing out of the window. 'The first building on the right is Reception, ask for Sally.'

As we leave the cabin the security guard picks up a different clipboard and goes out to talk to the driver of a lorry that's pulled up at the gate. Rose and I start walking and exchange an optimistic glance.

'Well this seems more promising than four unanswered messages,' Rose says. 'Maybe *your boyfriend* really can find us some jobs,' she muses more to herself than to me. It's not lost on me that her tone is a little sharp and I suddenly wonder if she's jealous but I know better than to ask.

We look around at immense fields of crops and irrigation systems. In the distance we can see dozens of commercial greenhouses, huge industrial units and storage tanks. The wide road we are walking along continues towards them and a sign states *Warehousing, Greenhouses and Maintenance*. Outside Reception a smaller road more suited to cars veers right and another sign states *Headquarters, Residences and Staff Facilities*. There are three redbrick two-storey office buildings directly in front of us, all with sliding glass doors and boxes filled with shrubs outside, beyond them I glimpse a small community. Rose and I exchange a glance; this place is far bigger than we thought.

We wait for another lorry to rumble past then cross the road and enter Reception. An impeccably groomed receptionist in a skirt suit stands up and smiles at us so we introduce ourselves.

'Welcome to DB Produce, may I take copies of your Resumés and Employment Authorisation Documents?' she asks.

Rose and I look at each other in relief; I remembered at the last minute to pick up our USB stick and I pass it to her. She gestures to a waiting area with black leather sofas.

We sit down and sip some water from a dispenser and before long she returns our USB stick, just as a cheerful woman in her mid-forties wearing a black skirt and red blouse enters and shakes hands with us.

'Hello, I'm Sally, Mr Brook's assistant. Would you like to come with me?' We follow her and I wonder if Adam's surname is Brook and if she's talking about him.

We cross diagonally to the second building, enter through the double doors and I'm immediately aware of the blissful air conditioning. She and Rose chat about how unusual the prolonged heatwave is and I hastily dust off my blouse as we walk up two flights of stairs. We enter a busy office with around twenty desks and Sally leads us through an open side door before leaving and closing the door softly behind her.

My heart flutters with nerves and a lump gets stuck in my throat as Adam rises from behind a desk. Is he a manager?

'Morning ladies, you got here ok? It's sure hot again today.' He smiles at us and holds out his hand. Rose shakes it, the first to recover from the surprise.

'Err yes, good morning, Adam,' she says politely, surprise unmistakable in her voice. He turns to me and I also shake his hand feeling beyond weird and not knowing what else is appropriate. His eyes are warm but professional and I try not to stare at him. To say he looks hot in a suit is a massive understatement.

'Take a seat and let's see if we can find you some work, shall we?' He shows us two seats in front of the desk upon which is a nameplate stating *A. Brook, Chairman.*

I'm stunned, although it would certainly account for the hysterics of his cousin Jenny and her boyfriend when I referred to him as 'Adam from the veg stall'. Oh dear God, at first I'm embarrassed, but then I reconsider. Why should I be? If they didn't tell me, how was I supposed to know?

'Adam, are you the manager here?' Rose asks him, she clearly hasn't spotted the nameplate. He turns his attention briefly to his computer.

'Just bringing up your documents. Ah, here they are.' He clicks on his mouse, then turns to answer her question. 'No, I'm the owner. My uncle, Jonathan Sims, runs our daily operations, but he's out of the state so I'm covering for a few weeks.' He's really down to earth when he answers, like we're in our front yard and talking about my bike, not a business the size of this. 'We're trying to keep it family run, my late father, Daniel Brook, started the company,' he says simply when he notices me staring at him a little. I blink and avert my eyes and try not to appear so shocked. He turns his attention to the computer.

'I thought you worked at the market?' Rose blurts out and inwardly I cringe.

Thankfully he just chuckles a bit. 'Yeah, I kinda do. The warehouse belongs to DB Produce and it's a PR thing for the town that my dad started years ago, it's become a tradition for the Brook family to be seen there.' Rose and I share a glance. He owns the market warehouse? That's news. No wonder he knew what documents were held on us in the office.

'Well, let's start with Rose, shall we?' He turns the screen so we can see it and he opens her CV. 'So, you were a veterinary assistant back in England?' he begins and I tune out. My mind is in turmoil, am I seriously starting to date the owner of a large corporation? Part of me is deeply awed and another is fed up that his stall wouldn't let me sell a few eggs when he must be so rich it's ridiculous. I also feel completely out of my depth, but oh boy, he does look great.

Then Rose agrees enthusiastically with something and I try to focus a little more on what they are talking about.

'How's your math?' Adam is saying. My eyes drift along the tailored cut of his navy blue suit jacket and I can't help admire how broad his shoulders look. The colour suits him, setting off his dark brown hair and hazel eyes attractively against the cream of his skin. The tattoo on his neck adds an element of rebellion against the otherwise conservative appearance.

'Good. I did an A-Level in maths,' Rose is saying. He looks at her a bit blankly and scrolls through her CV.

'Like a college diploma?' he asks, and she nods. 'Awesome, then come in tomorrow at nine and we'll start you on a three-month trial. You want to take a look around?' Rose beams at him. Adam presses a button on his phone and Sally answers. 'Sally, could you please take

Rose down to Finance to meet Susan and ask her to talk her through the benefits package for the invoicing administrator position? Rose starts tomorrow on the standard terms.'

Oh wow, just like that. Rose has got a job. Sally comes in and Rose follows her without so much as a backward glance at me.

A quiet pause settles in the room as Adam and I are left alone. My heart is beating erratically in my chest and as usual, I have no idea what to say. Should I be light-hearted and make a joke? Or should I be serious and ask him why he didn't tell me? I'm completely at a loss for the protocol of when you ask your new boyfriend for a job. Adam smiles at me and it lightens the tension in the room so I offer him a shy smile back, but I'm nervous and he can tell.

'Well that's one of you happy,' he says warmly, I think he's trying to make me feel more at ease and it works. Then he opens my CV on his computer, having recently finished college and only ever worked one Saturday job it's very short. 'So you took Music Production at college? Is that what you want to do?' he asks, his voice rising in surprise.

'Well a lyricist ideally, but I'll do anything. I appreciate it's not relevant here.' I speak a little too quickly and it's obvious I really just need a job. He raises his eyebrows at me.

'Did you seriously just tell me, you'd do *anything*?' I nod, completely oblivious to the look in his eyes. 'Like what?' he asks me leaning his elbows on the desk, his eyes alive with curiosity.

'I don't mind. Packing boxes, cleaning, washing up. Whatever there is,' I answer openly. He doesn't say anything and there's a pause. 'Are there any jobs?' I ask squeezing my hands between my thighs.

'Well, warehousing wouldn't work out and there are no vacancies in catering at the moment,' he says smoothly. I can tell by his tone it's a no and my heart starts to plummet.

'I just need some work,' I say, silently cursing that I sound so desperate. He leans his chin on his hands as he looks at me. I can't believe in a place this size, there's *nothing*. 'What about crop picking?' I ask brightly. He shakes his head.

'I can't see any positions that might be suitable,' he says gently.

'Ok,' I say quietly wondering if I am really *that* unemployable. I blink at him trying to look like it doesn't matter and he holds my gaze.

'Would you work for me personally, Ella?' he asks and hope blooms inside me. 'I'm looking for a housekeeper,' he says relaxed, but his eyes are sharp. 'Cleaning, walking my dog, cooking, laundry... whatever. Would you be interested in that sort of thing? It might help us both out,' he adds casually.

I nod straight away, I don't even think about it. I could do that, except the cooking maybe, I can't cook to save my life. It might be a bit awkward, though, I'd be dating my boss, but that's the least of my worries. His eyes shine at me and a smile touches the corners of his mouth.

'I can do all that except the food, usually what I cook is inedible,' I admit honestly and hope it's not a deal breaker.

'Ok, we'll leave the cooking.' His smile widens.

'What would be the hours?' I ask.

'Weekday afternoons, say three 'til six?' he says, amused, and adds, 'don't you want to negotiate the salary first?' I flush knowing he's right. I must look as desperate as I am and he smiles and puts me out of my misery. 'How does two hundred and fifty sound for fifteen hours a week?' I nod, I'd take any offer right now and it sounds pretty good, it's not like I've got a lot of housekeeping experience. 'And you're ok with big dogs? He barks more than he bites,' he says and his eyes are positively glowing at me.

'Sure.' I can handle a dog if it means I get paid.

'Then meet me tomorrow afternoon at two at the rear gate. No need to go all the way through front security, I'll give you a turnstile pass and a door key.'

I smile at him and nod, a little shocked I actually have a job. The relief is immense. His gaze lingers on me for a moment longer than necessary and he clears his throat and starts getting up, so I do the same.

'And on Wednesday night I'll take you out,' he states confidently. 'Where do you want to go?'

I blink at him in surprise. He wants to take me out, like on a date? My pulse pounds in my ears with excitement.

'A diner, a movie theatre?' he suggests when I don't respond.

'Oh, err, I've no idea!' I answer, flustered. 'Let's decide tomorrow.'

'Sure.' He rests his hand on my lower back as we walk over to his office door. The contact sends tingles rippling up my back and I want to turn and throw my arms around his waist but manage to control myself.

Rose and Sally are just returning from Finance, perfect timing. I smile at Adam in a gesture of goodbye and he winks at me and my tummy flutters in its usual response. Should I thank him for the job I wonder? Hmm… awkward. He tilts his head towards his computer.

'I better go,' he says. I nod and he returns to his desk, leaving the door open.

As Sally walks us back to Reception, Rose is chatting happily, thrilled she has a job and I can't say I'm disappointed either, but I don't join in. My head's overloaded with images of how gorgeous Adam is in a suit and what on earth I've got in my wardrobe to wear on a date. My heart pounds significantly harder on the way home than the gentle walk demands.

The rest of Monday and Tuesday morning pass in a flurry of activity. Charlotte's been checking the licensing and hygiene requirements and decided we can use the eggs to bake cakes. The change of business plan for our plot at the market has got us all in a spin. Charlotte's booked a hygiene inspection at the ranch so it's been all hands-on-deck cleaning. That's all of us except Rose, who gleefully left the house this morning to start her new office job, leaving us to do the dirtier tasks. I call Mr Jackson to ask about a larger pitch, tables and chairs, as Charlotte's plan is that we run an English tea shop. We also contact the coffee stand owner and strike a deal that we share the seating and costs if we agree not to sell coffee. Aside from that there's the utensils and ingredients to buy. By Tuesday afternoon I'm desperate to leave the house and meet Adam.

There's a turnstile gate in the security fence at the rear of DB Produce and it makes the walk ten minutes quicker than going through the main entrance. I'm wearing my baseball cap to keep the sun off my head and feel like I'm melting in my vest top and shorts. Everyone I've spoken to tells me the weather here is changeable and the heatwave is an exception; I hope so, I'm beginning to pine for rain.

Adam pulls up in his truck just a few minutes late and smiles at me through the windscreen as he parks and gets out. He's wearing tailored grey trousers and a short-sleeved white shirt; my eyes seem to get glued to admiring his physique and I hastily try not to stare as he walks towards me.

'Hey, baby,' he greets me as he reaches the turnstile and passes me a card to scan so I can enter.

Feeling ridiculously pleased, I accept the hand he holds out to me as we walk to his truck and smile brightly at him, it makes him pause to flick his eyes over my face before smiling back. His hazel eyes are so damn sexy, I divert my attention quickly for fear I'll blurt it out and tell him I think so.

'So, how's your day been?' he asks squeezing my hand.

'Manic! Charlotte's decided we're going to sell Cream Teas on market day, so she's got us all in a frenzy cleaning and organising,' I say light-heartedly, relieved for a normal topic of conversation to distract me.

'Cream what?'

'Oh you know, like English homemade scones, jam and tea.' I grin at the novelty of having to explain that.

'*Scones* and *jam,* you mean like *jelly?* That could be popular,' he comments, amused.

I get into the truck quickly, trying not to smile like an idiot as he opens the door for me. He's had the air conditioning on and it's blissfully cool inside and I notice again how impressive the interior of his truck is, with leather upholstery and high-tech dashboard. I try not to touch anything that I could break. Adam gets in and starts the engine.

'How was your morning?' I ask, my heart fluttering happily at seeing him again.

'Let's say I'll be glad when Jon's back, I'm too busy to be stuck in the office all day,' he says glancing at me as we start to pass through a few roads of small houses. He's *too busy* to be at work? What else does he do all day?

'So, do a lot of the farm staff live on site?' I ask him while looking out of the side window at what look like workers' accommodation.

'Yeah, about sixty per cent, mainly guys here for the labour, their families tend to stay in the cities and they go home at weekends, as do a lot of the office staff,' he says.

We drive towards the end of a road full of small detached bungalows where there's a line of mature trees. The trees run along the border of a worker's bungalow and then along the kerb of the street shielding what's behind it from the road. Adam slows the truck and we turn in through a driveway entrance in the trees. I'm immediately distracted by the green lushness of the lawn and surrounding shrubs. He must have one hell of a sprinkler system for it to look so good in this constant heat. I turn to look out of the front windscreen and see his house as we pull to a stop.

Oh wow, it's gorgeous. And big. I'm immediately embarrassed about the impression he must have got from the ranch on Sunday. I cringe as I remember the bills stamped UNPAID laying on the breakfast bar. He cuts the engine and looks at me and in return I raise my eyebrows at him.

'Are you expecting me to be able to clean the whole house, *every week*?' It's the first thing that comes into my head and perhaps a stupid thing to say, but I'm taking a mental gulp of air. 'No wonder you need a housekeeper.'

He rolls his eyes at me like I'm being cute then he gets out of the truck. I'm not being cute, though, the place is huge. He holds the door for me like a gentleman as I jump down, feeling like I'm stepping into an oven. I glow inside at the feel of his arm, which he slips around my shoulders as we walk to the front door.

The house is painted white and is built in three sections with a detached triple garage off to the left. The main house is two storeys and there are three large windows overlooking the front garden on the first floor and another two either side of a large oak front door on the ground floor. On either side of the main house, there are symmetrical extensions; these are only one storey with pointed roofs tiled in the same grey slate as the main house. I can't tell from where I'm standing how deep the main house is, but at a guess it's at least three times the size of our ranch.

He opens his front door and we enter into an octagonal entrance hall. There's a door to my right and then a staircase, directly in front of us is a large kitchen diner and another three doors to my left, which are closed. The hall floor is polished wood and it follows through to the rear kitchen. I blink as I take in my surroundings, but don't comment, swallowing my surprise while trying not to look awed.

Everything is finished to an exceptional standard and I'm beginning to realise how much money my boyfriend must have. It makes me feel insecure that we're worlds apart.

'How many bedrooms are there?' I ask trying not to sound fazed.

'There's six bedrooms and three bathrooms upstairs and a downstairs WC in here,' he says neutrally pointing at a door on the right of the kitchen. 'In here's a TV room.' He opens the door immediately to my left where I can see two large sofas and a TV, which more resembles a home cinema. At the second door he opens I see a beautifully presented dining room. 'This is the dining room, but I don't tend to use it,' he says shrugging and then turns to the right of the front door. 'In here's the lounge.' Inside is a square room with three large sofas positioned around a modern glass coffee table with a fireplace on the fourth side. Glass cabinets and bookshelves are positioned around the edge and my first impression is that it's opulent but not overdone, furnished artistically in creams and browns with the light from the large front window filling the room. An interior designer must have had a hand in achieving such an effect. I think of the bedroom I share with Sarah at the ranch and the cardboard boxes still pushed under the bed as we've run out of space to unpack the contents. Fuck! I'm out of my league here.

I'm taken aback at the size of the rooms and wonder how long it's going to take me to clean all this. Oh God, what if I break something? His house is more minimalistic than cluttered, but the lamps and artwork he does have look expensive.

He catches my eye and says, 'You ok, baby?'

I glance up at him and know he's already spotted the anxiety on my face.

'Yeah, umm, I don't have any sort of insurance, Adam. Should I get some? I mean, what if I break something? Are you going to be mad? I'll try not to of course, but…' I start babbling with nerves and looking around the room.

He tilts my face up to look at him and my skin burns where he touches it. He's smiling as he wraps an arm around my waist and pulls me against him. His body is muscular and firm and my heart hammers lustfully at the unexpected contact.

'Am I going to be *mad*?' he repeats back to me, raising his eyebrows as his eyes dance down at me. 'Accidents happen. Why? Do you think I'd deduct it from your wages or something?' He smiles; the way he says it, it's clear he wouldn't. He slides his hand from my chin around the back of my neck to caress my hairline. Tingles of pleasure race through me. Swallowing hard in response, I have to remind myself to breathe. I shake my head. The look he's giving me has my knees feeling weak and my arms wrap around his back automatically.

He tilts his head down slowly and his lips seal over mine, so tantalisingly soft I'm lost to the feel of them and close my eyes. As he kisses me, he tightens his arms around me and I feel light-headed. His kiss becomes more ardent and I groan, molten fire running hot inside me. When he pulls away, it takes me a second before my eyes can fully focus on him as desire rocks through me.

'Maybe I shouldn't work from home too often if you're here,' he says huskily, his breath tickling my lips. 'I don't think either of us would get much work done.'

My tummy hits the floor at the realisation of what he's implying and I pretend my cheeks aren't tingling with the familiar burn. He kisses my forehead affectionately and chuckles at my reaction.

'Well unless you want me to push you onto the couch, I guess we should go and see the rest of the house, huh?' He teases me.

Oh wow, I almost ask to take the first option.

I lower my eyes to his shoulder. Excitement rages through me at just the thought! Exhaling in amusement, he drops his arms from around me and takes hold of my hand.

'Come on, beautiful,' he says softly and the endearment makes my breathing falter. He thinks I'm beautiful?

He leads me into a kitchen, which is a marvel in modern design, finished in sparkling marble worktops and grey units with no handles. There's a large table in the centre and a sofa and coffee table off to the left-hand side. Aside from a deluxe blender like you make health shakes in and several large tubs of protein, there's very little in the kitchen that hints more about the man I'm with. Everything seems a little sterile and unused.

Beautiful arched floor-to-ceiling windows overlook a moderate sized back garden and there's so much light coming into the room it's stunning. Two doors on the far right are open and I can see one leads into a pantry and utility room and the other to a hallway in the direction of the extension.

In front of the sofa area, folding glass doors look like they would open fully to lead out onto a large patio area. I feel like I'm in a show room at an expensive shop. It's all gleaming chrome and shiny.

'Do you already have a cleaner?' I ask, a little awed.

'No, why?' Adam says and then catches my expression and realises what I mean. He shrugs a bit. 'I work away a lot and when I am here, I don't tend to spend much time inside, it's a big place to rattle around on my own with the dog so I tend to go out. I'm sure after walking Chase, laundry and groceries I've got enough to keep you busy, though.'

'You called your dog *Chase*?' I ask smirking.

My smile is contagious apparently as he smirks back. 'Yeah, *as a joke*, but it kinda stuck.'

Biting my lip to control my grin, I look around and see a door on the left of the room leading down another hall to the extension on that side.

'There's a gym through there, which you're welcome to use by the way,' Adam says nodding to the door I'm looking at and I raise my eyebrows, relieved he can't see my expression. A *gym*? We can't even afford to fill our water tank up. I feel like bloody Cinderella visiting the prince's palace. 'My home office is in the extension on the right.' He nods towards the other side of the room. 'I'm usually untidy when I work, so I'll do that room. But go right ahead and knock yourself out with the rest of the house.' He picks up two keys on a metal ring from the kitchen table and passes them to me. 'These are for you.' As I take the keys, his expression catches me by surprise. He looks like the cat that got the cream. 'I've got to get back to work in a bit,' he says apologetically, 'but I'll leave you to have a look around upstairs; any things you might need are in the utility room,' he says pointing to the room off the kitchen which I'd already spotted. 'But first I want you to meet a buddy of mine.' He smiles, watching my reaction.

'Your big dog?' I ask.

He takes my hand and leads me to the back door which he unlocks before we exit onto the patio. There's a huge barbeque under a cover and four large garden sofas around a central table.

It's a moderate sized garden with more mature trees surrounding it and a gate at the end. Considering the size of the house it's not as deep as it could be, but very wide and laid with lush green lawn like the front. Adam whistles and my attention is immediately drawn to a Saint Bernard who is scrambling out of a massive dog kennel and bounding towards us in delight. He's gigantic, although he looks adorable with his tongue lolling out. He barrels into Adam's legs and wags his tail so hard it looks like it could break off; his eyes are overjoyed to see his master. Adam ruffles his head and commands him to sit which he does obediently even though he's excited. Even sitting, the dog comes level with my chest, but then again, I'm not that tall. Adam looks amused at my expression.

'Do you think you can walk him?' he asks. 'I did warn you he was big, but he's remarkably well behaved, I promise he won't pull you over,' he says as the dog nuzzles his hand.

'Can I say hello?' I glance uncertainly at Adam.

'I sure hope so, Ella, I want you to look after him while I'm at work!' He laughs. I hold my hand out and the dog licks me like we're already friends. 'His treats and leash are in the drawer under the microwave,' he says. 'Walk him when you arrive or he'll bark until you do. For obvious reasons I leave him in the yard during the day.'

'What do you do with him when you're away with work?' I ask, remembering his earlier comment and registering a slight pang at the thought of him going away regularly.

'Jenny or my aunt come and get him, they spoil him and think I don't notice. They live right around the corner.'

'Do you have any brothers or sisters?' I ask.

'No, it's just me, and my aunt, uncle and cousin. I lost contact with my mom years back.'

'I'm sorry to hear that.'

He shrugs, then the dog shifts and sits on my foot, it makes me giggle and lightens the atmosphere.

'He's gorgeous, Adam.' I smile up at him as Chase rolls on his back playfully like an oversized puppy.

'Like someone else I know,' Adam says looking at me. I divert my eyes swiftly and bite my lip, not knowing what to reply. 'So I'll take you out tomorrow night?' He asks, stroking my face. I try to hide my shiver of pleasure as my skin comes alive under his fingertip.

'That'd be great,' I say focusing on the dog rather than looking at him directly.

'Anywhere you wanna go?' he asks, dropping his hand to dust dog hair off his trousers.

'Surprise me.' I smile at him.

'Alright,' he responds, apparently up for a challenge. 'So, I've got to get back to the office, baby, sorry. Help yourself to whatever from the fridge and do what you think, lock up when you leave as I'll be back late,' Adam says, his eyes still focused on me.

I nod, hoping I don't look disappointed that he's leaving. Perhaps it shows on my face, though, as he steps closer, pulls my hips against him and kisses me. My heart rate soars and my knees almost give out as he rocks my world out of orbit once again. By the time he pulls away my breathing is so erratic it's almost embarrassing, except that his is the same. He holds my face in his hands and presses his lips to my forehead.

'I'll see you tomorrow then,' he murmurs. I nod, conscious that my lips are still tingling and trying to hide my smile so I don't look overly keen. 'You be good for her,' he says with mock severity looking at the dog who wags his tail.

I watch him walk backward a pace and then turn to go back into the house, leaving me in the garden. I press my lips between my teeth and continue to hide my smile. I'm not sure who I'm hiding it from with just me and the dog here now, but I feel a bit stupid grinning to myself. I look down at Chase and he's watching me with bright eyes.

'You want to go for a walk then?' I say and he pricks his ears like he knows what I'm talking about. I think he and I are going to get along fine.

Wednesday morning passes in another blur of activity preparing for the cake stall on Saturday. Sarah came home from the supermarket this morning with some discounted pink aprons, a huge range of crockery and the ingredients we need. We used Adam's money for it and also filled up the water tank and paid some bills, it was a lifeline, almost literally. I hope the stall is a success so we can pay Reece back on Sunday, although with Rose and I now working at least the pressure has eased longer term.

I start work at Adam's early on Wednesday so that I can freshen up before he gets home. I've decided on a short but casual summer dress and strappy flat sandals, applied lashings of black mascara and small sparkly earrings and I'm pleased with my look. I'm just finishing brushing my long hair loose to my waist when Adam gets home.

When he walks in through the door and sees me, he blinks then tilts his head forward and widens his eyes, only half teasing. He clears his throat and I panic that I've done something embarrassing like got my skirt tucked in my knickers.

'Hi,' I say, fidgeting with a ring on my finger.

'You look real pretty, Ella,' he says appreciatively, adding good humouredly, 'who's the lucky guy?' His eyes glint in a way that sends my heart racing. I bite my lip and focus on something else; it seems a bit coy to say *you are* so I don't reply. Adam chuckles.

'I'll just go change,' he says dropping his keys and his wallet on the hall table but keeping his eyes on me for a moment before heading upstairs.

When he comes down he's wearing a tight navy blue T-shirt and a pair of low-slung Levi jeans that make his bum look amazing. The T-shirt emphasises his powerful shoulders and I struggle to take my eyes off him. Luckily he doesn't seem to notice me ogling him, he's too busy looking at my legs. His tattoos poke out from under his sleeves enticingly, like someone has run a black paint brush in patterns down his biceps. He takes my hands in his; he's put aftershave on and smells fantastic.

'Come on then, it's a half hour's drive,' he says and tugs me lightly towards the door and whistles.

'What is?' I ask, trying not to smile as Chase bounds past us. He's bringing the dog on our date?

'You'll see when we get there; it's a surprise.' He's giving nothing away and we get into his truck with the dog, who amuses me by sitting on the seat next to me, his head level with mine.

As he drives, we talk easily together, he asks me about my sisters and I tell him that Rose and I don't get along that well, she was always jealous of the relationship Dad and I had and can be quite argumentative which upsets me. I hate arguing.

We talk about the move from England and how Sarah is rapidly developing the same bossy big sister tendencies as Rose now that we're sharing a small room. He listens to me for a while and I start to wonder if maybe I'm waffling but he assures me I'm not. Is he just being polite? There seems to be so much going on behind those sharp eyes, it's hard to tell. He asks where Charlotte's ex is. I explain he walked out just after Amy was born, saying he'd found someone else and Adam surprises me with the strength of his reply.

'Kids should have both parents around while they're growing up,' he says firmly, not a trace of humour in his tone. 'He sounds like a prick to me.'

'Were your parents around much when you were young?' I ask him, immediately hoping I haven't touched on a sensitive topic as I remember he said he's not in contact with his mum.

'Not really, my dad threw my mom out when I was small, it's a long story but let's say they had some troubles. Then my dad got sole custody and shipped me off to various boarding schools as he was too busy running the farm.' He sounds a little bitter, so I decide not to pry further.

'So you were close to your dad?' he asks me, switching the conversation back to me. I nod but don't say anything for fear of getting choked up in front of him. 'Grace said you got upset about him when she spoke to you, so I didn't want to bring it up earlier, but I want you to know I'm really sorry for you, baby,' he says and reaches over to cover my hand resting in my lap with his.

I blink in surprise. I hadn't known he'd spoken to Grace about me and I'm touched at his sensitivity. I squeeze his fingers back.

'Thank you,' I say hoarsely and look away from his eyes down to his hand. I notice again the various scars on his knuckles and run my thumb over them, frowning a little.

'So what made you choose Music Production at college?'

I look up from his hand, distracted. 'I've always loved music, I'm not the best musician but I love writing it, especially lyrics,' I gush, unable to hide my enthusiasm.

'Do you play anything?'

'I've had lessons on guitar and I'm not bad, but mainly it's so I can hear the lyrics with music, you know?' I explain.

'Not really.' He smiles. 'I read business at university,' he says shrugging. 'It's interesting to hear you like the writing side more. That's your passion, right?' I smile at him and nod, pleased that he gets it; most people just think I want to be a musician. 'Don't you like performing?' he asks. I quickly look out of the side window.

'Err, I'm not great at being the centre of attention, I tend to clam up a bit,' I say honestly. He doesn't say anything, and I can feel his eyes still on me so I decide to change the subject. 'Which university did you go to?'

'Washington, then I travelled and spent a few years in Mexico.'

Oh wow, that sounds fascinating. It would also explain why his accent is not from the south, like Dan's, for instance.

'What did you do in Mexico?' A moment passes before he answers.

'I was in the automotive industry for a while, shared a house with two brothers called Carlos and Juan. But when my dad died, I had to come back and take the reins at the farm.' His tone is a little flat. I wonder if that wasn't what he'd wanted at the time.

'Why didn't you want to come back? Did you have a girlfriend out there or something?'

His reaction to that is a little odd as he smiles at me before he answers.

'I had several while I was out there, Ella, but they weren't what made me want to stay, let's just say they weren't like you.'

I'm not sure what to say to that so stay quiet and am relieved when he glances at the dashboard navigation and turns off the highway.

I look out of the window at the passing countryside and am surprised when we turn down a side road and he stops the truck. He reaches into his back pocket and pulls out an eye-mask like those for sleeping on a flight. He hands it to me and raises his eyebrows implying I should put it on. I take it and look at him uncertainly.

'I guess you're just going to have to trust me,' he says smoothly, so I pull the mask over my eyes and can't help but notice my heartbeat speeds up with the loss of one of my senses, and the truck starts lurching forward again. Around five minutes later, he pulls to a stop. 'Stay here and don't peak.'

'Ok,' I whisper and sit on my hands to stop from fidgeting. I hear his truck door close and a few minutes later my door opens. Chase leaps out and Adam reaches across and unclips my seat belt before lifting me out of the truck.

I squeal as it's unexpected, but he just says, 'Relax, I didn't want you to fall getting out.' He doesn't put me down, and walks a few paces before lowering my feet to the floor, by then my pulse is thrumming through my veins. He moves to stand behind me, slipping his arms around my middle again, and whispers in my ear. 'You can take the mask off now.'

I pull it off and gape at what's in front of me. We're on a slight hill, looking down onto the fields below us and there are miles and miles of sunflowers in bloom. I've never seen anything like it. It's magnificent.

'Aww wow!'

'Do you like it?' he asks, squeezing my waist a little tighter.

'It's amazing, Adam.' I'm truly stunned by the view. 'I had no idea.'

He chuckles a little. 'Tourist!' He pokes fun at me and I try not to grin. Then he turns me around and there's a picnic blanket and wicker hamper on the ground next to us; I'm overwhelmed. Christ, is this guy romantic or what? I cover my mouth with my hand.

'I thought we could eat supper here,' he suggests. 'You hungry?'

I nod shyly, keeping my fingers pressed to my lips. I wonder if I'm dreaming and going to wake up soon.

After a particularly healthy picnic, we watch the sun set over the fields of sunflowers. We've laughed and joked all evening with Chase sleeping quietly next to us on the blanket and I've been relaxed and not struggled to make conversation once. That's not like me at all, but there's a charisma to Adam that puts me at ease. He is sitting next to me with his arm around me when he nudges his nose against my head to get my attention.

'I don't want you to think I brought you here just for that, so I wanted to ask you first, if I could kiss you goodnight? Here, I mean, without your sisters watching.'

Oh God. Hot waves of molten lava rush through me and I almost melt, but we're really secluded here. I swallow as my pulse explodes into life.

'Is that ok, baby?' he asks coaxingly, tucking my hair behind my ear with his other hand and I look up at him beside me and nod. I can hardly say no if it's just a kiss goodnight, and besides, I don't want to say no, although I'm nervous.

He smiles in a way that makes my heart skip several beats and shifts so I'm suddenly being eased onto my back with his arm still around me. He lies down too, half over me and brings his face close to mine. My pulse is erratic and I look at him a little uncertainly.

'Relax, don't be nervous,' he says softly, so I try to loosen the tension from my shoulders. 'If you're not comfortable, you just say so, right?'

The way he says it is so confident and attractive, it takes my breath away as desire pulses hot inside me. When his lips meet mine, they are soft and gentle and I wrap my arms around his neck. As he deepens the kiss, I can't catch my breath and excitement makes my blood pound in my ears. Slowly his hand slides to my chest and I let him feel me through my clothes, desperately wanting to arch my back and press against him, but lacking the confidence to do so.

Oh wow, can he kiss!

I pull at his neck, dragging his mouth closer to mine and he groans. As his kiss intensifies, he unbuttons the front of my dress. My heart is pounding so hard I'm finding it hard to think straight. When my dress is opened low, he lowers his head and trails his tongue over my sensitised skin, slipping the straps of my dress and bra off my shoulders and freeing my aching nipples.

A dazed part of my brain is wondering if this is really happening and also asking me if I want it to, but then his mouth closes around my breast and pleasure shoots through me making me gasp and lose all train of thought. Oh God! My head lolls back as he sucks and sensation rocks me to my core. After a while, he pulls my knee to the side and kneels between my legs, still teasing my straining tip with his tongue. It feels amazing. Hot. Pulsing. Aching. When his mouth starts working his way back up my collarbone to my neck, I try to pull my bra back up, but he links his fingers through mine and pulls my hand away, pinning it to the floor.

'Don't cover up, baby, I want to look at you,' he says huskily and then rolls his weight on top of me. The erratic pounding of my pulse is overwhelming, but also exciting beyond belief. Adam pulls his T-shirt off roughly with one hand and I run my hands over his smooth shoulders as we lie together just kissing for some time. His weight pressing on my bare chest leaves me panting as much for air as with desire, and my eyes grow wider as I can now feel his erection pressing hard and demandingly into my thigh. Oh God, that feels so good, but my hands are starting to tremble and I know I'm not ready for more yet.

When his hand slides down my hip to my knee and then starts ascending on my inside thigh, things are suddenly moving too fast and I shake my head and put my hand against his face.

'Adam, not yet,' I whisper, feeling vulnerable as these new sensations surge through me. His hand pauses and then wraps around the back of my thigh instead. He pulls his head back fractionally and looks at me lying half-undressed underneath him.

'You don't want to?' His eyes are hooded and his hot breath against my lips makes my head swim deliriously. I fight the urge to run my tongue along his lip.

'I do, but I don't,' I whisper shaking my head, my eyes imploring him to understand, even if I don't myself. He raises one eyebrow but smiles warmly and I almost melt underneath him and change my mind. Almost.

'Which part of you does? I'll take that bit.' He teases and I can't help but smile as he takes away my apprehension. He nudges his nose against mine and my tummy turns over at his playfulness.

'That's better; I love it when you smile. We'll take it at your pace, baby, no pressure, right?' he says softly. I drag in a lungful of air in relief and nod, rapidly becoming mesmerised by him. Still smiling at me, he raises his hand and strokes my fringe off my face.

'So which part of you didn't?' He smirks, raising both eyebrows swiftly in fun. 'Are you still bleeding or is it just too soon?'

I blink at his directness and then flush pink as I remember him handing me my tampon in the market bathroom. I avert my eyes and shake my head highly embarrassed. He laughs loudly.

'Both huh?' He grins playfully.

I give him a push on his shoulder in mock frustration, trying to divert his attention away from my burning cheeks.

'No! The second one!' I mutter exasperated and start trying to wriggle out from under him, but it inadvertently just pushes him into a more intimate position nestled between my thighs, which highly amuses him. I push him again and he pins my hand down gently and deliberately presses his body down on me to keep me still.

'Well how about a last goodnight kiss then before you give me bruises?' His eyes are showing me he's entertained by me.

I roll my eyes at him but don't protest when he leans down and kisses me again. Everything about him is so appealing; the taste of his mouth, the smell of his aftershave and the weight of him on top of me, I soon lose myself in the kiss, so much so it's just as well he's the one to break away first.

'If I don't stop now, I'm going to start thinking that you've changed your mind,' he teases, but I notice his breathing is becoming increasingly irregular.

'I haven't!' I pant, not failing to notice the warmth igniting inside me at being here like this with him. He pushes himself back up and adjusts the bulge in the front of his trousers and I look away hastily and readjust my dress. He smooths my bra straps for me, enjoying watching me squirm under the attention before pulling me to sit up beside him.

'Sorry,' I mumble, hastily re-buttoning my clothes.

'Don't be, baby, I don't want to rush you,' he says softly to me, hooking his heavy arm around my shoulders. 'You're different to other girls I've been with and I don't want to fuck up, so it's *good* you said, ok? Never apologise.' His tone of voice tells me he means what he says.

'Different how?' I ask him, mystified.

He smiles down at me sideways with a strange glint to his eyes and shakes his head subtly to emphasise his answer.

'I'm just not used to… having to wait for it,' he says tilting his head as he studies my reaction and his lip curves up on one side as if to apologise for his terminology.

'Oh!' I gulp. 'Is it bad that I'm different? Are you going to get bored of me?' I ask, showing him all of my insecurities before my brain-to-mouth filter can kick in.

'No, baby, it's not bad! It's as far from bad as you can get,' he says firmly and I have to look away as I register the compliment.

'So, what were they like?' I ask, a little confused.

'Well, I'll tell you what they weren't,' he says, pulling me closer and I nuzzle into the warmth of his bare chest. 'They weren't good, they weren't honest, and they sure as hell weren't sheltered.' He's clearly implying that he thinks those are all positive characteristics I do possess. 'But like I said, I'm looking for a good girl,' he says softly then rests his face in my hair. I swallow and enjoy cuddling him back and we sit like that until the sun has fully set around us and the stars dazzle me as much as he does.

The rest of the week passes swiftly as we prepare for market day. Adam works late and has already made plans in the evenings which he couldn't change so I don't see him again until Saturday, but he calls me twice and after each call I'm glowing.

Except Sarah, who has a shift at the supermarket, the whole family come to the market for the grand launch of the tea and cake stall. I have to admit it's nice not to be here on my own, especially after Reece's visit last week. The team from the grocery stall have noticeably stopped giving me a hard time too, but I think it's more because I'm now seeing their boss rather than having my older sisters with me. Carson in particular has stopped leering at me altogether and even helped us set up.

The stall turns out to be really popular. Sharing the seating area with the coffee stand works well too as customers can buy coffee with their cakes if they don't want tea, so neither stall loses out. The coffee stand lady, called Mary, tells us next week she'll bring her niece to help clear the tables.

Adam turns up at the market around lunch time for a short while. I get the impression it's just to make an appearance as I remember what he said about it being a PR exercise. I'm balancing Amy on my hip and trying to entice some customers with a plate of cake pieces to sample, when I glance up and see him.

'Hello.' I beam as he joins us and flicks his eyes over me like he hasn't seen me for a year.

Yay, happy me!

'Amy, why don't you ask Adam if he'd like some cake?' She picks up a piece and squeezes it in her hand, holding it out to him.

'Cake?' she asks. She looks so cute with her bunches, I have to smile. It seems Adam does too.

'No thank you, sugar.' He lets her down gently, so she amuses us by stuffing it into her own mouth instead.

'You look pretty,' Adam says, his eyes attentively looking over me. 'I like the apron!' I roll my eyes, considering the pink frills disdainfully.

'I'm not wearing it through choice,' I whisper so my sisters don't hear.

'So are you heading over to Dan's later? I hear Hannah, Rose and Sarah are going,' he asks, changing the subject.

'No, I'm shattered so going to stay home with the children and give Charlotte a night out.' An evening at Dan's house really doesn't appeal. There's a slight pause as he considers this.

'Can I join you?' he asks.

Duh!

I smile, unable to hide that I'm pleased.

'You'd rather be babysitting than with your friends?'

'I'd rather be with you,' he states certainly. I beam at him, I can't help it, so he kisses me briefly on the lips. As he pulls away, I catch

Dan watching us from across the market, but he diverts his eyes swiftly when he sees I've noticed. Hmm, awkward.

'Ella, I just want to ask you something before I go,' Adam says, his tone turning quieter and my attention is immediately focused back on him. 'Do you have the full two thousand dollars for tomorrow?'

I blink at him, taken aback. I'm certain I never told him that.

'If you need anything, you only have to say and I'll make up the difference.' He's serious. 'Those guys are bad news, baby, I'm worried about you.'

My instant denial that everything is fine dies on my lips as I register the concern on his face, so I answer him honestly, trying not to be embarrassed.

'The market's done well today, with Sarah's wages, we're hoping we can cover it, but we'll know for sure later when we count up.'

He nods in response. 'Then you can tell me tonight if there's more you need?'

I nod.

'Ok, I'd better shoot, see you around nine then?' he says, ruffling Amy on the head. I nod again and watch him leave.

How does he know exactly what we owe and by when? How does he know that?

Chapter Five

After the girls have left and the children are asleep, I lock the doors and flop down on the sofa to rest my eyes. I think I must doze off as I wake up to the sound of a vehicle pulling up outside. The light is fading fast and I glance at my watch; it's eight o'clock and I wonder if Adam has arrived early. Rubbing my eyes, I walk to the front window and see an unfamiliar car outside. Reece is just a few paces from our front door.

Oh shit!

He's come a day early.

We counted the market takings and have seventeen hundred for him, not quite the full amount but I was hoping to take Adam up on his offer for the rest. Reece hammers on the front door and it makes me jump. When I don't answer, he tries the handle and I stand frozen, watching him out of the window. Reece spots me and a cold sinking sensation settles in the pit of my stomach as our eyes meet.

He points at the front door, clearly demanding I open it and I shake my head trying desperately not to look scared, though my heart is pounding. I open the window instead; it's far too small and high up to be a risk for him to climb through, so I figure it's safe.

'You said you'd come tomorrow,' I call, hating that I sound timid rather than a force to be reckoned with. Reece walks towards the window and looks at me stonily through the glass. 'We've got most of it, seventeen hundred,' I say. Personally, I think that's a great effort.

'It's two grand,' he says flatly. 'Pass the money out the window.'

'Tomorrow. You said two thousand, *tomorrow*. I'll give you the rest tomorrow and then it's finished.'

He looks at me and his eyes are ice cold. My hands tremble with the knowledge I'm here on my own with the children. Then I hear a click at the back door and spin around, slamming the small window shut behind me.

'Oh Christ!' I squeal, my hand clasping over my mouth.

There are several men at the back door. While Reece has been distracting me, they've been working the main lock, which has just given out. Adrenaline pumps through me as the door shudders with the force of their shoulders making impact. A single sliding bolt is all that's keeping it closed. I fly into Charlotte's room and grab the sleeping children in my arms. The only internal room with a lock is the bathroom and I hear the back door come crashing down with a shattering of glass as I dart inside. Amy is half asleep so I lie her on a towel on the floor and David sits down, barely awake.

A sob of terror escapes my throat before I can contain it. Think. I've got to think. If I stay in the bathroom with them, the men will find us all, but if I lock them inside, perhaps the children won't be noticed. Decision made.

'David, I'm going to lock you inside and then pass the key in to you, it's really important you stay here and keep quiet. Promise me?'

He nods at me, his eyes growing wider as we can hear the men inside the house.

I kiss them both and dart out of the room, grabbing the key from the inside of the door and then turning it in the lock from the outside.

'She's here!' Someone calls behind me, right before something hard slams into the back of my head. White lights blind me as the pain registers, and I slump to my knees. My thoughts are of the children and I watch my hand slide the key beneath the door like it belongs to someone else. Then everything goes dark.

There is noise around me, is it voices? I can't think through this fog in my head, I've never felt so tired. I try to listen but can't seem to wake up enough.

Aargh! I feel a sharp prick in my arm. I shake my head, frustrated. I liked my sleep and now I'm not as comfortable. I try to see what pricked me, but something is covering my eyes so I can't. Oh well, I'll worry about it later… I just need a bit more sleep.

'Give her some more, wake her up God damn it.' A voice growls nearby and I feel the sharp pain again. Ow!

I jerk my head up from where it's lolling on my collarbone and the ground moves like I'm on a swing. I'm dizzy and feel like I'm about to throw up. My senses start to rush back to me in a cacophony of complaints.

My head throbs, my knees ache, I'm freezing cold.

I instinctively want to wrap my arms around me, but my wrists burn and my shoulders scream in protest. Belatedly I realise my hands are bound high above my head; I'm kneeling but hanging all my weight off them. Fuck, they hurt. I whimper loudly and try to support my weight more on my knees.

Some men are arguing and it's hurting my ears. The haze in my mind clears a little more. I register the cold hardness of the floor under my knees and shiver so much my teeth start chattering. The men are getting louder and I feel someone's hands on my head, tilting my face up and untying the cloth around my eyes. When it falls away I'm immediately blinded by a powerful spotlight shining down on me, yellow circles float behind my eyelids and I jerk my face away. I try to raise my knee to stand up, but something digs into my ankles and I realise they are bound together.

Then I remember Reece at my house.

Adrenaline pounds hard and fast through my veins. I'm suddenly wide awake, like I've been sucked out of a dream by a tornado. I start struggling to pull my hands free and the pain in my wrists takes my breath away.

'It's ok, Ella, don't struggle, I'm getting you free.' Oh God, I recognise Adam's voice. It's stressed and urgent but I don't care, the relief to know he's with me engulfs me. Where *am* I? Then a large hand on my tummy and another on my side lift me, making my shoulders pulsate with the pain of lowering my arms. I register his skin is touching mine and I panic. Am I wearing clothes? Fuck, where's my top? Why are my eyes not working yet? I'm hoisted up and over Adam's shoulder, so my arms hang down his back and his arm steadies me around my waist. As the air is pressed out of my lungs, I try desperately not to throw up.

'Hush, baby, I've got you.' Adam reassures me over the commotion going on in the room behind me. I'm jolted around a bit, but I can't make out what's going on.

Another man is insistent. 'Well you can't just leave, you have to have her; they wanna teach her to have a bit of respect.' I don't understand what he's saying. My head isn't working properly.

I can feel the tension rippling through Adam's shoulder beneath me as he growls, 'Get the fuck out of the way, you've had the money.'

I'm so scared, I can't even cry. I stay still on Adam's shoulder and try to get my eyes to focus. They finally start cooperating and I look at the knotted rope binding my wrists to see if I can loosen them. Adam is shoved but he doesn't lose his grip on me, and we're ushered into a side room. It smells of stale cigarettes and it's freezing inside. I shiver violently. Everything about the room is grey, the faded white on the walls, the concrete on the floor, the metal bed frame. I think we're in a basement maybe as there are no windows, just a bare light bulb in the ceiling. The door slams shut with the thud of a bolt slamming across. It reminds me of a prison cell I've seen on TV. Adam doesn't put me down, though, just hammers against the closed door.

'Son of a bitch! Open it!' Adam thunders.

Oh fuck, he's so angry, it's frightening me more than a little. My eyes land on the bed again. It's the only furniture in the room and my blood turns to ice. Where the hell am I?

'Either you get on with what you've paid for or she'll be sold to someone else,' a man shouts through the door.

I realise with a jolt that he's talking about me. Has Adam *bought* me? Barely dressed and in a place like this, it's not hard to work out what for. Terror rushes through me and I try to squirm off his shoulder. Realising I want to be put down, Adam bends to lower my feet to the floor and then holds me up as I sway precariously. A shiver of fear and cold rips through me, and Adam wraps his arms around me to keep me warm.

'You've got five minutes, Brook, or she goes to one of three others out here,' the voice shouts through the door and then footsteps move away.

Adam puts a hand on my face, taking in my scared witless expression.

'It's ok, I've got you, Ella, you'll be alright now, baby,' he says. I'm still shivering so he runs his hands up and down my arms and then tries to loosen the rope binding my wrists. I cry out as it chafes my raw skin so he stops.

The only clothes I'm wearing is a red thong I don't recognise and nausea churns in my stomach. I'm numb, whether with shock, fright, or cold I can't tell. My head is throbbing. Adam pulls his T-shirt off and slips it over my head to cover me then wraps his arms around me again. It makes me feel slightly less vulnerable being covered, but I don't think I've ever been so scared in my life.

'TWO minutes!' the voice shouts again.

'What d-do they m-mean?' I ask him through chattering teeth, afraid I already know the answer.

'To get you out, I had to pay your debt.' His voice changes completely when he talks to me, it's softer and gentle. 'But they want you to work it off, literally. You know, to learn that when you should pay, you do. They're fucking sick bastards, Ella.'

'W-what does… that m-mean?' I ask shivering.

'They want me to fuck you, or they'll sell you to someone else who will,' he says looking me in the eyes. I almost gag with fear.

'D-don't l-let them.' I shiver. I can barely get my words out. Adam's eyes are fierce.

'Not fucking likely,' he growls protectively squeezing me to him. 'Can you trust me?' he asks directly, maintaining eye contact with me. I swallow the unsettled feeling inside me and nod.

Immediately Adam scoops my knees up from under me and lifts me onto the bed. He pushes me backward onto the mattress and the contact makes the back of my head ache. I freeze rigid as I register what he's just done. Oh Christ. This can't be happening. I must be having a really disturbing dream. Then Adam pulls the thong down to my tied ankles and I realise in a panic this is definitely real and burst into silent tears. He pushes my ankles towards my bottom, unfastens and pulls his jeans open and then he spreads my knees. I gulp in some air and squeeze my eyes tight, but the tears just spill out from under my closed lids.

'Shh, look at me, baby,' he whispers reassuringly. When I don't respond he tilts my face towards him so I open my eyes and blink the tears out of them. I thought I was scared earlier, but now I'm terrified. I'm actually trembling. There's an intensity in his eyes that renders me speechless. 'Trust me, Ella. I'll get you out of here, I promise, but it's got to look real,' he says urgently.

I stare at him uncomprehendingly. *Look* real?

He kneels on the bed and then covers my body with his, his weight crushing my bound wrists into my chest uncomfortably under his T-shirt. As he wraps his arm under my neck, sobs force their way out of my throat and I gasp for breath. When his hips rest intimately between my legs, I don't feel his skin against mine, though, just material. He still has his pants on. His beard grazes my cheek a little as his head moves low against my ear.

'I know you're scared, Ella, but I won't hurt you, we can just pretend love, yeah?'

Pretend... love?

I swallow as those words register and bury my face against his strong bicep. I murmur my agreement; I know if this doesn't happen then they'll bring someone else in to do this for real and, oh my God, I'd rather be here with Adam. I feel safe with him holding me.

Adam starts moving on top of me in a way that has me quaking and shocked. My lack of experience is evident in even this imitation of sex and I can't stem the flow of tears. I assume the mirror on the wall must be some sort of one-way window as there are no further demands for us to get on with it.

They must be able to see us.

I'm so appalled it's unreal.

Adam continues to move against me; he's so strong and powerful I can barely breathe underneath him... And I register he's getting hard through his pants. Oh sweet Jesus. This is turning him on for real? I'm deeply upset, hurt and scared... and he's getting hard? Perhaps it's irrational, but *that* suddenly frightens me more than everything else.

'Am I hurting you?' Adam murmurs against my ear as I start to sob a little louder, he eases his weight a little, handling me with more care, but I want to push him off me. I can't, though, or the gang will get someone else in here, I know it. Adam's mouth tries to find mine, but I turn my face away, tears rolling down my cheeks. At least if anyone is watching from the corridor it certainly looks genuine. Seeing my increasing distress, he kisses my forehead instead.

'Pretend, ready?' He breathes.

I don't know what he means, but when he thrusts hard against me a few times and fakes an orgasm, I gasp and cry louder, but I'm not pretending.

He collapses his weight on top of me and I can feel he's still hard against my thigh. Even if it wasn't real sex, I can't help but feel a little abused. Perhaps I'm just not thinking straight, I *know* he's trying to help me, but I can't help the way I feel. He kisses my cheek and wipes my tears away, but I keep my face diverted and I can't stop trembling.

'Can you g-get off?' I whisper hoarsely.

'Yeah, I'll get you out of here now, Ella, I think that looked real,' he says quietly to me, but his breathing is irregular. He eases off me, kneels up and adjusts his clothes with his back to the door, but I don't look. I feel utterly exposed and want to crawl away from him, but manage to bring my knees together despite the burn in my hips. Then Adam gently pulls the thong back up my legs. Automatically I want to say thank you, but I can't seem to bring myself to do it. I roll onto my side, gasping deep shuddering breaths, but I can't slow my heart rate down. He sits next to me and rests his palm soothingly on my shoulder.

'Can you sit up?' he says softly after a giving me a moment. There's a concern to his voice that wasn't there before. I don't turn to look at him but do manage to haul myself upright. Immediately he slides one arm under my knees and the other under my shoulders and lifts me, cradling me in his arms so my head is against his bare shoulder above the black tattoo of the lady's hand on his chest. I'm deeply unsettled, but it's still reassuring to be held. I'd rather be in his arms than anyone else's. He sits on the bed with me still shaking and sobbing and cuddles me against his chest.

'How you doing, baby?' he asks, running a hand in soothing circles around my back.

'B-been better,' I gasp, finally getting more control over my emotions.

'You're alright now, I've got you and they'll let you go,' he reassures me. When I don't reply he just leans down and kisses my forehead tenderly. 'I still need to get you out of here, so don't be scared if I shout, right? I want you to know, it's not really me. The stuff you might hear, I wish you didn't have to, so just don't believe it all, I guess what I'm asking is for you to trust me again.'

Trepidation starts to quiver in the pit of my stomach, but I nod in answer. Oh Christ. What's he scared I'm going to hear? What don't I know?

He stands up effortlessly with me still cradled in his arms and walks to the door.

'Open it!' he thunders through it.

I jump and close my eyes tightly against his chest. He's so aggressive! I'm sure as hell not going to complain, though, when he's on my side. A bolt slides and the door creaks open. I'm jostled slightly as Adam kicks it the rest of the way and it slams against the wall.

'Where are her clothes?' he growls at whoever is standing behind me. I bury my face further into his chest. I don't want to see anymore.

'They want a word. This way,' is the answer he gets back. It's a different voice than before; it's deeper and sends shivers through me. My heart sinks, oh dear God, please get me out of this hell! Disappointingly, Adam turns to follow whoever spoke.

I can hear blatant gasping and groans of pleasure coming from somewhere nearby as we walk along and I try not to throw up.

'Is that what I think it is?' the man escorting us asks, his voice quieter and less demanding this time. What's he talking about?

'Yeah,' Adam answers flatly.

'Do they know you're a member?' he asks, sounding slightly awed this time. A member of what I wonder?

'Yeah,' Adam grunts again then he leans down, bringing his mouth close to my ear. 'I'll handle the talking,' he murmurs, his voice soft when he talks to me. 'Don't say anything, right?' Yes, I decide it would be best if he did the talking, I'm more likely to just cry at them. I nod and keep my face pressed into his shoulder. That's totally fine by me. 'Good girl, I'll get you home soon,' he says keeping his voice low.

He's so strong and confident; I'm melting against him. Jeeze, my head is getting so messed up! Not ten minutes ago I wanted to crawl away from him. I can't seem to get over that he was getting turned on for real when I was tied up and upset.

Adam cradles me in his arms as he strides easily up two flights of stairs not even pausing for a breath. I hear a door open and I can sense there are several people in the room we enter but no one speaks. I close my eyes tighter; I don't want to see who's in the room.

'Brook,' a voice says respectfully.

'What the *fuck* do you think you're playing at?' Adam growls back, a ferocious energy ripples through his chest under my cheek. I stay silent and still in his arms. There's a pause; I assume the man is considering his answer. When he speaks, his tone of voice is still respectful and to my absolute amazement, it sounds apologetic.

'Brook, we didn't know you were involved, I'd have made sure it was handled differently.'

'The *fuck* you didn't, Parker!' Adam shouts at him. 'And all this shit since I arrived? Who the fuck do you think you are?'

I'm jolted in his arms as he kicks something. I think it's a desk as I hear a chair scraping back in reaction.

'It's just business, Brook.' The man's voice is apologetic again.

'*Just business?* That's a fucking insult! You dare to hurt my woman and think this is just business now?' Adam thunders with rage. I'm so scared I'm positively trembling and can't possibly screw my eyes closed any tighter. 'You went early and straight to her for the money when I told you to come only to me. You expect me to believe you'd go through *the fucking process* with her for two freakin' grand if she wasn't with me? It's fly shit! So don't fucking give me that *it's just business* bullshit. It's as personal as it gets!'

He kicks the furniture again and it scrapes on the floor. I hear a commotion behind me of people moving aside then the room falls suddenly silent. Adam swings me around so he's looking over his shoulder towards the men now.

Then I hear the unmistakable click of a gun being loaded. Oh Christ. I realise he's turned away so I'm sheltered by him. I curl into him, terrified. Adam can feel it and protectively puts a hand over the back of my head and pulls me closer.

'You pull that trigger and you'll all be deader than me, you know it.' Adam's voice is hard as steel and under complete control; frankly, it makes this all the more frightening. Then I think it's Parker's voice that speaks.

'Can't you see that on him? Now put the damn Colt away!'

Is he ordering one of his men to put the gun away? And see *what* exactly? The silence stretches for a moment and then the tension in the room eases slightly. I hope that means the gun has been lowered.

'I'll pretend that didn't happen,' Adam says icily.

'That would be appreciated,' Parker replies.

What the *hell* is going on?

'But for touching, Ella, you're fucking on my list now, Parker. You leave the whole family alone or I'll be sending El Jefe a message from Mexico, you tell him that from me.' Adam growls and there's another silence as everyone, except me, seems to know the significance of that.

'Understood,' Parker responds stiffly, but is that a trace of fear in his tone?

A moment later I feel someone put something soft in my lap and I jump but presume it's my clothes. I don't dare open my eyes to look. Then I'm swung around and Adam is striding back down the stairs. I feel him shove something with his shoulder and figure it must be an exit because the temperature, air and sounds around me change. Adam keeps walking and I finally open my eyes as we cross a car park. He stops by his truck.

'Baby?' he says softly and I nod. 'I've got to put you down to unlock the truck, can you stand?'

I nod. Adam puts me down and I feel gravel scraping my bare feet. He keeps one arm around me and uses his other hand to unlock the truck before opening the door and lifting me inside. He picks up my clothes from the tarmac where they've just fallen and passes them to me. Once the door closes my head swims and I gulp in some air in a panic. Who the fuck is Adam to make a gang like that sound apologetic? I fail to steady my hands shaking in my lap. A cold sweat breaks out across my forehead followed by a rush of nausea and I know I'm going to vomit. I hastily grab the door handle and push it open. In the wing mirror I glance at Adam on his mobile at the rear of the truck.

'We're out, you ready?' I hear him say right before I lean over and retch out of the door. I gag several times but thankfully my stomach is empty and Adam returns, supporting my shoulders to prevent me from tumbling out of the truck.

'It's just the shock, baby, it'll pass,' he says soothingly.

When I'm done, he lifts me further back and gets in beside me, closing the door. He turns off the interior light so the car park lighting illuminates patches of the interior, and he wraps his arm around me and just holds me for a moment as I collapse into him until the nausea passes.

I expect him to talk but he doesn't, instead he opens the glove box where the cupboard lighting reveals a handgun inside. I freeze at the sight of it. I know it's almost standard to carry one here, but it's not a sight I'm used to. Adam reaches inside and pulls out a leather pouch. I watch in horrified silence as he slides a curved blade out of it. Does he always carry that around in his truck?

He then pins my wrists on his thigh and uses the razor-sharp knife to slice the rope before discarding it. He turns my wrists over in his hands to look at them.

'Put some ointment on them when you get in, ok?' he says softly. Our eyes lock on each other's and I stare back wide-eyed and silent. His expression is so many emotions all at once: regretful, angry, protective. I'm so confused. He runs his hand down the side of my cheek and my skin comes alive under his fingertips. I don't know what to say or do and there's a pause as he tries to find the right words.

'That wasn't really me; you remember I told you that, right?' He speaks quietly, but I can tell he means it. What I can't tell is whether I believe him, there was just so much I overheard which I don't understand, like *a message from Mexico*, what the hell does that mean?

'Yes, I remember,' I whisper in reply.

He nods and then briskly holds out his hand indicating I should lift my ankles and the moment is broken. I shuffle back and he places my feet on his lap to cut the rope. Again he inspects them, but they aren't anywhere near as sore, I wasn't hanging my weight off of them after all. He puts the knife back in the glove box as I lower my shaky legs off his lap.

'I'll take you home soon,' he reassures me. He picks up my knickers from the pile of clothes then he puts his hands on my hips and starts to ease the thong down.

What the fuck? I freeze.

Does he think that's ok? He doesn't even blink an eyelid, just shifts me so he can pull the underwear down my legs. Without a word, he hooks my own knickers around my feet and starts to pull them up.

'I can… m-manage!' I gulp and hastily take over, my hands shaking by the time I finish. He places one hand over mine to hold them still. I jump a little at the contact. God, I'm a bag of nerves.

'It's ok, Ella,' he says gently. 'You're out of there now; I've got you, baby.'

Then he pulls the hem of his T-shirt that I'm wearing up and over my head. I fold my arms quickly and try not to gape at him, but he just holds my bra out ready for me to slot my arms into without so much as a comment. I pull it on swiftly, deliberately not looking at him. I know he's looking at my body and my heart is beating erratically, remembering what happened not half an hour ago. I wince at the pain in my shoulders when I reach behind me.

'Do you want me to fasten it for you?' Adam asks.

Oh Christ no! I shake my head and manage to join the clasp, ignoring the burn in my joints. Before he gets a chance to put my top on for me also, I tug the vest top on but I still feel naked, like his eyes are burning holes through it, he watches me shuffle into my shorts and slip my feet into my flat summer shoes. He then slips his T-shirt over his head and while he can't see me, I look at the tattoo on his chest, trying not to be distracted by how breathtakingly well built he is. It was the thing the men commented earlier, about *seeing* something that's got me wondering if they meant his tattoos. The one on his chest of a lady's hand is the most interesting, the thumb and forefinger are touching and I notice now that with the other fingers raised above it, it forms the shape of a letter 'd'. On the back of the hand to the right is lightly inked the letter 'm', which I hadn't noticed before. Are DM initials for something?

I divert my gaze out of the windscreen as he pulls his shirt down and a yellow glow in front of the truck catches my attention. There are flames flickering in the upstairs window of the building we just exited. My hand springs automatically to my mouth and I make a grab for the door handle, my instincts screaming at me to go and help, but Adam holds me still with a strong arm. Then the downstairs exit slams open and people come streaming out, many men and women in various states of undress. My blood runs cold as it couldn't be clearer I was in a brothel and I suddenly want to cling like a limpet to the man next to me for getting me out. I don't dare ask how he came to be there in the first place, though.

'We should call 911!' I gasp in shock and look at Adam.

'Yeah,' he agrees but makes no move to take out his phone. I stare at him aghast.

'Adam?' I whisper tentatively.

'It's alright, baby, they'll know already.' He points to various people already on phones exiting other buildings. 'I'm more worried about you. Are you cold?' He pulls out a hooded jumper from behind the seat and tucks it around my shoulders, but I stare out of the window at the blaze as he climbs past me into the driver's seat and starts the engine.

We're leaving? Surely we should be outside helping? Then I register his expression is carefully blank, thoughtful even, but ultimately not surprised. Did he know this was about to happen? Was that what his phone call was about? Dread rushes through me and he sees me trembling.

'Want me to turn the heat on?' he asks.

I'm wondering if he's just set alight to a building and he thinks I'm shivering because *I'm cold*? I'm astounded... and terrified. For some reason I don't want him to see how shocked I am.

'Yes please,' I whisper numbly.

He starts to drive slowly out of the car park as he adjusts the air conditioning to a warm breeze, but the chill is inside me. I have no idea where I am, but it's nowhere I recognise as near to our ranch.

My voice cracks a little as I try and speak. 'Do you know if... David and Amy are ok?'

He glances down at me. 'The kids? They're fine, Charlotte got back before I left them.'

'Before you left?' I croak.

'I heard Reece's guys might be paying you a visit and so I went early to check on you,' he says and looks down at me. I blink in surprise and then turn to look back out of the front windscreen. How would he have *heard* that?

'Thank you,' I mumble, meaning it. The reality of how much trouble I was in is dawning on me. He wraps his arm around my shoulders and squeezes. A few minutes of silence pass and then a call comes through to his car kit from a withheld number.

Adam looks at the dashboard and I notice the way his jaw clenches as he presses the disconnect button. A minute later the caller tries again.

'Do you think you should get that?' I ask tentatively. Adam doesn't look at me but connects the call.

'I'm not alone and you're on speakerphone,' is how he answers briskly. Huh? Tingles of apprehension run up my spine and I feel awkward and uncomfortable knowing he doesn't want me to hear this conversation.

'They did it. Do you want us to…?' The voice replies and trails off. It's a man's voice and he has a north American accent similar to Adam's.

'No, it's under control,' Adam replies. He pauses like he wants to say something else and then changes his mind. 'Like I said, I'm not alone right now, is there anything else?'

'Yeah,' the man replies quietly. He clears his throat and pauses. 'Can you get there by midnight, after you've dropped her? It's… critical, there's something new.'

'Yeah,' Adam replies curtly and then disconnects the call abruptly. I sit silently beside him, pretending to disappear into the seat. Who was that? He referred to 'her', so who knows I'm with him? After a minute Adam clears his throat.

'Ella baby, you said you trust me, can I trust you?' Adam says quietly. I nod quickly, there's no way I'm going to say no! 'Good. You didn't hear that call,' Adam says and although his tone is gentle, there's no mistaking the authority in it. 'You'll never repeat that you heard that, understood?'

'Yes.' I answer immediately, rapidly becoming freaked out. Adam hugs me tighter to him and I'm almost too self-conscious to even breathe.

'Good,' he replies and my heartbeat hammers.

We drive in silence after that and it's a while later when I clear my throat and concentrate my gaze out of the front windscreen, if I don't get this out now, I'm never going to.

'Adam, why didn't you… you know?' I mumble. I feel him glance sideways at me; he registers I'm deliberately not looking at him and returns his gaze out of the front screen.

'Ella, do you think I'd hurt you?' he asks, his voice unnaturally neutral.

'No,' I deny quickly, 'it's just you clearly wanted to…' My voice trails away.

'Are you upset about that?' he asks in that direct way he has. Yes of course I'm upset about that, *in that situation*! I don't answer him. 'Ella, I had you naked under me, of course I wanted to. I'm only human. I'd *never* hurt you, though,' he says bluntly. I swallow and squeeze my hands between my thighs. 'Ella, when I take your virginity, it sure as hell won't be because some sick bastard told me to and wanted to watch,' he says firmly. I take a gulp of air as a wave of faintness threatens me.

When I take your virginity?

'You say it like it's a certainty,' I counter. He's sending my nerves into free fall.

'What? Ella, you're *with* me, aren't you?' he asks, the surprise clear in his voice.

I nod, but I'm starting to think that perhaps I'd be more comfortable if I wasn't. He's a lot to take in right now and I'm way past what I can handle in one evening. I have so many questions building up that are unanswered.

'Then of course I'm going to take you to bed,' he says certainly, keeping his eyes on the road. I take a deep breath.

'Adam, I'm not ready for that,' I gasp.

This evening has proven that to me in a resounding way. I'm completely freaked out. He glances at me, so I turn further away to look out of the side window at the pitch-black side of the deserted highway.

'I know that, baby, we can wait. Tonight probably scared the shit out of you too,' he says.

You think? I nod in agreement, desperate to get home now.

As he drives me to the ranch he hugs me tightly to his side, it's intended to be supportive, but instead I feel anxious. I start repeating in my head the things I heard about him. He clearly knew those guys, well enough to know about 'processes' they follow. And who was that he wanted to send a message from Mexico to? What with the fire and the knife and gun in his truck, I'm so out of my depth.

I'm beginning to wonder who's the more dangerous company, the loan sharks who abducted me and tried to whore me out, or maybe Adam. My mega rich 'boyfriend', who even they seemed scared of. Did he really just have a building set on fire? That's what it looks like. And who was that on the phone? Someone who knew I was with him? Come to think of it, why won't he let me clean inside his home study?

My heart hammers like it's in my throat and I know I need to slow things down with him. A lot. It's like I'm driving towards a road closure and need to press the brakes.

It's resoundingly clear he cares about me and I thought I was getting to know him, but suddenly I feel like I really don't know him at all. Above all else, though, I feel safe when I'm with him. Oh God, I'm so confused.

When we get to my house, the lights are on and there's a car and a motorbike I don't recognise parked next to our van.

'Wait here,' Adam says to me and goes into my house on his own.

I sit trembling a little in the seat of the truck, my mind is in meltdown and Adam comes back after a few minutes and opens my door. I can't look him in the eye as he lifts me down without asking me if I need help.

'I'll take you to the bathroom, then you can bathe and try to warm up, the others know to give you some space until the morning,' he says trying to reassure me. I know he's trying to look after me, but I look at him numbly, still feeling unsettled.

He puts his arm around me and walks me inside. I see my sisters and Hannah on the sofas with three guys I recognise from the farm, but I don't know their names. My sisters are all wide-eyed and pale, but keep silent and I'm suddenly glad that Adam's asked them to give me a bit of space. I smile at them in a very wobbly way and let Adam lead me to the bathroom. I glance at the back door as I pass it and notice there are boards where the window used to be and it's back on its hinges. It probably explains what the men are doing here.

When we get to the bathroom, he walks me inside like he lives here and closes the door. His confidence is unnerving. Without speaking, he turns the hot tap on in the bath and puts the plug in.

'How are you doing now, baby?' he asks softly, leaning down a little to look into my face. I nod automatically and he strokes my cheek. 'Stay warm and try to eat something, it'll help. I'm real sorry, but I need to go, can I come over tomorrow?' he asks. I shake my head before I realise I'm doing it. I just need some space to think. 'I'll give you a call to see how you are then,' he says softly so I nod. I'm desperate to be alone. He kisses me and then leaves, closing the door softly behind him.

I turn the key in the lock once he's gone and sit on the toilet seat trembling. Grabbing a hand towel, I squeeze it against my mouth to muffle my crying as the bath fills. I don't dare let my sisters hear me or they would be crowding in and fussing, and I can't cope with that right now. Somehow, Adam knew that in advance and I'm grateful to him for his foresight. I cry silently for quite some time, but after a while I welcome the numbness that follows. It stops me from thinking.

During my bath, I wash blood out of my hair and realise how tender the back of my head is, so after my wash Hannah fetches me some painkillers. Sarah gives me a hot mug of soup and sits quietly hugging me while I drink it. Charlotte hurries about silently finding bandages and creams, and then Rose uses them to dress the rope burns on my wrists. She's as quiet as the others and her eyes are concerned, but none of them pepper me with questions. I fall into bed a few hours before the sunrise and notice that Charlotte creeps into the room before she turns in herself and kisses me on the forehead as I pretend to be asleep.

♡

On Sunday the girls break their silence and ask me questions so I answer a lot, but after an hour I feel a headache coming on and they get the hint that I don't want to talk anymore. Their concerned glances tell me that they are as shaken up about the whole thing as I am. It's suggested we go to the police, but we all agree not to. The money we borrowed might not have been legally obtained and we could unintentionally put ourselves in the spotlight and, quite frankly, we have enough to be dealing with right now.

Adam calls three times to talk to me, but I ask the girls to tell him I'll speak to him tomorrow. I don't know how I'm feeling, and wouldn't know what to say. I should probably just ask him the questions I have building up, but I lack the confidence after he already told me that what I heard wasn't the real him and asked me to trust him. The evening replays around my head in slow motion and eventually my mind can't cope with the subject anymore. I tune it out by spending the rest of the day on my bed, writing song lyrics in my pyjamas. I tell myself I just need to get my head together and tomorrow I'll be able to think clearly. Tomorrow is a new day and I'll pull myself together then. Just not today.

Chapter Six

On Monday I finish my housekeeping duties and leave Chase in the garden while I sit waiting at the kitchen table for Adam to get home. Curiosity got the better of me earlier, and although I told myself I wouldn't go inside, just take a peek from the doorway, I couldn't help trying the door handle to his study. It was locked, though, and I noticed a peephole fitted into the wood. It didn't help to settle my curiosity. I mean, who has peepholes fitted in internal doors?

By the time he's due home, I'm fidgety and my tummy is unsettled about seeing him after not taking his calls yesterday. He comes in and looks relieved to see me, but strangely he doesn't talk, just leans against the kitchen door frame. Perhaps he knows not to approach me. Do I look as jumpy as I feel? I look back at him apprehensively, for some reason I feel like a kid who's been caught making mischief by the headmaster. He looks tired, like he's been up all night. After some time he speaks.

'How are you feeling? I've been worried about you.' His eyes tell me he means it.

Oh shit, I suddenly feel guilty. After everything he's done for me, I shouldn't have made him worry.

'Better than yesterday,' I reply. Time to grow up and apologise. 'I'm sorry, Adam, for not speaking on the phone yesterday,' I mumble but keeping eye contact with him.

His eyes travel to my wrists, taking in the dressings wrapped around them and then back up to my face. I expect him to be annoyed and ask me why I didn't take his calls, but he surprises me.

'You've nothing to apologise for. Do you want to talk about it?' he asks softly instead. I swallow before I answer.

'No, I just needed some time. I'm fine now, though. Sorry again.' I feel like I'm staring at him so much my eyes are starting to dry out. He doesn't say anything for a moment.

'No one's expecting you to be *fine*. You don't have to pretend, especially not for me, baby. Why don't you stay for supper? We could talk. About anything you want or about nothing at all, whatever you want.' His voice is gentle, but a rush of anxiety bubbles up inside me and I feel vulnerable. It shocks me, I haven't felt like this since I was thirteen and Tom and his groupies used to corner me and steal my lunch money.

'Thanks, but I can't, Charlotte's cooking for me,' I lie rising to my feet, my voice a little hoarse. I've always been a crap liar and he crosses his arms and looks like he doesn't believe a word, but doesn't give me a hard time. 'I better get home.' I pick up my bag. The unsettled feeling in my tummy is increasing with every moment.

'You need a ride back?' His tone's a little flat. I shake my head.

'I brought my bike,' I answer quickly, crossing to the back door. I pause and look back at where he's watching me across the room. Whatever's going through me right now, I know I owe him a lot and need to get this out.

'Thank you, Adam, for coming to get me on Saturday.' I mean every word, but an unexpected rush of emotion suddenly consumes me, my heart slams inside me and tears spring to my eyes. Concern clouds all his features and he strides across the room towards me. I jump and try to open the door but don't manage to do it in time.

'C'mere,' he murmurs and wraps his arms around me, crushing me into his chest. 'You don't need to thank me, baby, I'd do it again tomorrow; I just wish you didn't have to go through that. Any of that.'

His arms around me feel so right; despite being deeply unsettled, he still makes me feel safe. It's such a mindfuck! I also want to push him away, knowing there's so much he hasn't told me. I gulp as I try to stop from breaking down in front of him. I'm stronger than this and need to get a grip. I wriggle a little out of his arms and push his hands aside.

'I've got to go,' I gasp desperate to leave.

'I'll see you tomorrow?' he asks concerned, but releasing me as I wish.

I nod and try to smile at him, but it's strained. He stands there watching me, so at a loss of what more to say, I turn swiftly and head into the garden where my bike is. I pull the door softly behind me and feel relieved when it clicks shut.

Overnight I have a nightmare, reliving scenes from Saturday. I wake up in a cold sweat in the early hours and can't get back to sleep. On Tuesday afternoon, I deliberately I finish work earlier and am gone before Adam gets home. My head is such a mess; I think Saturday freaked me out more than I want to admit. I know it's cowardly, but I just can't summon the confidence to confront him about all of my burning questions, although I do leave him a note apologising that I had to get home.

As cowardly as it is, I arrive early for work on Wednesday intending to do the same, but instead I find Adam working from home. He meets me in the hall as I let myself in and I freeze when I see him. Adam stops about a couple of feet away from me when he sees my reaction, his eyes narrowing slightly. As if that's not awkward enough, I then make matters worse; instead of acting normally and saying hello, I step back and blurt out, 'I wasn't expecting you to be home.'

'I live here,' he answers flatly, his voice perhaps a little too quiet, and then there's a pause as I wrack my brains to say something which might put this right. I come up with nothing.

'If you're working, shall I come back tomorrow? I don't want to disturb you,' I offer lamely.

'You're not disturbing me, Ella,' he sighs. 'I thought perhaps we could talk, about Saturday.'

My instinct is to bolt, but I know I can't avoid him forever.

'Ok,' I say reluctantly. 'Do you want to walk Chase with me?' I'd feel better if we were out of the house. He studies me and I know he can see I'm uncomfortable, he's too bright not to.

'Sure,' he answers. 'I'll put on some sneakers.'

Chase bounds up excitedly when I call him for his walk and I wait with him in the front garden. When Adam joins us, Chase starts to pull, so Adam covers my hand with his to take the lead from me. His touch is like a ripple of electricity jump-starting my hormones and I know I can't fool myself for a second that I feel differently about him. The attraction between us is as strong as ever, it's just my head that is having trouble.

'I'll take him if he's in the mood to pull,' Adam says and slips his arm around me before I can step away. I love the feel of his heavy arm around me, it feels safe, sexy and familiar but, paradoxically, I'm also uncomfortable and feel embarrassed about Saturday. I just don't know which way is up at the moment.

'So, as you've been avoiding me, I guess you're still pretty upset?' he asks as we walk out of his driveway and head right down the residential road of workers' housing.

God, he's so direct.

'Yeah, I guess I am.'

'I can't be there for you if you don't talk to me, Ella.' He sounds slightly frustrated, like he's unaccustomed to not being in control.

'Ok, what do you want to know?'

'Whatever you want to tell me,' he says, exasperated, and then takes a breath and softens his tone. 'Well let's start with what upset you most, yeah? Was it them breaking into your house and hurting you? Where they took you? Was it me?' He sounds like he genuinely wants to talk about this. I always want to be treated like an adult, so I take a deep breath and decide to start behaving like one. I can't run away forever.

'Yes, being attacked upset me, of course it did. But I was more worried about the children and then later I think it was being tied up that's really got to me.' I take a deep breath for courage; I *never* talk like this! 'I guess it touched a nerve from my childhood, that's all.'

Adam squeezes my hand and keeps his eyes front as we near the perimeter turnstile, perhaps afraid that if he looks at me, I might clam up.

'Did someone abuse you when you were younger, Ella?' he says keeping his voice gentle and undemanding.

'Not how you think,' I interject quickly. 'Not sexually, but yeah, a group of older boys on my estate used to pick on me. They would corner me whenever I was alone and hold my arms behind my back while they raided my bag. They were stronger than me and I guess being tied up and powerless brought it all back.'

'I'm so sorry, baby, I didn't know. I can understand you felt like that. When was this?'

'Most of the way through secondary school, until I was around fourteen, then the leader of the group, Tom, moved away for a few years and I guess the others found something else to amuse them.' I'm surprised at myself, I'm able to tell Adam about this so calmly, in fact it almost feels like a relief to open up to him. It's quite empowering.

'When you say for a few years, I guess he came back again? What happened then, did he quit hassling you?' Adam asks, still squeezing my hand.

'Oh, he apologised,' I say, my tone lighter now. 'Actually he admitted he'd always acted like a prick and surprisingly he started being nice to me. We were good friends by the time I moved to the States, he even offered to take me to my college graduation party as a favour when I didn't know who to ask. I guess, though, after years of trying to avoid the group, the damage to my confidence was already ingrained.'

Adam doesn't say anything for a while, just mulls that over.

'I'm pretty sure, Ella, it wasn't as a *favour* that he took you out,' Adam says frankly. 'If a guy doesn't want to take a girl out, he won't. Don't put yourself down, baby, you're fucking beautiful and I'm sure most of the guys in that group were just trying to get your attention but didn't go about it in the right way.'

I flush at the compliment, but don't look up at him. How can he say the sweetest things and be the same guy who has a huge knife in his truck and intimidates brothel owners? It doesn't seem to add up. I wonder for a split second if by opening up to him, it might encourage him to do the same. I almost want to ask him about the things I heard on Saturday night, but at the last second I chicken out.

'Ella, I have to ask, as you've been avoiding me, did *I* upset you on Saturday?' Adam says, keeping his eyes facing forward. We exit the turnstile, let Chase off the lead and he scoops my hand back into his. 'If I did, I'm real sorry, but they wouldn't have let you go otherwise, you do understand that, don't you?'

I pause, should I admit to him that he did upset me? I'm not sure I'm ready for *that* conversation yet.

'I know you helped me, you were amazing to come for me and get me out of there.'

'Of course I helped you, I'm fucking crazy about you,' he exclaims like it's obvious. 'But, baby, that's not answering my question, is it?'

Whoa! *Fucking crazy* about *me?*

Immediately I'm both elated and freaked out. I'm still missing so many answers to my questions, including not knowing how he might react if I confirm he did scare me. He took me way past my comfort zone when he stripped my underwear off and dry humped me in a brothel, then appeared to order a building to be set on fire, but do I say that?

No way.

'No, you didn't upset me,' I lie. Adam looks down at me walking by his side but doesn't say anything else.

We take Chase on a long walk; I think we both just want to be together while this tentative peace exists between us. We don't mention it, but I think we're both aware we seem to be balancing on a rope and neither of us wants to destabilise us. When we start talking again, we keep the subjects light. It helps me relax and I like holding his hand, but I know I'm still upset and I think he knows too, he never misses anything. When we get back to the house, he leaves me in peace and returns to his study.

When Adam comes home on Thursday, he finds me hanging up the last of his freshly ironed shirts in his walk-in wardrobe. As I'm reaching up, he comes inside and slips his arms around my waist. It startles me more than I want to admit, I'm so jumpy since Saturday, but I try to hide it.

'Hey beautiful,' he murmurs and kisses my neck.

'Hi.' I want to snuggle into him but don't. I'm on edge and need to know more about him before I encourage him to take our relationship further. 'Did you have a good day?' My heart is thumping by feeling his arms around me.

'It was boring, I missed you,' he mumbles, trailing his lips along my collarbone where it's exposed by my baggy off the shoulder T-shirt. Oh God that's heavenly! I almost rest my head back against his chest. He slips his hand under my top and cups my breast, and those doubts I have re-surface. I take a deep breath and try to turn to face him but he keeps me pinned in place by his arm around my waist. A week ago I'd have loved the feeling, but right now I'm not in the right frame of mind.

I pull his hand away from where it's sliding inside my bra and turn around. Thankfully he lets me, but immediately seals his mouth over mine, his tongue demanding attention. Oh boy, I want to kiss him back so much, he makes me tingle all over, but just not now. I don't mean to hurt his feelings but soon pull my mouth away; I'm too jittery and uptight.

'Adam, I don't want to,' I say breathlessly and he looks at me and sighs.

'Ella, you're freaked out 'cause you've had one hell of a week, I get it, but don't say you don't want to when I can see in your eyes that you do.'

I blink and after that statement desperately want to stop staring back at him, but I can't pull my eyes away first. Breathing heavily, I settle for shaking my head again.

'Bullshit sweetheart, I'm not buying it. You want me. I want you. There's no problem if you want to wait, that's fine, you just say so, but don't say you don't want to.'

'Fine! Then I want to wait, Adam. And I want to leave the closet.' My voice is emotional and almost cracks as my heart rate accelerates. He exhales heavily, it's not really a sigh but certainly reluctant.

'Sure,' he says and steps back, so I practically scurry down the stairs and he follows me into the kitchen. It's a minute or two before he speaks. 'Do you want a drink?' he asks, turning the coffee machine on. His tone tells me he feels rejected but I don't know what to say to make it better.

'No thanks,' I answer, hovering in the centre of the room awkwardly. I glance towards his study and see that for the first time, the door has been left open. Although all I can see is cream carpet and a desk, it makes me curious to see inside.

'Actually, Adam, can I ask you a favour? I haven't checked my emails since leaving the UK; do you think I could use your laptop?' He looks at me before taking a cup out of a cupboard.

'Sure,' he answers, casually, 'I'll go fetch it.'

'Ok.' I'm a little disappointed I won't see inside his office after all.

'Remind me to buy you a smart phone at some point,' he says and I raise my eyebrows at the offer.

A few minutes later he sets the laptop on the kitchen table for me, but then pours his coffee, collects his phone and comes to sit beside me. I can't help wondering if he thought I was going to snoop. I wasn't.

He opens up the browser for me and then turns his attention to his phone. I log onto my emails and blink; there must be some sort of error! Then I check the dates and times of the emails and they are all different. Perhaps I make a noise or something, as Adam's attention is caught and he peers over my shoulder.

'Looks like Thomas Chambers really wants to talk to you,' he muses but his tone tells me he's not pleased.

Yeah, it really does. Almost my entire inbox is from him. There are two from some of the older people from my salsa club, two from a college friend, which look like jokes, and several sales promotions. I can feel Adam watching my expression with interest and I look back at him blankly.

'I thought you said you didn't have a boyfriend?' he says more directly now.

'I didn't!' I exclaim, a little stunned. Adam just raises his eyebrows at me.

'Well with email titles like *missing you*, it looks like this guy sure has a hard-on for you. I reckon you better reply and tell him you're spoken for before he catches a flight out here to see you.'

I blink at Adam in surprise. He's serious. Oh God, he looks jealous! Wow, do I, Ella Peterson, actually have a boyfriend who cares enough to be jealous?

I nod quickly and then click the most recent email, from two days ago.

Hi sunshine,

I can't believe you've been gone for two months and I haven't heard from you, Ella! Just send me a phone number or an address, would you? I'm worried, you aren't even on Facebook! It's like you've disappeared! Are you ok? Are we ok? Did I piss you off or something to make you want to shut me out? I don't think I did, but I'm sorry if that's the case. I've got news by the way, I got promoted and there's a sales manager role based in Kansas that I could transfer into. It's quite some way from Groats Valley where you live, but the firm have offered to fly me out for a 'look and see' visit, probably towards the end of next month. I'll likely take some leave while I'm there, travel a bit and come look you up. Can you spare me your couch, sunshine? I'd love to see you, been thinking about you... a lot.

Tell me something about what you've been up to? Have you found a job yet? Send me some of your lyrics to read, I'd love that. Have you made any new mates?

Anyway, I hope you get this. Let me know if you're ok and send me your number so I can call you,

Tom

Oh holy fuck! I'm a little stunned. He's been thinking about me... *a lot*? I click reply and open a new message.

Hello Tom

Nice to hear from you. Sorry I haven't read all your emails yet or been in contact, I didn't realise you would worry, it's just we've had no internet since we moved...

Congratulations on your promotion, I'm pleased for you, I know how hard you work. And moving to Kansas? Wow, that's a surprise to learn we might be neighbours of sorts. You never mentioned moving to the

USA. Yes, of course we can put you up if you're visiting. I warn you, though, our house is small, shabby, and overbearingly crowded, so as long as you're not expecting the Ritz, or any privacy whatsoever (or a hot shower once Rose and Sarah have been in the bathroom first...) then sure, you're welcome to stay.

Since arriving in the States, life's been pretty shit until recently. We've really struggled to find work. I started running an egg business, which didn't go well, and we're up to our necks in debt. We borrowed some money from a loan shark and things turned nasty on Saturday, I won't go into the details but I'm really shook up about it. Things are just so different here, more real somehow.

Things are looking up, though, so I'm trying to stay positive. I met a great guy called Adam who I'm sort of 'seeing'. He gave me a job as his housekeeper and has an adorable dog, so now I'm working I'm going to start saving up for a car. He also gave Rose a job in Finance at his company, so she's thrilled about that. Adam's been fantastic about 'the thing' that happened on Saturday, so supportive. He's a lot older than me, though, and I want to get to know him a bit more, sometimes he's a little overwhelming (but in a good way).

Stay in touch, my address and phone number are below, but I can't promise I'll be online regularly.

Ella (aka sunshine...? Since when do you call me sunshine?)

I press send, read the emails from my salsa club and send a quick reply to them, then get up and use the bathroom. When I return Adam tells me a new email chime sounded so I open it, Tom has replied already. God, that was quick!

Hi sunshine

Finally, an email!

What the fuck happened on Saturday? Are you alright, love? I've been worried about you and it sounds like I was right to be. If you're not enjoying the States or need to fly the overcrowded nest, you can always move back to the UK, I have a spare room with your name on it and would support you while you get on your feet.

So you've got a new guy huh? How much older is he? And he's your boss and employs your sister? And he owns his own company? It's not surprising you're overwhelmed, just be careful, Ella, ok? In fact, can you give me his number or surname? I'd like to talk to him.

I'm definitely coming to visit, my boss authorised the flights this morning. Can't wait to see you.

Thanks for the mobile number by the way, I'll call you soon, it's quite late here and I've got to work tomorrow.

So glad to finally hear from you and hope things improve soon, call me anytime.

Tom

He wants to talk to Adam? I can rent a room from him in the UK? I'm not sure what to make of that, but I'm not about to send him Adam's phone number. I don't reply and minimise the browser, then get up to tidy away some cleaning utensils I've left out before I leave. I'm just finishing in the utility room when Adam comes in. He crosses his arms and leans against the door frame.

'What do you mean, you're *sort of* seeing me?' Adam asks, his jaw tense and his eyes fierce. My eyes spring up to his from where I'm kneeling by the cupboard, a little taken aback.

'Pardon?'

'You're *sort of* seeing me?' he repeats. 'And you need to get to know me better because I'm overwhelming? What the fuck does that mean? It sounds thoroughly underwhelming!'

Oh Jesus, he's really cross. My adrenaline kicks in and I'm suddenly indignant.

'You've read my emails?' I exclaim standing up.

'Yeah, I read your emails! You told your fucking childhood bully more in an email than you can say to me! You said you were fine after Saturday and then suddenly you're actually really shook up about it!

139

What the fuck, Ella? Why the hell can't you say that to me, unless it's *me* you're pissed at?'

'W-what?' I gulp, I hadn't really seen it from that point of view.

He storms up to me now and slams his hands against the cupboard on either side of my shoulders, caging me in but not touching me, but it's an aggressive move and I'm intimidated. He's a big man and towers over me, so I automatically press myself back against the cupboard door.

'So what are you pissed at me about?' he demands. 'That I wanted to fuck you? That's what you implied that night, isn't it? Well news flash, Ella, yeah, I want to fuck you! You're my girl, of course I want that, that's kinda the point isn't it? You're all I think about and the waiting is driving me goddamn crazy! This whole relationship is completely a one-way thing! It's got nothing to do with what I want!'

'I didn't k-know that.' My heart is pounding so hard I can barely get the words out.

'I'm not going to let Saturday drive a wedge between us,' Adam says firmly, 'but I don't want to be *sort of* your guy either. And I'm sure as hell not going to share you when you invite your fucking ex to come and stay with you. You think he wants to come all that way to sleep on your sofa? He wants in your bed, Ella, with you. Are you gonna let him or say no because you're *sort of* with me?'

I push on his forearms, but he's so strong I can't move him. I panic and in my jumpy state I slap him across the face before I know what I'm thinking. My reaction stuns me more than him; I've never hit anyone before. I immediately shove him and he looks at me stonily before lowering his arms. I push past him, heading for the door, but he sidesteps me and pushes it shut in front of me. I freeze and stare at him. A silence enters the room and the atmosphere is thick. I don't dare look him in the eye.

Oh Christ! Why did I have to hit him?

'I know it's a two-way thing, Adam. But I'm not ready for more; since Saturday I feel like I hardly know you and there's so much you're not telling me.' My emotions are on overload.

'Christ, Ella!' He slams his hand against his forehead in frustration. 'I asked you to trust me. You told me you did, that's just gotta be enough for now. I guess the real question is either you want me or you don't, but I'm sure as hell not going to share.'

'Then I don't want you,' I flare at him defensively, 'not if you're going to be like this and snoop through my emails.'

'You don't want me,' he repeats flatly.

'No,' I say stubbornly. More than anything I just want to leave, I don't do confrontation. The expression that crosses his face confuses me. He clears his throat.

'So you're pushing me away.' There's a cold glint to his eyes and he oozes power; in the confines of his utility room, the effect is overwhelming. I suddenly feel my age. I'm too young to know how to handle him, as always I'm completely out of my depth with him.

'Yes,' I snap.

'I didn't think you were like that, Ella. So you're going to be like all the others,' he mutters angrily. 'I thought you were decent and pure, I can't believe you're freakin' playing me. Jesus!'

What is he talking about? Does he mean his ex-girlfriends? He pushes down the handle and abruptly pulls the door wide. I don't wait for him to say anything else but dart through the doorway.

'*Ella?*' Adam shouts after me but I don't wait, I grab my bag and shoes and fly out of the front door. I run bare foot along the grass to the end of the driveway where I pause to pull my shoes on and look back at the house. Adam is gripping the door frame above his head and leaning on his arms. The stance is annoyed but casual.

'I quit!' I shout at him angrily.

'Not accepted!' he states back, his voice authoritative and strong.

Well just watch me. I spin around and the tears come hard and fast down my cheeks as I start to run home. I'm upset about Saturday.

I'm upset he seems to be hiding things from me. I wish with all my heart we hadn't argued and I really regret hitting him. I shouldn't have done that. And above all else, I'm so deeply upset we just broke up. I really like him and I'm gutted it hasn't worked out. Utterly gutted. What have I done?

I suddenly miss my dad like crazy, and I'd give anything for him to be here to give me a cuddle. I need him right now; my dad would have known what to say to make me feel better. The tears stream down my face so hard my vision blurs and I run blindly around a corner and collide straight into someone's chest. I'm sent reeling sideways and precariously close to falling over.

'Lord, Ella,' Dan exclaims in shock reaching out and steadying me by my shoulders. 'Christ girl! You alright?'

My breath comes in short sharp gasps and I manage to regain my balance, wiping frantically at the tears streaming down my face with the palms of my hands. Dan continues to hold onto my shoulders, I probably look like I'm about to fall down.

'S-sorry, Dan,' I pant, surprised at our collision.

'What's wrong?' Dan asks. I shake my head, but he's not to be put off with me looking like this. 'Tell me! Did someone hurt you? Is it about Saturday night?'

I blink. What? How does *he* know what happened? Embarrassment floods my cheeks. Does the whole world know? I shake my head quickly hoping to divert the conversation away from that.

'Adam and… I just b-broke up.' I'm trying desperately to calm my stricken heart rate down a little. 'Sorry,' I gasp, 'I should look where I'm g-going.'

'Aww I'm sorry to hear that,' he says gently and it takes me by surprise that he's so sympathetic. 'You want to talk about it?' he offers, gently massaging my shoulders with his thumbs as he keeps me standing up straight.

I shake my head, blinking more tears out of my eyes as I look up at him, more than a little taken aback. Talking about it would be good, I feel like my head is going to explode right now, but to *Dan*? I've always felt so uncomfortable around him.

'I'm a good listener.' He shrugs, still holding my shoulders but his eyes are kind. 'Maybe I can help?'

'I don't think so, not unless you have any clue about what Adam was talking about, because I don't!' I mutter breathlessly, dismayed that the tears just keep coming.

'What did he say?' Dan asks me.

'Something about *playing* him and being just like all the others,' I answer, my bottom lip trembling embarrassingly.

'Oh,' he says, but it's the way he says it that catches my attention. 'He said *that* about *you*?' It's clear that Dan might have an idea what he meant.

'Do you know w-what he's talking about?' I ask him, sobbing hard but trying to calm down. My hands are shaking and I know I'm embarrassing myself in front of Dan of all people, but I can't seem to stop.

'Come back to mine, we can talk,' he says quietly, dropping his hands from my shoulders.

'Do you know what he meant, Dan?'

He starts walking away and I stand hovering on the pavement with my bag. He doesn't answer me straight away but when he does, his voice seems kind.

'Come on,' he nods his head further up the road, 'we can't talk in the street about Adam's business, Ella, this is his plant. Come back to mine and clean yourself up a bit, we can talk there.' I'm so confused I don't question it; I follow Dan back to his place, desperate for some insight as to why Adam looked at me so coldly.

When we reach Dan's place, I'm in a daze and don't really register much about the house except it has a large front lawn and is a standard smallish worker's place. He gestures for me to go and clean up in the downstairs bathroom, so I take his advice and the blissfully cold water on my face does help me calm down. When I come out, I'm conscious I must look a red-eyed mess and I'm hiccupping, but at least the hysterical sobbing has stopped.

Dan lounges on the sofa with his knees spread and a cold beer in his hand. He holds out an opened bottle to me.

'I figured you could use a beer,' he says. I thank him and take the bottle absentmindedly as I sit next to him.

'Do you know what he meant by "all the others"?' I ask Dan. 'Was he talking about his previous girlfriends?'

Dan takes a long drink from his bottle then pulls out a packet of cigarettes and lighter from his jeans.

'Adam's got a bit of a track record for picking up trash for partners, Ella,' He takes out a cigarette, which he offers to me. I shake my head, so he changes his mind and puts it back in the packet again. 'I'm surprised he'd compare you to them, though, you're worlds apart, what did you do?' He looks sideways at me, his eyes curious as he tosses his cigarette packet on the coffee table. I twist so I'm facing him and can see his expression, placing a cushion on my lap so I don't flash my knickers at him as I cross my legs on the sofa.

'He thinks I invited my ex to come and stay with me, but he's not an ex, just a friend, we've never even kissed. Then I lost my temper and I hit him,' I mumble, ashamed. Dan raises his eyebrows at me and tries to hide a smirk. I'm clearly not a force to be reckoned with in his eyes. 'In what way were his exes trash?' I change the subject.

'Err, you better ask him for the details,' Dan answers vaguely, 'but I'll tell you that they weren't women I'd take home to meet my parents, if you know what I mean. Hell, one of them darn near tore him open.'

'What do you mean? Like, broke his heart?' I ask.

'Nah, she stabbed him! It was in Mexico, Rita was her name and she was high at the time, demanded cash for her next hit. He didn't want to touch that stuff, you know, after his mama nearly OD'd, so he said hell no. She went at him with a blade when he was asleep. It shook him up as you can imagine.'

What? I stare at Dan, dumbfounded. So much of that statement is deeply disturbing. My mouth drops open a little. He was stabbed by his girlfriend? And his mother nearly OD'd? He'd mentioned his parents had had troubles, but Christ!

'Don't tell him I told you that shit,' Dan says then, eyeing my reaction. 'He'll tell you 'bout that stuff when he wants to.'

'Or not,' I answer under my breath as it's not like he's good at opening up.

Dan doesn't respond, but his dark blue eyes study me as he swallows more beer. I drink some from my own bottle and the bubbles soothe my dry throat, even though I'm not keen on beer. I'm trying to get my head around everything Dan just said.

'What else did he say?' Dan asks after a few minutes pass.

'He said he thought I was *playing* him. What on earth does that mean anyway?'

'Well, fucking with him, clearly,' Dan answers. My eyes grow wide and I stare at him.

'I'm not. I mean we haven't, umm… I'm not…' I stammer and Dan's eyes grow wide to match mine and a smile pulls at the corner of his mouth.

'Ella, I didn't say you were fucking him, I said fucking *with* him,' he intervenes, amused. 'Like messing him around and shit like that. Why, you're not banging him then?' he pries directly.

I shake my head primly, what's the point denying it when my burning cheeks are already giving away the truth. Dan throws his head back and laughs.

'Well that's what he means by playing him then!' He grins. 'You've been together, what, a few *weeks* and you've not nailed him yet?' He laughs louder. 'Christ, for Adam that's a record, he must have blue nuts by now.'

I stare at him, shocked, and shift uncomfortably on the seat. Oh that's so crude. I put my bottle down on Dan's coffee table intending to swing my legs off the sofa and stand up. Dan puts his hand on my shoulder, and nudges me to stay put, he's still laughing but making an effort to stop.

'Sorry!' He sniggers and takes a calming breath. 'Really, I shouldn't have said that.' His apology seems genuine but his eyes sparkle with interest. I remain seated but avert my eyes, feeling awkward. He passes my bottle back to me so I take it.

'So you're not…?' he asks, deliberately letting his voice trail off suggestively.

'I'm not answering that,' I retort, his answering smile tells me he's worked it out for himself.

'Well, it's kinda relevant, don't you think?' he probes. '*Are* you playing him? I can see where he's coming from if you're not… you know.' He quickly adjusts his last words in response to the glare I give him. I drink more beer and don't answer.

'Why not?' he asks me nosily, shifting to give me his full attention. 'Have you never—'

'Can we change the subject?' I ask a little too brightly, cutting him off.

'Sure.' He grins. Oh God, how much more embarrassing can this get? 'You know, a lot of guys find that a real turn on,' Dan says smoothly, watching me astutely. I almost choke on my beer. Ok, I was wrong before, it could get more embarrassing.

'I don't know what you mean,' I mutter, trying to cut the conversation dead.

'Yeah you do.' Dan grins, teasing me, he's completely unperturbed by my tone. He's making sex-eyes at me and I feel like I'm about to combust. I rapidly redirect my gaze to the bottle in my hand. 'Well if you need any help with that, you just let me know,' he offers. I swallow with a gulp and look at him sharply.

'Pardon? Need help with *what* exactly?' Surely I've misunderstood? Dan leans an arm on the back of the sofa and smiles in a way that implies he's joking, but his eyes tell me he's serious.

'Popping your cherry, sweetheart,' he says confidently.

My mouth drops open and my cheeks flame. 'I can't believe you just said that.'

Dan laughs and shrugs it off, but he's looking at me in a way that's sending my nerves into turmoil. His eyes flick down over my exposed bra strap where my T-shirt is designed to hang off one shoulder, so I pull my top up self-consciously.

'Anything for a friend.' The bastard is acting like he's teasing me, but I can't be sure and wonder if I should just walk out. Perhaps Dan realises this and he clears his throat.

'Are you feeling better after Saturday?' He changes the subject and his tone loses the playful edge.

'You know… about Saturday?' I ask, aware of a sinking sensation in my stomach.

'Yeah, I saw him carry you out,' Dan answers not breaking eye contact. I stare back at him blankly. Dan was there? Was it Dan that set the building on fire?

'I wanted to ask you how you were earlier, but I haven't seen you.' He's still holding my gaze. 'And I thought it might be a bit odd to turn up at your house again, you know, since you're with Adam now… or were.' He shrugs, correcting his tense.

I look away quickly and drain my bottle of its remaining beer. 'Yeah, I'm ok now,' I answer, wiping my finger through the condensation on the glass bottle.

He reaches towards me and at first I think he's going to hold my hand. Awkward! To my relief, though, he plucks my empty bottle out of my hands instead.

'I was worried about you,' he says sincerely. 'We all were.'

'All?' I mumble, keeping my eyes on my lap. I think Dan can see I'm uncomfortable and he rises and heads towards his kitchen. I breathe a sigh of relief.

'Yeah, Car, Mig, Jordan, Owen and me. We were there. We were worried,' he answers coming back in from the kitchen holding two more beers fresh from the fridge.

He goes to hand the beer to me but as I reach out he lets go of it and it lands in my lap, beer frothing all over my skirt. I squeal and jump up as Dan hastily pulls his T-shirt off to mop it up.

'It's ok,' I say quickly taking over, aware he has his hands near more intimate areas of me, but my skirt is drenched.

'Sorry!' he apologises. 'I'll get you another.' He heads back into the kitchen to give me some space. When he reappears, he passes me another bottle, so I put it on the table with the other and look down at my skirt. 'You want to put it in the dryer for a bit?' he asks.

'Yeah, if that's ok?' I answer, looking up. I almost blink in shock at the sight of him with his shirt off. Wow. Dan is a man worth looking at. The tattoos of the naked women curve all the way up his muscled arms and over his shoulders, although they aren't to my taste, they are artfully done. His chest is sculpted and toned and he has one nipple pierced. I divert my gaze rapidly and think I was just quick enough for him not to notice me checking him out.

'Have you got any shorts I can borrow?' I ask him, flushing pink.

'They wouldn't fit you, Ella,' he answers casually. I nod, feeling awkward. Dan gives a carefree laugh at my discomfort, like I'm being cute. 'Don't worry sweetheart, I won't look. Go sit back under your cushion!' He smirks, turning his back to me and holding out his hand expectantly.

I peel off my skirt and pass it to him, glad he can't see me cringing with embarrassment. He takes the skirt and walks out to put it in the tumble dryer without looking behind him.

When he returns, I'm sitting on the sofa with cushions piled up modestly on my lap.

'So what music are you into?' Dan asks, sitting back down with an iPod in his hand as he passes me back one of my beers. He starts flicking through various tracks. Music? That's all he needed to say and immediately I'm off, lost in my favourite subject, keen to take my mind off Adam.

We talk for quite some time and I'm surprised at how easy it is. We speak about my salsa club back home, my song writing and he tells me he used to play guitar back in school. He has two young sons who live with his ex-wife. It's a surprise to hear he has children and is divorced, but then he is nearing thirty, like Adam. Hmm, my chest constricts when I think of Adam so Dan distracts me deliberately by cooking a pizza and fetching us more beer. He invites me to watch a band with him in a few weeks as he has tickets; it sounds good but I'm not sure I want to go alone with him so I hedge my bets and say maybe. It's reasonably late when I notice that it's almost dark outside.

'Oh gosh,' I squeal in surprise. 'I hadn't realised the time.'

'Everything ok?' Dan asks, leaning his head on the back of the sofa. I realise that I'm tipsy after so many beers, how many was it, five? Maybe more? I'm not used to drinking as it is and it'll be dark for sure by the time I've walked home.

'I better call my sisters to come and pick me up.'

'Oh, well I'd give you a ride but...' Dan waggles his eyebrows at me, raising his current beer in the air. 'You can stay if you like, on the sofa or you can take my bed and I can crash out here,' he says, shrugging indifferently. I look at him, surprised and slightly sceptical. 'It's better than dragging your sisters out to pick your drunk ass up, right? Besides, I want to hear more about your music,' he adds.

'No you don't.' I accuse him light-heartedly, making him chuckle.

'Well, I want you to show me some of those salsa moves actually,' he suggests playfully, then changes his tone. 'Seriously, though, you can stay. No problem.'

'Are you sure?' I ask realising I'm definitely too drunk to walk home alone and likely to get an earful from Charlotte for dragging her out in the van and wasting petrol. 'You wouldn't mind me on the couch?'

He starts laughing loudly at that and arches an eyebrow at me. I realise what I said and giggle, the beer giving me a welcome warmth that distracts me from my anxiety over arguing with Adam.

'Oh very funny,' I exclaim and blush at my oversight.

Dan grins, gesturing with his palms raised towards the sofa. 'Help yourself!'

'Ok, can I borrow your phone?' I ask and he digs his mobile out of his jeans.

Hannah answers the call and I explain that I've got talking at Dan's house and I'm going to crash on his sofa that night. Hannah's surprised, repeats it and immediately Charlotte comes on the line asking if I'm alright and if that's really what I want to do. I assure her I'm fine and just about manage to pronounce my words clearly. Dan watches, amused, as I have to confirm that he's just a friend. How embarrassing. Getting the third degree.

Charlotte tells me that Adam has called twice and my beer-induced serenity falters. I ask her to tell him that I'll call him tomorrow if he rings again and then we hang up.

'Mama's worried huh?' Dan teases, prodding me playfully. I roll my eyes at him.

'Yeah, they think I'm still fourteen,' I grumble, more to myself than to Dan. I'm getting a little tired of always being treated like a child, if it had been Rose or Sarah calling, they wouldn't have got the third degree.

We continue to talk some more about music and I'm relieved, thinking about Adam just upsets me. I'm actually beginning to feel grateful to Dan for distracting me. It's several more beers later, though, when I finally put my hand up to Dan and refuse yet another bottle.

'I'm drunk… enough!' I hiccup, as the room moves around me and it makes me giggle. 'How many of those do you… have anyway?'

I fail to not slur my words and know I'm going to have a hard time walking. He watches me with amused dark blue eyes that seem to be following my every movement.

'Aww, I usually keep a few crates for the Saturday night crowd,' he answers. I push my feet out from under the cushions and stretch my legs. He scoops up my ankles and pulls my knees to rest over his thighs. It's a casual movement and I don't think much of it until he leaves his hands high up on my bare thighs. Dan keeps the conversation going as naturally as before but I'm suddenly more self-conscious.

'I should… get my skirt,' I say and wonder if I should push his hands off my legs. Would that be an over-reaction?

'Ok.' He agrees, but leaves his fingers where they are, his thumbs drawing small circles on my thighs. Pleasant tingles run up my legs, but even in my relaxed state it seems a little too familiar.

'You know, Ella, you don't have to sleep out here; you could crash in with me. It's your choice, but it'd be more comfortable,' he says. His eyes are caressing me in such a way that I sit up and ease my legs off his lap.

I shake my head and the room sways precariously. 'Out here is fine, Dan, thanks though.' I get up and cross the room unsteadily heading for the bathroom.

When I come out Dan has started playing salsa music on his iPod in the living room. I totter into his kitchen to the tumble dryer and crouch down to pull the machine door open. I lose my balance and land on my bottom and can't help a giggle that escapes me. When I look up Dan is grinning as he leans casually against the kitchen wall with his arms crossed.

'Need a hand?' He laughs.

'Nope.' I giggle and pull my skirt out of the machine. I crawl onto my knees and have to lean heavily on the worktop to start pulling myself up.

'Here,' Dan says supporting my elbows to get me to my feet. 'If I didn't know better, I'd say you were drunk, Miss Peterson.' Dan smirks over his shoulder at me as he takes my hand and leads me back into the living room. He takes my skirt from me and tosses it onto the sofa, then slips a strong warm hand onto my waist under my loose fitting T-shirt. He keeps hold of my other hand, assuming a dance hold.

'Come on, I wanna learn some of those salsa moves,' he says light-heartedly, pulling me a little closer but leaving a gap. My eyes are on a level with his collarbone and I'd be lying if I didn't feel the pull of attraction to him. With his bare chest in front of me, muscular arms and a toned stomach, it's a struggle to keep my eyes off him. I blink and successfully divert my eyes back up to his face.

'Dan, I won't be able to dance.' I protest, trying to pull my hand free. I hiccup again and it starts us both laughing. 'And I need my skirt,' I add quickly. The music is playing a slow song and Dan starts swaying to the music.

'You look great without it.' Dan teases in a way I'm not sure how to respond to, so I do what I always do and blush. Dan starts dancing with me and I sway unsteadily, so he tightens his arms and holds me against him. I gulp as adrenaline surges through me at the contact. I blink at him, not sure what to say, but he keeps his eyes on mine and my tummy flutters nervously.

'I need my skirt,' I mumble, looking away from him. He lifts my hand in the air and gestures for me to make a slow turn underneath it. I said I wouldn't dance but he's encouraging me anyway. 'Dan, I have to put my skirt… on!' I protest, hiccupping again.

He doesn't answer but keeps his hand raised so I have to make the turn, but I shake my head at his persistence. When I have my back to him, his arms slide around my waist from behind me and he presses himself against my back. He's strong and holds me securely and it makes my pulse explode in my veins. I have to admit, it could feel rather nice if I hadn't just broken up with my boyfriend this afternoon. Dan is surprisingly pleasant company, but my heart is pining for Adam and I don't want to lead Dan on. I look over my shoulder nervously at him and he lowers his head to rest his chin on my shoulder, moving my body with his to the music.

'Dan?' I ask timidly. 'I think… this isn't a good idea,' I say trying to speak clearly, but the room is moving and my tongue doesn't want to cooperate.

He lowers his head and runs his lips over my collarbone where my T-shirt exposes one shoulder. His lips leave pleasant tingles along my skin but I don't want to be distracted and pull at one of his arms around my waist, but he tightens it instead.

'Dan, stop. I need to put my skirt on. I don't… want to lead you on. Don't… want you… to get the wrong idea.' I stumble over my words.

'Chill out, honey,' Dan starts kissing the skin under my ear. My breathing hitches up a notch and he presses his hips against my bottom; I can feel he's hard through his jeans.

I shake my head.

'No, I don't want to… can you stop? I think you've got the w-wrong idea, I'm really sorry.' I pull at his wrist. Immediately his arms leave me and I stumble forward as I'm released. I spin around, overbalance and slump sideways to rest my bottom on the arm of a chair that was luckily in just the right place. I see Dan sprawling on the sofa where Adam has just wrenched him off me.

Oh sweet Jesus.

A hot flush ignites my skin as I lay eyes on Adam standing tense and bristling in front of me. Desire pools low in my tummy. He looks so amazingly hot right now, tall and lean, his brown eyes burning as he glares at Dan who is still on the sofa looking back at him. Is this what beer does to your hormones I wonder? Adam is breathing hard and his fist is clenched at his side in an obvious show of restraint.

'She said stop,' Adam growls at Dan and I blink at the aggression in his voice and manage to stand up. It's surreal, like I'm looking through a window and not really in the room with them.

'Did she?' Dan says sitting up and then standing, squaring off to Adam. The two men stand glaring at each other. Adam is taller and more muscular, but Dan is not slight by any means and they both tower over me. Dan's iPod is on the chair next to me and I turn the music off. The silence is absolute for a moment.

'Two times.' Adam glares at Dan icily. 'She said stop two times, Dan. What the fuck are you playing at?'

'Salsa lessons,' Dan replies cockily and smirking in the face of Adam's anger. Instantly Adam's fist makes contact with Dan's jaw. My fingers clamp themselves over my mouth.

Dan staggers back and puts his hand over his jaw, but surprisingly doesn't retaliate. I stand frozen to the spot, although in contrast the room appears to be moving around me and I have to lean my hand against the chair for support. The men glare at each other. Electricity surges through the air until finally Dan speaks first.

'What the hell's got you all riled up anyway?' He accuses Adam, his southern accent noticeably stronger. 'You barge in here and act like I'm messing with your woman. She's not with you, though, is she? She broke it off, so what the fuck are *you* doing?' Dan retaliates.

Adam takes a calming breath and flexes his fingers from where they were still clenched, then for the first time looks at me. I look back at him uneasily, suddenly realising how bad this must look with me missing a skirt and Dan in only his jeans. I want to tell him this isn't what it looks like, expecting him to be angry with me, but his expression surprises me. Instead of the anger I'm dreading to see on his face he looks concerned.

'Are you ok, baby?' he asks me, his voice gentle.

I blink at him in shock and nod. His eyes flick down over my exposed legs, taking in my drunken demeanour and the many empty beer bottles around the sofa area. 'Get your skirt on, you're coming back to mine.'

What? Before I can form a reply, Dan answers instead.

'The hell she is! She's staying here tonight, with me.'

Uh oh, that sounds awful. I clear my throat and find my voice, but it's not as coherent as I'd like it to be.

'What he means is... Dan said I...' I hiccup untimely, 'could sleep... here.' I point at the sofa and wince thinking the words still didn't come out right. 'I mean, staying on the couch, on my own.' As I finish, my hand slips ungracefully off the arm of the chair but I manage to stay on my feet as the room tilts.

'I bet he did *say* that.' Adam glares at Dan.

Dan angles his head in the face of Adam's fury. 'What is it, Adam? You scared she might actually want to stay here rather than with you?' Then he directs his voice to me but keeps his eyes on Adam. 'Ella, you can stay as long as you like, sweetheart, he doesn't own you.'

I stare back at them both, unsure what to say, even though they are focusing more on each other than on me. The testosterone levels in the room are way over the top and any minute I think they are going to come to blows again. I slump into the chair and hastily pull my skirt on and also my shoes which are thankfully on the floor near me. The tension is now building and I'm starting to feel terrible; this is my fault.

'I'm really sorry.' I apologise to both of them, and they turn to look at me. I lean on the arm of the chair and pull myself to my feet, standing up precariously. 'I didn't mean to cause...' I hiccup, 'any trouble. Sorry.' I shake my head to show them I'm sincere and reach down to pick up my bag, but my hand misses and I snatch it on the second attempt. Adam comes to stand beside me and slips his arm around my waist seeing I'm unsteady.

'You don't have to apologise, Ella,' he says calmly and glaring at Dan. 'Come on, I'll take you back to mine,' he says and takes my bag from me.

'It's ok, I'll w-walk home,' I stammer.

'No you won't. You can stay here, Ella.' Dan intervenes, his voice getting louder.

'You're fucking dreaming if you think I'm going to let that happen!' Adam thunders at him, making me jump in fright. 'You fucking get her loaded when she's upset, get her half-naked and try to seduce her when she said no. If she's staying with anyone it's with me where I can look after her, you're fucking lucky I don't floor you, you piece of shit.'

'Well who fucking upset her in the first place?' Dan shouts back. I sway unsteadily on my feet and Adam slings my bag over his shoulder and bends to scoop my knees out from under me, cradling me in his arms. It takes my breath away and the room spins. I'm not sure what to say, although I think it's not the best idea to stay at Dan's after all, even if it's just not to cause more problems. My head lolls against Adam's shoulder and I breathe him in, he smells amazing, it's like his scent is fast-tracked to my hormones. I hook my arms up loosely around his neck, appreciating the way his muscles ripple under the fabric, and stare up at him. My eyes are drawn to the strong line of his jaw and the breadth of his neck.

'Well that's true,' Adam agrees with Dan. 'I did upset her, but at least I don't get her wasted to try and get her fucking panties off!' He strides out of the room with me in his arms.

When we reach his truck, I don't argue with him as he holds open the door and helps me climb inside. I watch him silently as he gets in the driver's side, my head resting against the back of the chair. There now appears to be two of him.

'Do you want me to take you home, baby, or do you want to come back with me?' he asks. My befuddled brain struggles to understand what he says and I look at him blankly. I'm stupidly drunk and I think Charlotte will lecture me for a century if I turn up like this. Adam looks at me expectantly and, when I don't answer, drives us to his place. He parks in his driveway and helps me out of the truck. I'm precariously close to falling over and he steadies me protectively.

'Sorry again,' I whisper, putting my hands on his biceps to try and stand up straight and failing. Oh my gosh, he has the sexiest arms and I squeeze them as I hold myself up.

'You haven't done anything wrong, baby, you're young, easily taken in and upset... And Dan's a manipulative prick who can't be trusted.' Adam vents as he looks down at me held up in his arms.

'I mean for hitting you too. I'm... s-sorry for hitting you,' I mumble.

'I deserved it.' He shrugs nonchalantly like it's of no concern. 'I was a prick for reading your mail and getting jealous. I shouldn't have said what I did either.' His eyes are burning down at me and I look away.

'I am sorry, though, Adam... for everything and causing trouble... again.' My tongue feels too thick in my mouth to form my words properly. He tightens his arms around me and then kisses the top of my head.

'As I said, I was out of line, baby. And if we can't make a mistake and drink a bit too much at eighteen, when can we, huh? Come on, let's get you to bed,' he murmurs and literally holds me up as I stumble along his driveway. I look up at him sharply as his words register and he notices my expression of concern.

'Ella, if you're going to be sleeping at a guy's house, it's damn well going to be mine,' he says arrogantly but softens his voice when he takes in my expression. I'm feeling vulnerable with him and the drink in my system isn't letting me hide it like I have been doing all week. 'Don't be worried, I know you're not ready for sex, baby,' he says softly and I breathe a sigh of relief.

Once inside, we pass Chase in the hall and Adam helps me negotiate the stairs up to his bedroom. I trip and stagger all over the place and am giggling loudly by the time I collapse flat on my back on his bed.

His eyes sparkle with amusement as my giggling increases and he strips my skirt and shoes off me and then pulls his own clothes off, leaving on only his pants. He comes and lies on the bed with me, smiling at my drunken laughter, pulling me into his arms and kissing my head. My heart rate explodes in my chest to feel him pressed closely against me and I can't stop my arms from wrapping around his broad shoulders. His skin is warm and smooth over hard muscles and I run my hands over them, the beer giving me confidence I wouldn't usually feel and pushing aside all my questions raised on Saturday. I just don't care about them at this moment, being with him is all I want.

'Did you know... I was at Dan's house?' I ask him, aware of the ache yearning between my legs, wanting to feel him inside me. Somewhere in my mind, I'm mildly freaked out by the intensity of the feeling.

'I was worried about you after you left, but your sisters said you weren't home when I called. I thought you just didn't want to speak to me so I drove over to your place to apologise. They told me you'd since called and where you were,' he answers absentmindedly and still smiling at me as I lie in his arms. 'You know, I think I am going to buy you a cell, it'd be easier.'

I'm not really listening, though. I feel like I'm melting inside with the way his warm brown eyes are caressing me affectionately.

'You know, you're a fucking beautiful drunk,' he says.

'A beut...iful drunk?' I ask him.

'Yeah.' He smiles watching my face but doesn't say anything further, just brushes my hair off my forehead. 'Listen, I know you probably won't remember this tomorrow, but about Saturday, I really don't want it to drive a wedge between us,' he says softly.

'Ok,' I answer him, slightly breathless. I could lie in his arms forever; it feels absolutely amazing after our argument earlier. He smiles at me, like he can see my mind isn't really on what he's saying. 'Did you know you've got a twin?' I mumble at him. He rolls his eyes at me and his smile is so sexy I'm mesmerised. 'Lucky me! Now I have two of you.' I giggle girlishly, finding my own joke hilarious. He leans his head down and bumps his nose against mine in response.

'Well there's only one of you and you're perfect,' he says huskily to me and I smile at him, not really registering what he said or the way he's looking at me.

'What were you doing at Dan's anyway?' He pulls my hair loose from its band and spreads it out over the mattress. He runs his fingers through it and his eyes are hooded.

'Talking 'bout you, and missing you, and actually trying not to think 'bout you... sorry,' I mumble incoherently but honestly, the alcohol's making me more open than usual. Oh my gosh, I can't stop staring at his eyes, they take my breath away. My gaze drops to his lips and my breathing shallows a little.

He caresses my scalp; it sends my insides into a quivering mess of excitement. He swallows as he looks down at me in his arms and tilts his head slightly before speaking.

'Ella,' he says carefully, his tone turning a little more serious, 'no matter what happens between us, you need to be careful around Dan.'

I nod, agreeing with him. 'It wasn't what it... looked like,' I answer him honestly and then hiccup.

'I know, baby, but even still. It might have turned out to be more than you expected,' he says, trying to give me a warning in as gentle a way as possible. I shake my head at him.

'No, it wouldn't, I can look after myself.' I say defensively. Now it's his turn to shake his head and he smiles at me endearingly.

'Ella, don't put yourself at risk by drinking so much. I worry about you and you wouldn't have got him off you,' he says gently.

'I would!' I protest, widening my eyes. He exhales in exasperation and then takes me by surprise by rolling on top of me, pinning me underneath him and pushing his knees between my mine. It's intimate and sexy as hell but unsettling so soon after Saturday and our argument.

'Adam!' I gasp as his weight crushes me and my pulse starts to pound in my ears.

'Mmm?' he answers smiling at me. My insides spasm with desire at the feel of him on top of me and the look on his face but I'm also apprehensive.

'You said…'

'And I'm not.' He finishes my sentence for me, enjoying the way I'm wriggling under him. 'Relax, baby, I'm just proving a point.'

'What?' I gasp, highly conscious of his cock hard under his pants as I squirm. My pulse starts to accelerate as I begin to get concerned.

'Get me off you,' he says to me gently.

'Adam!' I pant in protest. He notices my expression and kisses me affectionately on my forehead, resting his weight on his elbows by my head.

'Don't look so scared, baby, I won't hurt you, you know that, right? But you're worrying me that you're going to get yourself in trouble, so I want to see if you really can look after yourself,' he says. 'So come on, get me off you.'

I push against his chest and wriggle, but I can't budge him. He's not even holding me down or using his strength, he's just lying on me, although it's clear he's enjoying it. I shove him and push my feet against the bed to arch my back but he's just so much heavier than me, it's no contest. When I'm starting to look alarmed, Adam relents, albeit with a satisfied look on his face that he was proven right.

'Push one of your legs down straight against mine,' he says gently. I blink and do as he says. 'Now twist onto your side towards that leg and push my shoulder.' I manage it but it's hard to shift him as he relaxes. I hit him with my hand twice, but it makes no difference at all. Then I shove his shoulder and his body moves off a little and I wiggle back.

'Good, now you can pull your leg free.' He's amused at the efforts I've exerted to do it. I free my leg and he wraps his arm back around me as I lie panting next to him.

'And don't try and hit a guy, baby,' he says gently and I'm absolutely entranced by his voice. 'You'll just hurt your wrists. Use your elbows to hit instead and put your shoulder behind it, right?' His voice is deep and soothing and I nod at him silently, knowing he's trying to help me.

'Better?' he asks softly, stroking my hair and I nod, awed by his confidence. 'Good,' he says and then pulls me into a possessive cuddle that sends my heart into palpitations. 'I worry about you. First you get abducted and then I find you half-naked and drunk in Dan's arms.'

'Fair point,' I mumble.

'I meant it earlier, though, Ella, be careful around Dan, right baby?' I nod quickly, feeling more vulnerable than ever but at the same time safe and protected when I'm with him. There's an inner strength in Adam that pulls me to him, which I can't turn away from.

The room is spinning and I can feel my eyelids getting heavier by the second.

'Do you want to sleep now?' Adam asks, one hand caressing my back.

I nod sleepily at him and he helps me into his en suite and leaves me to use the bathroom. When I'm done, I climb into his bed as he goes to use the bathroom himself.

I'm wearing my underwear and T-shirt still and my bra is digging in so I take my top off and drop it on the floor, my bra quickly following behind. Oh that's so much more comfortable to sleep in I think, turning my back to the bathroom and snuggling into the bed.

When Adam returns to the bedroom, he pauses before getting in the bed beside me. He slips his arm around my shoulders and I snuggle up against his side and rest my cheek on his hard chest. It feels like heaven and I melt against him.

'Ella?' he says quietly.

'Mmm?'

'You've taken your top off,' he states, caressing my fringe off my face again.

'Wasn't comfy!' I mumble groggily. 'You mind?'

He exhales in amusement. 'Of course I don't mind,' he exclaims and pulls me tighter against him. 'It's just you're a little confusing sometimes.'

'Sorry,' I say rubbing my cheek against his chest and I squeeze him. He feels so amazing, his skin warm against mine, I just can't help myself.

'Do you just want me to hold you?' he asks, his voice rougher than previously. I nod sleepily.

'Sleep... well,' I mumble and let my eyes drift closed with the scent of his skin filling my head.

'Not freakin' likely,' he grumbles and rests his face in the hair on top of my head, inhaling deeply.

My head is pounding and I open my eyes, disorientated, my mouth feels like I've been licking carpet. Adam's skin is warm and his light dusting of chest hair is tickling my nose. His arms are wrapped around me as he's propped up against the headboard; he's clearly been watching me sleep while I lay on his chest, his eyes are warm and affectionate and make my tummy flutter excitedly. I'm startled awake by the sudden reality that I've just spent the night with him and I'm nestled up against him wearing only my knickers. Oh holy fuck!

'Good morning, sleepy,' he says smoothly and I blink and sit up flustered, holding the bed sheet modestly against my chest and wincing as my head pounds with the movement. Oh Christ... did we? No, I don't think so.

'How are you feeling, beautiful?' Adam asks, his voice a little rough but deep and sexy. Beautiful? My hair has tumbled all over the place and I must look a mess. My head spins as if on cue.

'I've been better,' I whisper hoarsely, unable to hide my embarrassment this early in the morning. What time is it?

He smiles and runs a hand through my hair, pushing my fringe out of my eyes and my skin tingles where he touches me. 'Yeah, hangovers are a bitch.'

I'm freaked out, what the hell am I doing here? Then memories of Dan's house and Adam's argument with him come back to me. Oh dear God! I remember Adam hit Dan because of me! My pulse pounds in my head and adds painfully to the effects of my hangover.

'Did you sleep ok?' I ask, struggling to think of something to say and feeling desperately awkward. Tickles of sensation ripple over my skin giving me nervous goosebumps. He smiles at me and shakes his head.

'Nah, I stayed awake most of the night to make sure you were ok,' he says frankly. 'You were pretty out of it.' With his hair tousled, I've never seen anyone look sexier in my entire life. But he's hardly slept? Now I feel bad. Again.

'Sorry,' I whisper as my cheeks burn with embarrassment. He chuckles softly.

'Don't be. I can think of worse ways to spend a night.' His eyes are telling me how much he enjoyed it. I clear my throat and look around the room, hugging the sheet against my chest.

'Err, did we…?' I mumble, my voice trailing off.

'Did we what?' He feigns ignorance; he knows what I'm asking. His hand in my hair massages my scalp and I want to lean my head into it but I refrain.

'It's just I'm… not dressed and…' I stutter.

'You're not dressed because you took your own clothes off.' He smiles. I flush as the hazy memory returns and I realise he's right.

'But are you asking if we fucked?' His relaxed attitude is in stark contrast to mine, it's clearly not the first morning *he* has woken up in bed with someone, unlike me. I nod and keep my eyes averted from his. He laughs. 'That would have been wrong on so many levels.' He leans forward and the feel of his warm breath on my skin has my senses on overload. He smells heavenly; I can't think straight.

'Ella, when I take your virginity, trust me, the next morning you won't need to ask me,' he says confidently.

Whoa.

My breath catches and my lungs stop functioning as I'm suddenly light-headed. I clutch the bedsheet to my chest tightly.

'Why, are you hoping that we had?' he asks me, taking hold of my free hand. There's a spark of optimism in his tone. He brushes his lips along my cheek and my skin ignites at his touch. 'Because I've been lying here hard all night and I'm up for it if you are,' he says only half teasing as he rests my hand palm down over his erection, large and stiff under the sheet.

My mouth drops open and my cheeks burn that in my innocence I hadn't noticed. I pull my hand away and he lets me but links his fingers through mine to keep a gentle hold on my hand. His sharp eyes flick over my face telling me he's reconsidering, following my reaction.

'Well how about you finish me off then, if you're not wanting to play yourself?' he suggests.

I'm in deeper than I know how to get myself out of and suddenly overwhelmed by everything. The surprise of waking up with him, knowing I caused a fight between him and Dan, my pounding head after the week I've had. I feel dreadful and it's all too much. I shrink back and shake my head sharply.

'Really?' he asks disbelievingly.

I tug my hand and he lets go so I wriggle back, staring at him. Oh gosh, how do I get myself into these situations?

'You're saying *no*?' he asks, raising his voice very slightly. Oh no, now I'm upsetting him. A rush of anxiety bubbles up within me. I slip hastily off the bed, taking the sheet with me. Adam stays sitting on the bed, his black pants still stretched tight in the front but he's not embarrassed like me, instead he looks stung. I grab my clothes hastily from the floor. He raises his eyebrows at me and his expression says it all. He thinks I'm immature and need to grow up.

'I'm sorry,' I say quickly, before rushing into the bathroom and closing the door.

Oh Christ. What a mess. What the hell am I doing? I drop the sheet and look down at my hands trembling in front of me. My head pounds and I feel a little sick from last night's drinking. I rinse my mouth at the sink and wash my face and then dress. Thankfully Adam has a comb in his bathroom and I manage to pull my hair into order and leave it loose, although it takes me a little while.

When I come out of the bathroom, the bedroom is empty and I leave his folded sheet on the bed before walking shamefully downstairs. I can hear him on the phone in his kitchen and stare up at the ceiling looking for inspiration on how I can explain my behaviour. Adam's voice carries through the open door.

'Yeah, around eleven?... Oh just leave them on my desk. I'll sign them and take them over when I get in, no need for you to go twice because I'm in late...' Oh God! I look at the hall clock and it's ten o'clock on a Friday and I realise I've made him late for work. Fuck! My heart bangs in my chest at my utter disregard for him. I feel like crap.

'Oh damn!' he exclaims. 'Tell her I'm sorry and reschedule for later today at a time that suits her. Do tell her I'm sorry, Sally, won't you? Just explain I had to take care of something important.' My heart drops through the floor with guilt. 'Right, ok, I'll see you in a bit,' he says and hangs up his mobile.

I walk timidly into the kitchen and pause to knock quietly on the door. He's wearing his office clothes, black tailored trousers and a blue short-sleeved shirt I ironed for him earlier in the week, with a silver tie. He's looks fresh and amazing; it puts me to shame and makes me feel out of place. He looks up at me and smiles, but it doesn't quite reach his eyes.

'Hey, baby. Do you want some breakfast?' He nods to some breakfast things he's put out on the table for me.

I stare at him, consumed with my lack of thought for him.

'Sorry,' I mouth at him, the volume in my voice muted.

He nods in acknowledgment.

'Do you want juice? I've left out some Tylenol if you need it,' he says watching me from the other side of the kitchen.

My lip starts to tremble as emotions build up in me again and I bite it between my teeth, taken aback that he's *still* being so nice to me. It dawns on me that regardless of what I heard or think I understood from events on Saturday, that Adam's always being good to me.

'You ok?' he asks and I nod quickly.

'Adam, you're late for work, I better go.' My voice is hoarse. 'I'm sorry again.' Gosh, I feel like I'm always apologising.

'It's ok, work can wait.' He reassures me and I desperately try to calm my emotions, but I'm struggling and I can feel tears starting to well up in my eyes. I'm such a mess. *This* is such a mess. And I've caused it. All of it. I should grow up and explain, but I just want to run.

'No, it's not ok; I'm interfering with your work.' I take a shaky breath and a tear slips down my cheek. 'I'm so sorry, Adam, *again*. I'm going to go.'

He takes a few steps around the table towards me but I step back before he reaches me. There's a moment when we both stand looking at each other and everything stops.

'Ella, don't go yet. I've sure loved having you here, I'm sorry about earlier, I just… shouldn't have assumed!' he says shaking his head as he speaks. 'Stay a while, yeah? Have some breakfast and I'll drive you home.' His eyes are willing me to stay.

I shake my head, grab my bag off the hall floor and turn to leave the house. My head is pounding and I feel on the verge of bursting into tears.

'Will I see you later?' he asks me calmly, following me at a distance to the front door as I walk through it.

'I'm not sure,' I say and walk down the path. Halfway down the drive I turn around, intending to apologise again, but he's already shut the front door.

The tears roll down my cheeks and I start to run home. That's always my answer to everything, run. Run from Tom and his crew when I was younger. Run from talking to Adam and putting things right between us. Run whenever something challenges me, I'm sick of it. Why the fuck can't I just change it?

On Friday afternoon I don't go to work at Adam's house. I try to convince myself it's ok because I quit, but of course I feel guilty. My sisters don't know that version, I just tell them that I've texted Adam to tell him I can't come today as I don't feel well. It's sort of the truth; after all I've got one hell of a hangover.

I think about Adam constantly. As if I haven't got enough to deal with after being abducted only on Saturday, then I have to go and mess things up even more than I had yesterday. I want to call him, but I don't, knowing he's at work and not having a clue what to say. And Dan... what on earth was I thinking?

Around three the house mobile rings and I rush to it thinking it might be Adam but the caller ID says withheld. When I answer, the call is still for me, but it's not the man I'm hoping it is, it's Tom. He's thrilled to talk to me, I can tell by how animated his voice is and it takes me by surprise, we talk for almost an hour and he asks me about everything, from Adam and my job, to the market, my song writing and above all what happened on Saturday. I give him a summary of that, no need for *all* the details! I congratulate him on his promotion and ask about his family and he confirms he's coming to Kansas in a few months and is looking forward to seeing me. By the end of the call I feel like I just spoke more to him in an hour than we did in several weeks before I moved away and he lived around the corner.

Late on Friday evening, just as I'm collapsing on my bed for the night, Sarah decides to start rearranging my stuff in our shared room and plays the 'I'm the big sister card' on me. I'm already short-tempered as I haven't sorted things out with Adam and I tell her she should have asked me first. It results in an argument, so the atmosphere at home isn't great and makes my mood plummet further.

On Saturday morning I'm looking forward to some space away from Sarah at the market, when the supermarket manager calls and re-arranges her shifts so she can join us. In the end it turns out to be a good thing as we make up as we load the van together, but it still grates that once again I'm treated like a child and I have to apologise to her, not the other way around.

By the time we leave the house, I'm on edge again about seeing Adam at the market. And also embarrassed at the possibility of seeing Dan. Did he seriously suggest he could 'pop my cherry'? What the fuck can I possibly say to him?

I spend the short journey silently in the back of the van so I don't take out my irritability on my sisters. When we arrive, Dan is clearly in charge of the groceries team and Adam isn't around. My reaction to that is mixed. Initially I'm relieved, but once that fades, I'm disappointed. I guess it's a feeling I'll have to get used to; he's probably not going to want to see me anymore after the way I keep acting. Why I can't I just talk to him? At one point I catch Dan watching me, he winks and my tummy turns over in response. I give him a half-hearted smile and turn away embarrassed. Christ, my love life is a mess.

During market set up, I relax a little and get chatting to the niece of the coffee stand owner, a friendly girl called Charlie who is the same age as me. We really hit it off and she rather cheers me up. We exchange phone numbers and she invites me to go out with her and some friends and I beam at her; it's about time I started making some girl friends. We are mucking about over whose turn it is to clear a table between our two stalls when I see Adam. My heart lurches and I stare back at him for a moment, surprised to see him. Charlie notices the change in my mood and the reason for it.

'Are you ok, Ella?' she asks, calming her good spirits to match mine.

'Yeah, fine,' I assure her, wiping a table as a distraction. She doesn't buy it. Oh God, what should I say to him? I've acted so appallingly.

'Don't worry about them,' Charlie says lightly, flicking her head in the direction of the grocery stall. 'Just avoid them, we do.'

I look at her. 'What do you mean?'

'Oh, it's common knowledge round here that Adam Brook is a guy you don't mess with,' she replies easily.

'Mess with?' Is this American for sleep with or aggravate I wonder?

'Yeah my friends and I,' she clarifies. 'Our mamas always say to steer clear. Just so we don't get caught up in any trouble, you know?'

I'm not sure I do know. 'Why? Are they trouble makers?'

She laughs at that. 'Well they certainly always seem to be involved in it. Dan Monks is the worst. Let's just say they haven't got the best reputation locally. Too many fights mainly.' She smiles at me, turning away now she's finished clearing the table she was working. It's obvious that what she said isn't anything she shouldn't have.

I watch her walk away and contemplate what she said for a moment. Too many fights? I remember the bruise on Adam's face when I first met him and decide to avoid looking towards that end of the market for the rest of the day while I try and get a grip on my emotions.

At the end of Saturday trading, Adam comes over as we start tidying away.

'Ella, can I speak to you?' he asks. My heart pounds but I walk over to him and stand watching the other traders as they're packing up. 'You didn't come to work yesterday.'

'I wasn't feeling well, did you get my text?' I answer awkwardly.

'Yeah, I got it,' he answers, a little too softly. 'Are you feeling better?'

I nod as I stare at the far wall and control the trembling in my bottom lip by biting it between my teeth. Why does he always have to be so mature about everything? It makes me feel even worse.

'I brought your keys back for you, in case you don't want me to clean for you anymore.' I try to control the overload of emotion in my voice, pulling the keys from the pocket of my blue summer dress. I offer them to him along with his security pass. I keep my eyes concentrated on his shoulder rather than look him in the eyes, my pulse painfully loud in my head.

'*What?*' he exclaims, but still keeping his voice low.

'I thought, maybe...' I stall trying to figure out how to phrase what I want to say. 'That maybe my quitting the other day might actually be a good thing... Give us some space so I don't keep messing you around.' I'm so quiet by the time I finish that I wonder if he can actually hear me. Some space for a while sounds sensible to me. It's my first relationship and I'm just not able to handle the emotional rollercoaster it's turning into.

I glimpse Charlie watching us from a few tables away but consciously don't look at her directly. Adam pushes my outstretched hand away and closes the gap between us, putting a hand on my chin to tilt my face up. His eyes pierce straight through me and my tummy drops through the floor.

'I told you, Ella, you can't quit, so whatever's going on in your beautiful head, you need to get over it or talk to me about it,' he states flatly.

I stare at him blankly. Beautiful head? There's that word again.

He brings his face down slowly and his lips touch mine making me feel giddy. Am I making things worse by not pushing him away? I'm so conscious about making a scene, though, especially with my new friend watching. I lean my head back from Adam subtly and wish I could control my pounding heart rate more.

'Adam?' My voice cracks and I have to swallow. 'Can't we be friends?' A flash of frustration crosses his face.

'I didn't mean to upset you, baby, if I took things too fast, if this is what this is about?' Adam answers. I shake my head, the last thing I want is for him to feel bad; this is my fault, not his.

'No it's not that, I thought we could try it for a while. I just keep messing up.' Oh God, that sounds so lame.

'No, Ella, you and I could never be just *friends*,' Adam retorts, but thankfully keeping his voice low. I suddenly feel like I'm twelve years old. 'I know why you said it but men aren't wired that way. If you're looking for *friends*, you shouldn't have said you'd be my girl and kiss me like you do, then I might have believed you.'

He runs his fingers through my fringe, pushing it slowly out of my eyes so he can see my expression. The contact makes every sense in my body tingle into awareness.

'But you did say that, and you do kiss me like that, so no more talk of *friends*, Ella.' He pauses and drops his hand to catch mine. 'We can talk about anything you want to, just let me in, Ella,' he says so softly and with such a confidence I almost melt. 'You need to tell me why you're running from this, but just so we're clear, you're still with me.'

My heart is pining to throw my arms around him.

My head is telling me there's so much I don't know about him that I should keep my distance. My emotions are so new and raw, but it's getting increasingly harder to keep running away. I almost open up to him right there in the market place and tell him exactly how freaked out I was last week.

Dan decides that exact moment is the perfect time to come and speak to me for the first time all day. His timing couldn't be worse. I'm not sure if he doesn't notice the tension between us and that now is not a good time, or if it's deliberate. Adam's jaw clenches and he diverts his eyes. I tug my hand self-consciously out of Adam's and turn my attention to Dan.

'Can you give us a minute, Dan?' Adam mutters, a clear undercurrent to his tone. Dan ignores him. Oh dear.

'Sarah and Rose are coming to my place later, you wanna come too, sweetheart?' He smiles at me but his eyes are too focused on my answer for it to be a casual invite.

'Err, sorry, Dan, maybe next time?' I answer, failing to sound casual. My skin is still tingling where Adam touched me.

Could this be any more awkward with Dan standing here? Adam then slips his arm around my shoulders and it makes me jump.

Yep. It could be more awkward.

'Sure she'll come,' he answers for me, looking at Dan.

'Adam, I think…' I start to object but the look he gives me cuts me off mid-sentence. His eyes are telling me *please, Ella, we could talk*. It takes all my effort to not throw my arms around him and cry my heart out. I suddenly want to offload, to tell him everything, but I can't. How can I possibly admit that being intimate with him after what happened last week makes me so nervous it's sending my knees to jelly? That I was freaked out that he knew Reece's gang so well too and I don't know what that means? I won't even think about the cryptic phone call afterwards when someone knew I was in the vehicle with him… or the fire… and what the hell is a message from Mexico anyway?

I know he's watching me. Those sharp hazel eyes probably watching the indecision play out on my face, but now isn't the time to talk. I shake my head and shrug out from under his arm, trying to convince myself that it's better to walk away. My subconscious questions my choice of words, as to whether it's 'better' or just 'easier'; *that's it, run away, Ella, that's what you're good at* it snipes at me.

'Excuse me,' I say to Adam and Dan politely, 'I have to help my sisters.' My voice is hoarse and I turn away too briskly. I know I'm being abrupt, but I'm turning into an emotional disaster and I need some time to think. I hear Adam sigh as I walk away but I don't look back.

When our stall is packed up, I wave a cheerful goodbye to Charlie. She smiles back a little hesitantly and then comes to speak to me.

'Listen, Ella, I sure am sorry, I hope you don't think I spoke out of turn before, I had no idea you guys were together,' she starts to explain, clearly talking about Adam.

'It's fine.' I smile. 'We're still going out soon, right?'

'Sure, I'll give you a call.' She looks relieved and then leaves with her aunt.

I make sure Sarah and I go into the bathroom together to freshen up, I don't want to be cornered by Adam again. I tidy up my make-up and brush my hair loose from its ponytail and use some deodorant while I'm waiting for Sarah to have a quick shower. I smooth down my summer dress, it's figure hugging and admittedly a bit on the short side but it keeps me cool in this constant heat.

When we come out of the bathroom we find Rose and Carson waiting, it seems Charlotte and Hannah have taken the children home in the van. I sigh, realising I'm not going home as I hoped.

'Didn't Charlotte wait for me?' I ask Rose.

'Oh, Adam told her that you were coming to Dan's. Sorry, El, we assumed you'd want to come. Charlotte's going to pick us up in the van later while Hannah watches the children.'

I've been ambushed. I look at Carson and raise my eyebrows.

'Adam said so,' he says shrugging. Oh, well if Adam said so! I sling my rucksack onto my back and follow them out of the warehouse, trying not to stomp like a child. We get into a battered old Ford that was once white, Sarah takes the passenger seat and Rose and I get in the back.

It's weird being at Dan's again. I notice the large artificial front lawn, it's the nicest thing about the place, and there's a crowd of around forty people gathered on it and a large barbeque set up on the concrete driveway. I hadn't realised it was such a big event and I'm relieved as I fully intend to blend into a corner and mope. Someone's got a stereo pumping out music, but I've got a headache starting so I direct Rose and Sarah to the furthest point away and we join a group sitting on blankets; it seems to be the area where the few girls that are there (and are under fifty!) seem to be gathered. The four girls we sit near are exceptionally welcoming, if anything they are too friendly for anti-social me, they're all wearing flouncy dresses and look like beauty pageant contestants. I smooth down my hair and wish I'd put on some more of Sarah's make-up earlier, making sure to tuck my work trainers under my skirt as much as possible. I sit further back from the group so I don't have to make chit chat, and start to people watch instead. I don't think I've seen so many middle-aged men wearing cowboy boots in my life!

I inadvertently catch Dan looking in my direction and he smiles and inclines his bottle towards me. Oh no, that's all I need. I sigh with the knowledge of having to have another awkward conversation in the near future.

Appetising smells drift over from the grill, but I'm not hungry. There's a bucket full of ice water the size of a bathtub in the middle of the lawn that each new arrival contributes drinks to and I feel awkward we didn't bring anything.

Adam arrives on foot with Miguel, each of them carrying a large crate of food. He is greeted by almost everyone as he makes his way to a food table to deposit the crates.

Despite trying to blend into the background, I'm conscious of constant glances in my direction. I wonder if people are just curious who we are, but when Dan brings us each a beer, I notice him looking at my legs and realise my dress has risen decidedly too high. I tug it down discreetly and hope that wasn't the cause of so much attention. How embarrassing.

A man with well-groomed brown hair walks over to us, he looks a little out of place in his shirt as the other guys are more casually dressed. A good-looking man wearing cargo trousers follows him, throwing glances at me. I smile politely and take my small notepad and pen out of my bag as a distraction, fully intending to be anti-social.

'Simon!' Rose almost squeals when she sees the guy in the shirt. 'Come and join us. Sarah, Ella, Simon works in Finance with me, he's from Guildford.'

I'm surprised at the warmth in her voice and wonder if they might have a thing starting, but then I notice he's wearing a wedding ring and hope Rose has more sense than that. He's the first English person I've met since I've been here. He sits down as Rose scoots up to make more room and he introduces the guy behind him as his brother Chris who's visiting him. Chris stretches out long legs as he settles next to me.

Uh oh. I'm starting to recognise that look on his face; it's constantly on Adam's. I smile, not knowing what to say as usual and start drawing in my notepad.

'Ella, is it?' he asks me holding out his hand. I nod and put my hand in his, but he surprises me by bringing it to his lips and kissing the back. I raise my eyebrows, embarrassed.

'Pleased to meet you,' he says lowering my hand and I can't work out if he's joking. Who kisses a girl's hand when they're introduced these days?

'Are you visiting for long?' I ask and hastily pull my hand back. I feel like people are watching us, I can certainly feel Dan's eyes boring into the side of my face.

'Only for two weeks, I'm flying home on Monday.' He's got nice eyes and a good figure under his tight dark green T-shirt, but the sparks aren't flying for me.

'Simon moved here six months ago, so I thought I'd come and check it out,' he says, but I'm distracted as a man and a woman come and sit down next to him, he scoots up closer to me to make room. Hmm.

'I'm Shane and this is Mandy. You mind if we join you?' the man asks.

'Sure,' I mumble as they sit on the fake grass opposite and he starts to talk to Rose. His girlfriend smiles at me in a friendly way and then eats her burger, leaving me to talk to Chris.

He's leaning quite close to me; it's disconcerting. What should I say? Think of something Ella! I glance at Sarah hoping she'll rescue me, but she's chatting to Dan and doesn't see me looking at her; Dan, however, is watching me curiously.

'So, have you moved here recently?' Chris asks so I turn back to him. I notice a black snake tattooed up his forearm, it's quite striking.

'Yeah, we're still settling in.' I'm flushing a little from the look he's giving me. I cast a concerned look at Rose, but she just smirks. Christ, if he gets any closer he's going to be in my lap. I shift my bottom back an inch and subtly lean away.

'So what are you writing in your notebook?' Chris tries again. I've been working on some new song lyrics but that's too private to share.

'Just doodling,' I say and bring my legs round to my side. I feel a little like a deer in the headlights and consider getting up on the excuse of going to the drinks bucket, but there's a white man with dreadlocks by it who looks a little off-putting.

'You're living with your sisters, is that right?' Shane asks me, nodding towards Rose and I'm grateful for the interruption. I guess in a small community like this that a family of English girls is bound to make it into conversation.

'And our friend and my niece and nephew,' I mumble for something to say and Chris in particular sits quietly waiting for me to elaborate, but my mind goes blank. I glance at my legs in case my dress is inappropriately adjusted, but thankfully it isn't.

'Ella, you want some food?' Dan calls to me and I see he's getting to his feet with Sarah.

'No thank you.' I pretend to be busy by putting my notepad back in my bag, using it as an excuse of somewhere else to look.

A shadow crosses the sun shining down on us as Chris puts his hand on my thigh and it startles me. I guess he's just trying to get my attention. I blink at him and know I must look a little fazed.

'Are you always this shy?' he asks and I flush and stare at him. Oh fuck, what should I say?

'No!' I answer too quickly and start fidgeting with the clip on my bag.

'It's just I was wondering why the prettiest girl here is hiding in the corner?' he says, caressing my thigh with his fingers. Hmm, so the hand on my leg isn't so innocent after all. I widen my eyes at him and push his hand. Then someone next to us clears his throat. Adam is standing over us holding a Coke and a beer and my heart leaps into my throat.

'Excuse me, you mind getting your hand off my girl?' he says in an everyday tone of voice.

Oh crap.

Chris removes his hand but scowls up at Adam and Mandy freezes mid-bite. Oh God, I seem to be inadvertently causing trouble again and it makes me feel like shit. I knew I shouldn't have come. I didn't want to come.

Shane and Mandy seem to magically rise to their feet and find somewhere else to be; when I glance at Adam, his expression tells me why. He's not pleased.

There's a bit of a pause and Adam sits down leisurely opposite in the space they vacated and passes me the Coke, stretching out his legs. He looks directly at Chris who is glaring at him.

'You need something, pal?' Adam asks him, unblinking.

'No.' Chris continues to stare. I focus my attention on the bottle in my hand, my heart hammering in my chest now. Rose coughs and Simon saves what could otherwise be an awkward scene.

'Rose, let's go and say hello to Janet, shall we?' He pulls Rose to her feet as he stands up. She looks briefly at me as Simon taps Chris on the shoulder.

'Come on, Chris, that's my boss, move,' Simon mutters, so Chris stands up reluctantly.

'I'll see you in a bit, Ella.' Chris goads, but thankfully Adam doesn't take the bait, and they walk away. It leaves just Adam and me with the inevitable awkward silence. My tummy plummets and then rebounds back into place. I look at the trees lining the street, trying to appear relaxed.

'So you came then,' he says leaning on one arm. His eyes are appraising me in a way that makes me feel almost naked. Like most of the men, he's wearing a sleeveless black top, which shows off his physique, combat trousers, which hang off his hips, and heavy boots; it's a masculine and sexy look and I try not to stare at him.

'Yeah, *someone* told Carson I had to come,' I mumble.

'I see you made a new friend.' I know he's annoyed by his tone. My pulse starts racing, I hate arguing.

'Not really, he just came over because his brother did,' I answer quietly.

'I'm sure.' Adam answers dryly; his tone implies I'm naïve and it annoys me.

'You can be as sure as you like. He did.' I snap back.

There's a pause and I catch the glance of the guy with dreadlocks again, he's leering at me so I look away, unsettled.

Adam might as well be the only person here, every nerve ending in my body is tuned into what he says or how he moves. It's overload to be frank, I feel like I can barely breathe.

'So are you coming back to work on Monday?' Adam asks. I look at him uncertainly, but let's face it I do need my job.

'Yes, if I still have a job?' I hedge, glancing around. I want to wrap my arms around him, just be with him and not talk about the disaster of this week, but on the other hand, he's still too much for me to handle. He sighs.

'Yes, Ella, you do, but on the condition you start talking to me and stop running away, you're not a kid anymore.' He might as well add *but you're acting like one*.

It touches a sore spot inside me, because I know he's right. I want to be more independent and treated like an adult, well I guess now is the time to try it, or I'm going to risk losing him. I know I've been avoiding him all week, but it's just because Saturday scared me and there's so much about him I still don't know, but he did ask me to trust him.

'Ok,' I agree.

'Why did you agree to go on a date with Dan?' he asks, taking me completely by surprise. I'm so stunned I don't answer. 'He's been telling me that he's taking you to watch a band.' Adam informs me. 'Are you going to tell me it's not true?'

His words are like a knife to my chest as I register he's hurt. I take a gulp of air and shake my head.

'It wasn't like that. I didn't think he meant just the two of us. I assumed a group would be going so I said maybe.' Adam is not looking at me so I put my hand over his, but he pulls his hand away and stands up.

Ouch.

'Just so we're clear, we are still together, so I expect you to act like it.' He walks off to join a group of men by the barbeque and it sends a chill like ice water through my veins.

I sit on my own for a moment. I feel like I'm losing Adam and the realisation hits me like a hammer in the forehead that I don't want to. I keep pushing him away and now he's starting to do the same. I guess I either need to put my concerns about what happened on Saturday behind me, or build up the courage to ask him about it but risk not liking the answer.

Decision made. Flipping finally! He'll explain if and when he wants to or maybe one day I'll ask him, but at the moment I'm going to trust him like he asked me to. I don't want to lose him.

Sarah and Dan join me, some time passes and I don't get any more visitors. When the light is beginning to fade and the music is turned up, the older people start to drift home in waves of cheerful goodbyes and so the number of women drops substantially. I stand with my sisters, although I don't contribute much to their conversation. I'm wondering how I'm going to make things right with Adam before I leave. I glance at my watch; Charlotte will pick us up in an hour.

I need some headspace away from the stereo, so I tell Sarah I'm going to get a soft drink; some guy she's talking to tells me that Dan's got Cokes in a pantry off the kitchen. When I find it, I push the door open and switch the light on. It's in effect a large cupboard. I've just taken out a multipack of Cokes when the door clicks shut behind me. I hadn't seen anyone in this part of the house and my heart sinks when I turn and see the man with the dreadlocks. He's tall and wearing a vest which exposes sinewy arms and he stinks of something like herbal tea mixed with cigarettes. A little alarm in my mind wonders why he shut the door. He flicks his eyes over my chest in a way that makes me feel uncomfortable, so I abandon the drinks on the counter and move aside to let him pass. Instead he slams me hard against a cupboard, smashing my hip into the worktop and so I cry out.

Fuck fuck fuck!

Adrenaline pounds through me and I shove him hard in the chest with both arms but he doesn't budge, instead he laughs.

'Aww, shug, you wanna play rough?' he says, amused, and tries to grab my wrists, but only succeeds in getting hold of one, so I slap him hard around the face, it makes my palm sting.

'Get off of me!' I growl. I remember Adam telling me to hit with my elbow and I manage to land it right on his cheekbone, satisfyingly it makes his head jerk to the side. Before I can land another blow, though, he forces both my arms behind my back and clamps my wrists tightly in one hand. It's all happened in a matter of seconds and suddenly his tongue is in my mouth and his other hand up my dress. My blood is pumping so hard I can barely think. Repulsion rips through me and I scream, but his mouth muffles it and tears explode down my cheeks as his fingers start exploring.

'Don't be like that, shug,' he breathes against my mouth, he tastes of whiskey and the cigarette smoke on his breath makes me feel sick. I try to kick him but he's literally pinned me against the cupboard. I propel my body forward attempting to unbalance him or at least dislodge his hand which is trying to get inside my underwear, but he barely moves, instead he moves his hand to his jeans to starts pulling the buttons open and I know I'm in trouble.

There's a substantial bang as the main door slams open and rebounds off the wall. The man looks up sharply and I seize the chance to scream as his mouth leaves mine. My lips throb from where his mouth was pressed so hard against mine and I can taste the metallic tang of blood.

'*Get your fucking… hands off me!*' I roar.

'Leave her be, Carl,' a voice demands from the doorway and I hope to see Adam, but it's Dan who's standing there. All I care about right now, though, is that the man still has his hand between my legs. Tears stream down my face and I head butt him, but he's taller than me so I only make contact with his shoulder and a pain shoots through my forehead. A loud cry escapes me.

'You going to make me, Monks?' The guy jeers at him. 'No? Then go jerk off someplace else.'

Carl moves his fingers lower and I try to sink to the ground, but he holds me still. Then Dan wrenches him off me and hurls him against the wall. In the absence of him pinning me, I land on my knees with a smack. Carl goes to right himself but Dan lands a punch in his face; he puts his whole shoulder into the blow and then follows through with another from his other fist. Carl goes sprawling on the floor in front of me and I stifle a scream as I jerk myself back from him.

Carl staggers to his feet with blood oozing out of his nose. He goes to throw a punch, but Dan knees him in the stomach first and then the men are grappling each other, slamming from one cupboard to another. I shuffle back into the corner, bring my knees up defensively in fear of them landing on me, then Adam appears in the doorway and wedges himself between them with his elbows raised.

'What the fuck's going on?' he growls and then spots me on the floor, crying. He swings on Dan angrily for an explanation.

'Carl was about to get *your girl* banged up,' Dan rasps as Adam's elbow is against his throat. Carl is shoving backward towards the doorway. Banged up? Does that mean pregnant? A shiver of fear runs through me.

'That true?' Adam asks me.

'Dan pulled him off... me,' I answer, my voice breaking just as Carl lunges through the door out of Adam's grip.

'Watch her,' Adam orders Dan and then sprints out after Carl.

Dan flops back against the cupboard and I collapse forward onto my hands, both of us gasping for breath. I adjust my underwear under my skirt immediately, not caring a damn that Dan is watching and then kneel to wrap my arms around myself to try and control their trembling. I start taking deeper breaths as my head pounds. Why does this keep happening to me? Somewhere inside me anger simmers hot and wild. What the fuck did I do to deserve this?

Dan crouches on the floor around a foot away from me and hovers uncertainly for a moment before he puts his arm around my shoulder.

'Hey, it's ok, Ella, he's gone,' he says, squeezing me gently. 'You'll be ok now.' I look up at him and blink away some tears. His eyes are concerned. I nod to acknowledge what he said, but my sobs tell him I'm far from ok right now.

'Aww Lord, he's cut your lip,' Dan says, tenderly wiping his thumb along my lower lip and time seems to stop for a moment as our eyes stay locked on each other. I'm unsure what to do next, but his expression tells me he's got something he wants to get off his chest.

'Listen, Ella, I just wanna say, about, y'know, how I've been around you at the market and at my place the other night. I figure I owe you an apology.'

I blink at him, momentarily silenced. That's not what I was expecting.

'Don't worry about it, I think you just made up for it,' I reply with a weak smile, probably failing in my attempt to lighten the mood. 'Thank you, for stepping in, I mean.'

Dan nods at me like it was nothing. 'Anytime,' he says sincerely.

'Ella?' Adam calls from nearby in the hallway and Dan drops his arm and clears his throat awkwardly. He stands up and takes a step back and I wonder if something has been said between them, I'm guessing so judging from Dan's reaction.

Dan crosses his arms and leans against the wall facing me. I push myself to my feet with shaking hands and Adam comes into the pantry and puts his arm around me protectively. It's not lost on me that Dan immediately averts his gaze from us.

'Are you ok?' Adam asks me, concerned, his breathing is erratic like he's been running hard.

'I'm fine,' I croak, seeing underneath his calm exterior that he's angry. Is he angry with me? Is he angry with Carl? Or with Dan again? I just don't know.

'Did you catch him?' Dan asks Adam.

'No, Miguel rang me, though, he caught him getting in his car, he's taking him to my place. I want a word.' His tone tells me it's more than just a word he wants.

Dan looks towards the open doorway before speaking.

'Did anyone out front notice what's happened? You want me to go tell her sisters or something?' His question is directed at Adam, not me. He's already turning towards the doorway to leave.

'No, the music's too darn loud, but don't do that, I'm guessing Ella could do without their fussing right about now,' Adam says as astute as always.

Dan glances at me again and then leaves without a word, which strikes me as odd and it's suddenly clear, Adam is calling the shots and Dan has been overstepping the mark. Once we're alone, Adam looks at me.

'Did he hurt you, Ella?' he asks, his eyes focusing on my lip as he tightens his arms around me. Tears brim in my eyes again, it seems Adam is like fuel on a fire when it comes to igniting my emotions.

'Only my hip, but he… tried to… touch me…,' I gasp in another breath, wringing my hands in front of me in an effort to get my words out but I can't, so end up looking away from him. Outside I may be blubbering, but on the inside I'm becoming increasingly angry. How dare he try to do that to me!

'Come on, let's go somewhere more private so we can talk,' Adam says softly, taking my hand. I'm upset and the last place I want to go is back to the party, so I follow him when he picks up a blanket slung over a chair in the kitchen and leads me into the rear garden. I register the lawn is artificial here also as it crunches under my trainers. My hand is shaking in Adam's so he runs his thumb over the back. Repulsive memories of Carl's hands on me flood my mind.

The light from the kitchen windows doesn't reach the end of the garden where Adam spreads the blanket out on the ground and sits down, giving my hand a gentle pull so I join him. I'm numb from shock.

'You ok?' He moves close to sit beside me and puts his arm around my waist. 'You're trembling.'

My mind is blank, but at least I've stopped crying. I don't really have an answer for Adam.

Am I ok?

On the surface I'm shaken, but inside I know I'm going to be fine. What I am is rapidly becoming furious at the injustice of this. A strength of will is building momentum inside me like an avalanche.

'What did he do?' Adam asks me softly.

I'm about to shake my head and say I don't want to talk about it, but screw that. I haven't done anything wrong and I'm not hiding anymore.

'He touched me... started taking off his trousers,' I mutter, deeply disturbed at what could have happened.

Adam's breathing turns deeper but he doesn't speak, just squeezes my waist reassuringly; we sit together quietly for a minute and I rest my cheek on his shoulder. God it feels good to be held by him. My head is thumping, my lip hurts and my knees are sore where I fell. After a while he leans down to kiss me on the mouth tenderly, but I pull back.

'Adam,' I say, my voice cracking a bit. 'Don't.'

'Don't *what*? I can't even *kiss* you now?' he asks, his voice raising a little. I want to say it's just that my lip is sore, but instead I blurt out the first thing that comes into my head.

'Everything's just such a mess,' I exclaim shakily. I rub my hand over my forehead. There's a strained silence as we sit together, the electricity almost audible as it crackles between us. Just being this close to him dazzles my senses. It's some time when Adam is the one to break the silence, keeping eye contact with me when he speaks.

'Ella, you want to know what I think?' He doesn't wait for me to reply. 'I think you're a walking magnet for trouble. Everywhere you go someone seems to be trying to get in your panties.' My immediate reaction is to start getting to my feet, but Adam holds onto my forearm. 'You just can't look after yourself.' He sounds exasperated. It's like he's reading my mind.

'Yes I can.' I mutter determinedly. I'm damn well going to start doing exactly that. That anger inside me is fierce. Ferocious. 'I even hit him with my elbow, like you told me!' I add indignantly and not without a sense of pride that I stood up for myself for the first time. Ever.

'No, you can't, Ella! Reece abducted you and I had to get you out of his fucking whore house. Dan had you stripped to your panties and now Carl. So how many assaults is that this week anyway? You're just not streetwise enough for this area.' His tone is frustrated. 'Christ woman. Can't you see I'm worried about you?'

That's it. Memories of being bullied surface from my childhood and something inside me snaps. It's not the area, it's me. It doesn't matter where I am; I seem to be a target. I can't keep blaming circumstance and bad luck, the spark inside turns into a roaring inferno. It's time I took control of my life and stopped running when it gets tough. Just now I started to stand up for myself. It's time I started to fight for what I want.

To fight my insecurities, including in my relationship with Adam.

And it's way overdue that I've finally started to fight for me.

I'm about to speak but he takes his hand off my forearm and puts a finger over my lips.

'No you don't. Just listen,' he says, and his voice turns much softer at his next words. 'I can't look out for you if you don't let me inside your walls.' He makes my pulse race, being this close and smelling like pine leaves after it's rained, musky but fresh like woodland.

'I know Saturday upset you, baby, but I can't be close to you and help you if you keep pushing me away.' His voice is so deep and confident, like everything about him it's incredibly appealing.

'I don't want to push you away,' I mumble through his finger on my lips, my eyes locking on his. He moves his hand.

'Say that again?' he whispers, leaning closer so his nose is almost touching mine.

'I don't want to push you away, Adam. Saturday scared the crap out of me; I needed a few days, that's all. And I'm wary of us, what we might be together, everything's so unknown to me, but I'm done running, Adam. I don't want to lose you,' I whisper. In the last half an hour it's like frightened Ella has disappeared and a stronger more determined girl has emerged. Adam takes that in for a second.

'How do you feel about Saturday now?' he asks me softly. I look back at him; his eyes turn my insides to jelly.

'I've still got questions, but you asked me to trust you and I do, so I guess you'll open up to me when you want to.' Oh my God, what a relief it is to make a decision.

'Finally. Some insight into how you're feeling.' He smiles. His change of mood takes me off guard. 'Why are you scared of us?'

My breathing falters and I swallow. 'It's a big step for me,' I whisper.

He moves his hand into my hair and presses his forehead against mine. 'Aww Lord, Ella, why didn't you just say so? I'd take care of you, baby, I wouldn't hurt you,' he says.

'I know,' I whisper and I mean it. I trust him.

'Kiss me,' he murmurs against my mouth, skimming his lips over mine. It feels sensational. His breath smells slightly of beer but it's not off-putting, it's masculine and attractive. I throw my arms around his neck and clamp my mouth to his and kiss him with a passion like never before. Sore lip be damned! He groans in surprise and holds my head as his tongue sweeps inside my mouth, devouring me.

'I've missed you,' he murmurs against my mouth.

'I've missed you too,' I reply, kissing him again. It's some time before we finally pull apart. There's an urgency building between us that I can't ignore anymore. The need to connect with him on a deeper level.

'You know I want you, Ella, I've wanted you since I first saw you, but do you want me?' It's a similar thing as he said before, asking me if I want him. I'm out of my depth, but I push it aside. It's time to take control of my life and, for whatever reason, Adam needs me to tell him.

'Yes, I want you,' I whisper.

He sighs and rests his forehead against mine again. 'That's all I needed to hear, baby. I can wait until you're ready, I just needed to know.'

He wants to wait? I take a deep breath for courage.

'What if I'm ready now?' I ask, trying to hide the tremor in my voice. He looks at me sharply and shakes his head.

'Ella, now isn't the time, you're upset,' he says and my heart melts that he's trying to put me first, like he always does, I realise.

'I'm fine, Adam, yes I'm shaken up, but inside I know I'm fine.' I take another breath. 'And I know how I feel about you. I don't want to push you away anymore.'

'Are you saying you want to come back to mine tonight?' His eyes are hopeful, but his tone dubious.

Oh Christ, decision time.

'Yes,' I answer. My heart is fluttering faster than ever and my nerves are on fire, but I know what I want and it's time to stop running.

Adam pulls me against him, pressing me possessively against his chest, nuzzling his lips along my jaw and down my neck. I pull my head back giving him more access before I even think about it.

'Just so we're clear,' he murmurs, 'because I sure don't want any misunderstandings.' His breathing shallows as his hand slides to my chest and my nipple hardens. 'I'm thinking that I'm going to take you to bed, Ella.' He's so self-assured, he takes my breath away. 'Does that match you're understanding of what you're saying, baby?' he mumbles, pinching my nipple lightly through my clothes and shifting me closer against him. I gasp at the sensations that rush through me. He's so strong and indomitable; it's so appealing.

'Yes.' I know what I want. I want him.

He smiles at me and it's so sexy a fireball ignites low in my belly. He presses his lips to mine and starts kissing me like the world's about to end. Tingles rush up my back and I'm light-headed as he coaxes my tongue to respond.

'Awesome,' he murmurs when he finally breaks away, his eyes glinting in satisfaction and a smile tugging at the corner of his mouth. I feel like a rabbit in the headlights and I stare back at him breathing hard. He gets quickly to his feet and holds out a hand to pull me up, and I put my hand in his.

Chapter Seven

Adam takes my hand and strides down Dan's back garden towing me behind him. We pass briskly through the house and I see Charlotte pulling up at the kerb in the van while Adam collects my bag. I go and tell her that I'm staying overnight with Adam and she's surprised but says it's my decision. Wow, that's new! Perhaps there's something to my tone of voice? When I turn around, I see Adam waiting and he holds out his hand to me.

I clasp his fingers in mine, my heart beating erratically, and I can't seem to look him in the eye. I might be finally realising what I want and who I want to be, but I'm also nervous as hell. He squeezes my hand and we start walking the short distance to his place.

Just as I'm leaving I catch Rose watching us and she glances away a little too quickly when she sees me notice.

'You're very quiet,' Adam comments after we've been walking for a few minutes.

I nod, he's right; words are quite beyond me. He soothes his thumb over the back of my hand. 'You still scared?' he asks, looking sideways to study my face. What's the point in lying? He'll see right through me like he always does anyway.

I nod and concentrate on walking on legs which have turned to jelly.

'I'll take good care of you,' he says softly. Oh God, I feel like I can barely breathe.

'I know you will,' I answer, barely audible.

We walk the remaining distance in silence and when we round the trees into his driveway, there's a truck, a jeep and a motorbike parked there. I hesitate and try to pull my hand out of Adam's, making him pause.

My heart is suddenly in my throat as I remember that Carl is here. Realisation dawns on me that I've got to go into a house where the man is who just assaulted me. I look at Adam, finally meeting his eyes for the first time since we left Dan's.

'You go in, I'd rather wait here,' I say. Adam tightens his hold on my hand.

'There's nothing to worry about, Ella,' he says firmly to reassure me. 'Do you not want to see Carl?' He's flicking his eyes over my face and correctly reading my expression. I shake my head at him.

'You're with me, aren't you?' he asks, closing the gap between us. 'Then don't worry, right? I'll look out for you,' he says kissing me on the forehead and then leading me up the driveway. As I follow him that fire inside me burns brighter. It's natural to be wary and I love it that Adam's protective of me, but I no longer need someone else to feel safe. I can damn well look after myself from now on… if I need to.

When I enter the house, I hear Miguel's distinctive accent and several other deep voices in the kitchen. I don't want to go in there, it's not cowardly, just sensible, so I pull my hand out of Adam's and shake my head firmly before slipping into the adjacent TV room and closing the door before he can say anything. My hands are shaking I'm so nervous, but I'm also sick to death of running and others looking after me because I can't myself.

Thankfully the light is already on and I see Chase is in the room, sitting up and wagging his tail to see me. He's such a welcome sight! I back away from the door and sit down next to the dog, my ears straining to hear what's going on. As always, with his home cinema and plush new sofas, Adam's house makes me feel like I've stepped into a reality which is so different from mine I can't possibly relax.

I scan the room for something I could pick up as a weapon if Carl came in, but there's nothing.

Deep voices boom through the wall and there's a loud expletive followed by a tremendous bang, which makes me jump. It sounds like someone fell through some furniture. Fuck! I screw my eyes shut and hug Chase, not ashamed to admit that I'm frightened. I wonder fleetingly if I should try and sneak out of the front door, but decide against it.

The shouting continues for a short while. It sounds like there's more men next door than I first thought. Sometime later, it seems apparent that people are leaving and doors are closing. I can hear engines start as they pull away from the front of the house.

The door opens. I'm apprehensive of who's coming in so I hug Chase tighter and it stops him from bounding to his feet to greet his owner. Adam leans on the door frame and folds his arms, unintentionally enhancing the curve of his biceps.

'You can stop hiding now,' he says meeting my eyes and watching me as I cuddle his Saint Bernard. Adam has a small cut over one eyebrow but otherwise his face is unscathed. 'Carl's about to leave, I've asked him to apologise to you, do you want to see him?'

I feel immediately vulnerable and I hate it. I hate that that creep has made me feel this way. Adam sees me hesitate.

'If you don't want to see him, that's fine, baby, no pressure.'

'No, I do,' I answer, rising to my feet and walking out of the door before I change my mind. I have to say, though, I'm glad I've got Adam and a huge dog behind me.

When I enter the kitchen, Carson and Miguel are standing with their arms folded on either side of Carl who's slumped in a kitchen chair and it gives me no pleasure to see he's a bloody mess, literally. He's holding a towel to his nose which is streaming blood and one of his eyes is so swollen it's half closed. I glance at Adam in shock and he shrugs.

'Dan did most of that,' he says, correctly reading my expression, but I do see now his knuckles are reddened. 'Carl, you got something to say to Ella?' Adam says in a tone which says *don't fuck around*.

Carl looks right at me and says, 'I'm sorry, Ella.'

I don't know if he means it and I don't care. He's only saying it because a group of men have beaten him into it. I hold his eyes and don't back down, a steely voice inside me tells me I can do this, that I need to do this. For me. I'm no longer that scared school girl who runs away from bullies.

I walk over, casually pull out the kitchen chair next to him and sit down, ignoring the adrenaline pumping through me. I rest my elbows on my knees and lean forward, my face just inches from his and I can smell the herbs on him again, he reeks of it. What *is* that anyway? To my amazement, he actually pulls his head back a little.

'Do you think I give a shit if you're sorry or not?' I demand, my voice quiet but cold as ice. He blinks at me and doesn't reply, but I can tell he wasn't expecting this. 'You may be bigger than me, but you're weak. You'll never be stronger than I am. You need to dominate others who are smaller than you to make yourself feel better, because you know you don't measure up, but you don't scare me. I pity you. You're pathetic.'

Then I lower my voice so only he can hear me. 'And if you ever lay a hand on me again, I'll claw your fucking eyes out.' He blinks at me but I can tell he knows I mean it. I do.

I lean back, my skin crawling that I was so close to him and then I stand, carefully tucking the chair under the table.

'Tomorrow you'll receive a visit from the police. I hope it was worth it.' I say blandly and turn to leave the room. I'm so desperate to get away from him that my hands are trembling, so I clench my fists and hope no one notices.

'Ella. The man said he's sorry,' one of the men in the room says, clearly about to try and talk me out of that.

I look at him with fire raging inside me. I don't know his name, but no one gets to tell me how to live my life. Not anymore.

'That's not your decision.' I cut him dead. I don't wait for anyone else to say anything, but walk past them all out of the kitchen, giving Adam a light squeeze on the shoulder as I pass. I head straight upstairs, Chase following behind me and I go to the landing window. I feel immensely proud of myself, but my hands are still shaking with adrenaline. It's a few minutes later when they leave and I'm watching them when Adam comes up and finds me. He doesn't say anything straight away, just slips his arms around me from behind and cuddles me. I take a shaky breath and put my hands over his around my waist.

'I'm proud of you,' he says resting his chin on my head as we watch the vehicles pull away, 'that couldn't have been easy.'

'Thanks, it wasn't.' I murmur, but God, it felt good. Liberating.

'Are you alright?'

'Yeah, I am.' I'm surprised at myself because I really do think I am. I'd go as far as to say I'm almost feeling good. He presses a kiss into the top of my hair.

'Do you want to talk?'

'Nope,' I answer brightly. He tightens his arms and stands holding me for some time, neither of us speak.

'Listen, Ella, if you're upset and have changed your mind, about tonight, it's really ok.' His voice is gentle and I know he means it. I swallow and try to relax my shoulders.

'Thank you, but I haven't changed my mind,' I say turning to put my arms around his neck. My heart rate soars and plummets and soars again.

He looks me in the eyes, I think checking to see if I mean it, and then smiles and closes his mouth over mine. I press myself against him and kiss him back. I love the way he's holding me, like he's never going to let go. Then he pulls back, takes my hands in his and walks me the few paces to his bedroom. My pulse explodes with anticipation and I know he can see I'm nervous, but he doesn't comment on it. His hands engulf mine and they are strong and warm, but I see that his knuckles are slightly swollen.

'Are you ok?' I ask him, gesturing to his hands and he gives me a half-smile in reply.

'Yeah, baby, it's nothing,' he says closing the bedroom door.

Without speaking he immediately kicks his boots off and then his socks and T-shirt follow as he throws them on a nearby chair. His chest is so perfectly sculpted, with a light dusting of hair over the tattoo of the lady's hand on his chest. I wonder again what DM stands for and why he's got it tattooed on him.

I can't control my eyes enough to stop drinking in the sight of him as he stands in front of me. The tattoos on his neck and biceps are eye catching, like tribal patterns, and I want to run my hands over them and feel his skin but instead I hastily drag my eyes away, self-conscious because he's watching me.

'I'm going to freshen up,' he says nodding towards the adjoining bathroom while watching me. I nod and focus my gaze on looking around his bedroom. Anywhere but his eyes! He walks leisurely into his bathroom, leaving the door open, and runs the tap, rinsing his hands and splashing his face. I catch a glimpse of my face in a mirror on his wall, my sore lip actually looks ok and I smooth my hair down quickly, ignoring the flushed look to my cheeks. While he finishes in the bathroom, I stand fidgeting with the pocket of my dress and study the white window blinds like they are fascinating. I wish I could calm down.

'You want to take some clothes off?' he says when he comes out of the bathroom, but his eyes are soft and playful. Electricity sparks between us, with his hair slightly damp it looks darker, matching his hazel eyes. He's so tall and broad shouldered with a strong neck, tight chiselled stomach muscles… I almost drool.

I sit on the bed and take my trainers off, deliberately letting my fringe hang over my face while I try to gain some composure. He empties his pockets onto the chest of drawers and pulls his belt free from the loops before facing me. Every nerve in my body is standing on end. Is this is really happening? I can't quite get my head around it.

He kneels on the floor and pushes my knees apart to get closer. His expression makes my tummy turn over with butterflies. He angles his head so his lips meet mine and his tongue pushes into my mouth as he embraces me. I raise my arms around his neck, his skin is so smooth; he feels amazing. He pulls me against his hard chest, his mouth demanding more and I kiss him back.

'So,' he murmurs when he pulls his lips away, 'you've finally stopped fighting this, huh?' His free hand starts undoing the buttons on the front of my summer dress. I nod, distracted as the slight scent of his sweat mixes with his aftershave and leaves me light-headed, it's just so *him*, I can't help but breathe in deeper. With my dress fully unbuttoned now, his hands slip behind me and deftly unclip my bra and he pushes the straps down along with my dress. I try to act like he hasn't stripped me down to just my knickers and wrap an arm modestly across my chest, knowing that my pink cheeks are betraying me. He chuckles deeply and it's so attractive I almost melt.

'I guess it's that time when I need to you to tell me yes,' he says, casually, nuzzling his way along my collarbone and then confidently pulling my arm away from where I'm covering myself. He links his fingers through mine and holds my hand gently. 'I think we'll be great together,' he whispers.

My skin feels like it's on fire where his lips touch it and my nipples harden like bullets as his mouth works slowly down my chest. I don't answer; I'm having trouble focusing as he flicks his tongue against my nipple, making me gasp.

'I know you're shy, baby, but I need to hear a yes,' he murmurs, oozing confidence. He starts sucking and spasms of desire course through me, and when his hand cups my other breast I arch my back, pushing myself against him.

'Yes,' I utter breathlessly. He kneels back to look me in the eye, I want to cover my chest again but he tightens his hold on my hand on the bed beside us. My heart flutters uncontrollably at the burning intensity in his eyes, it's a little unnerving to see exactly how turned on he is, knowing I'm about to let him closer to me than anyone else. What if he loses control and hurts me? My thoughts set my nerves on edge but at the same time molten fire sears between my legs. I trust him I remind myself, I wouldn't be here with him if I didn't.

'You want to take the lead from here?' He teases me after a moment, his eyes glinting in amusement, he knows the answer already; it's obvious I'm nervous.

I roll my eyes as I smack him lightly on the shoulder and shake my head. It makes him laugh and he tilts my chin to look me in the eye again, smiling wickedly.

'I thought not.' He grins as he runs his hands up the outsides of my thighs and hooks his fingers into my knickers on my hips. He doesn't pull them down, but I know he might at any time and my pulse accelerates. I focus on his impressive stomach muscles and try to breathe normally.

'Don't be nervous, Ella, it's only me, right?' He reassures me and brings his lips up close to my ear. 'Everyone has a first time once, baby,' he murmurs. 'Mine was in a car park when I was fifteen.'

Oh dear God. I swallow. Now is not the moment for me to be reminded how much older and more experienced he is if his aim is for me to relax. He ducks his head so he can see under my fringe hanging like a curtain to shade my eyes and he smiles warmly at me. It coaxes me into a shy smile back and his face lights up at my response.

'That's better, beautiful, your eyes are so pretty when you smile.' He's not giving me fake flattery; he's genuine. His words make me blush but I don't look away and he gives my knickers a light tug to ease them under my bottom until they stop halfway down my thighs as he's kneeling between my legs. It's so damn sexy; I try not to stare at him quite so awestruck. He strokes my hair back from my face and tucks it behind my ear.

'You need to relax, baby, or I'll bruise you,' he says gently. I gulp and nod, keeping my eyes glued to his as my breathing shallows. As his eyes wander down to my chest I notice that his own breathing is far from controlled, I've been so caught up with how I'm feeling, I hadn't noticed.

He undoes his trousers, leisurely pushing them down along with his underwear. I don't glance down, though, for fear of blushing profusely and embarrassing myself. He leans in closer to me and skims his lips across mine, his beard brushing softly against my skin. My mouth opens a little and my breathing quickens.

'I told you I'd take care of you, you trust me, right?'

'Yes.' I breathe immediately. I do trust him.

'Then relax, it hurts a bit the first time but I'll be gentle with you, we'll do this together,' he whispers against my mouth and I almost convulse on the bed. His breath is sweet and warm and he dazzles me. A large part of my brain is wondering if this gorgeous man is really here, with *me*.

He slips his hand down between my legs and I gasp sharply as pleasure shoots through me as his fingers start to explore. He groans loudly when he feels how slick I am, I'm already burning for him to touch me. When his eyes lock with mine, they are smouldering and he pushes his middle finger inside me. I shudder against his hand, I'm on fire inside and I move my knees a little wider as he strokes me. He keeps eye contact with me and it makes it so much more intense. He leans forward and I pant against his lips. I just can't control my breathing and my back arches forward as my hips move against him with a will of their own. His eyes are telling me how turned on he is as he watches and I gaze back at him feeling utterly under his control.

I moan on a wave of pleasure as his palm glides excitingly over me. My legs shake and open further, and my knickers dig into my thighs. He pushes a second finger inside me and I gasp. I've no idea what expression is on my face, but it makes him pause to look at me.

'Will you touch me?' he says huskily, his eyes are filled with lust. I look back at him dazed, with his fingers inside me I'm having trouble thinking straight. 'Please, Ella, you're driving me crazy,' he pants.

I run my hand down over his flat stomach and notice as I do the slightly raised skin of an old scar. Then my hand moves lower and I clasp my fingers around him, surprised at how thick and hard he feels under such smooth skin. He's much bigger than I'd imagined. I don't know what he likes, though. Oh God, I'm going to have to ask him. I sit up so my face is against his neck and he can't see the flush in my cheeks.

'Adam?' I whisper uncertainly. 'Show me?'

I feel him swallow as he registers what I said and he immediately pushes his tongue hard into my mouth, demanding and primal in his need to connect. He pulls his fingers out of me, wraps his hand firmly around mine and starts moving it up and down his erection. His breathing changes and he groans but doesn't stop kissing me.

I do as he shows me, but I'm struggling to match the passion in his kiss and I break my mouth away to rest my forehead against his shoulder.

'Like this?' I whisper, embarrassed, moving my hand and squeezing.

'Not so hard, I don't want to come,' he answers huskily and wraps an arm around me while burying his face in my hair. He leans against me as pleasure rushes through him and it boosts my confidence to know how much I affect him.

After a while he climbs onto the bed and pulls me to lie next to him, pushing my already discarded clothes to the floor. My hand continues in the rhythm he showed me, and he pulls my knickers the rest of the way down more urgently, his eyes are locked on mine. We look at each other for a moment and the feeling is intense, to see the need in him and knowing I want to satisfy it. He trails his hand over my hip and then I sigh with pleasure as his fingers slip deep inside me again. Tingles ripple from my head to my toes and my thighs tense as I crave more.

'Do you like that?' he murmurs huskily, watching me wriggle against him. I moan, throwing my head back as new intense sensations consume me. 'That's your G-spot, baby,' he murmurs, moving his finger slower but firmer and concentrating on that spot. The excitement inside me builds and my hips grind against him faster, becoming lost in sensation. My body has taken over. I throw my arms around his shoulders, close my eyes and cling to him; I've lost all control as my hips rock against his hand. My mind goes blank.

'You want me to make you come, baby?' Adam asks. Oh God, hot pulses of lava build inside me and I whimper and nod, my cheeks flushed, words beyond me.

Adam pushes higher inside me, clamps his mouth over mine and pushes relentlessly against *that* spot inside.

Oh my God!

I spread my knees as wide as I can, my mind spins and white lights flash behind my closed eyelids as my hips buck wildly. My pulse explodes as searing heat rips through my core and I convulse around his fingers. I moan loudly and he kisses me deeper and harder, then he strokes his thumb firmly over the sensitive nub at the front of me and I shudder.

'Adam!' I cry out against his mouth, unable to contain it.

'That's it, baby, fuck yeah,' he encourages as I cling to him as pleasure blindsides me again. He leaves his hand inside me as aftershocks rock through me then withdraws it, wrapping his strong arm around me and pulling me onto his chest.

He kisses the top of my head affectionately as I lie trembling and panting in his arms. Tingles ripple down my back as he caresses my skin and cradles my head with the other hand, cuddling me close as my senses start to return. I open my eyes and know my cheeks are burning, so I snuggle up against him more and hope he won't notice.

'Was that your first orgasm or do you touch yourself?' His voice is deeper than usual. I nuzzle my face into his chest, still trying to calm my breathing down. He can tell I'm deeply embarrassed, though, and trying to hide from him. 'Come on, Ella, tell me,' he encourages me light-heartedly, squeezing my shoulder a little.

'First,' I mumble against his skin and I feel his chest expand in satisfaction.

'Well I'm thrilled it was with me,' he says and strokes my hair off my face. Then without warning, he scoops me up into the centre of the bed. I lean on my side and watch as he takes from his bedside table a small bottle, which he throws on the bed, and a foil wrapper. He opens it and rolls a condom onto his thick erection. My adrenaline pumps hard through me, am I really doing this? I *want* to stare at him, he's gorgeous, but I'm suddenly intensely shy and can't even look. Then he confidently pushes my thighs apart before kneeling between them and I gulp in some much needed air. I feel his eyes raking over my body hungrily.

Oh Christ, this is intense.

'Aww, Ella, you're so fucking beautiful,' he groans, his accent more pronounced. 'You could make me come just looking at you.'

I meet his eyes and I'm taken aback by the desire burning in them. It's dominant and fierce and I'm mesmerised by him. I always am. He puts a hand on my shoulder and pushes me to lie flat on the bed and then covers my body with his, his chest crushing me into the mattress.

My heart pounds aggressively and desire pools hotly between my legs.

Oh God!

Every inch of my skin in contact with his burns with desire, I can barely breathe.

'You're very quiet, baby.' He breathes out against my lips. 'Are you ok?' His voice is concerned. I nod in answer, too overwhelmed to speak. 'If you've changed your mind, you can still say no,' he says, his voice is gentle and his eyes are focussed on my face. Oh sweet Jesus! My tummy bungee jumps and I shake my head, already trembling and unable to hide it. Don't stop now!

'No, I want to,' I reply, my voice hoarse with nerves.

Adam exhales and kisses me again, it's demanding but slow and I kiss him back as he rolls me into a better position underneath him.

He handles my body like it's his property, it's confident and sexy and makes the heat pulse deep inside me. My thighs quiver as I feel his erection prod gently between my legs. His weight on me is infinitely masculine and I feel pinned down and enveloped by him, but it feels good. It feels safe. It feels right.

When he leans on his elbow to ease off my chest, I gasp for air and watch curiously as he picks up the bottle and squirts gel onto his hand. He smooths it between my legs, making me jump in shock at the coldness. I widen my eyes at him.

'It'll help,' he reassures me, his eyes hot with lust. He takes his time to smooth the gel around and my breathing is soon coming in short sharp pants. My head lolls back onto the bed as the most exquisite sensations course through me.

'Adam!' I gasp unable to take any more. I feel like my entire body is going to combust under the heat if he doesn't stop that soon. My cheeks are flaming and I quickly cover my face with my hands, which are on the verge of trembling.

'Don't be shy, Ella,' he says, pulling my hands away gently, 'I want to watch your face as you lose it.' His voice is soft and caring.

Oh dear Lord.

I melt.

Then keeping eye contact with me, slowly and firmly, he pushes his hips forward and begins to enter me. I tense up as I feel him stretching me, *there*. Oh holy crap, it starts to pinch and I gasp.

'Relax, love, or I'll hurt you,' he says breathing shallowly and looking down at me under him, his expression a mixture of tenderness and pure male satisfaction. He wants this badly.

I suck in air and pull my knees up in the hope that it will ease the discomfort, but it doesn't. He pushes a little deeper and as it starts to hurt, the threat of unwanted tears starts to prick my eyes. Ouch! I push my head back into the mattress and whimper; I can't help it. He feels too big for me and my legs are trembling now.

'I won't push all the way in yet,' his murmurs and rests his forehead against mine. 'I can see that's hurting, baby.'

I blink in surprise. *What?* He's not even fully in yet?

I stare at the ceiling and he keeps still to let my body stretch as he focuses his attention on me. It makes me feel exposed emotionally. He kisses me on the nose, looking at me ardently.

'It's ok, love,' he says and then he moves his hips, slowly pulling out a little way and then pushing back in again, taking his weight on his elbow by my head and making his muscles flex. My legs shake again and it really stings.

'Oh God, Adam!' I practically whimper; I can't contain it.

'You feel that, baby?' he says softly, pausing again, 'you're *my* woman now, but you know that already, don't you?'

I nod silently, panting hard as he pushes a little further in. Embarrassingly a tear spills out of my eye and rolls down my cheek. He leans down and nudges his nose along the tear track and kisses me on the cheek. It's such an affectionate gesture it awes me.

'Don't cry, baby, it'll pass,' he reassures me. With the arm he's not leaning on, he wraps his fingers around the inside of my thigh and slides his hand up to cup my bottom, effectively lifting and holding my hips even more intimately against him. He's still watching my face intently and must be able to feel me shaking. It's overwhelming! I close my eyes and wrap my arms around his shoulders, burying my face against his neck. His breathing is uneven and I can feel his heart hammering in his chest as he lies on mine.

'That still hurt?' His voice is less controlled, but he's keeping his hips still. It's just so intimate, he feels big and hard inside me, but also warm and smooth and the pinching is lessening now. He's so strong and can easily hurt me, but he's being so caring and tender, just as I knew he would be.

'It's a bit better,' I whisper, cuddling into his strong neck, revelling in his weight on me

'Can I push in fully?' He breathes against my forehead, kissing me there and I nod. Then I feel him stretch me more, pushing all the way in deep. I gasp, clinging to his shoulders and he groans.

'Aww!' I exclaim panting hard, I can't help myself.

'You alright?' he asks. I nod quickly but my shaking thighs are telling him what he needs to know.

'You're stretching me,' I squeak at him.

He pulls his head out of my grip and looks down at me, it's so sexy I can't help but stare at him. He moves his hips around slowly, taking his time, his skin burning with heat under my hands. His lips cover mine and his kiss is sensual but demanding.

'That still hurt?' he asks when he pulls his mouth away, I shake my head a little.

'Good, 'cause taking it this slow is gonna kill me.' He exhales but is smiling at me as he pulls out slowly, then pushes in again. This time he doesn't pause, though, but carries on moving, deeper than before, making me squirm against him and screw my eyes tight against his neck.

'Aww, Ella, you're so goddamn tight,' he mumbles, his voice broken.

'Sorry,' I whisper into his shoulder and he pushes into me slightly faster.

'Sorry? Don't be sorry, being with you is the biggest turn on of my life,' he groans. My eyes spring open, resting my cheek against his neck. *Really?*

His plunges into me a little harder now, clearly his need to move becoming more urgent. I know how he feels, being crushed underneath him as he holds me like this is creating the most sensational feelings, but I'm still tender.

Adams kisses me more ardently as he presses me down and buries himself deep inside me; he's being so caring, though, it makes me light-headed. On and on he moves, sensually, slowly, deeply. Tingles of excitement crash through me from my core.

'No more talk of splitting up, you're mine now,' he commands and I agree breathlessly, overwhelmed by him as always. In response Adam rocks my hips against him, his mouth taking everything he can get from mine. My centre aches with the feel of him so deep and I wriggle under him. 'Baby, I can't go slow anymore!' His breathing is ragged and his eyes blaze down at me.

'Ok,' I pant.

He relaxes on top of me and starts thrusting harder. Oh my! He's so possessive! Soon the last of my discomfort has eased away and I'm pushing my hips rhythmically in time with his, ripples of pleasure seep through me, and I pull my knees wider. I rest my hand against his face and our eyes stay locked. I've never felt closer to anyone in my life, both emotionally and physically.

'You're so fucking beautiful,' he says and my heart glows; I want to tell him he is too, but it wouldn't sound right. He runs his hand down my side to cup my breast and tease the nipple; it makes me ache with tension. I throw my head back onto the bed and moan; I just can't contain it any longer. I want to scream and thrash against him but I hang onto my control by a thread.

'Is that nice?' He smiles, sounding pleased with himself. I look at him with hooded eyes, unable to hold back any longer and start moving against him harder, but he surprises me and holds my bottom firmly in an iron grip, keeping me pinned still. I gasp as sensations rock through me; I want to move against him. I'm burning to move against him. And he's stopping me. I moan with pent-up desire, no longer conscious of how wanton I sound.

'Greedy girl.' He teases me, crushing me so I can't move and playing with my nipples, pinching them.

'Adam!' I groan louder and try to arch my back off the bed towards him. I can't stop myself. Then he moves his hips slowly around, making me whimper with pleasure and cling to him, my body soft and moulding to his.

'I want you to lose control with me,' he says taking short sharp breaths. Oh my word! I think I already am. I can see from his eyes how much he wants me and he tightens his hold on me.

'What… about you?' I gasp.

'Only after you, beautiful.' He breathes heavily, rocking his cock against *that spot* inside me deliberately. My legs go numb and I can't think straight. I pant helplessly on the constant verge of crying out. He thrusts into me quicker and the sensation has me raising my legs high and wide in the air and closing my eyes.

'Adam!' I gasp, overwhelmed as he takes more control of my body than I can.

'I want to feel you come on me, go on, baby, relax, I've got you,' he says. I bury my face into his neck. 'Is that what you want?' he asks.

'I want to make you happy,' I whisper in reply and cuddle into him further, my emotions on overload.

He takes a gulp of air and I feel him look down at me sharply but I hide my face against him so he can't see my expression. My outstretched legs are quivering. He closes the gap between us and crushes me into the mattress again. I'm losing all train of thought. Then he starts kissing me slowly, deeply and stops thrusting, leaving me absolutely suspended on a cliff edge and shaking.

I moan desperately as he runs his hand over my breast and then starts moving again, but it's not fast like I want, just enough to bring me over the edge slowly making my orgasm even more intense. I scream and cling to him as the room flashes before my eyes, my legs tense and my body convulses as my hips ride him. His strong arms envelope me as he holds me.

'That's it, lose control,' he murmurs against my lips, watching my face as I come hard, then he pushes his tongue inside my mouth and starts thrusting harder and faster than before, prolonging my pleasure.

I pant uncontrollably against his lips but he doesn't stop moving, just pounds into me harder, but doesn't hurt me. I screw my eyes tight and suddenly shatter in sensation again at the same time as him. He lets out a guttural groan of ecstasy as he finds his release and collapses on top of me, resting his forehead on the duvet above my shoulder and heaving for breath.

Oh wow.

When I finally open my eyes, I'm thankful Adam can't see my face as a few tears trickle down my cheeks. I'm not upset, just overwhelmed and I swipe them away before he sees.

'Are you ok?' he pants, his breath tickling my neck and his body still crushing me.

'Uh huh,' I manage to get out in affirmation.

'I didn't hurt you?' he asks, his voice deeper than usual and sincere.

'No,' I shake my head, gasping also.

He sighs in satisfaction and I expect him to get off me, but he stays exactly where he is and starts kissing my neck. It's not the passionate kissing of a moment ago, when his tongue massaged my skin alluringly, now he's giving me small pecks up and down my neck. I raise my eyebrows up at the ceiling in surprise, safe in the knowledge he can't see. His fingers move into my hair and he works the tiny kisses up my cheek and pauses with his nose almost touching mine. He holds my head gently between his hands, cuddles into me and pauses, watching me. I stare back at him, completely unprepared for him to show me this level of affection. He smiles at me in the sexiest way, completely confident and not at all embarrassed, if I wasn't already short of breath, the look in his eyes would make me. I try to pull some much needed air into my lungs.

'You're squashing me!' I pant, not sure what else to say.

He takes more of his weight on his elbows but keeps me pinned where I am and continues to look at me. It throws me completely and I have to look away, not sure what to say or do and he starts playing with my hair, twiddling a lock between his fingers before kissing me on the forehead.

'I loved feeling you come on me,' he says quietly.

I'm quite stunned at his directness and considering he's still inside me, I'm also acutely embarrassed and immediately feel my cheeks burn. He kisses me yet again, but on the cheek now.

'Don't be shy,' he whispers, and of course I blush even more.

I look at him and he's grinning at me. Then he gently pulls out of me, but doesn't move away. I wince a little at the sensation and remain silent. What the hell does someone say after losing their virginity anyway?

'You're perfect,' Adam murmurs looking me in the eyes.

Perfect? I'm so far from perfect I wonder if he's really seeing me. Maybe if I was more experienced I'd know what to say in this situation, but I'm not, so I just blink at him. Adam seems to be studying every inch of my face.

'You want me to let you up?' he asks, probably noticing I'm becoming flustered at the level of attention. I nod, still keeping quiet. He smiles and pushes himself up to kneeling position and I divert my eyes when he pulls the condom off. 'Aww Christ,' he mutters, 'the condom split, baby.' Adam meets my eyes.

Oh fuck! I sit up in concern. Liquid oozes out of me and I bite my lip. Eww!

'It's alright, I'm healthy and I'll drive you to a drug store for a pill,' he reassures me, relaxed.

'Ok,' I exhale and glance down. My cheeks flame yet again as I see I've bled. My blood is on him and down my thighs. 'Sorry,' I whisper self-consciously, shuffling back from him to pull my knees together. I have to use my arms to do it, it's like my legs are made of lead. He chuckles softly and shakes his head at me.

'It's natural for your first time,' he says and his eyes glow wickedly like he's pleased with himself. 'And stop apologising for everything.'

I hope like hell that I'll stop blushing soon. I concentrate on the bedspread rather than meet his gaze. 'I guess I'll have some washing to do,' I mumble to lighten the mood and he laughs again and tosses the condom into a nearby bin.

'Come on, let's get you cleaned up,' he says affectionately and gets off the bed, taking me by surprise by scooping his arms under my knees and back to lift me up. I giggle and hug him tightly so I don't fall, and when I look at his face there's an expression that I can't interpret. It's intense and possessive for sure, but there's something else too. When I continue looking at him, he kisses my head again and looks away. I can't help feeling it's so I can't see his eyes.

He strides to the main bathroom across the landing and lets me lower my legs to stand in the bath. I scoop my hair up and twist it around enough so that it stays in a bundle on top of my head and when I look at him my breath catches in my throat. I bite my lip as I realise he intends to get in with me. It's obvious from the way he's watching me.

He turns the hot tap on and waits for it to warm up before putting in the plug and then gets in, tugging my hand so I sit also, with my back against his chest. It's a squeeze to fit between his knees and my shoulders are a little tense, so he works his thumbs into the knots of my muscles and it makes me tilt my head to one side as the water starts to fill the bath. Oh that feels good! We stay like that until the water starts to cool down and Adam hugs me close and washes me down which makes me squirm.

'You don't have to do that,' I mumble as his hands move between my legs.

'Oh yes I do,' he replies confidently. 'I'm going to touch you as much as I can.'

His response does nothing to ease my heightened sense of self-awareness.

We get out and he wraps us both in fluffy bath sheets and rubs me down. When I raise my eyebrows at him he just smiles in that way he does, kisses me on the forehead again and continues anyway.

'You kiss me a lot,' I state softly.

'Yeah,' he says and his eyes glint at me in amusement. 'Was that fixing to be a question?' I love the way his accent stretches the words out.

I shake my head quickly and look around the room instead. Adam leans forward and his breath tickles the skin on my neck and he scoops back a loose lock of my hair hanging over my shoulder so he can get closer to my ear.

'You're everything I want,' he says quietly, 'so damn right I'm going to kiss you.'

He's so direct!

'Now come to bed,' he says taking my hand. I swallow and hesitate. He wants to do that *again*? I'm a little sore! He sees my apprehension and smiles at me, rolling his eyes. 'You've slept with me before, baby,' he says. Oh! My cheeks flame that I assumed something else. I'm going to fall asleep with him... As he says, I know I've slept with him before, but I was drunk. I nod and try to hide that I'm out of my depth again.

'Can I borrow a... toothbrush?' I ask him tentatively, quickly swapping the word T-shirt in my head. He nods towards the bathroom cabinet.

'I'll go change the comforter,' he says and winks at me, then pauses and asks, 'do you need your bag?' I flush and smile back at him shyly and he leaves the room, returning a minute later with my bag and then leaves me again in the bathroom.

I take out a spare pair of knickers I carry in my bag and a sanitary towel and put them on, thanking heaven it's one of my nicer blue lacey pairs, not my grey cotton ones. I notice as I brush my teeth that my hands are trembling slightly. I tell myself it's no big deal to spend the night with him to calm myself down a bit. What's the big deal about going to sleep anyway? It's just so... intimate.

I pause outside his bedroom and see Chase on the floor at the end of the bed, he wags his tail making it pretty obvious I'm standing there so I can't delay anymore and walk quietly inside. Adam has already used the adjoining bathroom and is lying on the far side of the bed with a lamp on; it makes what's clearly a man's bedroom look surprisingly cosy with the blinds drawn. I don't look at Adam, my heart's pounding a little too hard in my chest to realistically think I'm going to get any sleep. He flips the summer duvet back (which has now been changed) to expose the sheet on my side. I sit on the edge of the bed and pull my feet up, trying hard to relax.

'I don't bite,' he says gently and I slip my feet under the duvet. He turns the lamp off and I'm about to lie down when I feel his strong arms close around my waist. 'C'mere,' he says and pulls me down so he can wrap his arms around me with my back pressed against his hard chest, his cock nestled between my bottom cheeks. It feels out of this world to be held close by him but I'm still a little on edge and he notices.

'It's just me, baby, right?' he says, cuddling me close. I nod. He nuzzles his face into my hair and seems to sigh with pleasure and relaxes against me. I'm a bit surprised again; he's so affectionate.

'Good night then,' I whisper.

'Night, Ella,' he answers, and there's a pause. 'I just want you to know, tonight was special for me too. I've never wanted anyone as much as you.'

What? Did I hear that right? I swallow in shock and try to sit up in order to turn to face him, but he tightens his arms and stops me.

'Go to sleep, baby, it's late,' he says softly and kisses my neck. My heart is pounding so hard it's like it's inside my head, and I wonder how on earth I'm going to be able to sleep when he just said *that*!

He strokes his hand down the side of my neck and the caressing motion slowly helps me relax and, along with his body heat keeping me warm, I eventually start to drift off into oblivion. As I do, I think perhaps Adam may pull me closer to him and kiss me on the shoulder, but I'm not sure what he murmurs.

Chapter Eight

When I wake up, I'm alone in Adam's bed and I can hear voices downstairs. I push myself groggily into sitting position, wrapping the duvet around me because I'm naked except for my knickers. My intimate areas ache with awareness of the night before and I can't help the smile that creeps onto my face as heat floods my cheeks. Oh Christ, it still seems a little surreal.

I take my rucksack into the bathroom with me and refresh my sanitary towel, then dress quickly in the previous evening's clothes. Thankfully my hair is in the mood to behave so I leave it loose before applying lashings of black mascara which I find in my bag.

Adam's voice is coming from the kitchen and I wonder who he's talking to. When I enter the room he's wearing only a pair of low-slung jeans with a brown leather belt. His sculpted chest muscles and tattoos hold my gaze before it wanders down over his toned stomach.

I think I've died and gone to heaven.

He glances up and sees me staring at him and I can almost feel the electricity arc in the space between us. The cut across his eyebrow from last night's fight with Carl looks sore; it makes him look rugged like a guy from the wrong neighbourhood rather than the owner of a large company. He holds his hand out and pulls me into a tight embrace and plants a kiss on my mouth.

'Good morning, beautiful,' he mumbles.

I lean back from him after I return his kiss, flushing a little and look to my right to see who he was talking to.

Dan is leaning against the kitchen worktop with a cup of coffee. He's wearing a *Wildcats* T-shirt which is stretching tightly over his arms where he is tense, and his jaw is set in a way that says he's far from happy.

'Good morning, Ella,' he says civilly. It's too formal for Dan, and even without his eyes confirming it I would know he's pissed off. He's not surprised to see me there, clearly Adam told him I stayed.

'Hi, Dan,' I reply, looking elsewhere, he can be quite intimidating when he's cross.

'Do you want some breakfast?' Adam asks and pulls a chair out for me. Aww, he's so sweet sometimes. I sit down and take in a subtle breath as I'm tender where I make contact with the chair. Adam walks into his kitchen area and starts making toast and cutting fruit. He's made some sort of health shake too; it's green and looks disgusting.

I ponder why Dan is here. Does he usually come by for breakfast? I can feel his eyes studying me as he sits in the chair opposite, his knees wide and his head tilting back on one side as he continues to watch me.

'I can see you're feeling better now,' he says. I widen my eyes at his disparaging tone and look at the table. For a second and I have to wrack my brain as to what he's talking about. Thankfully he jogs my memory.

'After Carl fucked off you were understandably a little shaken up, I can see that Adam's taken your mind off things, though,' he says dryly.

Oh gosh, the last time I saw Dan, he'd just watched me get assaulted and wrenched Carl off me. I nod and pick at some of my nail varnish, I feel so awkward it's unreal. I clear my throat a little and decide not to reply.

'Adam, can I help?' I ask, hoping it will give me an excuse to leave the table.

'No, almost done,' he replies dropping toast onto plates for Dan and I then bringing the fruit and health shake over for himself.

I see that the coffee table usually by the sofa at the far end of the room is missing and there's dirt on the floor where the people in the room last night kept their shoes on. I guess I'd been so preoccupied with confronting Carl, I didn't notice. I see Chase is in the garden.

'Dan came by to see how you are today.' Adam explains Dan's presence in a normal tone of voice, but I can feel his eyes focused on me, watching my reaction.

I glance up instinctively and regret it. As my eyes meet Dan's a rush of embarrassment washes over me at the images he must remember of me yesterday in the pantry.

'I'm ok, thanks,' I answer looking away and starting to wish Dan would focus on something else. Adam puts a glass of juice in front of me and smiles when he catches my eye. Bam! It's like a switch turns my hormones on.

He sits next to me then links our fingers on the table top and squeezes my hand while he talks to Dan. It's not lost on me that Dan has noticed our joined hands, so I sip my juice and pretend not to notice. A little later I subtly pull my hand free; why make the situation with Dan more awkward? The undercurrents are washing off him in waves, but either Adam's oblivious or ignoring it. I suspect it's the latter.

Adam presses his knee against mine as he and Dan talk about a meeting that's happening soon. Dan is particularly interested and his tone of voice leads me to think it's a big deal. They mention the warehouse and someone called Carrie who will pick them up as usual. They're vague, though, and I'm curious.

'Who's the meeting with?' I ask, seeing no harm in the question.

Dan raises his eyebrows and pauses with his coffee cup to his lips, but he doesn't look at me.

'It's better if you don't ask,' Adam says and puts his hand back over mine, holding my gaze. A sense of power and dominance quickly take precedence over the relaxed lover of a moment ago.

'Sorry, I didn't mean to pry,' I say softly, quite taken aback by the sudden change in him.

'It's fine, baby,' he says, his voice a little softer, but his eyes don't lose that withdrawn glint. 'It's just there are other businesses I'm involved in that you don't need to know about. Just don't repeat anything you hear.' I blink at him and nod. He squeezes my hand reassuringly.

'I want us to be clear from the outset, that's all. So if you want to ask about something, you talk only to me, ok?' As he states this, his voice could be called gentle but there's no mistaking the authoritative undertone.

'Ok,' I agree immediately, no way am I about to argue. He smiles at my response.

'That's my girl,' he says softly, then significantly quieter but I know Dan can still hear he adds, 'I don't want you to get caught up in things which might get you hurt.'

I nod numbly and wonder what on earth he's involved in. I feel in over my head again, it's becoming an all too familiar feeling.

Satisfied with my answer, Adam turns his attention back to Dan and resumes their conversation. I instinctively try to gauge what Dan's reaction is, but he's deliberately avoiding eye contact with me. It looks like Adam's word is law.

I'm quieter for the remainder of breakfast and Adam acts like nothing was said; after a while Dan gets up to leave.

'You need a ride, Ella? I've got a spare helmet with me,' he offers naturally. I notice for the first time a motorbike helmet on the kitchen worktop and look at Dan, surprised. I didn't know he rode a motorbike.

Adam answers for me. 'It's alright, I'll drive her.' There's a possessiveness there that makes my heart beat quicker. 'We need to make a stop,' he adds. Oh, the chemist. I nearly forgot.

Dan nods and picks up his helmet and strides towards the front door, calling, 'See you later then, Adam, the guys are arriving around eight,' over his shoulder. They've clearly got plans for tonight.

Dan pauses in the doorway and I feel his eyes on me so I deliberately don't look up. Adam answers with a 'yeah' and Dan closes the door after him, leaving us alone.

I wait for him to speak first. I feel like I've overstepped some invisible mark and I'm expecting to be told off. Adam's eyes are warm, though, and he takes my hand and gets to his feet, pulling me up with him. He wraps his arms around my waist and my pulse explodes at the contact with his bare chest. It's not what I was expecting, so I look up at him hesitantly, struck again by how much taller than me he is.

'You're very quiet, beautiful,' he says softly.

'Yeah, just tired. Someone kept me up late last night,' I reply coyly and attempting to avoid the elephant in the room.

'He can keep you up every night if you let him,' he replies smiling. I think he means it. My insides quiver with arousal at the way he's looking at me.

'And how would he do that, living two miles away?' I jest, tilting my head on one side as the tension inside me begins to ease. His gaze flicks over my face and he swallows before answering.

'Yeah, that might be a problem,' he admits, tightening his arms. His tone is light-hearted, but his eyes are serious. 'Perhaps you should consider moving in at some point.'

I raise my eyebrows. 'Huh?' I ask him inarticulately, thrown off guard. He's got to be joking, right?

'At some point,' he repeats, intending to lessen the impact of what he said and correctly judging my reaction as overwhelmed. My heart thuds hard and I'm momentarily speechless.

'Umm Adam? We're still getting to know each other, I mean, you know, in terms of living together,' I rephrase quickly.

He places a finger on my chin and tilts my face up so I have to look him in the eye and my tummy turns over like it's in a cement mixer.

'Don't look so freaked,' he says. 'I said *at some point*, ok?'

'Ok,' I answer, and he leans down to my level and seals his mouth over mine.

Every sense in my body comes alive and he fists his hand gently in my hair, pinning my head still. I melt against him as I kiss him back and his tongue delves hungrily into my mouth. He handles me gently like I'm fragile, but is also demanding and possessive, like he's claiming me as his. His hand slips under my dress into the back of my knickers. It's like I've been running hard the way my pulse ramps up and when he finally pulls his lips away, his eyes show a desire that is burning and fierce.

'Are you bleeding?' He meets my eyes with a confidence that makes me take a sharp breath. My cheeks flame as I realise he must be able to feel the end of my sanitary towel. I drop my gaze and push against his strong arms to release me, suddenly mortified.

He laughs like I'm endearing.

'Don't be shy, Ella!' He coaxes me. 'I only ask because I want to take you upstairs again, but I won't if you're sore. It doesn't bother me if you're bleeding, baby, but I guess it might bother you, huh?'

Oh jeeze! He's relaxed and upbeat after years of experience and it's a stark contrast to me as I wriggle in his embrace. He tightens his arms around me and seems amused as he plants a light kiss at my temple. 'Well, next time then, if you're shy now,' he says, angling to look down at me, so I bury my face against his chest and nod. I can tell he's still smiling at me and I squeeze my arms around him, trying to hide my face. We hug for a while and he caresses my shoulder, then when I'm finally more composed I let go of him.

'Come on, I'll take you to a drugs store and then out to lunch later.' He smiles down at me.

'I haven't got any money,' I respond automatically at which he rolls his eyes.

'Then I guess we'd better offer to wash the dishes.' He teases me and I can't help smiling. 'I'll just grab a shirt,' he says, stroking his finger tip down my cheek and then pausing. 'Um, Ella? I just wanna ask you something. I wondered, would you want to come to a works thing with me at the end of the month?' he asks changing the subject completely.

I look at him uncertainly.

'I thought you didn't want me to ask about your work?'

He lowers his head to my level, bumping his nose against mine.

'No, I don't want you asking about my *other* work,' he says gently. 'And that's only 'cause I don't want you to get hurt, that's all. But this is a DB Produce networking thing. A dinner we host each month,' he says, nudging his nose against my jaw line. 'It's a nice restaurant and you'd brighten up my evening, baby.'

It sends tingles of pleasure up my back. I'm flattered that he'd ask me to something like that and I push away my doubts about what he's not telling me.

'I wouldn't embarrass you?' I ask.

'What?' His eyes become more serious.

'Well, I mean, I've never been to anything like that... and I'm guessing I'll be the youngest person there.'

'Ella, *I'm* usually the youngest person there,' he says confirming my thoughts. 'Is there something else?'

Why does he have to be so perceptive? He's so good at reading people. I take a deep breath and decide to open up a little.

'It's just, I don't really find it easy to socialise.' I clear my throat a bit. 'I clam up sometimes; I wouldn't want to make you look bad, Adam.' I say honestly. That independent streak inside me pushes forward, though, and tells me it's about time I started to get over it and here's a good opportunity.

There's a pause as he considers what I said and then he unexpectedly nuzzles his lips down my neck, nipping me gently. My pulse increases exponentially and excitement bubbles low in my belly, but I resist the urge to press against him.

'I've never met anyone like you. You shouldn't worry about stuff like that, Ella, just be who you are and if other people don't get that, fuck 'em! They're not worth bothering with.' He exudes an inner strength that draws me to him. 'Is it that you're just shy?'

'Probably, but mainly just with men I don't know, that's all,' I answer him honestly.

'Well I'd look after you,' he says more gently, keeping his eyes on mine. 'You wouldn't have to talk to anyone if you didn't want to, except me of course,' he adds lightening the mood. It makes me smile as he intended but I decide he won't have to. I need to look after myself and if talking to a group of strangers is going to help me build that confidence, then I'll do it. Time to stop hiding.

'Ok,' I answer, 'I'll come, if you're sure?'

'I'm positive,' he states, clasping his fingers around mine. 'Come on, let's go out.'

My gaze lingers on his swollen knuckles and I pause. 'Adam? Is your hand ok?' He looks at his hand and shrugs.

'It's alright, baby, I've survived worse.' He dismisses it casually. Charlie's words come back to me *too many fights* and I remember his bruised eye when I first met him, and also his calm reaction to the brothel fire. I wonder again how rough his lifestyle is. I realise I'm staring at his hand. When I glance up, our gazes lock. I tug my hand but he holds onto it and leans closer, his breath tickling my cheek. It's amazingly appealing and I feel a little dazed.

'You're looking at my hand a lot,' he states, his tone deeper and quieter than usual.

'Sorry,' I mumble. The way he's looking at me has me fixated on his eyes.

'Don't be.' He leans closer again so our lips almost touch.

'Does it hurt?' I ask, caressing my thumb over his knuckles. He shakes his head but guilt surges up inside me anyway. I go to touch the small cut above his eyebrow with my free hand but hesitate and let it fall back to my side.

'I'm so sorry, Adam,' I say quietly. 'That's my fault. I hadn't realised...' My voice trails off at my own self-centredness. He raises one eyebrow at me.

'It's not your fault, it's Carl's fault. And no, it doesn't hurt,' he says, tilting his head on one side and, regarding my reaction thoughtfully, he pauses a moment. 'I noticed when you saw Carl messed up last night you were a bit... unsettled.' He seems to choose his words carefully. 'Are you not used to seeing that kind of thing?'

I shake my head quickly and look away.

'No, my dad didn't let me go anywhere that...' But I can't think how to phrase what I want to say. I clear my throat and try again, mumbling awkwardly 'not really' instead.

There's another pause and Adam watches my reaction astutely.

'I guess still being a virgin you didn't hang out with many guys back in the UK?' I'm a little shocked by his bluntness and raise my eyes to his.

'Why do you say that?'

He shrugs his shoulders casually.

'Guys scrap,' he says as a simple explanation, waiting for my answer. It's like there's a lot more going on behind those sharp eyes than what he's saying. I blink at him, overwhelmed by the way he's looking at me. 'Your *friend* Tom didn't scrap, huh? He just picked on the little girls or what?' I notice the way he emphasises the word 'friend'.

'Yes he was just a *friend*, and I don't know if he got into fights, he never told me if he did!' I answer a little defensively, although I'm not sure why.

'Is he the reason you're shy around guys? Or was it because your father was over protective?' Is he a mind reader or something? My cheeks take on a little colour, confirming the truth. Adam gives a half-smile and shakes his head a little. 'I bet your father told you to stay away from guys like me specifically, didn't he?'

I avert my eyes, focusing on the tattoo on his neck.

'Guys like you?' We're so close; it's sending my pulse into overdrive. He chuckles a little in amusement.

'Yeah, Ella, older guys who scrap and want to fuck their daughters don't always go down well with over protective fathers,' he says lightly.

'You're being silly.' I exclaim. 'It's not like he wouldn't have let me have a boyfriend.'

Adam smiles down at me.

'Let me guess, one your own age, maybe a college guy who's studying math or some shit?' He grins at me and sees from my reaction that he's hit the nail on the head. Then his smile fades a little as he considers something.

'So you weren't playing me?' he says softly. 'All that pushing me away and pulling me back again, I thought you were a cock-tease, but you really are as pure as I thought to start with.'

Pure? I blink at him. His level of understanding me is so spot on as always.

'I'm just *me* Adam,' I reply and ignore the pounding of my heart as he leans in the final inch and kisses me softly.

'Well it's looks like I've got my good girl like I wanted then,' he says against my lips. I want to kiss him, hard, but force myself to pull back slightly instead and take a steadying breath.

'So how come you're always getting into trouble anyway?' I venture, hoping it's not obvious I'm trying to dig a bit deeper. His walls come up immediately, though, he's far from stupid.

'I'm not in as much trouble as it sometimes appears you know.' There's something about his tone that makes it sound like he wants me to believe him.

'Uh huh,' I respond nonchalantly, concentrating my eyes on where I'm running my finger over his sore knuckles.

'So that's a scar on your stomach from an operation then?' I ask casually, wondering whether this plucky girl inside me has always been there. There's a quiet pause as he looks at me then smiles and leans close to bump his nose against mine.

'I think Dan's been sharing secrets that aren't his,' he says. Oh damn! I look up at him guiltily and nod. I'm a crap liar anyway.

'Yeah, he might have said something, but I was wondering about it anyway,' I answer honestly and deciding now is definitely not the time to bring up what Dan also said about his mother overdosing.

He looks down at me like he's on the verge of saying something, but looks away.

'You know, baby, sometimes people aren't always what they seem; you should remember I said that. It's the lesson I learnt when the woman in question gave me that scar,' he says a little cryptically. It leaves a strained silence between us as he's clearly not going to elaborate further, so I return my attention to his hand.

'Speaking of scars, do you want me to dress your hand for you?' I ask, changing the subject a little. He rolls his eyes at me, implying that the damage there is such a minor thing it's of no consequence.

'I did this looking out for you,' he replies instead, gesturing to his injured hand and keeping his tone serious. The look in his eyes is so intense. I wish I were more equipped to deal with this... *with him!* I look back at him, remaining quiet. 'Tell me again that you're my girl,' he says abruptly, 'like you did last night.'

'I'm your girl,' I answer quickly, my pulse racing.

He nods in agreement.

'Damn right. Come on, let's get some lunch... and an emergency contraceptive,' he adds lightly. I gulp and watch him as he goes upstairs to get a T-shirt.

Adam drives to a chemist and buys me a morning after pill, which I take straight away, and after that we go for a walk before he treats me to lunch at a Mexican restaurant. When I say treat, I mean it. After weeks of cutting back, to eat out is a luxury and the food is delicious. He's great company and the anxiety I felt this morning at breakfast is soon forgotten.

Instead of taking me home after we've eaten, I ask him to drop me off at the police station. At first I think he's going to talk me out of it, but to my surprise he doesn't and is even supportive. He drives me there without a word. When we pull up outside he asks if I'd like him to come with me, but I shake my head. This is something I need to do myself. I kiss him goodbye and tell him I'll call Charlotte to pick me up later.

Giving the statement to the police is not as daunting as I thought it would be and I'm relieved a female officer is on duty. I tell them I don't want to press charges, but would like the police to speak to Carl and she says she would look into it. Over an hour later I leave the police station and find Adam still waiting outside to take me home, a used disposable coffee cup in the holder. I'm touched he waited for me. When he drops me off, he kisses me goodbye and I can't help but smile as I watch his truck bump its way back along our driveway. The glow soon disappears, though, as I walk inside, straight into chaos.

Charlotte has been up most of the night with David and Amy who have picked up a tummy bug and Hannah is currently being sick in the bathroom. By mid-afternoon, Charlotte, Sarah and Rose are all ill and I'm kept busy looking after everyone. By the early hours of Monday I've also caught it and spend several hours being sick. Knowing I will not be able to work that day, I call Adam's mobile mid-morning, hoping to hear his voice to cheer me up, but it goes straight to answer phone so I leave a message.

'Hi Adam, it's Ella. I'm not well so can't come over today, sorry, I hope it's not a problem, just feeling rotten. I hope your hand is ok now. I've been thinking about you. Hopefully I'll be back to normal tomorrow and will be round as usual. Bye.'

An hour later I get a text back from him. *Sorry, was in a board meeting. Feel better soon baby.*

I spend the rest of the day in my pink pyjamas, lying on my bed. When I feel up to it, I quietly re-work the lyrics of a song I'm writing and by dinner time I'm contemplating a bath and an early night when Hannah knocks and pokes her head around the door.

'How are you feeling?' she asks me in her warm and concerned way, she's not looking great herself but far more recovered than yesterday.

'Ask me another one,' I grumble but smile to show I appreciate her asking.

'I just came to say there's a delivery for you, on the front porch.'

I'm not expecting anything. I sit up and the movement makes my tummy ache.

'For me?' I ask before getting slowly to my feet and heading to the front door. There's a ginormous bunch of the most beautiful red roses in a glass vase wrapped in cellophane placed in the middle of the porch, but no one is around. I look back up at Hannah who's followed me to the door and is smiling broadly.

'Are you saying those are for me?'

She nods at me and laughs. 'That's what the envelope says.'

I go outside and pick up the envelope clipped to the cellophane which is addressed simply *Ella*. Inside is a small white card with a sunflower on the front. I bite my lip to hide my smile as I remember my first date with Adam. I turn the card over and there are just a few handwritten words in elegant script.

Thanks for a special evening. Hope you feel better soon beautiful. Adam x.

I look at the roses; they are stunning. There must be fifty stems here and my mood lifts considerably. No one has ever bought me flowers before and let's face it, these aren't just *any* flowers.

'Wow!' I look at Hannah, shocked.

'I know,' she exclaims, admiring the flowers.

That evening I call Adam's mobile and have to leave another message to thank him for the wonderful flowers. What is he doing that he's always too busy to answer his phone? A while later the family mobile pings with a text.

Glad you liked them. Hope you're feeling better baby, thinking of you. A x.

It makes me grin stupidly and I go to sleep feeling decidedly happy for someone who's still feeling ill.

I go to work on Tuesday afternoon, feeling much more my usual self. When I see Adam's truck in the drive, I hope he's at home but find myself disappointed.

I've just finished walking Chase, who I'm deeply fond of, and am emptying the washing machine when Adam's answering machine connects a call and it goes to speaker phone. The message is brief.

'Adam? It's Carrie. I know I'm late calling, but I can't pick you guys up as something's come up, sorry, talk to you later.' Then the line disconnects.

I stand in the kitchen and raise my eyebrows in surprise, she sounded so curt! I press play on the machine to hear it again, wondering if I'm misinterpreting it. The machine plays a different message, though.

'Ella? It's Adam. Pick up if you're there… Ok, if you get this, can you call my cell and tell me if Carrie has left a message? She's late picking Dan and me up from the warehouse. It's important, so give me a call if she's left a message. Thanks, baby.'

The machine states the message was left at 3:15pm and Adam sounds stressed. Then a second message starts playing automatically. At first all I can hear is rustling, like his phone is in his pocket and then I hear Adam speak in the background.

'Hell! Dan, get down, they're inside!' And then there's muffled shouting and I know something is wrong. Christ! Is that *gunshots* in the background? I listen to more of the same until the message times out, my heart slamming anxiously. The machine tells me the message was left at 3:22pm.

I find Adam's number and call him back, but I get a 'this number is unavailable' message. Why is his mobile suddenly not working? I glance at my watch. It was fine only twenty minutes ago when the last message was left. I don't have Dan's number and wonder what I should do. Should I find someone and ask for help? Call the police maybe? No, I decide I can't do that; Adam was very clear to keep things to myself and my tummy lurches as I realise they must be at the meeting he and Dan were talking about. The one for his *other* business. I can feel my adrenaline starting to kick in a little and wish I knew more about it so I would know how to help.

I look around the kitchen in a state of mild panic, and notice Adam's truck keys. I haven't driven since passing my test in the UK and never on the right, but maybe I could drive his truck to pick them up? Trepidation runs through me at what I might find at the warehouse, but I can at least go and take a look. If I don't like it, I'll stay in the vehicle.

I grab the keys and my bag, head out of the front door and get in the truck. I study the controls and adjust the seat and mirrors; this thing is huge in comparison to the little Nissan I learnt in. I'm so nervous I almost get back out again. Jeeze, I hope to God that I don't crash his shiny truck. I have no idea if his insurance will cover me either. Can you go to prison here for driving without insurance?

I take a deep breath to calm down and turn the engine on. The engine doesn't start. It takes me a full five minutes to work out I need to press the brake pedal down because it's an automatic, and by the time I work it out my hands are shaking. I put it into drive with the lever and ease the truck slowly out of the driveway.

Once I reach the site security gate, the guard waves me to a halt. I recognise him from my many entrances through this gate when I've come on my bike, but I can't remember his name. Luckily, though, he seems to know me.

'Hello, Ella,' he says. 'Does Adam know you're taking his truck out?'

'Yes of course.' I smile. 'I'm picking him up from town.'

'Drive safe then,' he says pleasantly and flips a switch which makes the gate rise.

'Thank you,' I call out of the window successfully faking a cheerful persona, before pointing the truck in the direction of town. I drive incredibly carefully, perhaps a bit too slow really as I get beeped twice by frustrated drivers stuck behind me. I calmly let it pass over me; quite frankly I've got enough to contend with already. I'll be amazed if I make it all the way to the market warehouse to be honest. I just hope I don't run out of fuel, the gauge is saying it's running low.

I slow down and pass the warehouse in order to park on the road side a short distance from the car park entrance. It's reasonably quiet here when the market is not on, so I jump out and leave my bag inside out of view, popping the keys into the back pocket of my jeans shorts after locking the truck. I walk warily along the pavement and consider what I should do next, my heartbeat considerably quicker than usual. I've been so concerned about actually making it here I stupidly haven't given much thought to what to do once I got here. The heat of the afternoon doesn't help me think clearer either and I can't tell if I'm sweating from that or anxiety.

I can't see anyone around, so I open the gate and walk across the car park. There are several vehicles parked, but I scoot around them and head towards one of the pedestrian entrances. For a moment I consider going back to the truck to see if Adam still has his gun in the glove box. Maybe I should bring it? Then I dismiss the idea as ridiculous. I don't even know how to use it and I'm more likely to be a danger to myself.

I reach the door and pause outside to listen before blundering inside. A large hand seizes me by my shoulder.

Bloody hell!

I'm spun around. I just manage to hold in a squeal of alarm as I recognise the tall bearded man in front of me. It's the same guy who had been with Reece at the market weeks ago, when he came enquiring about the money we owed. I know he recognises me, I can see it on his face.

I glance past him and spot a man in jeans and a black T-shirt swiftly crossing the carpark, breathing hard. I could have sworn there was no one around a moment ago. I'm about to scream to him to help me, but he disappears from my line of sight, almost like he was never there at all. My assailant clamps his hand tightly over my mouth, cutting off any chance I'd had to cry out as his other hand grips the back of my head.

'*Tu estupidez es impresionante,*' he snarls under his breath then he reaches past me, swings the door open and pushes me through. I fleetingly consider resisting, but I'm already inside before I get a chance. It's quiet and darker inside and the door opening abruptly as we enter causes some commotion. Several men shout something tersely in Spanish, and then the tall guy behind me answers.

'Found her outside; she came alone!' Again I'm shoved forward a few paces but I pull my shoulder away to stop him pushing me. I squint trying to look around, my eyes adjusting as the doors are all shut against the bright sunshine and the lights are off. I'm aware of the entrance door reopening as the guy behind me leaves.

I blink and look ahead of me. My heart freezes and then starts beating in overdrive. There are at least eight men standing in the open space in the middle and three of them have guns pointed at me, another is in a chair smoking. Two men are lying on their sides on the ground in the middle. It's Adam and Dan. My heart leaps. Fuck!

I can see they are gagged with their hands cuffed behind their backs, but I can't see their faces. I turn sharply to the men pointing handguns at me and stare at them, hardly daring to breath. I recognise Reece standing to one side of the group. He's shaking his head at me in a way that implies he's either amused or astounded at my stupidity, and I resist the urge to run at him and scratch my finger nails into his stupid spider's web tattoo. Arsehole.

The nearest of the three men strides towards me and levels his gun at my chest from a couple of feet away. I'm unable to hide the terror in my eyes so don't even try. He's dark skinned, wearing jeans and a dirty vest which shows off an overly lean body. He's not young, maybe in his late forties? Another man with slicked back brown hair, combat trousers and a red T-shirt joins him to stand closer to me. It's too close for comfort; adrenaline pumps in my head and I can smell his pungent body odour.

The guy in the chair looks distinctly Latin American, dressed in trousers and a casual long-sleeved shirt despite the heat. I guess he's in his late forties also and has black medium length hair pulled back into a small ponytail at the top of his neck. His voice is heavily accented when he speaks.

'And who are you?' He pronounces every syllable slowly and perfectly. I open my mouth to reply, but Reece answers for me.

'This is Brook's little English squeeze, Jefe, the cause of all the trouble.'

Adams growls from the floor and tries to sit up but one of the armed men kicks him hard in the stomach, making me wince as I watch. He points his gun at Adam.

'*Cállate!*' the man demands.

Adam can see the gun from the position he's lying in and quietens. The guy in the chair, who was referred to as Jefe, raises his eyebrows in a decidedly flinty way. He angles his head towards Reece as he replies, but leaves his eyes pinned coldly on me.

'Is that so?' he says in the same slow and deliberate way. 'Check if she's carrying,' Jefe orders the guy in the red T-shirt near me, who approaches and moves his arms forward to start patting me down or feeling me up, I'm not sure which. I really don't want him to touch me and I raise my hands quickly and take a step back.

'I'm not! Really!' I say quickly.

Adam groans on the floor at the sound of my voice and I notice Dan's shoulders slump. The man in the chair looks disdainfully at me, pushes his chin out and up in a way which clearly tells me to take my top off to prove it.

'Do it, or we will anyway,' he says bluntly, his accent strong.

I gulp and slowly take the hem of my top and pull it over my head, leaving me standing there in my black bra and shorts. I hold my top in my hands out wide at my sides and turn in a circle to show him there really isn't a weapon concealed. There are a few whoops and jeers and someone in the room whistles in appreciation but I'm too scared to notice who.

'Come forward and put your hands on your head,' he commands, smiling sleazily. Something tells me this has turned from a threat to a source of entertainment. I do as I'm told, I'm not stupid, and walk more into the centre of the warehouse towards him. I'm frankly not in a position to argue.

'And what are you doing here, *Adam's girl?*' the man in the chair asks, now satisfied I'm not armed. Thank goodness I left Adam's gun in the truck. They might have shot me. As I approach him, I notice he has a sizeable stack of notes in the hand not holding his cigarette. I avert my eyes quickly. I've no idea how much cash it is, but it's an awful lot; I'd struggle to get both my hands around it.

'I came to give them a lift,' I say lamely, glancing towards Adam and Dan on the floor. I notice that although Adam is tense, Dan doesn't seem to be moving much but I still can't see their faces from this angle.

'Well they do not require a ride at present,' El Jefe answers slickly. A few of his men chuckle at his tone, as he intended.

Adam tries to shout something at us through his gag, but the guy with the gun brings the butt of the handle down hard on the side of his head and I flinch at the sound of the impact. Jesus Christ! That was hard! Adam groans and quietens.

El Jefe takes a long drag on his cigarette and blows the smoke over his shoulder as his eyes rove over my body. It gives me the creeps, but the whole room is doing the same so it's not like he's the only one. He flicks his cigarette onto the floor and rubs his shoe on it.

'Why don't you come over here and sit with me,' he says patting his lap. It's not really a request and I stare at him, unable to hide my fear. I really want to shake my head but I don't dare, although my feet won't seem to move.

'Come on.' He instructs me like he's coaxing a pet and I know I have to move. I walk over and sit gingerly on his knee and once I do, the men aiming guns at me lower them. He unsurprisingly smells of cigarette smoke.

From this position I can finally see Dan and Adam's faces, they're both awake but Dan is clearly the more beaten up of the two and seems to be quite hurt. Both of them have bleeding cuts on their foreheads and Adam has the inflicted welt from the butt of the gun on the side of his temple but it seems to be mainly covered by his hair. I deliberately don't look either of them in the eyes, but I know they are staring at me intensely.

'You can put your hands down,' Jefe says quietly to me in his thick accent and, still clutching my top tightly, I lower my hands to my lap and hold them together trying to hide the fact they are trembling. I lean as far from him as I can manage, looking straight ahead. To my surprise and utter relief, though, El Jefe does not actually touch me.

'So, do you know where this is from?' he says picking up the very large stack of notes held together with a thick elastic band. I shake my head and don't look up to meet his eyes.

'This is Adam's money, which I am taking in recompense for my burnt business, which I think you are the cause of, if I'm not wrong,' he replies, his pronunciation stilted. Oh dear God, he's clearly talking about the brothel. Is all of this here today my fault? Are Adam and Dan hurt because of me?

'Do you think it is fair recompense, young lady?'

I nod immediately but Adam kicks off again, the same guy boots him hard in the stomach and I wince, my hand flying automatically to my mouth before I can stop it. The guy starts to kick Adam repeatedly and I turn my face away unable to bring myself to watch. I'm shaking and although I know my reaction is telling them I'm scared, I can't seem to stop.

'Enough!' El Jefe tells him. 'You're upsetting our visitor.' He sounds amused and caresses his palm down my arm; it makes my skin crawl. The guy stops kicking Adam and I subtly lower my trembling hand from my mouth, my shoulders radiating tension.

'Adam seems to be a fortunate man,' El Jefe says smoothly.

'He has money.' He raises the stack of cash in the air.

'He has loyal friends,' he says indicating Dan lying on the floor and looking pretty messed up if I'm honest.

'And he has a pretty young woman.' Now he runs his hand up through my ponytail, letting my hair slip through his fingers. I don't react to it so he places the palm of his hand on my shoulder and runs it down my back to my bra strap; it makes me jolt upright in the hope that sitting up will lessen his hand's contact with my skin. It doesn't.

'Today I will relieve him of one of the three,' El Jefe says to me directly and I look sideways at him as a shiver runs through me to my core. I stupidly notice he has really long eyelashes. It's amazing how the mind focuses on the details when it's terrified. His eyes, however, are dark and hard.

He's talking to me, but it's clear his words are intended for Adam. I'm becoming even more anxious, if that's possible, that he might be referring to me. Then I see him smile lazily.

'Today I will relieve him of the money,' he clarifies, and I take a steadying deep breath in relief and hope he doesn't notice. Usually I'd feel like bursting into tears, but surprisingly, anger is my overriding emotion in response to my fear. I want to ram the palm of my hand into his chin.

'If he interferes with my businesses again, though, I will relieve him of another,' he says deliberately looking at me, taking his hand from my back and letting his fingers move slowly over my collarbone to caress my cleavage at which point I look away. He's obviously goading Adam who can see what he's doing; making it clear that I'll be the next of the three he'll take if Adam retaliates. Adam, however, doesn't seem to get that it's just bait and reacts like a volcano going off, shouting incoherent words through his gag and trying to get up.

The guy with the gun slams the butt of it against his shoulder, and then does it again. El Jefe seems to think that's enough and goes to stand up. I don't need telling twice and spring up off his lap like a rocket. I run to the spot between Adam and the man and shove him hard with both hands on his chest before I even know what I'm doing. It makes him take a step back in surprise and I hear several guns click as they are loaded and aimed in my direction. My adrenaline is pumping in my ears and everyone falls silent, curious to see what will happen next.

I have no idea what to do now; I can hardly rugby tackle him to the floor. So I hold my shaking hands up, having seemed to drop my top en route. My gesture is clear and unthreatening; I'm beseeching him to stop. Instead he backhands me across the face and I literally go flying a few feet and land with a smack on my side, knocking the wind out of my lungs in the process. My hand springs to my cheek which is smarting like hell. For a moment the room turns a disturbing shade of black and then the light becomes normal again and my lungs sting as I struggle to breathe. I blink and flex my jaw and prop myself up on my elbow to glare at the guy who struck me. God that hurt!

None of the gang is speaking or intervening, and he looks like he's about to continue his assault on Adam, who's currently going mental on the floor. One of the others is pinning him on his back by a foot on his shoulder but having a hard time doing it.

I'm dizzy and wheezing but, fuck this, I'm not going to stand by and watch him beat the crap out of Adam when he can't defend himself. I get shakily to my feet and walk back to the guy, who stares at me like I'm stupid.

I'm starting to think he might be right.

I slowly place my hand on the forearm he's holding the gun with. There's no threat or mal intent there; I just want him to stop.

I plead quietly so only he can hear me. 'Please, just lower the gun, please.'

He doesn't listen, though, he's all fired up and aggressive.

'You wanna take my gun sugar, that right?' he sneers at me loudly.

What? Is he joking? He jerks his elbows out and his shoulders forward and glowers at me. I stare at him, calm on the outside and quaking on the inside.

'And what would I do with it?' I ask, hoping my voice doesn't portray the terror I'm feeling. 'Do you think I'm going to take all nine of you on, standing here in my bra? Seriously?' There are ripples of laughter from the others standing around, and it goes a long way towards lightening the otherwise dangerously tense atmosphere.

'I don't even know how it works,' I add, looking distastefully at the gun before returning my gaze to him; again there are more laughs, although I didn't intend to amuse anyone.

He clearly doesn't care for the entertainment factor I've unintentionally created and pushes me hard in the face. I go straight down, landing on my knees right by Adam's head. There's another pause as everyone waits again to see what will happen next, and I crawl to sit in front of Adam. I'm holding my face where the guy struck me for the second time. He raises his arm, making a clear threat to strike me again; I screw my eyes up in anticipation of the blow and put an arm over my head protectively, but I don't back down. I don't move away from Adam and stay exactly where I am.

'*Enough!*' El Jefe commands in a voice that none of his gang is going to argue with. 'I said enough, Lopez!'

To my absolute relief my attacker backs off and I lower my arm from around my head and collapse from my knees onto my bottom next to Adam's shoulders. My hands are shaking so much I try and hide them.

'Brook, you freakin' yaller dog, you always let your women defend you?' The guy called Lopez jeers at Adam.

Thankfully Adam is sensible enough not to try and respond. I reach across and push against the leg of the guy who's pinning Adam's shoulder to the floor with his boot. He gets the hint much quicker than the first man and removes his foot and takes a step back. Perhaps he complies because I'm gentle. If I'd shoved him, he surely wouldn't have moved.

I pull Adam by his shoulders so his head rests on my lap and wrap my arms around him protectively. I do not dare look down at his eyes, although I know he's staring at me, instead I keep my eyes trained on the one called El Jefe who's watching us.

He comes over and crouches down near me, his eyes now on the same level as mine. He pauses as he studies me, it sends a chill through me and the smell of his cigarettes lingers unpleasantly in my nostrils. I try not to appear confrontational as I return his gaze. For me that's not usually hard, but right now I have to make a concerted effort. I'm so damn angry.

When he speaks it's in Spanish and his attention is focused on Adam. I don't understand a word, but Adam clearly does and looks him straight in the eyes and nods. I remember Adam telling me that he spent a long time in Mexico before his father passed away and he had to come home. I get the impression they know each other well. They hold a conversation, even though it's more than a little one sided, and there are various glances in my direction but I just look back at El Jefe blankly. What on earth is he saying? I glance over at Dan and notice he seems to have understood also and is looking at me with an odd expression on his face. Then El Jefe makes me jump by running his finger down the side of my cheek and I return my attention back to him abruptly; his touch makes me shiver.

'You are very brave young lady,' he says once again pronouncing every syllable, and he produces two small keys from his pocket and tucks them into my bra between my boobs. I hate the feel of his fingers touching me and my shoulders tense up in response; aside from that I manage not to react and I'm proud of my self-control.

'You wait until you hear the car horn, before you unlock the handcuffs, ok?'

I nod. He's letting us go?

El Jefe indicates the door I entered through and there's a general exodus of all the men. He leaves in the middle with the bundle of cash, and one of the armed men walks backwards at the rear, keeping his gun aimed in our direction. He waits inside the door for a moment as several engines kick into life and I watch him apprehensively until he finally leaves and the door swings shut behind him. I hear a car door close and then the engine revs and finally there's a beep of a car horn. I sag in relief but my hands start shaking violently as I take one of the keys from my bra; Adam sits up so I can access his handcuffs behind his back. It takes me a few attempts to get the key into the lock and when I finally do, it's the wrong one. I have to do it all again with the other key, but eventually Adam's handcuffs click and spring open. His reaction is like a grenade going off and he springs to his feet and starts tearing at the gag tied at the back of his head.

'Do you want some help?' I ask him timidly but he shakes his head and growls something unintelligible. I shiver and decide to keep my distance so shuffle over to where Dan is lying and staring at me. I get the key into his handcuffs and as they spring open he groans as he regains full movement in his shoulders.

'Fucking *son of a bitch*!' Adam thunders from my left as he finally gets his gag off and I jump in fright, my eyes going straight back to him. 'They hurt you, baby? They'll pay for that, I'm telling you; I'll make them fucking pay for hurting you.'

He's absolutely furious. I've never seen anyone in such a rage. I continue trying to untie Dan's gag, deliberately looking away from Adam.

Then Adam is crouching next to me. Electricity courses through me as he places his hand on my cheek and turns my face so I have to look at him. I stop breathing and stare at him, startled. His eyes are burning, like a caged beast being tormented. My cheek throbs under his light touch, so I pull back a little and he notices.

'Are you hurt? Tell me,' he asks, his voice overwrought, and he starts looking me over intently and turning my face to the other side to check for himself.

'I'll be fine.' I gulp, too intimidated to admit I am hurt in case it enrages him further. I lower my eyes from his so he can't see the fear inside me shining out of them. Then I feel like I'm zapped with lightning as he thumps his fist hard against his thigh and stands up swiftly. He utters something under his breath, clearly not intending for me to hear him. The blood drains from my face as my brain registers not only what he says but, more relevantly, the rage with which he spits the words out.

'You shouldn't fucking be here,' is what he muttered. It's like ice water being injected into my veins.

Oh Christ. He's angry. *With me?*

My heart pounds as dread seeps through me. I know he didn't intend for me to hear him, so I pretend I didn't and bite my lip; I hurriedly turn my attention back to finishing untying Dan's gag with fingers that are trembling so much I can barely control them. Throwing the gag on the floor, I concentrate on Dan. The glimpse I get of his face before he masks his expression startles me. There was an intense focus in his eyes as he drank in every moment of our exchange. But what startles me most isn't that he was watching me, it was that he was studying Adam. It was Adam's reaction that had held his attention.

Dan flexes his jaw and casts his eyes back to me. He's lying motionless and looks awful. From a cut on his brow there's a small trickle of blood running down towards his eye, so I wipe it away with my finger.

'Thanks,' Dan says gruffly and then immediately groans with pain and screws his eyes shut, his hand over his ribs. I get onto my knees and prop my leg under him to support his head.

'Is it your ribs, Dan?' I put my hand on his face to get his attention. He opens his eyes and stares at me leaning over him for a moment before nodding.

I swallow the rising fear I can feel building in my throat as I register again the anger behind Adam's words. *You shouldn't fucking be here.* I decide I need to focus on Dan now, I can think that through later.

'Can you stand up on your own?' I ask him to distract myself. I stroke his face, trying desperately to concentrate on him rather than on the turmoil of my emotions. I don't know what to do to help him and feel useless.

'No,' he says gruffly. I look to Adam for help.

He's standing a few feet away, both his hands thrust into his hair, clearly trying to calm down. When our eyes meet, anger dominates his harsh expression and I recoil, but this time physically, my heart pounding in my chest. He's seriously intimidating and I divert my eyes straight back to Dan. Immediately he comes back to me, resting a hand on my shoulder.

'Hey, it's ok, Ella, I'm not hacked off at you,' he says and I can tell he's making a huge effort to control his voice. I nod to say I've heard him.

'Dan's hurt, can you help me lift him?' I whisper, ignoring the tremble in my voice. 'They might come back.'

Then our eyes meet. The look on Adam's face is fierce and my breath catches in my throat, I have to make an effort to continue to breathe.

'Move out the way,' he says quietly and runs his hand around the back of my neck in a caress that's so firm it shows his tension. He bends and supports Dan under the shoulders. 'On the count of three,' he says and Dan nods.

Adam supports his weight over bent legs and lifts Dan to standing position. Dan lets out a sharp gasp as he's moved, but otherwise says nothing, although the pain he's in is obvious from the narrowing of his eyes and the stiffness of his shoulders. Dan wraps his arm around Adam's shoulders and Adam supports him as they start moving towards the door. It's clear to all of us the urgency of leaving.

'How did you get here, Ella?' Adam asks, leading Dan. I hurry to pull my top on.

'I drove your truck.'

Adam raises his eyebrows at me. 'I didn't know you could drive? Why didn't you tell me?' he says.

I don't think he looks angry, well not about that at least. I guess he has bigger issues right now.

'It didn't come up,' I answer, hurrying ahead to cautiously open the door, thankfully outside it looks clear. I hold the door wide as Adam helps Dan out, he's walking ok but is clutching his ribs and grimacing.

'You want to go to ER buddy? I'll pay,' Adam asks Dan as we leave the warehouse. The sun is glaring after being in the dim interior and we're all squinting. Dan shakes his head.

'No, will be alright after some rest,' he mutters.

I'm looking about anxiously and point in the direction of where I parked. I'm quite astounded at how well I seem to be coping with the fact I was just being held at gunpoint, I guess adrenaline's keeping my wits sharp, although my hands are refusing to stop shaking.

I run ahead; the truck looks ok from what I can tell so I unlock it and open the passenger door. I glance back quickly to check if the men are coming and see Adam gesturing something with his free hand behind his back where Dan can't see. Huh? I blink and look again with more attention, but Adam has moved it back to support Dan's arm slung around his shoulders and is looking at me.

I frown. What was he doing?

'You alright, Ella?' he asks softly, distracting me.

I nod and in my heightened state of anxiety, I think perhaps I imagined it. Maybe he wasn't making hand gestures at all. Although that's certainly what it looked like.

Between us, we manage to get Dan in the truck and buckle him in. I hold out the keys to Adam but he shakes his head.

'You drive,' he says. I wonder if perhaps he's more hurt than he looks and I flick my eyes over him, concerned.

'I'm not a very good driver…' I start to protest but Adam is already in the middle seat, his head back and eyes closed. I nervously take the driver's seat and try to calm down. I'm gripping the steering wheel so tightly on the way back my hands ache, and I wince frequently when other drivers use their horns at me in frustration. I must be driving worse now than on my way here. Adam's had his eyes open for a while and has been watching, surprisingly, without comment, thank goodness, I need to concentrate.

'Dan, should we go to a chemist and buy some pain killers?' I ask.

'A drugstore? Nah, I've got pain relief. But thanks, Ella,' he says gruffly, taking a breath, 'for giving us a ride I mean. I know you came for Adam, but even so.'

Something about his voice isn't right, it's too quiet and it leaves us sitting with an awkward silence hanging in the air. I glance over and see he's still looking out of the opposite side window, but before I can answer, Adam pats Dan on the leg twice in the way guys do. I return my eyes quickly to the road. Perhaps they have a deeper friendship than I'd previously thought. Adam's warning to me that I should not trust Dan springs back into my mind and I'm confused. If they're such good friends, why would Adam warn me?

Perhaps it's to try and divert us from the fact that we've just been held at gun point, beaten up and he was robbed, but it's Adam who breaks the uncomfortable silence.

'Just head to Dan's place, Ella,' he says.

'Ok,' I answer, concentrating on the road.

'She knows the way,' Dan mutters dryly, clearly alluding by his tone of voice to last week when Adam found me there… in his arms.

Wow, was that a low blow I wonder? Adam seems to think so as he squeezes my thigh in response and we both stay quiet.

I slow the truck and pull up at the security gate to DB Produce. The same guard as earlier comes out and smiles when he sees me returning with Adam in the truck; perhaps he was getting concerned I'd stolen it. Instead of flicking the switch to raise the barrier, he walks over to the driver's door, so I lower the window.

'Mr Brook, I wanted to let you know that Mr Sims has just got back,' he says looking at the blood on Adam's brow and welt where the butt of the gun made impact. The guard doesn't alter his blank expression at all and I get the impression this is far from the first time Adam has turned up looking like he has been fighting.

'Thanks, James,' Adam answers, courteously.

James looks over at Dan and carefully controls his expression. 'Shall I send Barry round to Dan's house, sir?'

'Yeah, please,' Adam answers. The guard nods and takes a step back to flick the barrier switch. I'm conscious of Adam's fingers caressing my thigh as I start the truck moving forward and he seems to have relaxed a little now we're back on site.

'How long have you been driving, Ella?' he asks to break the silence.

'Not since I passed my test last year,' I say concentrating on my speed. Adam lets me focus for a moment.

'Are you insured?' he asks me softly.

'What?' After what I've just witnessed in the warehouse, with an armed robbery taking place over a stack of money which was clearly gained illicitly, he's asking me if I'm insured to drive? Is he serious? *Now* he wants to play the law-abiding citizen? The man is a mass of contradictions. 'You're worried about your truck?' My voice is strained and a little incredulous at his timing.

'No, Ella, I'm worried about *you*,' he answers flatly. 'What if you were in a car wreck? You shouldn't have come to pick us up with no insurance.'

Oh.

'Well I got your messages after Carrie left a voicemail on your answering machine and didn't know who to ask to help, so I just jumped in the truck, I guess I didn't really think it through,' I answer, keeping my eyes on the road.

'What do you mean, messages?' Adam asks me sharply. 'I only left you one.'

'No, you left two, but I think the second was unintentional. It sounded like you were in trouble,' I explain.

'You thought we were in trouble and *then* decided to come and get us?' Adam raises his voice. '*On your own?*' There's an undertone to his voice which indicates more than just surprise, is it concern? I glance quickly at his face and decide no, it's not concern, it's more than that, he's angry but trying to hide it from me.

You shouldn't fucking be here. His words from earlier return to me like a knife in my back. I suddenly feel like I should justify myself.

'Well I assumed you were doing something you wouldn't want everyone at the farm offices to know about, so I didn't want to start asking around as you told me not to.' I shrug. 'So I came myself to see if I could help in some way. I wasn't planning on going inside, but the guy in the car park surprised me.'

There's a pause and I can feel Adam and now Dan both looking in my direction.

'I didn't mean to make things worse,' I mumble apologetically. I continue looking ahead, but the silence from the other half of the truck starts to stretch. 'I wanted to help and couldn't think of what else to do,' I add self-consciously. 'Where did the money come from anyway? Are you selling stolen goods or something?' I ask nervously before I lose my courage, keeping my eyes deliberately looking forward.

Dan clears his throat in such a deliberately fake way that it implies Adam's busted, and then looks back out of the window again. Adam runs his hand up my bare thigh and it makes me jump, sending tingles of electricity through me at the unexpected contact.

'Ella…' Adam says in a tone of voice implying that I shouldn't ask.

'Ok, you're right; perhaps it's best if I don't know.' I immediately back down.

He squeezes my thigh reassuringly and starts caressing his fingers around the top of my leg; it feels lovely and makes me squirm in my seat.

We finally pull up at Dan's place and I carefully reverse onto his driveway so he hasn't got far to walk. Once the engine is switched off, I close my eyes and breathe a sigh of relief to let out some of the tension inside me.

Thank God I can stop driving now.

Thank God we're all alive.

I know Adam hasn't taken his eyes off me for the last minute but I don't look at him, it's too unsettling. Instead, I unclip my seat belt and swing open the driver's door, leaving the keys on the seat for Adam before jumping down. While I walk around the truck, Adam leans across and opens the passenger door, gets out and then starts helping Dan. He groans sharply with the movement and Adam leans down under Dan's shoulder to help him walk.

'Ella, my door keys are in my pants pocket,' Dan says. I hurry to take them out and run ahead to open the door before Adam helps him inside.

It feels strange to be back at Dan's place and I'd rather wait outside instead of bringing back memories of Carl, but with Dan hurt I think that would be selfish when I should stay and help. Adam manoeuvres Dan onto the sofa and I fetch him a glass of water for something useful to do.

Adam pulls out his mobile from his pocket and grimaces when he sees its screen is smashed. Well that would explain why it wasn't working earlier.

'I'll be back in a bit, I need to make a call,' Adam says glancing tentatively at me.

Yeah, I bet you do.

My eyes lock with his and my tummy lurches; all I want in the world right now is to throw my arms around him and cry my eyes out at the shock of what's happened. Clearly that brave young woman I turned into for a while has now turned and fled. I take a deep breath and nod mutely, wondering again what I've got myself involved in.

'Will you wait until I'm back before you leave? I want to talk to you,' he asks. I nod and then he's gone, hurrying through the front door, clearly having no intention of letting me hear the conversation he's about to have or who he's going to call. I look back at Dan who's now slouched on the couch and watching me. He looks so rotten I go over and sit next to him, leaving a comfortable gap between us.

'How are you feeling?'

'Like hell,' he answers, but there's a strange glint in his eyes so I turn away feeling awkward.

'Can I get you something? Some tablets or...' My voice trails off as I can't think of anything, but he shakes his head.

'Barry will be here soon,' he says as if that will solve all the problems and I guess Barry is some sort of first aider. 'He sure cares about you, y'know, he wants you real bad,' Dan says, abruptly changing the subject and clearly talking about Adam. I look towards the far end of his living room and don't respond straight away.

'What are you expecting me to say to that?' I'm at a loss for words and highly aware that only a few days ago he himself offered to take my virginity for me.

Hmm. Awkward much?

'Nothing. And I can see you want him too, I just want to make sure you know what you're getting into with him,' he says, his strong southern accent stretching the words out. My heart jolts in my chest.

'And what is that exactly?' I ask a little defensively and deliberately keeping my eyes on a table opposite me.

'Well don't you wanna know what this afternoon was about?'

I take a subtle deep breath. Of course I want to know, but at the same time a voice in my head is screaming at me that maybe I'll regret it if I do. Surely Adam would tell me himself if he wanted me to know? But then again, I was in real danger earlier and although I'm making a conscious effort not to think about it yet, I know that later I'm going to be a trembling mess with a thousand unanswered questions once I let the lid off my emotions. I swallow and haven't reached a decision of whether I want to know or not, when I look at Dan. Perhaps the war I'm waging inside between my curiosity and this sense of foreboding is apparent on my face. I'm not sure, but Dan flicks his blond hair out of his eyes and decides for me.

'He's supporting the drug cartels in Mexico, Ella.' Dan's voice is calm and cool and I stare at him, stunned. My shoulders jerk back from him automatically.

'*What?*' Now I've heard it all! Dan is jealous I spent the night with Adam, that's what this is about. 'Do you expect me to believe that?' I start to stand up to leave, but Dan takes hold of my wrist.

'Stay, Ella, just hear me out,' he says quietly. I stare at him, my pulse pounding in my ears as I realise he's serious. 'I'm not trying to upset you; I've been wanting to talk to you alone since last week.' He pulls my wrist and I reluctantly sit back down on the sofa.

'Dan, if you're going to bad mouth him, at least come up with something plausible!' I bite at him.

'Ella, I'm looking out for you. You don't know him like you think you do. He's involved with some heavy shit and you need to hear this.'

There's something about his voice that catches my attention and, despite the thundering of my heart, I now want to hear what he has to say. Even if it's just so I can brush it aside later.

'Say what you want to, but make it quick, I'm not staying long.' A voice in my head is warning me not to listen. Another is asking me what Dan's motive is for wanting to tell me this.

'It's true, Ella. He's selling pesticides to south of the border.'

I nod to acknowledge I've heard him but don't look up. When I don't reply, Dan continues.

'Ask him outright if you don't believe me. He over-orders and then sells them on for cash as they can't source the quantities they need for production without raising suspicion.' Dan takes a deep breath and gingerly moves his hand placed over his ribs, as he's obviously hurting; it brings my attention back to him. 'It's why El Jefe didn't fuck him up today; he knows Carlos would take him out if he messed with Adam.'

'Who's Carlos?' I ask, dreading the cold chill starting to seep into me.

'Carlos is Adam's buddy from when he lived in Mexico, they're real tight and you could say his family is... well connected,' Dan says. 'Think about it, Ella. You think just anyone can walk into one of Reece's establishments and pick you up and they'd let him walk out of there with you unscathed? It's bullshit! You saw the money today. That was payment for two loads, I drove the second truck, Ella; I saw what was loaded in it.'

I suddenly feel dizzy and sick. I swallow the bile rising in my throat. There's a ring of truth to what he's saying that I can't help but recognise.

'He's a member of the *Discípulos de la Muerte*, haven't you seen his tattoo with their initials?' Dan asks.

'He's a member of *what*? I don't speak Spanish,' I mutter irritably, my head pounding.

'Death's Disciples, the most notorious gang in Mexico City, surely you've heard of them?' Dan says like everyone in the world must have heard of them. I shake my head but want to burst into tears as I remember DM are the initials on his chest tattoo.

'So that means you're involved in it too?' I ask Dan quietly, trying hard to think logically and failing.

'Nah, I just store the excess chemicals as I'm told to, Ella. Adam's my boss, sweetheart, and I need this job to support my ex with the kids.'

There's a knock on the door and it abruptly halts our conversation as a man calls out 'Dan, it's Barry.'

Dan looks at me for a second and I look back at him blankly, my head feels like it's spinning. I swallow and flick my fringe out of my eyes. He sighs and looks towards the front door.

'In here, Barry!' Dan calls out and grimaces with the effort.

The door opens and a balding middle-aged man who's a little overweight comes into the room carrying what looks like a doctor's medical bag and looks surprised to see me there. I smile, although after this afternoon I've never felt less like smiling in my life, and I get to my feet.

'I hope you feel better soon,' I say genuinely to Dan and put my hand briefly on his shoulder. He nods at me and I turn quickly and leave through the front door before he can say anything else.

Oh dear Lord! Was he lying? He must have been lying; it seems too farfetched to actually be true.

There's a large dark red car parked on the drive behind Adam's truck and I guess it must be Barry's. I find that Adam has not locked his truck, although the keys are gone from where I left them on the seat. I'm relieved and take my rucksack out and close the door. The heat from the sun has faded considerably and for the first time since I've been here, I shiver slightly from the breeze and pull on a cardigan from my bag. Perhaps the season is finally starting to change and the heatwave is ending.

I walk onto the large expanse of fake grass where I sat with my sisters for Dan's barbeque and find a spot to the far side near the fence. I sit down to wait for Adam, my hands still shaking in response to everything that's gone on this afternoon and my mind in turmoil. Scenes from the warehouse and words from Dan swim around my head and my cheek throbs where I was hit.

Then to make matters worse, as if I wasn't emotional enough, I start thinking about my dad and what he would have said if he'd found out about this afternoon, although thankfully, I'm too numb to start crying. It seems life here is just one thing after another. Perhaps I should move back to the UK. At least I'm less likely to be shot there.

A short while later Miguel, Carson and Adam's cousin Jenny all arrive at Dan's place by foot and walk briskly up the driveway. They don't see me sitting quietly by the fence and I don't call out to them either, I need the time alone to try and clear my head. I sit for a long time until I finally consider myself calmed down and realise I'm actually quite cold and the light is starting to fade fast from the sky. It gets dark late here, so my sisters will start to worry soon if I don't get back.

A large black saloon pulls up at the kerb outside Dan's a few minutes later. The passenger's door swings open and Adam gets out, as does an older man from the driver's side. Finally.

They walk quickly towards the house and when they don't see me, for some reason, I don't call out to Adam. Something about the man with him doesn't make me feel comfortable to do so. I'm guessing he must be Jonathon Sims. He's tall, looks quite fit and has light brown hair and is dressed in tailored work trousers and a shirt with no tie.

They are almost at Dan's front door when Barry comes out. The three men talk but I can't hear what they say, they don't seem downhearted, though, so I guess the news about Dan is not too serious. Adam seems keen to get inside and then looks agitated when

Barry says something. At that point, Barry spots me and points me out to Adam, who spins around and smiles so warmly when he sees me, a warm rush spreads through me in response. His uncle looks at me curiously but doesn't approach. Adam comes over immediately; he's cleaned the blood off his face from earlier and changed his T-shirt, he looks a lot better than I thought he would.

'What are you doing out here alone?' he asks as he crouches down next to where I'm sitting. 'I thought you'd left,' he says, clearly relieved I hadn't.

'Just getting my head straight in the quiet,' I mumble. His hazel eyes shine at me in the half-light and he nods, but I can't seem to stop staring at him.

'You wanna come inside?' he asks me holding out his hand and standing up. I shake my head to the question but take his outstretched hand and let him pull me to my feet. I'm a little stiff from sitting in the garden and rub my arms to warm them up as I've got goosebumps.

'Actually, I'd almost given up on you and was about to go home,' I answer, studying him. My eyes are trying to drink in every detail of his face, like I know our time together is on a countdown.

He hugs me close and starts rubbing my arms to help me warm up and it feels great; I don't think about it, I just throw my arms around him and rest my face against his chest. I feel his throat move as he swallows in response and he kisses the hair on the top of my head, enveloping me in his arms.

'Are you ok?' he asks me quietly, resting his chin on my head. Now he's here, I realise I'm not ok at all.

'No, but I'll get over it.' I snuggle into his chest further and I can't stop myself, I squeeze him tighter against me, it feels so wonderful to suddenly be in his arms. I realise how much the events of the afternoon have shaken me up and I want to be close to him. I don't want to believe the things Dan said. I don't want to ask him. 'What did you want to talk to me about? I'm cold and want to get back before the light goes completely,' I ask him, breathing in. He smells of deodorant, fabric conditioner and that fresh woodland scent that's unique to him. I close my eyes as I cuddle him.

'I wanted to make sure you were alright, baby,' he says softly. 'We didn't really get a chance to talk earlier and I was worried.'

'You were worried, *about me*?' I ask. 'That's the wrong way around given what you must have been up to today!' I feel him nod.

'I worry about you all the time,' he says flatly. He pauses and holds me tightly then adds, 'And I wanted to say if anything like that occurs again, don't take this the wrong way, but don't come, Ella. I sure don't want you anywhere near those guys again, especially not for me, I can take care of myself. You hear me?' He kisses my hair again, so I nod in reply. There's clearly more he wants to say, though, so I glance up at him expectantly.

He leans his head back to look at me and suddenly it's like the rest of the world around us goes into slow motion and then fades away. The wind stops blowing and the leaves on the bushes stop rustling. It's just us, and our gazes lock onto each other's so firmly it's like we'll never look away. I cease breathing and my heart flutters out of control and the ground seems to shift under my feet, making me sway a little. His breathing deepens and we stay locked in our own little bubble. Slowly he brings his mouth down, his lips close over mine and the sensation makes me quiver. The ground tilts precariously as I cling to him and kiss him back like never before, I just can't seem to pull myself close enough to him. He groans and responds by pulling my hips up tight against him. When I'm light-headed from the lack of air, I finally pull back. Resting my hand on the side of his face, I stare up at him; I've surprised myself as much as him. What on earth is he doing to me? This is intense. Is it just my body's reaction to the stress of the afternoon?

'Come back to mine?' he says softly caressing my face with one bent finger and smiling at me, his eyes are so attractive, I'm dazzled by him. Then Dan's words come back to me in a rush and fear of learning whether they are true stabs me through the heart.

'I can't,' I whisper, shaken by the intensity of my response to him and the events of the afternoon. A tidal wave of mixed emotion comes crashing through me, shaking my very soul as I pull away from him and take an unsteady breath. 'Not today.'

Adam looks concerned and suddenly wary. 'Sure, ok,' he says quietly, but there's a world of thoughts passing behind his sharp eyes, I just can't read what they are.

'Can I ask you a favour?' I ask.

'Anything, baby.'

'Can you ask someone to call Charlotte to come and pick me up? I want to go home now,' I say softly. There's a flicker of comprehension in Adam's eyes.

'Of course I will, but tell me something first. What did Dan say to you to put that look on your face?'

My heart misses several beats and the ground feels like it's suddenly rushing up towards me. I take a deep breath. The oxygen to my brain allows me to keep standing and I regain my composure, but only just.

'Nothing,' I whisper, my eyes locked to his.

He looks at me for a moment and nods, appearing to be satisfied by my answer and I breathe a small sigh of relief as he leans forward and presses his lips to my forehead.

'I'll go call your sister.' His breath is warm against my skin. 'But don't lie to me, Ella,' he says softly, before turning to walk into the house. I watch him go, my heart slamming painfully against my ribs.

Chapter Nine

On Wednesday morning I wake in the early hours, damp with sweat from my nightmare. I'd been tossing and turning all night, my mind replaying the scenes from the warehouse and Dan's words around and around.

I've barely slept and by sunrise I'm up and showering. After carefully applying some make-up to hide the hint of a bruise appearing on my cheek, I spend the morning quietly gardening in the vegetable patch and looking after the chickens. My mind is busy doing what it does best when it's in crisis, and by late morning I have most of a new song in my head, I'm just struggling for a chorus. I get myself a cup of tea and my notebook and then settle down on a blanket outside, some way from the house so I'm not disturbed. I'm definitely not in the mood to talk to anyone right now.

I flick through the book and find the lyrics to earlier songs I'd written when Adam first kissed me, and my heart pounds erratically as I consider the conversation I'm going to have to have with him later after work. I can't live in denial and ignore what Dan said. I need to speak to him.

I've finished work and am feeling uneasy sitting at the kitchen table waiting for Adam to get home. I hear his keys in the door and try to swallow some of my apprehension as he comes into the room.

He looks so good in his navy blue shirt and tailored fawn trousers, I can't help but ogle him. You'd never think he'd been assaulted and gagged just a day before. His eyes are a little cautious as he looks me over, no doubt taking in every aspect of my posture and expression in the usual quick assessment he makes of me with his eyes.

'Hello, baby, how's your cheek today?' he asks immediately, putting his laptop bag on the floor near the doorway and dropping his keys on the table.

'Hi, not too bad,' I mumble as he pushes his hand into my hair and turns my head a little to study my face intently. Tingles shiver down my back at the caress of his fingers on my scalp and I take a deep breath. 'Are you ok?' I ask him softly.

He gives me a lopsided casual grin. 'Yeah, I've had far worse.' He says it like it's silly of me to ask such a thing. I raise my eyebrows at him and decide that perhaps I'm better off not asking any more questions.

'But what about you?' he asks again like he didn't believe me the first time, then he runs his hand down my cheek. 'You're more delicate than me.' The look he gives me sends a jolt to my heart and then straight between my legs. I have to take a gulp of air and look away.

'I'm fine, really.'

He leans down and presses his lips to mine and I kiss him back. We're drawn to each other; I can't deny it. I can feel the pull of him race through my whole body and I know he feels it too. I can see it in the way he looks at me. It's like my blood hums when he's near me and I'm disappointed when he pulls away, although he leaves his face just inches from mine.

'I meant it yesterday, Ella, don't come after me again if you think there's trouble, go find Carson or Owen, I don't wanna see you get hurt, especially over me,' he says and I can tell he means it.

'Isn't that the other way around? If it wasn't for us borrowing the money in the first place, then no one would have…' I start to explain but he puts his finger over my lips.

'Hush, baby, this goes way back before you, so don't blame yourself.'

A silence settles and I struggle for something to say. Now would be the opportune time to ask him if what Dan said was true, but I can't bring myself to do it… not yet. The sense of foreboding in my heart is warning me that I might not like the answer I get.

Adam pulls out a chair and sits down in front of me, spreading his knees wide around my chair and holding both my hands in his.

'Tell me something, why did you come to pick us up yesterday?' He says it in a tone that is soft but considered, like he's been thinking about this a lot.

Our eyes meet and my tummy flips over quite suddenly at the look in his eyes as he watches me for my answer. I only hold his gaze for a second before I look away, but I'm significantly more flustered when I do. The expression on his face was intense, but I can't pinpoint the emotion. Desire for sure, given the way my heart rate is thundering in my chest. Concern and regret possibly also? The silence resumes when I don't answer and my anxiety levels start creeping up. What is he thinking? His look was so fierce… and worried.

'I don't know,' I mumble.

'Yes you do,' he answers softly. 'Tell me.'

'Because I was worried?' I answer, but it comes out more of a question.

'And?' His voice is still soft and confident. He runs his finger down my cheek again and my palms break out in a cold sweat. I want to look away but I can't. He has me fixed in his sights.

'Because I care about you,' I mumble quietly.

'And you'd do anything for me? Enough to knowingly put yourself at risk?' he asks, his voice caressing and seductive. I don't think about my answer, I'm mesmerised by him. I just nod and stare back.

He breathes out heavily and his face becomes a carefully controlled mask, blank of all expression. There's a moment of silence and neither of us breaks it. It seems to last an uncomfortably long time and my heart starts to pound increasingly harder the longer it lasts. A sense of numbness is spreading up from the floor, I've lost the ability to move my toes and my knees are starting to feel loose. I'm relieved to be sitting down.

'Are you going to tell me what was going on yesterday?' I ask him to break the silence and my voice comes out as barely more than a whisper.

'No, Ella, but I'm sure Dan's filled you in,' he answers, his intelligent eyes holding mine and telling me he knows he has.

The chill seeping into me moves higher, through my thighs, which suddenly lose their strength, and into my tummy. I feel sick and then I can't seem to draw in enough breath. I'd grip the table, but Adam is still holding my hands, caressing his thumb over the back of one.

'So let's speak about that. What did he say to you?' Adam asks me with an air of authority that I don't want to argue with. My hands are starting to shake a little so I pull them out of Adam's and slide them onto the seat under my thighs. I take a deep breath.

'He said you're illegally… umm,' I take a deep breath and clear my throat a little, 'supplying pesticides,' I say tentatively.

'To whom?' He casually rests an arm on the table and leans back in his chair. His face is so blank it's beginning to scare me. Icy fingers seem to leave trails up my back and my throat is suddenly too dry.

'Friends in Mexico,' I whisper, feeling compelled by him to speak the truth. When he fixes me with his eyes like that, I can't help but give in. I'd give him anything he wanted when he looks at me like that and I'm out of my depth. I always am when I'm with him.

He says nothing and the absence of words speaks volumes. I don't need to explicitly say the drug cartels that Dan mentioned; the understanding between us as we look at each other says it all.

'Can I ask something? Do you love me, Ella?'

I hold my breath and stare back at him, wide-eyed and trying hard not to tremble. I'm feeling giddy. I'm certainly head over heels for him. But love? I think I do, but I'm not sure. It's very soon and the events of the last twenty-four hours are too overwhelming for me to think about that just now.

'I don't know, Adam,' I whisper honestly. I can't ask him the same question, although I'm dying to know the answer, I'm just not confident enough to do it... or handle the answer if he says no.

He runs his thumb down my cheek again in a soft caress which adds to the sensation of dizziness. He nods, accepting my answer.

'Well how about another question. If I asked you to have a little faith in me, could you?' he asks softly. I gulp and my world starts spinning out of control. Oh Christ. I can't answer that, not without knowing if what Dan says is true or not.

'Is it true, Adam?' I ask breathlessly instead. 'Are you doing what Dan said? Are you involved in the *drug trade*?' My heart is suddenly pounding phenomenally and I hold my breath; it's the moment of truth and I don't want it be, it's too soon. Far too fucking soon.

'I can't answer that truthfully, Ella, so I'm not going to,' Adam says, keeping his mask of control firmly in place.

Oh hell. It's like my world just shattered. I clasp my hand over my mouth and drag a rasping breath in through my fingers as the kitchen tilts to a precarious angle.

I'm a good person, I try to look out for people and never willingly hurt them and I can't support what he's doing. It goes against everything I was raised to believe was right.

'Oh Christ, Adam!' A rush of tears immediately rolls down my cheeks. I hadn't even realised they'd been welling up inside me. I shake my head as I stare at him and he looks back at me, completely expressionless and under a tight reign of control.

'I can't...' I gasp, failing to find the words; I shake my head again. 'I just can't...' I stammer, gasping for breath as tears cascade down my face. Adam's eyes burn with regret, but his mask slips solidly back into place so swiftly I wonder if I really saw it.

'I know you can't, baby,' he says softly, 'you're a good girl and that's what I…' He clears his throat and doesn't finish what he was about to say. 'I know you can't,' he finishes gruffly instead. 'There's something I can't either,' he says quietly, but his voice is so controlled. How can he be so under control? I'm rapidly dissolving in front of him. Do I mean so little to him? The sensations creeping up through me finally reach my head and the room spins around me. I gulp and grip the table for support, bracing myself for what he's about to say.

'I can't have you running after me and getting into trouble,' he says. 'You'll get hurt in my world, baby, and I can't have that. I meant it when I said I wanted to look out for you, I meant it. But I can't do that if you put me before yourself.'

I stare at the table and gag reflexively under my hand which has sprung back to cover my mouth. I feel sick. He's breaking up with me? I look up at him, in shock. I know I can't be with him when his principles seem so different from my own, but I'm a very long way from being ready to let him go.

What can I possibly say to that?

'I think it's best if we go to that friends status like you wanted. It's better for both of us,' he says, his eyes expressionless and clear. He's cutting me loose? Just like that?

Is he really that indifferent? Then I notice there's an energy in the way he's holding his shoulders and a tension in his hands which hints at a deeper level of emotion than perhaps he's displaying.

I blink the tears out of my eyes and look up at the ceiling, trying to get a handle on my emotions. It's for the best I tell myself, but it doesn't help.

'If that's what you want,' I mumble, taking in a shaky breath. I wipe more tears away from my eyes now as they continue to fall and he puts his hand on my shoulder consolingly and it completely undoes me, the tears start flowing faster. 'I can't believe Dan was telling me the truth,' I exclaim shakily and blinking. 'I thought he was lying.' I start to rise to my feet when Adam squeezes my shoulder and presses me down to hold me still for a moment longer.

'Ella,' he says, an urgency in his tone that catches my attention. 'Don't trust Dan. Promise me?'

I blink at him and then push his hand off my shoulder.

'Should I put my trust in you instead, Adam?' I throw at him shakily, thinking *I used to*, until two minutes ago.

'Yes,' he says unwaveringly. 'Yes, you should trust me. Have a little faith in me, Ella,' he emphasises, his eyes losing their mask and imploring me to believe him. I get to my feet, shakily I admit, leaning hard on the table next to me.

'I can't do that.' I gasp among my tears, trying hard not to let my voice break. Not anymore.

'I understand,' he replies quietly and the control with which he speaks is like a sharp slap in my face.

'So I guess this is goodbye then?' I say shakily, picking up my rucksack and shrugging it on.

'Goodbye?' he asks, surprised. 'No, this isn't goodbye!' I look at him, confused. 'We're going to make this friends thing work, Ella,' he states adamantly. 'And besides, you still have a job here.'

I blink at him. My job. I hadn't even thought about that.

'You said you and I could never be friends,' I say defensively. 'You said it would never work. I can find another job… somewhere,' I add, knowing that won't be easy.

'Then I guess things will have to change, 'cause I'm not losing you out of my life,' he asserts. Oh God. I feel myself completely ripping apart down the centre. My knees almost give way and an eruption of tears bursts from me. Immediately Adam's arms come around me, pressing me into his chest and I long for the feeling of reassurance and warmth that I usually feel, but there's nothing. Just an emptiness that's about to swallow me whole.

'Stay a while?' he asks quietly, holding me tightly against him. My heart wants to say yes but my head is shouting *no, keep your distance*.

I shake my head and push on his arms to release me. He doesn't. 'I want you to stay, Ella, just until you feel better,' he murmurs into my hair. 'Don't leave like this.'

So I give in and stay, but my knees go weak and we find ourselves sitting together on the kitchen floor, and stay exactly where we are for ages. Him with his arms around me, and me not pushing him away, but knowing that I should. We don't talk. My mind is so busy registering that I've lost him it takes a while for me to calm down. When I do, I try to work out what's going on in his head. Why are we still sitting on the floor? If he wants to be just friends, why is he still holding me? Is there something he wants to say? Then as if he's reading my thoughts, he breaks the long silence.

'I know it doesn't seem like it, Ella, but I *do* care about you,' he says. 'You can come to me about anything and I'll try and help, ok? Whatever it is, doesn't matter, just know you can come to me, anytime.'

'But just as a friend.' I almost choke, clarifying our new situation. He doesn't answer me.

I free myself from his arms and get to my feet, but he doesn't stand up when I do, just stays sitting on the floor. A part of me wants to rewind the whole conversation and pretend it didn't happen. Another part wants to ask him if he'd stop doing what he is, for me. If he wanted to do that, though, he'd have offered, wouldn't he? The largest part of me, though, the loudest and most forefront in my mind, wants to leave. It's time to walk away; I can't be with someone who's involved in that. I can't. I won't. I can't drag my family into that world either.

Our eyes lock for a moment as I look at him; his expression is still blank and controlled. I swallow and look up at the ceiling, hoping for inspiration for something to say, but as always there are no words, so I pick up my bag, turn and leave. He lets me. For once I don't feel like I'm running away, more like making a decision and moving on.

I cry the whole way home, walking slowly, barely seeing the ground as tears blur my vision and sobs wrack through me so hard I have to stop and crouch down for fear of falling.

When I get home, I'm desperate to find Charlotte, but instead I find the next best thing, Hannah. She takes one look at me and does exactly what I need her to do. She throws her arms around me and lets me cry my heart out without asking questions. From the way I'm crying, she already knows why.

'I'm so sorry, Ella,' she says, rubbing my back in circles. 'Tell me, what can I do?' She sooths me when my sobs finally subside.

I shake my head.

'There's nothing, Hannah, nothing you can do. It doesn't matter anymore; we're not together. It was my decision too,' I mumble, but the words leave me feeling hollow inside.

'Oh, El!' She sighs empathetically and hugs me tighter. 'What are you going to do?'

'What I always do, cry a lot then pick myself up.' That determination inside me to get back on my feet is overwhelming and strong. I know I'll do it; I can now depend on myself. I don't need anyone to look after me; I'm not a child. I look up at her, my eyes still swimming in tears and I see the sympathy shining back at me in hers.

'But it hurts, Han, it really fucking hurts!'

Later that evening, I avoid my sisters and finish my song. I now have the chorus and the ending for it, even if it isn't what I wanted the ending to be.

I SHOULD HAVE KNOWN BETTER

I might not say it, but I know how I feel
I'm elated, 'cause inside this feels real
It's like my skin ignites, when I think of your touch
And my pulse explodes; it's such a rush
You are like a bolt of lightning out of the blue
And now the flame that lights my world, only burns for you

So it doesn't matter what he said
It doesn't matter what you do
Nothing else matters, as long as I'm with you

You blow my mind
You blur my lines
You chased me and I was thrilled to be caught,
But life sucks, when you meet the man you want,
And he's not who you thought.

When you touch me, you ignite my desire
I never knew, that I could feel this on fire
You took me further than I'd been before
You stretched my limits, making me want more
And then you crushed my hopes of a future with you
When you lied by omission and then confirmed it was true

It didn't matter what he said
It didn't matter what you do
Adam, I thought it didn't matter, as long as I had you

You blow my mind
You blur my lines
You chased me, and I was thrilled to be caught,
But life sucks, when you meet the man you want,
And he's not who you thought.

You've knocked me off my feet,
Literally pulled the rug out from underneath,
You've sent me reeling but still wanting you
It's left me questioning us, having to think things through,
Now my tears have put out my light,
My world is a darker place, in perpetual night.

It matters what Dad said
It really matters what you do
It matters, that I didn't see through you

You blew my mind
You blurred my lines
You chased me and I was thrilled to be caught,
But life doesn't suck,
So when the man you want pulls you down,
You have to get yourself back up.

It matters what you said
It really matters what I do
It matters, that I feel stupid to have fallen for you

FALLING FOR YOU SERIES
CONTINUES IN PART TWO

Believe in me

♡

When circumstances force Ella Peterson's life in unforeseen directions, she finds herself living at the DB Produce plant and trapped in a relationship with a man she doesn't want, while relying heavily on the man she does. Ella's desire to support herself is pushed to the limit as she struggles to make ends meet. She soon discovers that Adam was right all along, Dan is not to be trusted. But then, Adam Brook isn't what he led her to believe either. Not at all.

Caught in a tangled web of coercion, deception and desire, Ella is compelled to stay in a relationship with Dan, not to supply the information he wants from her, but because if she doesn't, she won't be able to help the man she loves. Once Adam finds out that Ella is carrying his baby, though, all bets are off. But how will Dan take the news that Ella is stronger than he thought?

Suddenly the tables turn and it's Adam that needs to rely on Ella.

Keep reading for a sneaky peak.

Prologue

The first hint of an autumnal breeze tickles my face as I sit on the grass with Chase in Adam's back garden. The sun is out, but like my mood most days, it's no longer bright and warm. The dog fetches his ball and returns to push it into my hand; he crouches down and waits attentively for me to throw it again, so I do. I'm so fond of him, he feels like the only friend I have in the world who I can really talk to.

It's been a month since Adam and I broke up. And it's been rough. A month of hell. It's been so bad I've almost sworn myself off men completely.

The first week after we broke up, I saw him most days while I carried out my housekeeping duties and he was friendly, but distant too. It was worse than if he'd been horrible; being physically close to him but with that tension between us smoothed over by niceties and smiles, like everything would be fine. It was too much. Far too fucking much. By the time I got home each evening, I cried myself to sleep and woke up exhausted from bad dreams. After a week of this, I told him I couldn't do it anymore and tried to quit working for him, but he wouldn't let me, so we agreed he would be out when I came over from now on.

I was sceptical, I thought he wouldn't manage it, especially now that his uncle is back and he is no longer needed in the DB Produce offices every day. I thought he'd have to be home more, but he's been out every day in the last three weeks and today is no different, it's just Chase and I here. We communicated by handwritten notes for a while and then one day when I arrived, he'd left me a post-it attached to a new mobile phone. The note said he'd pay the bills as a bonus to my wages as he was frustrated he couldn't contact me if he needed to. I throw the ball again and decide it's time to go, rubbing Chase behind the ears affectionately before I collect my bike and leave through the rear gate. I cycle home with a heavy heart as usual, not looking forward to my new friend Charlie taking me to the karaoke bar called Hot Shots in town again tonight. My thoughts are stuck on Adam constantly and Charlie tells me it's good for me to come out and have fun, so like last week, I agreed to go again. I wouldn't say it's not fun exactly, more like I'm a spoilsport, but I don't want Charlie to give up on me, she's the only girl friend I've made since I arrived in the States with my sisters, so I'll keep on agreeing.

At least when Adam was around that first week after we broke up, I didn't miss him so much. I can't win. And I remind myself again that it's better this way, that this was my decision too. He's not the man I thought he was. At least my heart can begin to heal now. But it hasn't. It hasn't even begun and I still cry every night.

I'm wearing my tight jeans with the rips up the thighs and a tight blue camisole and black heels. Charlie and her friend Isabella have stylishly pinned my hair up for me and enthusiastically applied me with make-up. According to them, I look great, but I don't feel great. I feel like shit. *They* were having such a good time trying to make *me* feel good, though, I didn't have the heart to stop them; they're fast becoming good friends. At least I'll blend in as I'm wearing similar clothes to them. Charlie isn't drinking as she's driving her dad's car tonight, but Isabella and I have already had a few glasses of wine at Charlie's house before heading out. We won't be served alcohol once we're at the bar as we're all under twenty-one, and our wrists will be stamped at the door when we show our ID, but at least we're allowed in.

Last week I saw Dan out with Hannah's partner Miguel, he spent most of the evening offering me things. A drink, a dance, his jacket if I was cold, a lift home on his motorbike, etc. There's always been a certain tension between Dan and I, so at first I felt awkward, but he took my refusals in such a spirit of fun, I lowered my guard a little and eventually accepted a Coke from him with the promise of a dance next time I saw him out. I'm hoping if I do see him there again tonight that he'll have forgotten that last part. Although it's a favourite hobby of mine, I'm not really one for dancing these days.

An hour after we arrive at the bar, the karaoke is turned off and the lights dimmed as the dance floor fills up to the sound of chart songs. Isabella and Charlie have met up with more friends and are soon wiggling and dancing like the best of them, but they dance so differently here. I feel self-conscious and out of place, so I hover at the edge of the dance floor and smile encouragingly whenever they throw glances in my direction.

A nice guy wearing black jeans, a loose button up shirt over a T-shirt and cowboy boots has been standing next to me for ten minutes. He's trying really hard to engage me in conversation, but as he's finding out, I'm not much of a conversationalist and it's getting so strained it's painful, but he doesn't seem to be deterred.

'So, do you wanna dance?' he asks me again and this time he picks up my hand and tries to encourage me to follow him onto the dance floor, smiling. I shake my head and try to pull my hand free.

'No, really. Thank you, but I'm happier watching.' I say again, but he continues smiling and pulling me forward anyway.

Strong arms wearing a leather jacket circle my waist from behind and it makes me jump in surprise as I'm hugged close to the man behind me.

'She's promised this dance to me,' Dan says, leaning his chin on the top of my head and I feel his chest shudder against my back; he's

265

laughing at the expression Mr Nice Guy pulls as he drops my hand and turns away discouraged.

I shake my head in exasperation and pull Dan's arms from around my waist before turning sideways on to face him.

'That was mean, Dan,' I exclaim, but the slight smile on my face tells him I'm far from upset that he's scared away my admirer. The guy was becoming annoying.

Dan looks down at me and smiles as he leaves one arm around my waist, his blond hair hangs in his eyes as usual.

'Yeah, but it was effective.' He grins. I roll my eyes and go to turn away. 'Oh no you don't,' Dan says mischievously and tightens his arm. 'Come on, you better dance with me now so he takes the hint.' He smiles before pulling me onto the dance floor. I follow him reluctantly, but feel awkward, like people are watching me.

'Dan, I really can't dance like you guys do here.' I start to protest, just looking at the bumping and grinding going on around me is making my cheeks flame.

'Then I guess I'll have to teach you,' Dan responds, wrapping his arms around my waist to pull me against him and starting to move us to the music. I remember the last time he tried to get me to dance and a lump forms in my throat at the memory, it was followed by the first morning I woke up with Adam. No, I'm not going there. I shut the thought down quickly.

Encouraged by the good-natured whoops and cheers from Charlie and Isabella to finally see me dancing, I relent a little. And I have to admit, Dan does look hot in a leather biker's jacket.

'One dance,' I say sternly to Dan and he grins at me as he starts to sway his hips against mine.

It's half way through the dance when that sensation of being watched prickles the skin on the back of my neck and I instinctively look towards the bar. My heart stills and then kickstarts back into life in double time. Again, my body responds before my brain has a chance to catch up and I find myself looking straight into the most amazing dark hazel eyes that could only belong to one man. A hot flush creeps up my skin and tingles along my throat as I look back at him. It's been three weeks since I've seen him and it has to be now that I run into him. *Right now?* When I'm dancing with Dan? Life is cruel sometimes.

He's staring at me intently, it's like a searing heat suddenly burning me when before I was frozen; from the distance across the busy bar I can't tell what his expression is, but he's not listening to the attractive blonde girl leaning up and saying something into his ear, that's for sure. That's when I notice, he has his hand resting on her lower back as they stand close together at the bar. I can't look. If my heart pounds any faster, I'm in danger of passing out. I turn my attention back to Dan.

'Sorry, Dan, I think that's enough dancing for me tonight, I'm going to head home.' I attempt to step back.

Dan looks down at me, but instead of loosening his arms around me, he closes the gap between us.

'Don't go because of him, Ella. Stay, have some fun. In fact, stay to prove to yourself you're capable of picking yourself back up and having fun without him.' Dan encourages, clearly knowing that Adam is in the bar and that I'd just spotted him. I look at him curiously, how did he know exactly the right thing to say to me to get me to stay?

He raises his arm in an overly romantic gesture, indicating I should make a turn underneath it and he smiles at me. 'Come on, dance! You might actually have some fun without meaning to.'

I sigh, but decide to take him up on his offer and make the turn as he intended. My mind tells me perhaps it's time to start thinking about living again, not moving on exactly, it's too soon, but just living. My heart tells me it's not going to be that easy.

Acknowledgements

I'd like to give my heartfelt thanks first and foremost to you, my readers. Your enjoyment means the world to me and without your support it is difficult for indie writers to reach new audiences and continue to write. Please therefore support new authors by leaving reviews or sharing good books with friends on social media. Your support means everything and I'd be extremely grateful.

I'd also like to thank my husband and children who supported me during the many hours I spent writing this book and acknowledge the excellent work of my editor, Deborah Blake, for her attention to detail and valued advice.

To the many friends who listened to me and read my drafts, please know that your time, enthusiasm and feedback was much appreciated and I'm grateful.

And finally, I'd like to give a very special thankyou to my best friend Jenny, who argued with me, laughed with me and encouraged me from draft one. I couldn't have done this without you Jen, so thanks for making the experience so much fun.

For more updates on new releases and future offers, please subscribe to my mailing list and check out my blog on *www.juliafirlotteauthor.com*. I can also be found on Facebook, Twitter and Instagram.

I really look forward to hearing from you and wish you happy reading.

Lightning Source UK Ltd.
Milton Keynes UK
UKHW010829280220
359503UK00001B/12